Planted

C. T. Collier

The Penningtons Investigate, Book One

Asdee Press

Cover design by Dave Fymbo
Imprint logo by Karen Sorce
Series logo by Lia Rees

place. Big guys having a fight in there would have trampled everything, not just the tree in the middle and a couple roses bushes next to it."

"Thank you, Mr. Woodard," Lyssa said. "Why would someone want to steal it, do you think?"

"That little tree cost a bundle, ma'am. Mr. Tuttle told me never to tell his wife what he paid for it. That's the only thing I can think of that explains how that tree went crooked. I know my men planted it straight and made sure it was in the ground for life." He shrugged. "Though I could have told you that tree couldn't live long in this climate. And I did tell Mr. Tuttle that."

"I'm sure you did, Mr. Woodard."

"Yes, ma'am, but there was no changing his mind. Stupid waste of a pretty little tree, if you ask me. And Woodard Nursery caught flak from half the Tompkins Falls Garden Club because of that tree."

"What kind of flak?"

"Half of them said I never should have agreed to plant the tree in the first place. The other half said that Tuttle woman was arrogant, thinking she could make it grow here, and she deserved what she got. A dead tree."

On her way back to the car, Lyssa reflected that Rikki Tuttle got a lot more than a dead tree that night. Something happened that made her son stay away from Tompkins Falls the rest of her life. She rested her forehead on the steering wheel, suddenly overwhelmed with sadness for the two young men who'd gone missing that night. Whose blood was on her gun? Who'd been killed and which of them had pulled the trigger? *I have to know.*

Chapter 13

"Ah, deep breath." Kyle let his lungs expand with ocean air. His nose tickled in the salty mist.

Lyssa inhaled deeply and coughed.

"Having trouble with this peace and calm, are you?" Kyle only knew from her giggles that she'd heard him over the thunder of an incoming wave.

"I can't remember the last time I took a deep breath."

He exhaled two weeks of worry about her. She was herself again, swinging her sandals and digging her bare feet into the sand with every step.

She wrapped her arm around his waist and nestled against his side, and he braced her shoulders. "We can't easily snuggle like this up on your cliff path, can we?" she asked.

"Not if we want to live. By the way, it's our cliff path now, Mrs. Pennington. Well, ours and the Duke of Cornwall."

"I can't wait to be back there with you."

In fact, there were many hiking trails he'd yet to explore with Lyssa. "Perhaps this summer we'll get onto the paths through wildlife areas."

"It won't be long now. When I've talked with your gardener, we've only talked about rose cultivation. Is everyone well?"

"Terrible flu this winter, all through the western counties, but everyone at Pennington House stayed well. Mum's had some of her pals visit, and she's eager to get outdoors now the camellias and rhododendrons are in bloom."

"Sounds heavenly."

"It is, my love. But I saw a yellow crocus the other day on someone's lawn in College Heights." He held up one finger.

"Just one?"

"One brave yellow crocus."

"Darling, you were very quiet when we boarded the plane last night, and you haven't talked much since. What's that about?"

"Mostly, I'm relieved to have Paul named CIO. That means I'll be finished with the job soon and able to give my energy to affairs in Cornwall and the business. I'm mulling it over. But let's leave that conversation for tomorrow. I've been wanting to ask you how you feel about making Pennington House our home after your contract is finished in two years and two months?"

"We're counting in months now, are we? Yes, of course I want Pennington House to be our home base."

His breath released in a whoosh.

"I haven't worked out how I'll use my expertise from there," she added. "We talked about the improbability of my holding a full-time university job, even if it's mostly online teaching and independent research. And I've seen firsthand that my undergraduate students need more handholding than I can give them from a distance. Perhaps grad students are more self-disciplined, I don't know."

"What about that delegation from your fan club that turned out for the wedding?"

Lyssa's laugh, like a chorus of songbirds at dawn, sent a cluster of plovers scurrying toward the dunes. "You're referring to the two—count them, two—women you invited by name?"

"They made it known through the coastal grapevine that they'd seen your public broadcasts, thought the redhead who frequented Pennington House was one and the same as the Savvy Spender, and were eager to meet you. I just helped it along a bit."

"It's good that you did. We had a chat about the ways I might reach more of the women in the south west of England. They want customized teaching in financial literacy, and they'll help me understand their needs. I intend to pursue that, and I've been emailing back and forth with them. But I've had no time for workshop design or materials. I'm afraid I'm going back to Cornwall empty-handed."

"You'll have time after classes end. Sweetheart, do you think something local like that will suit you?"

"As opposed to?"

"Oh, say, star of your own internationally syndicated public television program on financial literacy?"

"You're being silly. I want to be useful, not famous. Besides, when my contract in the UK ended, I promised myself I'd never again use a straightening iron on my hair." She shook her red waves, tightening into curls in the moist sea air.

He gathered her into his arms. "My love, you make everything lively and fun. That's what I first noticed about you, the quality I first fell in love with."

She held him tight. "I can't imagine a lovelier compliment."

He kissed her deeply. It wasn't until the incoming tide licked their bare feet that they were aware of time passing. "I hate to spoil this, but we need to head back and get dressed for our lunch with Janet Tuttle."

"I suppose."

He took her hand in his, and they trekked back toward the resort. "On the bright side, since Janet won't be drinking this early in the day, we can count on reliable answers to all our questions, eh?"

Janet Tuttle looked precisely as Kyle had expected. Ramrod straight and severely coifed.

"We can talk here as long as we want," she told them, with a sharp-eyed look around the nearly empty dining room of her ladies club. "Most of our snowbirds have flown to their homes in the north by now, so it's quiet. My ride is coming at two o'clock, and I'm perfectly happy to wait for her alone if we finish before that."

"Thoughtful of you, Janet, to have us meet here," Kyle said. "We've disrupted your life with our inquiry, and we want you to be as comfortable as possible."

"This little place of ours was a favorite lunch spot when Rikki was still alive." She dabbed at the corner of her eye with a handkerchief.

The three-story clubhouse had a commanding view of the Atlantic on one side, and of a private golf course on the other. It was probably a golf resort, not just a ladies' meeting place.

"We'd meet our friends here, sometimes play cards after. The winter before last, we had two horrible weeks of wind and rain. This was our haven. The valet service meant we could drive under the covered entry and let the valet worry about parking."

He couldn't bear to listen to her prattle until two o'clock. He took charge by summoning a waiter and suggesting they order drinks and hear the specials. Janet liked that idea.

Their drinks arrived: Janet's bottle of Pinot Grigio "for the table" and Kyle's tea service for two. After telling the waiter they needed more time with the menu, Janet produced a thick book, which she placed on the table between Kyle and Lyssa. "You asked if I had photos that would help you know more about Vince. This was Rikki's photo album of his early years, through his college graduation. Mostly snapshots, but they'll give you an idea."

Lyssa drew the book closer to her and slipped her phone out of her tote. "I wonder if you mind my taking a picture of one or two things that might be particularly helpful to us?"

"Of course, dear, go ahead. And ask me any questions you want. Kyle, you and I can discuss the terms of Tommy and Rikki's wills." She covered his hand with hers.

Kyle smiled his consent and withdrew his hand, but resigned himself to some toadying to get the answers he wanted from her.

Lyssa turned the album on its face, opened the back cover, and paged through the empty leaves to the photos of Vince's college graduation.

Kyle leaned closer. "Cutting to the good stuff?" he whispered.

She told him, "Except there's nothing after Tompkins College."

No photos of Vince and Patty arriving at the Tuttles on May 19th five years ago.

"Janet, when did Rikki move down with you to Myrtle Beach?" he asked.

"It's complicated. Rikki wanted to stay in her home after Tommy died, which was late spring three years ago, but it didn't work out for her. She missed Tommy, and she was mad at Vince for not helping out at the end."

"Vince didn't come even after the funeral to support his mother?"

"Certainly not." Her tone was acerbic. She poured a full glass of the wine and drank a mouthful before continuing. "She and I got very close then. I was still living in Tompkins Falls and just coming here winters. She started coming with me for the winter. We both loved the beach and the ladies club. Rikki and I got along so well we decided to buy a condo on the shore in Myrtle Beach and move here permanently, which we did that fall. We split the purchase price, put the condo in both our names, and shared the expenses. Our agreement was the survivor would inherit the condo in full."

"I do want to know more about Rikki's will, now you've brought it up. But let's start with Tommy's will, since he died before her."

"My dear departed brother." She leaned toward Kyle, forearms on the table. "Yes, he was very smart with his will."

Kyle sat back and raised his teacup as a barrier. Her breath was strong with alcohol, more than the few gulps she'd taken at the table. "That would be so helpful, Janet."

Lyssa had turned to a page with a photo of Vince and a young man who looked very much like him. When Janet noticed her snapping a picture, she offered, "That's Nate Westover with Vince. I'll tell you a story about him later. Don't let me forget."

"Do tell us now," Kyle said.

Flustered for a moment, Janet pulled her elbows closer to her body and slugged more wine. "I assume you know about Bill and Margie being killed in the rockslide?"

"The Westovers? Yes, terrible tragedy."

"Well, after they were killed, Nate was not himself. Rikki said he needed the Tuttles—all three of them—to be his family, which was completely unrealistic."

Kyle thought back to the Weaver twins saying Nate made the group of friends feel like family.

"My brother and his wife cared about Nate, of course, but the boys were out of college now, and it was time to separate from family, move forward with their lives. In fact, Vince started working on his master's degree right after graduation, at that state college. Nate planned to do the same, but he was still recovering from his injuries and had to delay one term."

"Back to the story I started to tell you, I didn't know any of this until Rikki and I were living together, here in Myrtle Beach. She said that one weekend after the rockslide, when Nate was just back on his feet, he burst into Tommy's house on a Friday evening, just as Tommy and Rikki were finishing their meal in the dining room. They always had a family meal in the dining room, every night of the week. Vince was leaving for a date. Nate was furious that Vince was going out without him. Vince couldn't get him to see reason, Rikki said, and Vince finally left the house so he wouldn't be late for his girl."

"He walked out, leaving Nate behind?"

"Yes, of course. He couldn't be rude to his date. Well, Nate got agitated. He started yelling, said terrible things to Tommy and Rikki about how everyone had abandoned him, even his best friend. Then he told them what it was like to watch his parents die. Bill had shoved Nate free of the slide and was immediately buried by the rocks. Nate told them he'd watched his mother take a boulder to the chest, before she was lost from view under the slide. Can you imagine?"

"Horrible," Kyle said. Without thinking, he took a breath that expanded his own lungs to the max.

"Tommy and Rikki couldn't calm him down. He started shouting at Rikki, 'Tell me how it felt when she couldn't breathe!' He rushed at Rikki and choked her with his bare hands." Janet twisted in her chair and darted forward toward Lyssa. "Just like this." Janet's gaze fixed maliciously on Lyssa's throat, her hands hovering an inch away.

Lyssa backed away from the hands thrusting toward her. As she scrambled to her feet, her chair crashed on its side.

"Sweetheart." Kyle stepped between the two women, blocking Janet from Lyssa's view. Lyssa stood, gasping, her hand on her throat. "Janet was only demonstrating, you know that."

"I do know." Lyssa sucked in a ragged breath. "But that was the nightmare, Kyle. The hand rising from the garden and choking me. The woman screaming. It was Rikki in the dream." Trembling, she let him fold her in his arms and said, "I need to be excused for a few minutes."

"We should leave."

"No, we need this information. Please, can you carry on? I just need my phone first. It's next to the album."

"You're sure you'll be all right?"

She nodded. "I'll call Gianessa." She pressed a number on her phone and stole out of the dining room through one of the French doors to a covered porch.

"Did I scare her, Kyle? Will she be all right?"

"She'll be fine, Janet," he said through his teeth. He wondered if she'd done it deliberately.

He stood a moment longer, watching his wife. Once she was settled into conversation, he righted her chair and returned to his seat.

Janet had drained her glass of wine, and the steward was refilling it for her.

Lord, give me strength. He owed it to his wife to ask all the right questions before Janet was blotto. "Was Nate's attack on Rikki reported to the police?"

"Yes, it was. Tommy bashed Nate over the head with a heavy candlestick and knocked him out, then called 911. In the end, though, Tommy and Rikki decided not to press charges, on the condition Nate get some kind of inpatient treatment. I don't know the details. The whole thing was hushed up. Rikki didn't say so, but I suspect Vince persuaded them, because Nate was his friend and they both wanted so badly to be teachers. Having an assault on his record would not do."

"Indeed." *Is that what the police are covering up?*

"Rikki would not allow Nate in the house after that."

Kyle nodded. That tallied with what the Weavers had told him.

"And Tommy laid down the law with Vince not to associate with Nate. Of course, Vince may have defied that. He was a grown man, after all. Given his behavior the next year, maybe it didn't even bother him that Nate had done that to Rikki."

"I feel sure it bothered him very much," Kyle said. He tuned out for a moment. His gaze swept the porch for Lyssa. *Where has she gone?* He could just make her out through the blinds, talking on the phone, pacing at the far end of the porch.

Janet's voice droned on. He watched his wife.

Lyssa pocketed the phone, stood with her hands braced on the rail for a moment looking out at the ocean, and then walked the length of the porch to a set of French doors that returned her to the dining room. He rose to meet her. With a weak smile for him, she held up her head like royalty. He kissed her cheek and, as he seated her, whispered, "You tell me what you need, and we'll leave when you say so."

"Right now I need to eat." She grabbed a roll and a packet of butter from the basket in the center of the table. After slathering her roll with butter, she lifted her menu like a shield between herself and Janet. *Or perhaps Janet's wine?*

Kyle stepped to the waiter's station.

"Once Rikki sold the house," Janet was saying when he returned, "she moved in with me in Tompkins Falls, and then we decided to make our home together here." *She's talking in circles now.* Her eyes shifted right and left, as if startled to see Lyssa back in her chair and Kyle just taking his seat. "As I've said, yes." She rearranged the two spoons of her place setting.

"You mentioned, Janet, that Tommy's will left the house on Seneca Street to Rikki," Kyle said. "Can I assume he left everything to his wife?"

"He did. His will had read that way all along, while Vince was still a student, and he hadn't changed it. They didn't expect Tommy to die. Had he given it any thought after Vince graduated, he might have put something in trust for any children Vince might have, but he didn't. And my dear brother knew I was well set, thanks to my late husband's estate." She touched her perfectly coifed hair. "Not only was he generous, he never objected to my keeping my own name."

"So Tommy's will was simple. Rikki inherited everything," Kyle said. "By any chance, did Vince come to town to acknowledge the terms of the will?"

"Not after Tommy died, no. I suppose he had to sign something to allow probate to go forward. That's all that was required, I'm sure. Would you like to speak with the attorney?"

"I would very much, if he would agree."

Janet made a note in her day planner. "I'm just reminding myself to call Hector to give him permission to answer your questions." Kyle handed her one of his business cards and asked her to write Hector's full name and phone number on the back for him. He eyed her address book and watched her pen to be sure she got it right.

"And did Rikki use the same solicitor? Er—attorney?"

"We both used an attorney here in Myrtle Beach." She paged to that entry in her address book and jotted it down for him. "Lovely man. Very young and smart about estates."

"And Rikki left her share of the condo to you, as you've said. How did she dispose of the rest of her estate, Janet?"

"She left a generous sum to me and substantial amounts to her church, to the college—Tompkins College, that is— and to several charities." Janet chortled. "Nothing to the Tompkins Falls Garden Club."

Lyssa chuckled, and Kyle squeezed her hand.

"Nothing to Vince?"

"Some token, on the lawyer's advice, in the form of a donation to Tompkins College in Vince's name."

Easy enough to verify.

Janet drained her wine glass, and the steward bustled to her side. A waiter at Janet's other shoulder asked them, "Are y'all ready to order?"

"We certainly are," Kyle said. "I'll have the tuna steak salad. Janet?"

"The club sandwich. Light on the mayo."

"I'll also have the tuna steak salad," Lyssa said. "And hot coffee, please. Right away. And I'll want the strawberry shortcake for dessert." She mouthed to Kyle, "Want to share?"

"Lovely." Kyle gathered the menus and handed them, along with his credit card, to the waiter. "Janet, you must have dessert, too. We insist."

She agreed to a thin slice of cheesecake "with fudge sauce covering the top. You know how I like."

The waiter smiled deferentially and departed.

"Janet, in what ways were Vince and his father alike—looks, temperament, interests, any way at all?" Kyle asked.

"They looked nothing alike, except the big nose. I had it, too, the Tuttle nose. Tommy always had a joke to tell about noses. As for me, once I finished college, got a job, and saved enough, I had cosmetic surgery for it. That was the difference between Tommy and me. Vince hated the nose as much as I did, by the way. I wouldn't be surprised if he'd got rid of it by now."

She explained that Tommy had been director of public relations and development at Tompkins College. One of the Westovers, she thought, worked at the college, too, and both boys had full scholarships, a benefit offered to children of employees who qualified for admission. "Yes, I remember now. Margie was a professor of whatever that science is that deals with rocks and volcanoes and that kind of thing."

Probably Margie Westover had looked forward all her life to the opportunity to hike the Vermillion Cliffs. *Ironic she died in a rockslide.*

"Was Vince a funny fellow like his dad?" Lyssa asked. "He looks quite serious in his pictures." She smiled at the waiter who'd deposited a carafe in front of her. He poured a full cup before departing. She brought it to her face and held it with both hands, blowing across the surface of the steaming liquid to cool it.

"Vince was more serious, and he was often embarrassed by Tommy's jokes, as children can be. Did I tell you they were both tenors? Tommy sang in the church choir. Lovely, clear voice. Vince had it, too, but he never developed his talent. He took his education very seriously. Although he played basketball and baseball with his friends, he didn't play on a team at school. He preferred his art. No one knew where that came from, but he showed talent at an early age. Here . . ."

Janet set down her wineglass, sloshing a bit on the tablecloth, and rummaged in her purse. She brought out a card-sized envelope. Tucked inside was what looked like a much-handled page from a sketchbook. She positioned a drawing on the table in front of Kyle. "That's Tommy and me at the rail of the paddle-wheel steamboat, *Canandaigua Lady.*"

Tommy, shorter than his sister, sported a potbelly, a jaunty captain's hat, and a wide warm smile. Janet, tall and slender, wore a tight smile, but a long scarf at her throat blew free in the wind that tugged at her stiff hairstyle. Kyle wondered if Vince had added the scarf detail. The thought made him smile. *We must find him.*

"Vince was ten or eleven when he drew that. He had long fingers, elegant hands. Tommy used to say he was born to hold a paintbrush."

Lyssa snapped a picture of the drawing.

"Delightful memory, for you to have, Janet," Kyle said. "Sweetheart, what have you found in the album?" She'd been paging quickly the last few minutes, and he saw that the photos now were of Vince as a young boy.

"I'll show you." Lyssa scooted her chair closer to him and he stroked her back as she scrolled through the pictures on her phone.

Most were of Vince and Nate, often with their arms around each other's shoulders. Vince might have been an inch shorter than Nate, no more, and Vince's big nose stood out in every picture. Indeed, they were inseparable as lads. His chest ached now he'd come to know the two boys through photos and stories. *Where are they now?* Was one of them dead at the other's hand? He shook his head, unwilling to believe it. He preferred to think it had just been some accident with the gun, something that needed to be covered up for the sake of their careers. Not a fatal shooting. *Good Lord, not murder.*

One picture showed a smiling Westover family and Vince. The family wore hiking gear, while Vince wore a sports jacket.

Lyssa held out the screen so Janet could see. "This must be when the Westovers left for their fatal trip out West?"

"Yes, Vince was invited, but he had a good-paying job for the summer, and he needed the money for his master's program."

"Fortunate," Kyle said. He scrolled backward and once more held the phone screen for Janet. "The boys are a little younger here. Vince and the Westovers are in hiking clothes, as if Vince were going with them on a trip. Did he sometimes join the Westovers on hikes or vacations?"

"Usually, yes. They were outdoor enthusiasts, and so was Vince. Tommy and Rikki were homebodies. I don't believe my brother ever took a vacation except to work on the house. Rikki and I did some traveling, but the only time Tommy came along was to Charleston and Savannah to see the gardens and eat good Southern cooking."

Kyle opened his mouth, but Lyssa spoke first. "Janet, I'd love to hear more about Vince's art. Did he paint?"

Janet reached for the album. "May I?"

Lyssa shrank back, and Kyle caressed her shoulder.

Janet paged to the center of the album. "Here!" she said triumphantly, just as the waiter emerged from the kitchen with a tray laden with their meals. The waiter hesitated, set the tray on a nearby stand, and stood tapping his foot.

Janet's finger stabbed at a photo of a teenaged Vince and a graying Tommy standing under an oil painting. "That's Vince's portrait of his father, my brother Tommy." She stood the album on end for them to see. "It hangs over my fireplace now. It's a beautiful likeness, and it reminds me of better times."

Kyle remarked, "He's captured his dad's fun-loving spirit, hasn't he?"

Lyssa snapped a picture of it seconds before Janet slammed the album shut and dropped it to the floor beside her. "Come," Janet said with an imperial wave of her arm to the waiter.

At his wife's request, to counter the nightmarish lunch with Janet Tuttle, Kyle took them shopping at boutiques in a nearby tourist town—sandals for him and shell jewelry for her. She bought long silk scarves, deep blue for Manda and herself, sea green for Bree, and violet for Gianessa.

After stashing their shopping bags in the car, they walked hand-in-hand on a mile-long stretch of golden sand, went together to a five o'clock AA meeting in the next town, and only then drove back to Myrtle Beach for dinner.

It was nearly seven-thirty when a table opened up for them at the restaurant. Housed in what had been a seafarer's home, the shoreline restaurant had been the top pick of the concierge at their resort. "Best meal on the coast," he'd told them, adding that it served only dinner and was famous for its local seafood.

Finally seated and supplied with menus, Kyle turned a charming smile on their pert, blonde waitress. "Any chance you'd have a proper pot of tea for us?"

"I'll see what I can do for ye," she said. "Madam, anything more than the tea for ye?"

"You're Irish?" Lyssa's eyes lit up with a smile.

"I am that."

"Kyle's mother is from Bantry, and my ancestors came from Dublin."

"I'm just over from Cork meself. Studying in Wilmington, working down here on me breaks." She curtsied. "Me name's Katie. I'll do my best about the tea and be back for yer order."

Lyssa stroked his hand. "Thank you for going to a meeting with me and skipping your brandy tonight."

"Without you sober, I have no life," he said, his voice thick with concern. The thought of being married to an active drunk like Janet was too repulsive to contemplate.

"I'm glad you understand." She leaned closer for a kiss. "I was so conflicted with Janet, wanting to carry the message of recovery to her but barely able to stop myself from gulping down her wine. Her hands reaching for my throat nearly sent me over the edge."

"Clever of you to use your menu as a shield."

She grinned. "It blocked out the smell along with the sight."

"You never said who you were talking with on the porch."

"I called Gianessa but there was no answer. Same with Manda. I tried Joel's cell and he picked right up. While we talked he looked up AA meetings for this area, and I told him about Nate's attack on Rikki Tuttle. He agreed something has been suppressed by the police. He's going to contact the old chief directly and try to get us an appointment with him."

"That must be Chief Barker. He's mentioned him several times when we've talked, and I gather he helped Joel get sober all those years ago. If anyone would know about a troubled young man in Tompkins Falls, it's Barker. We're lucky, aren't we, that your first two phone calls didn't work out?"

"I'd call it a God Thing."

"Quite right. How's the tea, Katie?" he asked as the waitress offloaded a large white teapot from her tray and set two mugs in front of them.

"Don't tell a soul," she said, keeping a conspiratorial eye on the tables around them. "We've a stash of Bewley's for those who request it."

"Brilliant."

"Mind now." She lifted a finger to her forehead. "If it sits too long, it'll go bitter on ye. What can I get for yer dinner?"

Lyssa ordered the blue crab cake, and Kyle decided on the scallop special. "I'll put that in straightaway," Katie promised with a bright-eyed smile and hurried toward the kitchen.

"This calls for a big tip, my darling." Lyssa winked.

"Absolutely."

"Life's good." Lyssa squeezed his thigh. She took the mug he'd filled for her and inhaled. "I love this fragrance. After I came back to Janet's table, I wasn't paying much attention. If you fill me in, we'll fit it together with what I learned yesterday afternoon in Geneseo and from the garden club meeting and Woodard's Nursery."

"Perhaps the most important thing was that the Tuttles eventually agreed not to press charges against Nate for his attack on Rikki, if he agreed to get inpatient treatment."

"For his mental state?" Lyssa took a sip of tea and sighed. "Good black tea."

"The way Janet said it, I think so. Though Toffee Winkel had thought it might be for alcohol or substance abuse."

"Perhaps all of the above."

"The concern was, if he had a history of violence and instability, that would end his hopes of a teaching certificate."

"And they were right," Lyssa told him. "Somehow the field placement office at Geneseo found out and denied him placement."

"You're serious?" Kyle's eyebrows rose.

"I don't know exactly what they heard or who from."

"Would Vince have told them?" Kyle asked. "I'm not sure I trust Janet's claim that Vince was the driving force in keeping Nate's record clear of the assault charge."

"But why would he rat out his good friend, especially when they had similar goals? He understood the consequences." Lyssa took another sip of tea.

"If they'd stopped being friends, though, and he wanted to avenge the attack on his mother . . ." Kyle squinted out the window at the waves rolling onto the sand beach. *There must be floodlights along the building.* If they'd known that when they arrived they might have taken another walk in the surf while they waited for their table.

"Vengeance doesn't fit with my picture of Vince."

"Nor mine. Perhaps someone in the police department, someone who had children, let something slip out of a desire to protect schoolchildren," Kyle offered.

"Or someone at the treatment facility, perhaps for the same reason. There might even have been mandatory reporting, if they knew Nate was enrolled in a program leading to a teaching degree. He was probably already matriculated before he left with his parents on their fatal trip out West."

"Janet did say Nate and Vince had planned to start their programs together," Kyle said. "But Nate was still recovering when the first term started. He delayed one term. What would that mean? When would summer classes have started for a graduate program?"

"I looked at the schedule. For the teaching programs, the first summer session begins mid-May, and a second session starts around Fourth of July."

"So Nate probably started classes in July and had to drop those when he went into treatment late that summer."

"No, didn't Toffee say it was fall when she found him passed out on the front porch?"

"Yes, and Nick helped get him into treatment. I suppose that time frame might be inaccurate. She was on Demerol when we talked with her."

"Either way, his professors said he persisted with his courses and did well with them. He actually finished the program except for student teaching."

"That's to his credit, isn't it?" Kyle's fingers trilled on the tabletop. "I really wonder what his and Vince's relationship was like at that point. It's possible, since Rikki was all right, that Vince was a strong supporter for his lifelong friend. We've no way of knowing which way it went, do we?"

"Actually, Ralph at the coffee shop in Geneseo where Patty worked, thought Vince and Nate were best buds until Patty came between them, which was in the spring."

"This part is all new to me." Kyle sat up straight. "Let's hear more about Patty."

She summarized what she'd learned from the college and from Ralph. "Then Patty moved in on Vince, and he fell hard, Ralph said."

"And Nate went ballistic, eh?"

"No, although he was jealous, he was just cold to Vince after that."

Kyle finished his cup and poured more tea for them. "That doesn't add up for me. I'd expect two young men to have at least one head-bashing, body-slamming fistfight about it, and Ralph would have heard if they had. Those downtown merchants spread the word when there's trouble."

"Come to think of it, Ralph was cagey with his answer. He said they hadn't gotten into a fight in his father's restaurant."

"Code for something else, exactly." Kyle sat back.

"And saying that Vince fell hard for Patty tallies with Tommy's observation that Patty had her hooks in his son, doesn't it?"

He nodded. "Let's suppose Vince planned to marry Patty, brought her home to meet his parents, and Nate tracked them to the Tuttle home." He used his fingers to trace the action on the tablecloth. "Once the parents left, Nate barged in with his father's gun, and dispatched Vince."

"No, that doesn't fit the facts," Lyssa said. "Vince went on to purchase the condo and become an award-winning teacher and so on."

"And we've the same problem if we say Vince dispatched Nate. So, let's say someone else was killed with the gun. The three of them had all the time they needed to clean up the blood, get the body out to Nate's truck, bury the gun . . ." Kyle paused for a moment and shook his head.

"What?"

"Where did that lunchbox come from and the oil cloth and the leather pouch?"

"You're right, we've forgotten all that."

"The manner of the gun's burial has to make sense in whatever scheme we choose." At Lyssa's nod, he said, "To continue. They had time to wrap up the gun the way they did, bury it, and take off–Nate driving his own truck, Patty and Vince in Vince's Honda."

Lyssa cocked her head. "Or maybe Patty liked driving pickup trucks. She seems more the type."

Kyle laughed. "You're getting punchy. Either way, we need to verify Nate and Vince are still alive and doing whatever they're doing. Patty, too, for that matter. We need to ask Nick Nunzio if he ever hears from either of the boys."

"Yes, and Bree's asking around for Nick's watering hole. We're planning to have a conversation with him. Back to the unknown victim, we need a scenario to fit that. How could someone other than the three of them have been in the Tuttle home the night of May 20th, five years ago?"

"Quite right. Let's start with Toffee's guess. Suppose Vince had a party that Saturday night, and something happened at the party. Although the Weavers insist there was no party or they'd have been invited."

"Whatever." She waved a hand.

"Right. Something happened at the party that had to be covered up or Vince himself would end up with a record that would prevent him from teaching in public schools."

"You're on to something."

"At the same time, let's remember that Nate wasn't around Tompkins Falls much after he disappeared for that month of treatment. He might have been ordered to stay away from his neighborhood and been viewed as a pariah by his friends. The Weavers were very close-mouthed about him."

"I hadn't thought of that angle. It makes sense."

"So Nate, who wasn't invited to this hypothetical party, barges in with the gun, waves it around at the people who used to be his friends, and Vince wrestles it away from him. The gun goes off, and someone is shot. It doesn't much matter whom, but it's a big problem and it has to be hushed up. One of the partygoers might have known a physician who would treat the wound without reporting it. Something like that." He opened his hands for her feedback.

"Smashing." Lyssa seized his arm. "Vince buried the gun to hide the evidence—don't know why, don't care—and then drove into the sunset with Patty to start his new career with a clean record." She lifted her mug and set it down again with a moan. "There's the rub. Vince didn't come back to town ever again. Why?"

Kyle held up a finger. "Perhaps that was the bargain he made with whoever helped him out."

"Perhaps it was Nate who helped him out."

"Yes!" Kyle slapped his hand on the table.

Lyssa gasped.

A hush fell over the dining room. She turned apologetic eyes toward her fellow diners, rose from her chair, and lifted her hands in appeasement. "So sorry, everyone. My husband and I are cooking up a murder mystery weekend. We apologize."

Kyle had covered his face with his hands, and he only ventured out of hiding when chuckles at the nearby tables gave way to the normal sounds of clinking silverware, conversation, and hearty laughter.

"Nice save, sweetheart." He scooted his chair closer to hers.

"Are you blushing?" Her teasing deepened the warmth in his cheeks.

"Good Lord. To go on, Nate held it over Vince's head, because, after all, he could divulge the secret anytime he wanted, and Vince's teaching career would be over."

"Brilliant, darling, but why deny Vince access to Tompkins Falls?"

"To deprive him of contact with his friends," Kyle said.

"I don't understand."

"Payback, because Nate had been ostracized by those same friends."

"That works entirely, except Vince could easily have invited those same friends to Green Bay, and the Weavers never heard from their best bud. We're missing something."

Kyle kicked off his sandals and dug his feet into the sand as they set out. He savored the sight of Lyssa's sapphire eyes sparkling in the early morning light, and the waves of her red hair dancing in the fickle wind. "Eager to be going home, my love?"

They'd had Sunday brunch at their resort, checked out at noon, and decided on one more walk on the sand. Their pilot had scheduled the return flight for three o'clock to give himself time for eighteen holes.

"Not at all. I'd rather stay with you on this beach until we fly to Cornwall."

"And I as well." Kyle kissed her temple. "Though I am looking forward to letting go of the day-to-day responsibilities as interim CIO. Paul's eager to ramp up."

"Do you think Paul will do a good job? I know you said everyone's excited about having him step into the role. Didn't you have another excellent candidate? What happened with that?"

"In fact, he was the one interviewing when you stopped by my office. You heard the laughter and the high spirits. Everyone gave him high marks, but he wanted twice what we were prepared to pay, and he wouldn't budge. Honestly, I'm glad, as it's a message to the college staff that we're willing to promote from within."

"You've done a heroic job for the college, darling. Will you miss it?"

"Mostly not. I've enjoyed being around the students, though, and I'll miss that youthful energy and ambition. And I've enjoyed being a mentor to Paul, just as I have been for Geoffrey at Pennington Secure Networks."

"Is that working out, having Geoffrey play a larger role in your business?"

"Yes and no. I couldn't have been in Tompkins Falls with you all this time without his hard work. However . . ."

He delivered a five-minute state-of-the-business report that had Lyssa chewing on her lower lip. He'd learned from his financial person, just before they left for Myrtle Beach, that quarterly profits were down. Again.

"That's a significant drop," she pointed out. "You're worried, aren't you?

"Yes. Something's not right. I'll need to get my hands back into it somehow, without ticking off Geoffrey to the point of quitting." He stepped behind her and massaged her shoulders. "And you've just tensed up. Out with it. What are you worried about?"

"Between shoring up Geoffrey and getting things in order on the Pennington estate," she said, her voice straining to be cheerful, "will you abandon me in Tompkins Falls for the better part of two years, until my contract runs out?"

He swung her into a tight hug. "Of course not. Is that all you think of me?"

"I'll miss you horribly whenever you're gone."

"I'll not only miss you, my love, I'll worry about you as well."

"Worry about me? Whatever for?"

Chapter 14

"Drop us in back, if you would, Joel," Kyle requested. "Come in for coffee?"

Joel navigated the narrow drive between the Pennington house and the neighbor's fence. "No, thanks. Manda's waiting for me."

Lyssa said from the backseat, "Our love to Manda. Thanks again for all you did to make this trip possible, Joel. It was exactly what we needed."

"Good to hear." As the backyard came into view, Joel glanced to his left and hit the brake prematurely. "Tell me he didn't . . ."

Kyle gasped.

"What?" Lyssa asked.

"Sweetheart, it looks like Harold—"

"He planted the roses!" Lyssa wailed. "Joel, you didn't ask him to, did you? Kyle?"

Two no's came from the front seat, voices uneasy.

Lyssa climbed out of the car and circled around it to the garden. In the fading light, seventeen rose bushes sat tall and proud in the perfectly mounded garden, their tiny leaves ruffling in the evening breeze. Water issued silently from the center hole of the new stone fountain, flowed through the channel cuts in the granite top, and sheeted down the sides.

Lyssa squatted beside the roses and reached one hand forward.

"Careful, they might have been dusted," Joel warned her.

She drew back her hand.

Behind her Kyle said, "Are you terribly angry, sweetheart?"

She shook her head. In the presence of the roses, with the barely discernible bubbling of the fountain, peace filled her heart for a long moment, until a gust of wind reminded her there was unfinished business with this garden. Even the several-hundred-pound granite block that replaced the tree in the center could not suppress the lingering horror of the gun and the hand she'd imagined reaching up from the soil.

Her hand went to her throat, unbidden, and she shivered.

"Lyssa," Joel said behind her, his voice strained, "I just spoke with Harold, and he misunderstood. I take responsibility, and I am very sorry it happened."

"I am, too, Joel," she said with a catch in her throat, "but it's hardly something we can undo."

Kyle squatted beside her and tucked a strand of hair behind her ear. "Sweetheart, I know you're disappointed, after investing all that time and energy learning about the cultivation of roses."

"I'm actually more concerned about Bree. She had her heart set on learning to plant a garden. I'm not sure how to tell her or make it up to her."

"Harold has left the unused materials. Perhaps you and she can plant a few more roses close by the patio? Just a thought."

"Maybe. I'll call her tomorrow and see if we can go to a meeting together."

A metallic clunk from the driveway brought Kyle to his feet. "I'll get the bags, Joel," he called across the yard.

Lyssa knelt by the garden for another minute, contemplating the fountain. Finally, she whispered, "I will find out what happened here and why the gun was planted here. That I promise."

Kyle was waiting for her on the patio, her carry-on over one shoulder, a cluster of shopping bags in one hand, and their single suitcase standing beside him.

She fished out her key and offloaded her small bags. "You expected fireworks from me, didn't you?" she asked as she unlocked the French door and held it open for him.

"I did." He met her eyes. "Is your calm just a cover for a coming eruption?"

"No. And I'm very sorry for my behavior last week. I completely lost my sanity." She caressed his face and leaned in for a kiss. "The bright side is, with classes starting tomorrow, I wouldn't have much time for planting."

"True."

"Are you hungry?" She checked the refrigerator. "We have cheddar and apples."

"That sounds right. I'll check emails, if you don't mind. And, before I forget, Joel said he reached former chief of police Barker, and he's willing to talk with us, but only if Joel is in on the meeting."

"That's odd. Did he say why?"

"No, but it's not a problem for me. What do you think?"

"Fine with me. When are we doing this?"

~ ~ ~

"I know you've got news I'm not going to like," Bree said as they left the Happy Hour meeting Monday at six o'clock and headed for their cars.

"I hate this," Lyssa muttered. She straightened her spine. "When Harold installed the fountain, he planted the roses, too. It was a mistake, but it's done. I'm horribly sorry, Bree."

"I already knew. I drove by yesterday to see how the fountain looked, and he was just finishing."

"Did he say anything? Did you?" She crowded closer to Bree as a car squeaked past them in the narrow aisle.

"No, I was so upset, I just left."

Lyssa gave her shoulders a squeeze. "I feel so bad. Working on the garden meant as much to you as it did to me. Kyle suggested we get more roses and plant them close to the patio. Or something like that."

"Sure, that would be good." Bree looked at her sideways, her eyes twinkling with mischief. "But I have another idea for how you can make it up to me."

Lyssa grinned. "Do tell."

"I want to take the lead when we question Nick Nunzio, and I think we should do it Wednesday at the start of happy hour at the Manse Lounge, where he hangs out with some of the teachers."

"Brilliant. How did you—?"

Bree tugged at Lyssa's arm as a car backed out next to them.

"How did you find that out?"

"I asked a few teachers I know from the Bagel Depot. I'm telling you, that place has its finger on the pulse."

"And if they're smart they'll make you a manager as soon as you get your degree in December. So Nick is a regular at the Manse Lounge on Wednesdays?"

Bree nodded. "And I guess he's pretty popular because he buys rounds."

"Mr. Big Spender?" Lyssa dug her keys out of her jacket pocket and clicked the remote to unlock her car.

"Exactly. The girls said most of them wouldn't hang out there if he wasn't buying."

"So what else did they say? Does Mr. Nunzio have a girlfriend?"

"I guess he dates around. Only the young and beautiful." She rolled her eyes. "And once he's slept with somebody he moves on."

"Ugh." Lyssa had trouble reconciling the picture Bree had painted with the slightly overweight middle-aged man who'd answered the hot pink door of 54 Seneca when she and Kyle had done their goodwill tour. "He's not even good-looking."

"Funny, none of them said that. But they all said he goes first class all the way. Weekends in New York City or Toronto to see plays, dinner at fancy restaurants. Stuff like that."

"That doesn't add up. He grew up on Seneca Street, and he's a teacher. Unless he's got an inheritance all out of proportion to that, I don't see how he affords that lifestyle."

Bree was nodding. "Exactly what I was thinking. So, here's the plan. I'll flirt with him shamelessly, and you quiz him to find out where the money's coming from."

"Okay, but we're really trying to find out what he knows about Nate and Vince, right?" Lyssa said. "Nick's not the only big spender we're interested in. Vince shouldn't have had the money for that condo in Green Bay."

"Right. Maybe there's a connection, Lyssa."

"Like, Nate got a huge settlement from the rockslide and is sharing it with his buddies?"

"Maybe." Bree opened the front door of her tiny blue car and tossed in her purse. "Or maybe Nate's buddies, Nick and Vince, knocked off Nate, and they managed to cover it up so they could go on using his money."

"You are not going in a bar without me." Kyle's cheeks were rigid, and his gray eyes were thunderclouds.

"Kyle, how is Bree going to flirt with Nick if you're sitting at the table? You're being ridiculous."

"And you're flirting with disaster." He shoved the last dinner plate in the dishwasher and muttered, "Two sober women climbing all over a big spender with a potbelly in a bar."

"I have a legitimate reason to do this. I'm sober and I'm working my program. Bree is, too."

"Oh, and what are you planning to drink?" He shut the cover of the appliance with a snap.

"They make yummy espresso drinks at the Manse Lounge. I checked." She took a step closer to him and softened her posture. "I'll sip a cappuccino for the half hour we're there. Bree will probably have a tonic water or something."

"I don't want my wife hanging out in a bar without me. It's non-negotiable. Even if you weren't an alcoholic, I won't have it." He crossed his arms over his chest.

She stroked his arm muscles, her gaze admiring. That was her sister's tip for defusing a situation with one's spouse. "Darling, what's really going on?"

He sucked in a breath and forced it out. "It—it's unseemly."

"Talk to me. Are you worried about my sobriety?"

"In part, yes." He backed his hips against the counter and uncrossed his arms. "You were over the edge last week, and that's not healthy."

"Agreed." She held her tongue after that. As a teacher, she knew wait time worked better than a barrage of prompts.

"Your mission," he said, "is to understand their money story, correct? Vince's, Nate's, and maybe Nick's as well."

"Well, this mission is to find out all I can about what Nick knows about Vince and Nate and, yes, to follow their money stories."

"Why do you need Bree?"

"Bree is there to keep things light and to distract Nick as needed."

"So you've got a little act all worked out," he muttered.

She concentrated on her breathing, Gianessa's number one trick for staying calm in any argument.

He shifted on his feet. "There's a lot of money, too, isn't there, my love?" He tapped a rhythm on the face of the lower cabinet doors behind him. "Vince used big money to buy a waterfront condo he couldn't reasonably afford on a teacher's salary. Nick's wearing a Rolex, driving a Mercedes—"

"Is he?" she asked, surprised.

"I saw the wristwatch when we went to his house for our neighborhood tour, and several times I've seen him roll out of the driveway in a yellow two-seater. Nice car, by the way.

And Bree's telling you he buys rounds at the Manse Lounge for his modestly paid teacher friends. And he takes women to New York and Toronto for theater weekends." He braced her shoulders. "Please, my love, do not let Bree become one of those women for the sake of your investigation. Peter and Gwen would never forgive us."

"I agree absolutely."

"You said yourself, you think it's all connected, that the money Vince and Nick are spending might well be Nate's. His inheritance, the proceeds from the sale of his family home, and any settlement that might have resulted from the rockslide."

"Just a little theory of mine, yes," she said.

"And one possible corollary to your theory is that Nate might be dead but undeclared as such?"

"Yes." Suddenly, she was too shaky to stand. She slid onto the nearest stool. "God, this isn't a game."

"Precisely. Which means you're putting yourself in danger by confronting Nick about Nate and Vince."

"But—"

"Hear me out, my love. I think I'm better qualified than you to judge if Nick is evil or just greedy, which is why I want to be present when you and Bree take him on. Let me finish."

She nodded, her fingers pressed to her lips.

"I want to see the expression on Nick's face when you're questioning him," he told her. "I want to see what he does with his hands, which muscles he moves, and how he holds himself. I want to hear his tone of voice."

Hands gentle on her shoulders, he leaned close to her. "If I have to disguise myself with an eye patch or wear the uniform of a Swiss Guard or hide behind a potted palm, I will do so."

She giggled, and he drew her into his arms.

"But I will not let you go into the lion's den, except under my watchful eye."

"Now I see. Yes, that's a much more solid plan."

Kyle made a rasping sound in his throat and whispered, "Thank you, Lord."

"So, how will we pull this off?"

Kyle eyed the six-foot, black-haired beauty in the tight black pants and green sequined top. "You'd better hope your brother doesn't show up here tonight."

"I'll take that as a compliment," Bree said pertly. "Where are you hiding?"

"In plain sight." He scanned the room. "I'll take that high top no one wants." He gestured to a table along the far wall with a single high-back stool.

"You're going to be a chick magnet looking like that." Bree ran her eyes over his suit and fingered his tie.

"Hah. I'll have my wedding ring in full view, and . . ." He dispensed with his jacket and tie, roughed up his styled hair, unbuttoned his shirt collar, and stuck a few pens in his breast pocket. "I'll pretend I'm a nerd with my head buried in my iPhone. In reality I'll be bombarding my wife with texts."

Bree's laugh turned a few heads. "If I didn't know better, I'd say you've done this before."

"Nonsense, I'm making it up as I go along. Can you grab a table that gives me good sight lines?"

"Okay, but not too close. We don't want Nick to spot you."

"The only time Nick Nunzio and I met face-to-face, his eyes were all over my wife. I doubt he'll remember me, unless I open my mouth. Then my accent would give me away. What's your hand signal if you need my immediate intervention?"

"I need a hand signal?"

"You do. How about grabbing your throat and coughing a bit?"

Bree demonstrated, and he gave her a pat on the shoulder.

"Outstanding. Where's my wife? Tell me she's not wearing a floozy outfit, too?"

"Floozy?" Bree cocked a hip and swept her hand from head to toe. "I'll have you know I'm hot tonight."

"I got that, trust me. And so did every straight guy in the place."

He glanced at a pudgy gentleman who'd just arrived in the archway into the lounge. The man's eyes were assessing Bree.

Kyle lowered his voice and spoke quickly. "That's Nick heading right for you. Navy jacket. Take the table two away from mine. Have Nick sit where I can see his profile and see Lyssa's face." He hurried to his solitary perch on the sidelines and tapped on the preferred table as he passed.

Lyssa watched Bree and Kyle's exchange from the safety of the hallway outside the Manse Lounge. Nick Nunzio stood in the archway a few feet in front of her, scanning the room. Bree flashed a smile in his direction. He sucked in his gut and smoothed back his hair as she glided onto a chair.

Bree set her purse on the chair to her left. *That's the place she's saving for me.*

Nick started forward, and Lyssa trailed a few steps behind, hoping he wouldn't look back. He moved in, and Lyssa held her place, listening.

"Was that guy bothering you?" Nick touched Bree's shoulder with just his fingertips. His voice was deep and soulful.

It was a convincing act, but it turned Lyssa's stomach. She signaled a passing cocktail waitress and gave her order. "I'll come to the bar for it, but I also want to order a drink for the gentleman when he gets low." She pointed to the table where Nick stood and dropped an extra twenty on the tray.

"Whatever floats your boat, honey." The waitress tucked the bill in her back pocket.

Bree was saying, "No worries. That guy's harmless." She fluffed her shining black hair. "But you're someone I'd like to know. I'm Bree." Elbow on the table, she held up her hand to him.

Customers jostled Lyssa on their way to claim nearby tables, but she stayed where she was and enjoyed the show.

Nick took the hand Bree proffered as if it were a precious object. His gaze swept the length of her arm and the breadth of her chest before making eye contact. "Nick Nunzio. Buy you a drink, Bree?"

Bree tipped her head at the tall glass of tonic water and lime in front of her. "I'm set for now, Nick. Join me?" She gestured at the empty chair.

Nick set down his schooner of beer, the foam still settling, and made himself comfortable. "You're expecting someone?" he asked with a glance at the purse on the third chair.

"My friend's running late. And you and I have a lot to talk about, I can tell." She sat tall, crossed her slender black-clad legs, and gave a little twist that focused Nick's attention on her sequins.

"My pleasure," he said, "unless your friend is a jealous fullback?"

"You're funny," Bree told him and feathered her fingers on the back of his hand. "I like that in a man. What do you do, Nick?"

"I teach here in town."

"I knew you were a good guy. What do you like about teaching?"

Nick rambled for a few minutes about helping adolescents shape up and reach their potential. "How about you, Bree? What do you do?"

"I'm working on my bachelor's degree in business, and I have a job at the Bagel Depot." She finger-waved in the direction of the doorway, and Lyssa sprang forward, pretending to be out of breath. "Nick, I want you to meet my good friend, Lyssa. She's a lot of fun."

Nick turned with a smile, frowned briefly, and looked askance at Bree.

"Sorry to be late, girlfriend." Lyssa panted as she gripped the back of the chair. "Listen, I don't want to crowd you two." She looked at Nick and gushed. "Hey, look who it is! Aren't you my neighbor, Nick the teacher? How lucky! I've been hoping to run into you. I have some burning questions for you."

"Whoa," Bree squeezed her hand. "Sit down and relax. You'll scare away my Nick, and we're just getting to know each other." She patted Nick's arm.

Lyssa shrugged off her suit jacket and arranged it on the back of the chair. "I sound like an old married woman, don't I? You two carry on. I'll be right back." She fetched her espresso drink from the bar in fifteen seconds and walked slowly back to the table, straining to hear the conversation.

Bree had her drink in hand and was saying, "I hope you got away for spring break, Nick. Your job is stressful."

Nick's eyes closed and a smug smile dominated his fleshy face. "Four days of uninterrupted beach time with my brother in Florida. I tell you, the women . . ."

Bree made a rude noise through her straw.

Nick coughed and flashed a smile at her. "They've got nothing on you, honey. Every night, it was fish on the grill and dancing at a tiki bar my brother hangs at. That's what I call heaven."

"I envy you." Bree lifted the lime wedge from the glass and squeezed it into her tonic water. Nick watched with fascination.

"Poor woman, you had to work all week?"

"Yeah, but I like the job. The Bagel Depot is where things happen all day in a small town. Friends catch up. News travels. Rumors spread. In fact, it was a couple of high school teachers who told me this is the place to come on Wednesdays. I keep telling Lyssa she needs a break."

Lyssa slid onto her chair and plunked her glass mug on the table. "She talked me into coming tonight." She gave Nick a sunny smile.

"How did your husband feel about that?"

Lyssa rolled her eyes. "We had a bit of a row, but he saw my point. I couldn't let Bree come alone, after all, could I?" Her gaze flashed briefly to Kyle, and his geek disguise made her laugh. "Imagine running into you," she said to Nick. "Have a good time in . . .Where was it you went?"

"Florida. It was heaven. Why don't you ask those burning questions now?" His curt tone implied, *then you can leave.*

Lyssa opened her eyes wide and raked back her red hair, the sign to Kyle that she was about to ask Nick the first question. "Well, I'm dying to know if you've kept in touch with two of your students from our neighborhood. Vince Tuttle and Nate Westover? Vince lived in our house, and I've been told he and Nate were really close friends."

Nick fussed with his coaster and took a swallow of his beer. "Ah, just right. If I don't wait for the foam to go down, I start sneezing and can't stop."

Bree laughed. "Isn't he funny?" Bree jiggled Lyssa's arm.

Lyssa gave a polite nod and folded her hands on the table, as though she had all night to wait for Nick's answer to her question.

Nick squirmed under her gaze.

"Hey, girlfriend, this is really important to you, huh? Nicky, tell us about those two guys."

He gave his glass a quarter turn and exhaled. "What can I tell you? Nate, I knew well. Vince, not so much. Vince wasn't in my English class, because he was in an honors program. Nate and I stayed in touch after he graduated and moved away."

So he's alive? She smiled genuinely this time. "You know, it turned out the gun we found in our backyard was Nate's father's. Nick, have you any idea why it was put in our garden or who might have done it?"

Nick paled and shifted his bulk on the chair. "I knew he had the gun. I told him to put it in a safe deposit box with the papers from the estate. It doesn't make any sense that it

ended up under your tree. How do you think it got there?"
He drilled her with a look.

Lyssa paused for a second and wished she'd seen that
question coming. *God, help me out here.* "You know, they
never recovered the bodies of Nate's parents," she said, not
sure where this new idea was coming from. "The memorial
service was held while Nate was still in the hospital. Maybe
Nate needed closure. Maybe he and Vince buried the gun
together. Wrapped it in favorite things from their outdoor
adventures with Nate's parents. Could that be what
happened?"

"Seriously?" Nick gave a hollow laugh.

Lyssa kicked herself. She hadn't thought of that
explanation until this minute. It could be the truth, but she
wished she hadn't blurted it out right then so it derailed the
discussion.

"Like I said, my friend Lyssa needs a vacation." Bree's
soothing tone put a reluctant smile on Nick's face.
"Girlfriend, what else did you want to ask Nicky?" Her voice
thinned and rose an octave.

Lyssa swallowed her gaff and gave Nick her most
charming smile. "I'd love to know what Nate is doing now
and where he's living."

"Why?"

She scooped a fingerful of cinnamon-sprinkled foam
from her cappuccino and considered her answer as she
licked her finger. "I think it must have been horrible for
Nate to lose his parents like that, and I know he planned to
be a teacher." She let her voice become more serious and
more intimate with each phrase. "I really believe his skill,
and the compassion he's sure to have developed from the

tragedy, could be powerful in the classroom, for any age group. "Would you agree, Nick?"

"Yeah, and I'm the one who gave him the chance to prove it. You know, he's really a good teacher. I'm proud of him. He calls me every so often, and we talk teaching. Not that I can tell him much. He teaches elementary."

Lyssa's hand shook so badly she had to hold her glass mug tight with both hands. "Did he stay in this area?"

"No, and I'm glad. He and his folks were real outdoor people. One of their favorite vacations was to the Door Peninsula in Wisconsin. I visited Nate when he first got a place there. It's exactly right for him. You should see it."

Lyssa felt dizzy with the new information. She was glad to hear it but, if it was true, it shot holes in all their theories.

"Tell us about the house, Nicky." Bree's excited voice coaxed a smile from him.

"Okay, so, it's a log house." He opened his hands expansively. "But instead of being compact and rustic inside, it's luxurious. Huge windows, thick rugs, fantastic kitchen with an indoor grill, the works. It's right next to Whitefish Dunes State Park, on two acres, and it has a phenomenal view of Lake Michigan. Plenty of birding, fishing, and hiking. The place is made for Nate. You know, I'd love to get back out there to see him. Maybe this summer." He swallowed a third of his beer.

"When's the last time you were out there?" Lyssa asked.

"Must be three years now."

"I don't know much about that area of the country, but doesn't it snow a lot? He must have a tough commute to school every day, don't you think?"

Nick shook his head. "He says it's just minutes to his school." He took another long swallow of beer.

"Are you an outdoorsy person, Nick?" Bree asked, her smile showing even white teeth.

Lyssa's covert gesture to the waitress to bring Nick his next beer got immediate attention.

"I like fishing, and Nate's shoreline is the place for that."

"Wow, shoreline?" Lyssa remarked. "That must have cost a bundle."

"Let me tell you," Nick said as he swiveled toward the bar and jerked in surprise to see the waitress heading right for him with a full schooner.

"I read your mind, Nick," the waitress said smoothly and traded glasses with him. "Another schooner of ale. We don't want our friend Nick to go dry."

"Did someone buy me this?" He looked around at the neighboring tables.

The waitress winked before turning away. "I'll never tell," she said and added a few hip swivels on the return trip to the bar.

Nick watched her hungrily.

"You must have a secret admirer, Nick," Lyssa said. "What did you start to say? Something about Nate's luxury house on the water?"

"It must be gorgeous," Bree said.

"And expensive," Lyssa added.

Nick's smile was smug. "Nate's rolling in it. Between his parents' life insurance and the payout from the accident, he's sitting on millions."

"Is he really?" Lyssa asked, her tone as excited as Bree's. "Are you sure?"

"If we had a laptop I could show you."

"Seriously?" Lyssa drew her iPad from her tote bag and set it on the table.

"Show us, Nicky." Eyes round with excitement, Bree shimmied her sequins.

Nick puffed out his chest, and curled his fingers in a gimme motion. Lyssa finished keying in her password and activated the Internet browser for him. He entered the address of an investment company well known for its mutual funds. Lyssa craned her neck to see every keystroke. He logged in as Nathan Westover with a long complicated password she couldn't follow.

Once in Nate's account, the display showed five funds with assets totaling more than twenty million dollars.

"You can actually use his accounts?" Lyssa asked.

He slid the iPad closer to her and gestured to the screen. "My buddy Nate is good to his friend Nick, because I took care of things when he had a breakdown after his folks died. I stuck with him through treatment and stood up for him when he wanted to teach."

"This is unreal, Nick. I can't believe you have unfettered access to his money."

Nick shrugged one shoulder. "We made an agreement back when I helped him out. I'll never withdraw more than a certain amount in a month." He drank more beer, belched, and pointed to the screen. "Go ahead, neighbor. Click on that money market fund and look around. You'll see that some of the transfers have my initials, NJN."

Bree bounced on her chair. "I'll bet your middle name is James. Right?"

Nick focused all his attention on Bree. "Joseph." His hands slid across the tabletop and grabbed hers.

"I love the name Joseph." She leaned closer and showed some cleavage. "Nicholas Joseph. What a beautiful name for a son."

"And what does Bree stand for?" he asked.

Lyssa tuned out the conversation and concentrated on the opportunity Nick had handed her. As she scrolled through the transactions for the current year, she noticed withdrawals tagged NJN every month, each between one and several thousand dollars. Nice deal Nick had going. Did the IRS know about this? Occasional transactions for substantial amounts carried the label VTT. *Vincent Thomas Tuttle?*

An alert in the corner of her screen made her look up. Her view of Kyle, two tables away, was partially blocked by Bree. She glanced at the alert and realized he was texting her.

What are you looking at? he asked.

Nate's accounts, she replied and added the name of the company. *Regular amounts to VTT and monthly withdrawals by Nick.*

WOW.

But I'm stuck in this year. She wanted to see if Nate had purchased the condo for Vince.

Kyle told her what menu to look for, and she dug back to the period when Vince would have moved to Green Bay. In August of that summer, transfers had come into the money market account from the other four accounts, more than one hundred thousand apiece. Then a single transaction, a check of nearly five hundred thousand, carried the tag VTT.

Got it. How can I make a screenshot?

Home and Power together. They'll go to your camera roll.

Lyssa took her screenshots, glad the shutter-click blended into the noise around them. She scanned forward from August looking for the purchase of Nate's shoreline home on the Door Peninsula, but she saw no purchases over one hundred thousand for the two years after. She rolled backward and found it in early May the same year as Vince's condo purchase.

Nearly two million dollars on May 10th. Five years ago.

Ten days before the gun was buried under the Laceleaf Japanese Maple tree.

Her whole body trembled. She couldn't make sense of it and didn't want to think about the implications right now. *Breathe.* She made screenshots of the large transfers and did the same for Nick's thousand-plus amounts in the current year. Finally, she captured the opening screen for Nate's account showing his five funds with the account numbers and current totals.

Conversation at her table was quieter than it had been. Lyssa started to log out, but her stomach did a dive when she realized she had missed one important screen. She nudged Bree's foot, glanced at Nick, and clicked into Nate's account-profile screen.

Bree came through with a remark that got Nick laughing.

There in front of Lyssa was Nate's mailing address, a post office box in Sturgeon Bay, Wisconsin, and a phone number with the Tompkins Falls 315 area code. She took one last screen shot just as an alert came in from Kyle, *Get out now.*

She exited the mutual fund, and jumped into her personal email account.

Nick, one elbow on the table, was watching her. "What are you doing there, neighbor? Helping yourself to a million or two?"

Lyssa's laugh sounded shrill even to her ears. "Absolutely, Nick, couldn't resist." She angled the screen so he could see. "Go ahead, log back in, and check for yourself."

He did. Bree wore a worried frown. Lyssa watched Nick's actions from a polite distance, hoping Kyle was correct that her screenshots were out of sight somewhere. Kyle's gaze was on her. She drew strength from his nearness and arranged her face to appear calm and collected.

Apparently satisfied Lyssa had not made any transactions of her own, Nick started to return the device to her.

"Wait," Bree told him, her tone urgent. "You need to log out, Nicky."

He gave her an admiring once-over. "I like the way you take care of your friends, Brigid," he said. "Can I buy you another drink?"

Bree's short for Brigid? "That's my cue to leave you two alone." Lyssa rose and lifted her bag from the floor to the chair. After shrugging into her jacket, she tucked the iPad away.

Nick watched the device as it disappeared into her tote.

"How much is that gizmo? I want one," he said.

While Nick's eyes were on Lyssa's tote bag, Kyle sidestepped past their table, keeping his back to Nick, and disappeared behind Lyssa in the direction of the archway that led to the hall. While Lyssa gave him a few more seconds to exit, she told Nick, "It's called an iPad, and this is the mini version. The Apple Store at Eastview will be happy to show you all the choices. I hope you'll enjoy your new iPad as much as I have mine."

When she hugged Bree goodbye, she whispered, "You're brilliant. Watch yourself with him."

She trembled all the way across the lounge and broke into a run as soon as she'd cleared the archway.

She met Kyle in the parking lot. He wrapped an arm around her shoulders and ushered her to his car. "Unbelievable. Let's get you home. Will Bree be all right?"

"She can handle herself. Now that you've observed Nick with a keen eye, what do you think?"

"I don't trust him for a second, my love."

"I don't either. And I'm more and more worried about Nate. Nick and Vince are using his money right and left. If Nate's still alive he's being very generous, and I'm not sure why he should be. And Nick said something about fixing things so Nate could teach. If it's true, I'm glad Nate is teaching, but whatever they did was probably underhanded, maybe even illegal."

"Set that aside for now, my love. Were you seriously logged into Nate's millions?"

"Yes. When I show you those screenshots, you'll see."

"Hank Moran will want to see, too."

"So will the IRS, but do we really want to get Nick in trouble that way?"

Chapter 15

Joel had set up the meeting with retired police chief Barker for Friday, before the workday, at the Cushman home on Chestnut Lake. Kyle's only agenda was to learn all they could about Nate Westover and his history with the Tuttle family. He suspected Joel had an agenda of his own, probably something that would strengthen and inform his position as a community leader.

Joel had asked the Penningtons to arrive fifteen minutes early. After a pleasant greeting, at the front entry, he led them into a serene blue-and-gray living room, to an intimate conversation space. An antique settee upholstered in dove-gray suede had a view of the Cushmans' courtyard, alive this morning with songbirds in and out of the thistle feeder and butterflies fluttering from one flowering bush to the next. Two chairs, both covered in French-blue suede, faced the settee, one chair larger and cushier than the other. Each had a view of the lake.

Joel told Kyle and Lyssa, "I thought we could chat a few minutes, just the three of us." Joel's formal tone was off-putting. *What's that about?*

Lyssa glanced at Kyle with a question in her eyes, and he shrugged one shoulder.

After a summary of Barker's distinguished record in Tompkins Falls, Joel said, "He and his wife can dance rings around the rest of us. When we had his retirement party at the Manse summer before last, the two of them brought the house down with their jitterbug."

Kyle smiled politely. "We appreciate your humanizing him."

"Will Manda be joining us?" Lyssa asked.

"Manda is swimming, and she wants to talk with you for a few minutes before she dives in. Something about a thrift shop."

Lyssa made a fist pump. "Be right back."

"Joel, what's your stake in this?" Kyle asked. "We want to support you, of course."

Joel gave him a puzzled frown. "I'm not sure what you mean."

"We were surprised when you said the chief wanted you to be in on the meeting."

"I assumed he wanted me here to run interference for him. To be honest, I hadn't thought much about it."

"So you're a neutral party?"

"Not entirely neutral. I have deep respect for both parties here this morning. Lyssa's doing better?"

Was he being cagey, or was that really all he knew? He set it aside. Before Kyle answered Joel's question, though, he noted Joel had managed to cut Lyssa out of their pre-meeting chat. No way would he let Lyssa's grave concerns be eliminated from any and all of this morning's discussion.

"For a day or so, she was convinced the gun was buried the way it was as a ceremony of closure for Nate Westover following his parents' death, but around two this morning she had the granddaddy of all nightmares. Her screams would scare a Banshee. Terrifying." His stomach clenched at the memory.

"She and I both feel strongly that someone's been seriously hurt or killed with our gun and the shooter has not been brought to justice. She said at breakfast she will go to any length to know the truth about what happened, as will I. We're counting on Chief Barker to fill in some gaps for us."

Joel's expression reminded Kyle of the deep lines he saw in his own mirror this morning, lines etched beside his mouth and eyes. *I scored a point with that.* "Any chance we'll hear the whole story from the chief today?" he asked with an edge to his voice.

"He'll say as much as he can. Communicate your specific needs. Be open with him. And withhold judgment."

Kyle's back stiffened.

Joel cautioned, "I know you and Lyssa are frustrated that the city police haven't pursued the gun. Their focus has been Richie Davis, and he's, thankfully, out of jail now, with his gun permit revoked indefinitely."

Best give a little. "I understand you stepped up to cover Richie's legal fees. I'm sure that was much appreciated. Why did you?" He was grateful no one had filed a lawsuit against Lyssa since the shooting. Kyle had had no communication from the Davises, and all was cordial between the Penningtons and Mrs. Winkel and her sister, Mary.

"Dick Davis has done work for me around my properties for years, and I recommended him for the job at your home. It was the least I could do to support them during this ordeal. I'm pushing for probation and community service for Richie, and I've asked Dick Davis to volunteer Richie's services in Mrs. Winkel's yard."

"Very generous of you, and your strategy helps both Richie and our neighbor. I hope this morning's session helps Lyssa and me."

"Remember, Barker's no longer in charge."

"Ah, good point. About us judging Barker, let's have you cough if you hear one of us going down the dark path of blame," he said in dramatic voice that made Joel smile. "And please break in with clarifying questions."

The doorbell rang.

"Chief Barker, five minutes early," Joel said. "Now you see why I had you come even earlier."

Kyle laughed as he excused himself to find Lyssa, who was talking with her sister from the deck of the Cushman's indoor saltwater pool.

"The chief's here, my love. Hello, Manda."

"Hey, Kyle. Good luck," Manda said. "Lyssa, I'll catch you after he leaves."

As they retraced their steps, Kyle summarized his conversation with Joel. She whispered that Barker probably had plenty of influence, even if he no longer had authority.

His hand rested on her lower back as they reentered the living room. While Joel spoke privately with Barker, Kyle's gaze turned briefly to the view of Chestnut Lake. This morning, the water was an angry green, swept by a strong southerly wind, and dotted with whitecaps. *Lord, keep my anger in check.*

He whispered to Lyssa, "We'll learn what we can from him, shall we?" Her answering smile gave him confidence in Team Pennington.

Barker had a proud bearing that might have begun on the football field or in military service, but Kyle would bet he still maintained it through disciplined rigorous exercise. And jitterbugging. The image made him chuckle to himself.

Joel ended the private exchange with Barker and introduced everyone.

Barker held out his hand to Kyle and gave it a firm shake. When he only nodded to Lyssa, she held out her hand and waited until he shook it before giving him a warm smile.

Score one for my wife.

Joel motioned Kyle and Lyssa to the settee, and let Barker have the more comfortable seat, before taking the chair that sat at an angle to Lyssa. Seated, Joel's and Lyssa's knees were inches apart. Kyle trusted Joel's intent was to support her, not intimidate.

Joel opened with, "I suggest Kyle and Lyssa spend a few minutes bringing us up to speed on what they're looking for and what they've done so far to find the answers on their own."

Kyle nodded. "Exactly. Lyssa will lead us off."

Barker narrowed his eyes at her.

Lyssa paused at the top of her inhale and stiffened. Kyle brought his mouth close to her ear and whispered, "Intimidation tactic. Give it right back to him."

With her outbreath, Lyssa gave Barker her loveliest smile and sat tall. In her strong teacher voice, she told him, "Chief, we're grateful you've agreed to meet with us this morning. Kyle and I have been investigating the matter of the gun discovered in our backyard. We feel compelled to know why it was planted in our garden five years ago in such a bizarre way. And by whom. And we need to understand what crime was committed with it before it was buried.

"We've learned a lot, but our investigation is taking more time than we can reasonably give it, and we're *emphatically* not qualified to investigate a crime."

Kyle covered his mouth to suppress a chuckle.

"We need whatever help and information you can provide. Kyle will frame the situation." She turned to Kyle with a smile that took his breath away.

"Thank you, my love. Chief Barker, we're sensitive to the privacy issues concerning Nate Westover, and it's not our intention to spread gossip. Because the gun was owned by Nate Westover's father, because it has human blood on it, and because of the manner in which it was buried, we're concerned that Nate had a role in whatever happened that Saturday night.

"Perhaps he was the victim, perhaps the perpetrator, perhaps something else. We're aware the police blotter had nothing that weekend for our neighborhood but, given that you were chief of police at the time and were, we understand, acquainted with Nate, we're hoping you have knowledge that can help us uncover the truth and put the matter to rest."

Barker tapped his thumbs together without comment.

"This is not idle curiosity on our part. My wife, Lyssa, is plagued with nightmares. Severe, deeply disturbing dreams, related to the victim or victims." Lyssa reached her hand toward him, and he held it protectively. *Is she acting?* No, her breathing was a little ragged.

"Further, I'm concerned that, now the gun's been unearthed, we're in danger from whoever put it there. If someone killed or gravely injured a person on our property, and then covered it up for five years, what's to stop them doing harm again, to us, as we fumble around, looking for answers? We need your help in a very specific way."

The chief settled back in his chair. His eagle-eyed gaze shifted from Kyle to Lyssa and back. "Let's hear what you've discovered so far, together with the sources for your information."

Kyle glanced at Lyssa.

"We've done so much," she said to him. "Where should we start?"

"I'll start, shall I, with our tour of the neighborhood and our visit to Toffee Winkel in her hospital room?"

She smiled and withdrew her hand.

Joel cleared his throat. "Mrs. Winkel is the neighbor shot last week when you unearthed the gun?"

"Exactly. Thanks for that clarifying question, Joel. Safe to assume the chief is familiar with the shooting?"

Barker nodded.

Kyle continued, "Our attorney Harriet Feinstein asked us to speak with all the neighbors on the block to apologize for the shooting and to assure everyone Mrs. Winkel was recovering, emphasizing that Lyssa had saved her life with quick action. As we talked with our neighbors, we gathered enough information to know that Nate's parents, the Westovers, had been killed in a rockslide and that Nate had survived the accident but not without injury. From Hank Moran of the state police, we learned the gun had been registered to Nate's father and had human blood on it.

"That last gave us serious concern. We began digging deeper for answers, starting with our next-door neighbor, Mrs. Toffee Winkel, the woman shot." Kyle related the details supplied by Toffee, emphasizing Nate's disappearance that fall and Toffee's speculation that he was in treatment.

The chief asked questions concerning Nate's occasional presence in the neighborhood. Kyle supplied the answers. When the chief nodded for them to continue, Kyle handed off to Lyssa to fill them in about her visit to the Tompkins College Alumni Office and her subsequent visit to the college in Geneseo.

She summarized what she'd learned and added, "Concerning Nate's failed effort to earn a teaching certification at Geneseo, Janet Tuttle contributed a vivid description of Nate's attack on Rikki Tuttle, Vince's mother, six years ago. That is, the year the boys graduated from Tompkins College and some time after the rockslide. We know that incident was reported to the police, and apparently nothing came of it, except that it affected Nate's attempt to become a certified teacher."

"That's—" the chief said.

"Let me finish," Lyssa countered. "According to one of the faculty we spoke with, Nate apparently did very well with his courses at Geneseo, even though he struggled with pain from his injury and from emotional issues. Yet, in spite of his good grades, Nate was denied a placement for student teaching."

The chief glared at her and then at the lake beyond.

She continued, "Persons at Geneseo would not reveal who had tipped them off about Nate's, quote, unsuitability for placement, end quote. All we know is, it was verified with the authorities and, because of it, Nate was unable to fulfill the requirements for teaching certification. Regardless, he continued to take all of the courses in the program, finishing those in the spring term. Vince graduated. Nate did not. Vince got a job in Green Bay.

"We think it's important to note that Nate lived with a friend, Patty Beck. Sometime during the spring semester, Patty became Vince's girlfriend. Vince brought her home the weekend before Memorial Day weekend, unannounced.

Vince's parents had planned to be out of town, and they kept to their plans. When they returned on Sunday, May 21st, Vince and Patty were gone. Nate's truck had made an appearance in the driveway the night before. And the little tree, under which the gun was found, had gone crooked."

The chief shifted in his chair.

He's listening. Kyle pressed Lyssa's hand to encourage her. She continued her narrative, though her voice was growing hoarse. She revealed all the details they had unearthed about the fateful weekend, including Vince's total absence from Tompkins Falls the past five years.

"Fast forward. Our online searches revealed almost nothing about Vince, Nate, or Patty Beck, except that Vince Tuttle is successfully teaching in Green Bay, his wife Patty works in the hospitality industry, and Vince has served on the board of his luxury—yes, luxury—condo complex on the waterfront. No sign whatsoever of Nate Westover. I had pretty much concluded that Nate was the victim that fateful weekend.

"However, Wednesday evening I learned that the apparent monetary source of Vince's condo purchase was Nate Westover's sizable investment portfolio, and Nate is apparently alive and well on Wisconsin's Door Peninsula. For which I am grateful.

"In short, Kyle and I have identified when, where, with what weapon. The night of May 19th five years ago. The guest room in our home. The gun. We know who some of the players were." Her chin came forward. "But who was the victim, what exactly happened, and why was it covered up? And, by the way, who pulled the trigger? We need to hear whatever you can tell us, Chief Barker."

The chief straightened and leaned forward, his hands clasped between his knees. "Before I ask how you managed all that, tell me what led you to believe Nate Westover is alive and well."

"Lyssa, can you?" Kyle asked. She was stroking her throat.

Joel held out a glass of water to her. He leaned close as she sipped and said something Kyle couldn't catch. It got a smile and a nod from Lyssa.

"Take your time, Mrs. Pennington," Barker told her, though his voice conveyed urgency and his shoulders bunched like a linebacker waiting for the snap.

Lyssa placed her palms on her knees and her fingers clenched the fabric of her long silk skirt. "Apparently Nate is living on the Door Peninsula in Wisconsin, near Whitefish Dunes State Park and teaching elementary school nearby. I don't know where he teaches exactly. I will have Kathy Regis look into that. She found Vince's school for us."

"Kathy Regis?"

"Our librarian here in Tompkins Falls. She has access to public information around the country, such as statistics about schools and teachers. She's been very helpful with many aspects of our search."

"Go on."

"Nate currently has more than twenty million dollars in mutual funds, and about two million from those funds, we believe, was used to purchase his home on two acres of shoreline on the Door Peninsula." She shuddered. "It's chilling that the purchase was made just ten days before his deceased father's gun was buried in our rose garden."

"Your evidence?" Barker said sharply.

"The transaction history in his money-market account, together with a report of an actual visit to the property several years ago."

"And that visitor was?"

"A former teacher of his."

"From Geneseo?"

"No."

At her rebuff, Barker's head snapped back. "Am I correct in assuming this same visitor also has access to Nate's investment accounts?"

"You're correct."

Kyle opened a bright pink folder on the cushion beside him, Lyssa's cache of screenshots, spreadsheets, and notes.

Joel shifted in his chair. *This piece might be new to him, too.*

Lyssa tried and failed to smooth out the wrinkles she'd made in her skirt.

Barker's left eye twitched.

Kyle held out a copy of one of the screenshots from Lyssa's exploration of Nate's accounts. "The first shows Nate's address in Sturgeon Bay and his cell phone number."

He passed Barker the second screenshot. "This is the transaction Lyssa is referring to that we believe that is the purchase of the house on the Door Peninsula."

He handed over the third screenshot. "And this transaction we think was used to purchase Vince Tuttle's condo later the same summer, before Vince began his teaching position in Green Bay. Notice it's labeled VTT. Vince's middle name is Thomas."

"These screenshots were taken by you, Mrs. Pennington?"

"That's correct."

"And they've not been altered in any way?"

"Correct."

The chief stood abruptly and strode to the wall of windows overlooking the lake.

Kyle, Lyssa, and Joel rose from their chairs a second behind the chief.

Lyssa retrieved the screenshots from the floor where Barker had dropped them. She neatened them and set them on his chair.

"You're pale, sweetheart. Are you all right?" Kyle touched her shoulder.

Joel's gaze was also on Lyssa.

"I will be. Can you speak for us for a few minutes?" Her hands trembled as she fumbled in her purse. Without waiting for his reply, she held tight to her phone and exited to the courtyard.

Joel tipped his head toward Barker, still at the window with his back to them. "I think we've made our point."

Kyle noted the phrase "our point." Perhaps Joel was in their corner after all. *And I need him to be.*

Lyssa paced the courtyard, phone to her ear. "You see how this affects her," Kyle said to Joel. "She doesn't know yet that I have to go out of town for a week or more. If there were any way to avoid it, I would. I will try to persuade her to come with me, but I doubt she'll agree. Could she stay with you and Manda while I'm away?"

"Of course. Trouble in Cornwall?"

"No, a client up in arms. It could have disastrous consequences if I don't jump on it."

"I understand." Joel gestured to the chief. "He's ready to continue."

Barker reentered the circle of furniture and stood stiffly, hands behind his back.

"Chief?" Joel prompted.

"I'm not making sense of this relative to what I know." Barker's voice was gruff. "You already know about Nate's breakdown, and I can add some details and tell you the agreement we reached, and why. However, I cannot and will not give details of his diagnosis or treatment. And I'll point out the extent to which your report indicates a violation of his agreement with us."

"Very helpful, thank you." Kyle's heart hammered in anticipation.

"First, I want to place this in context. During the twenty-plus years I headed the department, we had our share of traumatized teens, male and female."

"Including me," Joel said. "The chief's actions were essential to my long-term recovery."

Barker acknowledged Joel's statement with eye contact and a grimace that might have been an attempt to smile. "We learned over the years, collaborated with agencies in the area, sought grants, initiated programs. I did what I could within the scope of my authority. My goal was to provide the support our young people, damaged in whatever way, might need to move forward and live to good purpose.

"Along the way, I made errors of judgment, and Nate Westover was apparently one of those. You know about Nate's attack on Mrs. Tuttle?"

Kyle nodded. "And according to Janet Tuttle, Vince's parents decided not to press charges."

"We urged them to press charges for the boy's sake. Finally, instead of dropping the matter entirely, they attached several conditions. One was for Nate to get inpatient psychiatric care for his aggressive impulses, which he did. Another was to stay out of the neighborhood."

"But he didn't," Kyle interjected. "Toffee Winkel found him passed out on his front porch one morning in the fall, and she sometimes saw him walking in the neighborhood after dark when she was out with her dog."

Barker's sharp-eyed gaze bore into Kyle's. A rumble sounded in the chief's throat. "Had he been on probation, we would have monitored him, but he was never charged. That was a mistake. The Tuttles, probably at their son's urging, knew a record of violence would ruin Nate's chances as a teacher, and they decided not to charge him with assault."

"But somehow his program at Geneseo found out about the attack on Mrs. Tuttle," Kyle said.

"No," the chief thundered. "There were no leaks from my department and none from the psych center. I checked on both after Nate called me from Geneseo to complain. And I spoke with the college on his behalf. Nate was denied a placement in the schools because he had several arrests in Geneseo for drunk and disorderly. Bar fights."

"We had no idea," Kyle said, and the chief nodded.

"The college wanted to know if I was acquainted with Nate and if he had a record in Tompkins Falls. I told them he had no record and that I supported his efforts to recover from the trauma of his parents' violent deaths. I told them everyone here believed he had promise as a teacher. They chose not to take a chance on him. Nate ruined his own chances with his record there of drunk and disorderly."

Kyle chewed on that until a movement by the door to the courtyard drew his attention. Lyssa pocketed her phone as she reentered the room. She perched just inside the door on a delicate chair with a needlepoint seat cover. He motioned to her to join them, but she shook her head.

"As I say, I'm disturbed by what I'm hearing," Barker said. "I had another long conversation with Nate after Geneseo's final refusal to place him in the schools for his practicum. It was clear he wanted to teach, and he knew his aggression and drinking in Geneseo, not in Tompkins Falls, had ended his chances in New York State. I urged him to continue with his courses, get more treatment, eliminate the use of mind-altering substances, and start fresh somewhere else."

"You knew Nate had a great deal of money at his disposal?" Kyle asked.

"It stood to reason that he did. I knew he had covered his own admission to the psychiatric program. He owned his parents' house, mortgage-free. Both parents had worked as professionals, lived well within their means, and had life insurance policies.

"The settlement from the accident must have been a million or more. I understand the guide had been warned to avoid the trail they took that morning." He shook his head. "Terrible waste. Senseless tragedy. I wasn't worried about Nate's finances, so much as his stability."

Joel asked, "Apparently, Nate then leveraged his courses at Geneseo to become certified in another state, specifically Wisconsin?"

"I'm skeptical about that," Lyssa spoke up.

The men stood. As she rejoined their circle, Kyle and Joel made room for her. "New York is not the only state that's strict about qualifications. Wisconsin also has very high standards."

"So how Nate became certified to teach is still an unknown?" Joel asked. He motioned for all of them to retake their seats.

"Correct," Lyssa answered.

"Chief, what do you know about the relationship between Nate and his lifelong friend Vince Tuttle after the Westovers died?" Kyle asked.

"As I recall, and I reviewed the police report before I came here this morning, just before he attacked Vince's mother, Nate was angry that Vince was leaving for a date. That tells me Nate did not respect his friend's priorities. Worse, Nate acted out his untreated PTSD on Vince's mother in the Tuttle home. Yet Vince argued for his parents not to press charges. Vince cared strongly for Nate, but, in my view, it was a one-way street."

"And yet, Nate apparently bankrolled the purchase of Vince's condo. What do you make of that?" Lyssa asked.

"Your evidence suggests that's true, I agree. Perhaps it was a peace offering from Nate for his abuse of Mrs. Tuttle. I'm only speculating. Perhaps it was payment for a larger favor we don't know about. Maybe it was a private loan." The chief shrugged. "To me, the data points don't give us a clear picture."

So we're back where we started.

Barker shook his head. "Without going to Wisconsin and talking face-to-face with the two young men, there's no making sense of it."

"And you'll see to that?" Kyle asked.

"No, I will not." Barker burned him with a look.

Lyssa huffed, and Kyle stroked her back, as much to calm his own anger.

251

Barker drew himself up and puffed out his chest. "I will, however, advise the authorities to talk with Mrs. Pennington." His gaze bore into Lyssa's wide-open eyes. "Unless she names the person right now who has visited Nate Westover's home in Wisconsin and who has access to his investment accounts."

Lyssa reached for her sister's hand as Manda strolled into the living room, her hair still wet from her swim.

"You okay, Lyssa? I heard shouting."

"I'm glad it's over." She stood with her back to the settee, her gaze on the stormy lake. "Kyle always says the lake matches his mood. God's got it exactly right for me this morning."

"I saw Barker's car drive away a minute ago. Joel looked grim." Manda set down a fresh carafe of coffee and poured refills. "How do you think it went?"

"Intimidation tactics." Lyssa waved her hand in dismissal, but she felt the heat in her cheeks. "We got maybe three additional pieces of information."

Kyle put away his phone. "If that," he fumed.

Joel, who had walked Barker out to his car, returned now and Manda handed him a steaming mug of coffee.

"Perfect, thanks," Joel said. He bussed her cheek.

"What do you think, Joel?" Lyssa asked. "Will he have someone question Vince and Nate in Wisconsin?"

"No. This meeting has shown me that I need to forge new alliances, now that he's retired. I should have done it months ago. Other than a few personal connections, I have no ties with the city police force. That's a mistake."

"Nevertheless, we're indebted to you for this interview, Joel" Kyle said.

"Yes, thank you," Lyssa said. "We had too high expectations."

"You said there were three new points of information, my love. What was helpful to you?"

"One, he let slip Nate's diagnosis was PTSD. Two, Nate paid for his own hospitalization. Remember, Nick Nunzio implied he had taken care of it? And, three, we know Nate's troubles at Geneseo were of his own making. No one from the Tompkins Falls police department or from the psychiatric center scuttled his chances at a teaching degree. That was important for me to know."

"Why, sweetheart?" Kyle asked.

"I care about that young man. With different timing, he'd have been one of my students. Both Vince and Nate, for that matter. They were close friends, both of them passionate about becoming teachers. If not for the rockslide, they'd have remained friends and shared teaching experiences and outdoor adventures.

"Part of me wants that to be their reality today. It's why I tried so hard to believe the gun was buried by both of them as a way of laying to rest Nate's parents after their violent death. That's what my heart wants, but my head won't let me get away with it."

Manda's arm came around her shoulders. "I saw you in the courtyard. Was that Gianessa you were talking with?"

"Yes." She puffed out a laugh. "Telling her a much longer version of what I just said. The truth is, we still don't know what happened that Saturday night five years ago, and I can't make sense of Nate's money story."

"Sweetheart, I think it's a mistake that you wouldn't give Nick Nunzio's name to Barker."

"I agree," Joel told her. "Why did you refuse?"

"Calculated risk. If the city police come after me for it, it's an opportunity to tell them what they should have found out through their own investigation and also to pressure them to help us. But I doubt they will. They don't really have to ask me anything."

"What do you mean?" Joel asked.

"Barker took the screenshots with him, and we didn't black out any of the transactions, including Nick's withdrawals. How many teachers at Tompkins College or Tompkins Falls High School have the initials NJN and live directly across Seneca Street from where Vince and Nate lived?"

Chapter 16

"I'm sure you haven't stopped for lunch." It was one o'clock the same day when Lyssa placed a zippered thermal bag on the cluttered table in Kyle's office at the college. "I have grilled shrimp salad with ginger-orange dressing. Pumpernickel rolls with lightly salted butter. And a thermos of tea."

"Brilliant. Did you do all this for us?"

"I did. It relaxed me. And I know you're stressed about something that has nothing to do with our mysterious gun or our unsatisfactory interview with Chief Barker this morning. I have until my four o'clock class. If you have some time, let's eat and talk."

For just a second, he looked like a deer caught in the headlights. He recovered with that lopsided smile that always made her lighten up. "I have time, my love, and I'll make space." He consolidated the stacks of papers on the table into one leaning tower. "Those can go on the floor." He pointed to the books on her chair.

"When you no longer have an office here," she said as the half-dozen volumes thudded from her hands to the floor, "will you recreate this mess in our little room in the front of the house?"

"Would that be the room that's currently crammed with all your books and the wedding gifts?" he asked.

She laughed. "And the cedar-shrouded racks with all your clothes, don't forget."

"You're saying I have a larger wardrobe than yours?" He poured each of them a steaming cup of tea.

Delaying tactics. "Darling, the entire world knows you have a larger wardrobe than mine." She took the tea he offered and wiggled to a comfortable position on the hard chair. "I rotate three academically appropriate skirts with two jackets, mixed up with six blouses and the occasional appearance of a blue cashmere turtleneck you gave me two Christmases ago." She speared a shrimp.

"You need a good shopping spree. Come with me to London next week."

Her fork poised in midair. "You're going to London next week?"

"I didn't mean to blurt it out that way." He pinched the bridge of his nose. "We need to talk, sweetheart."

"It's serious, isn't it? We should probably eat first so I don't get all weepy." She bit off her shrimp at the tail and chewed.

He nodded and swallowed some salad. When the meal was nearly gone, he told her, "I got a call from Bern at four this morning."

"Bern as in Switzerland? And you didn't wake me?"

"Correct. You were finally back to sleep after your nightmare, and you had early-morning classes."

"Do you have a client there?"

"My first, best, and highest-paying client has his headquarters there. His techie was unable to resolve a technical issue with our support person, which has never happened. So, Problem A, something has gone horribly wrong with tech support at Pennington Secure Networks."

"And Problem B?"

"Long story short, Rudolf, my client in Bern, called Geoffrey who, according to Rudolf, acted like a complete prick. Which is when he called me, in a lather."

"I can imagine."

"If he pulls out, it means millions, sweetheart, and it may be a domino effect."

"He's that influential?"

"I can't allow it to happen. I'll be back as quick as I can." He sighed. "Our esteemed college president and the provost are not happy about my absence."

"Are you worried?"

"They can put a sock in it, my love."

"I agree. Your business is our financial base, not this temporary CIO job."

"Nonsense, we'd be fine without Pennington Secure Networks. Which, by the way, was Justin's winning argument when he convinced me to take on the CIO position."

"Well, nonsense to that." Lyssa slammed her fork on the table. "Your business is not a hobby. You've put years of brainpower and creative energy into it. And you know full well your family money can't sustain an estate like ours and support the local economy, plus afford your luxury lifestyle, and give us the money we need to raise a family. I'll earn whatever I'm able, of course, but your business is our financial base, Kyle."

"I suppose you're right."

"Don't patronize me."

"Sweetheart, I'm really not up for analyzing my money story at this particular moment."

"Well, fortunately, I've just finished doing that." She heard her snippy tone. "Sorry."

"Are you angry that I'm going away?"

"No, honestly, I'm annoyed with myself that I can't drop everything and go with you. I want to support you, and I'd rather be anywhere but Tompkins Falls right now. Will you have to fire Geoffrey?"

"I don't know yet. After the drop in first-quarter earnings, I'm inclined to demote him, in which case he'd quit anyway. I will give him the sack if it's the only way to appease Rudolf."

"Best go to Bern first, see for yourself what's happening before you hear Geoffrey's side. But make sure Geoffrey knows you're with the client he ticked off. Make him sweat."

"My thoughts exactly. You're not only pretty, you're smart."

She tapped his shin with her toe and smiled as a blush warmed her face.

"And I may need to call on other clients while I'm on the continent. I'll be away a good week at least." He reached for her hand. "Sweetheart, I wish you'd tell everyone to put a sock in it, too, and come with me."

"I know, but I really can't leave my students this time of year."

"Are they panicked?"

"Half of them, yes." She withdrew her hand and went back to her salad.

"How do you handle that?"

"I tell them those who study pass and those who pass go on to fame and fortune." She winked at him and speared the last shrimp. "This is good with the ginger dressing."

"So it's money that motivates today's students?" Kyle asked.

"It motivates my economics students, at least. And I've already started review classes three times a week, through the end of semester. Is it worth my coming for a weekend?"

"You'd no sooner get there than you'd be on a plane heading back." He exhaled forcibly. "Lyssa, I don't want you alone in the house while I'm away."

She closed her eyes. *God, don't let him coddle me. I hate that.* She told him, "If I don't stay, I'll feel like a ninny."

"Please consider staying with Joel and Manda. Joel was receptive when I brought it up."

"Was he?" She read the worry in the deep creases of his forehead and resolved not to add to his burden. Still, she'd need to keep her plan to herself, and it would be harder if Manda and Joel were watching her.

I'll just have to be very clever. "Maybe I will stay with them."

His answering smile came from the heart.

Lyssa cleaned out the refrigerator and loaded up her car Sunday morning, with Manda's help, while Joel drove Kyle to the airport.

"You're sure you have enough clothes and supplies for a week or more?"

"If not, I can come back." Lyssa shrugged.

"Not alone, you won't," Manda said snappily.

"Bossy." Lyssa made a face at her sister.

"I love you, Lyssa. Joel and I are very worried about you."

"Well, Kyle and I are, too. Besides, you may decide to throw me out if I have a rip-roaring nightmare."

"It's that bad?"

Lyssa nodded, her gaze on the middle shelf of the refrigerator. "What about this new bunch of spinach? We'll use it, won't we? And the goat cheese?"

"Sure." Manda packed them in the cooler. "Aren't you supposed to tell the police you and Kyle are away?"

"I'm not telling the police anything unless they ask. And so far they haven't. Besides, I think Kyle said something to someone."

"Is your neighbor home yet? The one who was shot?"

"Yes, we went over last evening to talk with her and her sister, Mary. They'll keep an eye out." She put her hands on her hips. "The rest goes in the trash, and we're done. I'll make another pass at the window locks, if you'll check the front door and the door to the basement."

"I hear your husband's out of town, Mrs. Pennington."

The man lurked by her left shoulder, his voice too quiet for other diners at Lynnie's to overhear.

She shifted her gaze from a student essay to the leg of his gray pants and the hand marked by scars he'd probably earned on the street. Restless fingers played near his hip, making her mindful of the gun he carried somewhere on his person.

She sat up straight and smiled into Hank Moran's sparkling green eyes. "Is that a fact, Officer?"

Hank chuckled and gestured to the empty chair. "May I?"

She nodded and cleared a few inches of space for him, hoping he'd stay long enough for coffee.

"You're not staying alone in the house, I trust?"

"No, I'm with my sister and brother-in-law."

"And they are?"

"Manda and Joel Cushman. I forget I'm not the only person new in town who doesn't know who's related to whom. Was it Bree who told you Kyle's away?"

"No, I called Kyle myself to update him on the state-by-state progress on unclaimed bodies. When he answered his phone in German, I wasn't sure I had the right number. Did you know your husband speaks German?"

"You make it sound like he's a spy. Yes, he can fake his way through most European countries. I pick up accents quickly but not languages. Have you found a body?"

"We've had three states respond. No matches so far. Still, it's progress."

"It is, yes." The knot in her stomach uncoiled, and she drew in a deep breath. "Thank you. The truth is out there, and you've renewed my hope we'll find it."

"Fill me in on your investigation," he said and took the mug offered him. "Thanks, Lynnie."

Lynnie placed a metal pitcher on the table and smoothed down her green-and-cream striped apron. "Skim milk, no sugar, right? Anything from the pastry case?"

"You wicked woman," he said with a rumbling laugh. "I'll have a bowl of oatmeal with a sliced banana."

"For real?" Lynnie asked.

"Doctor's orders. Fiber and potassium to start the day."

"You got it. Anything more for you, professor?"

"I'm all set, thanks." She told Hank, "I stopped at the library yesterday and asked Kathy Regis to search her database of Wisconsin educational institutions one more time. We couldn't find Nathan Westover teaching at any public school, even registered preschools. She'll work on private schools as time permits."

"Kyle hinted you dug up more on Nate with a neighbor's help and then went head-to-head with the former chief of police. Tell me about that."

She fished in her tote bag for the right folder and spread it open on top of the student essays.

"Hot pink?" He fingered the tab of the folder and wiggled his eyebrows. "And unmarked. Must be classified."

"That's to keep it from disappearing into my sea of essays. Sorry, they're out of order." She shuffled the screenshots so the overview of Nate's multiple accounts was on top, followed by his contact information and the significant transactions in chronological order.

Hank paged through without comment as he spooned his steaming oatmeal. "Tastes good, Lynnie," his deep voice called across the dining room. "How did you get these, Mrs. Pennington?"

Lyssa gave him the full version of their interlude with Nick Nunzio, including Bree's sequins-and-skinny-leather-pants routine. Hank's booming laugh drew attention from nearby tables. Lyssa added, "Kyle thinks she should be a copper and go undercover."

"Most undercover work doesn't have the class of the Manse Lounge. But, you're right, she has a cool head under pressure now that she's sober."

"She told me once you had something to do with that."

Hank shifted on his chair and toyed with the handle of his mug. Instead of replying, he signaled for the check and gathered the screenshots into Lyssa's pink folder. "Bear in mind, Mrs. Pennington, the neighbor you baited may alert Nate Westover someone's been looking through his investment portfolio."

A thrill of fear shot through her, but it was quickly overshadowed by red-hot anger. "Bree and I wouldn't have been baiting my neighbor if the city police had been doing the job we need them to do."

"All the more reason to watch your back."

When Lyssa's phone rang at noon, she hoped it was Kyle reporting on his first day in Bern. It was Manda alerting her that power had been interrupted in the College Heights neighborhood the night before. "Joel just heard. I know you had timers set, right? I'll meet you at your house after work to check on them and then we'll go on to Happy Hour."

"Except I have my review class, so I'll be later than that. I'll just swing by the house whenever we finish. It will still be light, so you don't need to bother."

"Lyssa, if you go alone, Joel will call Kyle."

"Seriously?" When there was no answer, only huffy breathing, she said, "All right. I'll call you." She made a face at the phone.

"You're welcome," Manda said.

"Thank you." Lyssa laughed and ended the call.

Lyssa's review session ran late, and it was dark by the time she finished with her students. When Manda's phone went to voicemail, she said after the beep, "I'm going to swing by the house right now. Besides resetting the timers, I want to get my rain boots and a tin of tea. Call me if you get this in the next few minutes." She put the car in gear and rolled out of her parking space.

The College Heights area was quiet. Cheery lights glowed in the houses.

Except her own house. Lyssa stopped the car across from 57 Seneca and killed the engine and headlights.

The only light at her house was a narrow beam panning the window of the guest room. Sweat broke out on her forehead and her heart caught in her throat as she imagined the soil-covered hand rising from the garden and searching for her.

With a flashlight? Get real, Lyssa. That's a burglar.

She gulped. Someone had broken into their home and was looking for what?

Their most valuable possession was the baby grand in the dining room. Not easy to steal. Kyle had his laptop with him, and she had hers. His Lexus was in the garage. *Better double-check that when Manda gets here.* She was wearing her only valuable jewelry, an emerald-and-diamond engagement ring and diamond-studded wedding band. But Kyle had expensive clothes, shoes, tie tacks, cuff links, and assorted rings that added up to tens of thousands.

A minute later, the guest-room window darkened, and a faint glow illuminated the window in the small front room. The window brightened. The flashlight swept in an arc, right to left. It steadied in the area where Kyle's suits hung in covered garment racks. The beam lowered toward the floor.

What was down there? Shoeboxes. *Come to think of it, where's his jewelry box?*

She pressed 911 and told the operator where she lived. "I'm across the street in my car and I can see a burglary in progress. Someone is in the small room in the front of the house on the second floor, apparently looking through my husband's clothing and accessories." She listened and replied, "I will absolutely stay in my car and on the phone with you."

The seconds ticked by, and the flashlight remained steady. Maybe the burglar had set it on a perch while he rummaged through Kyle's things. She didn't dare make a second call to Manda on her phone while she was on with 911, so she drew out her iPad and sent an urgent email to both Manda and Joel. "Robbery in progress at my house. I'm on with 911 waiting for police to arrive. Safe in my car, no worries."

When she looked up from the screen, her house was dark, except for a faint light on the first floor at the back of the house. As she watched, the light was extinguished. "He's leaving the house by the back door," she told the 911 operator.

A shape appeared on her driveway. "He's coming toward the street now." She scooted down in her seat and peered over the rim of the steering wheel. An overweight man hesitated in the shadow of the bushes, looked left and right, and shrank back, eyeing her car. She snapped the button to lock all her doors and held her breath.

Her side mirror picked up the pulsing red light of a police car, still a block or so away, its siren silent. The man on the driveway tensed.

Worth a try. Lyssa stood her iPad on the dashboard and triggered the video camera as the burglar sprang forward and streaked across Seneca Street into Nick Nunzio's driveway and disappeared behind Nick's house.

A light went on inside, toward the back of Nick's house, and then another in the upstairs hallway. The ambient light in one bedroom darkened, as if he'd entered the room and shut the door behind him. A dark form appeared at the window for a moment and then melded into the drapery.

She told the operator, "The man ran out my driveway, crossed the street to number 54, Nick Nunzio's house, came into that house through the back, and he's now watching the street from an upstairs bedroom. I think it actually is Nick. Same body type, though I wouldn't have guessed he could move that fast."

A Tompkins Falls police cruiser, its red lights bathing the street, parked behind her VW. The headlights illuminated her car and highlighted her in the front seat.

Swallowing her vulnerability, she told the operator, "The police are here now."

She ended the call with a press of her thumb. How had Nick known she and Kyle were away? What had he been looking for? What had he taken?

Or was Nick making mischief, paying her back for the charade at the Manse Lounge last week? Had he guessed Kyle was involved and left something icky in his shoeboxes?

She'd know soon enough. She breathed deeply to slow her galloping heart. One of the officers headed to the back of Nick's house, and the other started toward her car.

A flash of headlights caught her attention. Manda's Volvo bolted through a four-way stop and screeched to a halt directly across from Lyssa's VW.

The officer backed up, unholstered his weapon, and crouched behind his open door.

Manda leapt from her car, leaving the driver's door open and the alarm chiming. She tugged on Lyssa's door handle, yelling, "Are you okay?"

"Step away from the car," the officer barked at Manda, his gun trained on her.

"She's my sister," Manda spat back at him.

Lyssa spilled out of her car and hugged her. "I'm okay, Manda," she said, tears flooding her face now that she had the comfort of a loved one. "It was Nick, and I don't know what he was after or what he did inside our house."

"Who's Nick?"

"Our neighbor, right there." She directed her hand toward his house.

"Oh my gosh, Lyssa."

"Kyle will go ballistic."

"Which one of you is Mrs. Pennington?" the officer's voice shouted over their strangled words and sobs.

Lyssa raised her hand and faced the officer. "I'm Lyssa Pennington. This is my sister Manda Cushman. That's my house," she said, waving to the darkened façade.

She snuffled her nose. "And the man who was inside our house is now upstairs. There." She pointed to the darkened window of Nick's front bedroom, where, as they watched, a shadowy form retreated from sight.

With Manda gripping her hand, Lyssa climbed the stairs and inched into her master bedroom. They'd been cleared to enter the Pennington home and asked to identify anything missing.

Although the bed was undisturbed, Lyssa said, "Imagine if I'd been sleeping here when he broke in."

"Don't go there. You're safe staying with Joel and me at the lake."

"Can I ask you to go through my dresser, while I check my closet? Remember, the policewoman said he may have left something or taken something."

Lyssa's hanging clothes were undisturbed, but her tote bags and purses lay in a heap on the closet floor. She held each one under the closet's ceiling light and ran her hand into each pocket and around and under the insert at the bottom. "They're all clean." It was her habit to empty every compartment before putting them away each time. That probably pissed him off.

Manda had found nothing out of place in the lingerie chest or the small chest of drawers that served as a nightstand on Lyssa's side of the bed. Lyssa examined Kyle's nightstand. "He forgot to take the Dennis Lehane book with him," she said, noting the bookmark a third of the way through. The contents of his chest of drawers had been disturbed, but nothing seemed to be missing. "Everything else is okay."

They started down the hall together, but Lyssa gave the door to the guest room a wide berth. "I can't go in there. Manda, can you check it, please? I'll be going through the things in the front room."

The stack of boxes with their wedding gifts was undisturbed, but each of the three covered garment racks had been unzipped, and one of Kyle's cashmere suit jackets lay crumpled on the bottom of its rack.

She lifted it with loving hands, pressed the cloth to her cheek, and inhaled his gingery fragrance. Then she fitted the coat on its hanger and hung it on the back of the door so the wrinkles could fall out.

"Nothing odd in the guest room," Manda said. "What's the story here?"

"Gifts are undisturbed, but the thief has been in Kyle's wardrobe. I don't think any suits are missing. They wouldn't fit Nick. We should go through the pockets, and I'm concerned about the boxes that are tucked under the racks. The light was focused down there most of the time."

"What's in the boxes?"

"Shoes mostly. His lifetime supply of Italian leather loafers." Her laugh had a hysterical edge. "But his tie ornaments and cuff links and rings must be somewhere down there. They weren't in his dresser. Can you check the boxes, right to left? I'll work around you. Then we'll have our answer for the police."

In the first clothing rack, she found so many pocketed treasures she grabbed a shoebox lid to hold them. By the time she reached the third rack, she had a mound of chrome-and-gold pens, monogrammed handkerchiefs, miniature cameras, flash drives in the shape of robots, intricate metal puzzles, and a signet ring. Although she'd long since concluded Nick hadn't fished in Kyle's pockets, she continued her search out of curiosity.

She found a tiny notebook in the suit coat he'd worn when they had shrimp salad in his office. Her name was on every page of the little notes about someplace they'd been, something they'd done, some silly thing she'd said. Each entry was dated, starting with the day they'd met, in London at a faculty soiree on the University of Chicago London campus. A tear fell as she read the last page, dated Friday. His heart was heavy, he'd written. He'd tried to persuade her to go with him to Europe but had to settle for leaving her in Joel and Manda's care.

She closed the cover on the small book and brushed at a few more tears.

"You were reading so intently, I didn't want to interrupt," Manda said. "What is that?"

Lyssa sank to the floor beside her. "Notes Kyle makes to himself." Her face warmed with love for her husband an ocean away.

"About you?" Manda's arm came around her shoulders.

Lyssa nodded and tucked the book in the pocket of her silk skirt. "Did you find something missing?"

Manda repositioned a carved mahogany box between them and opened its tiered compartments for Lyssa's inspection.

"It's his jewelry box," Lyssa said, "but where are his cufflinks and watches?"

Heavy footfalls on the stairs announced the arrival of an officer. "About finished up here, Mrs. Pennington?" a male voice called to them.

"In here," Lyssa yelled. "We've found my husband's jewelry box empty."

Lyssa snapped pictures of the box with its remaining contents. She closed the compartments and propped up one side. "One of these carvings opens a hidden drawer," she told Manda. She pressed a few ivy leaves with no results. When she jiggled an acorn, an inch-high drawer slid open, revealing gold chains and a tarnished pocket watch. "Thank God his father's watch is still here."

She rose from the floor, picked up the box, set it on a corner of a low bookcase, and opened it for the officer. "This is my husband's. Normally, there would be cuff links, tie tacks, and watches," she said, pointing to the empty tiers. "Many of each. More than I recovered from his pockets," she said with a gesture to the box lid, filled with things she'd found in the pockets.

"More than all that? You're sure?" he said, staring at the mound of treasures.

"I'm very sure."

"We're questioning Mr. Nunzio, but he denies having been in the house. This finding is grounds for a search warrant of his home. Will you be able to identify pieces that might have been stolen from your husband's jewelry box?"

"I'll know a few things, but Kyle's the one who'll know everything at a glance. He's in Europe, but we can Skype with him if you turn up anything. I'm sure he'll want to help."

Lyssa dumped Kyle's pocketed items into the jewelry box and took it with her for safekeeping. The officer motioned for them to precede him down the stairs.

Out in the fresh air, on the front porch, Lyssa welcomed her sister's arm around her shoulders. "Thank you for being here. Kyle's going to freak. Can you take this a minute?" She handed off the box and pressed her husband's cell number.

"Do you want him to come home?" Manda asked.

Lyssa shook her head. "Hello darling," she said in response to Kyle's mumbled greeting. "Is that German you're muttering?"

"Lyssa, what's happened? Are you all right?"

"I'm fine and very sorry to wake you, but we have a situation, and I need your assistance for just a few minutes. Then you can go back to sleep."

"Sure you're all right?"

"I'm perfectly fine. We've been robbed, Kyle, that's all. I'm with a policeman, and Manda is by my side."

"You weren't in the house?"

She patiently explained the circumstances and assured him she'd not been in the house. "Bottom line, I was waiting in my car for Manda, who arrived the same time as the police. Kyle, our burglar may have taken your cuff links and watches, unless you have the whole lot with you."

"I've only one pair and one watch along for the trip. Can you hold a moment?"

"What?" She shook her head. "I'm not sure what he's doing," she told the policeman. "But he confirmed items have been taken."

Kyle came back on the line. "Sweetheart, I've sent you an encrypted file, an inventory of the box, with photos and valuations, that I maintain for insurance purposes. Will that help?"

"Brilliant, yes."

"My love, they didn't get into the hidden drawer, did they?"

"I checked, and there are half a dozen or so gold chains and your dad's pocket watch."

"That's good then."

"How are things going?"

"Bern is quiet again, and I'm off to Munich in the morning. Rudolf warned me it's ready to explode. Do you need me to come there?"

"No, no. But we may need to Skype with you, if the inventory doesn't satisfy."

"If you must. Have you any idea who our thief was?"

"It was our neighbor with the pink door, Kyle." She held the phone a few inches from her ear.

"Nick? Bloody hell! That's what I get for asking him to keep an eye out while I'm away."

"I believe the officer heard you say all that. You told Nick we'd be away? You didn't give him a key, did you?"

"Of course I didn't give him a key. But you remember, he said neighbors watch out for each other. I fell for that one, didn't I?"

"I'm surprised you trusted him at all after what we learned last week. When did you tell him we'd be away?"

"Friday morning. Partly I wanted to gauge his reaction after our charade at the Manse."

"Did he say anything about that?"

"Not at all. Did he take anything besides the jewelry?"

"No, nothing, as far as I can tell. They're getting a search warrant, and I'll be asked to identify items, so the inventory will be a help." She tucked the phone close to her ear. "How will I know the encryption key?" She'd need a code to open the file.

"You'll find it in the coda in the Brahms sheet music."

"Are you serious?" Lyssa laughed, and her body flooded with relief. "I love you so much."

"I as well, sweetheart. Your laugh tells me you're all right. Love to Manda and Joel."

"Back to sleep now. You have important work to take care of in the morning."

"So this is Nick's bedroom? The décor's not very romantic, is it?" Lyssa remarked to Manda. Nick was still in the company of Tompkins Falls' finest.

A navy duvet lay formlessly on the bed, and wrinkled shirts adorned a plaid armchair. "He's a love-them-and-leave-them kind of guy, I understand." She glanced out the window to the street below. "I'm sure this is the room where our thief was hiding when the police arrived last night."

Someone behind her cleared a throat, and she turned her best professional face to the policewoman. "Good morning, Officer."

"Mrs. Pennington, we've recovered a number of items that may have come from your home. In addition to half a dozen watches in the pocket of the suspect's jacket, he also had on his person a pouch, which contains small items of men's jewelry. I will lay out the items, and we need you to identify anything you recognize as your husband's. Are you capable of doing that without your husband present?"

"I am." Lyssa took from her purse several pages from the inventory Kyle had sent, with photos of his cufflinks, watches, rings, and tie tacks.

The officer glanced through the pages and asked where she'd gotten them. Lyssa explained he'd emailed a file the evening before when she'd alerted him to the theft. "The green check marks are items I found in his pockets when we looked through the house last night.

"Very helpful." The officer spread a cloth on top of Nick's dresser. As she placed items on the cloth with her gloved hands, she instructed. "Officer Dansko is video recording our actions and voices. You may point to items you recognize as your husband's, but do not touch or move anything. That's my job." She set out half a dozen watches and loosened the strings on a leather pouch.

Lyssa gasped and reached for Manda's hand.

"What's wrong, Lyssa?"

"B—before we look at the items"—she cleared her throat—"it's important for me to know if that pouch belongs to Nick—sorry, to the suspect—or if it was supplied by the police?"

"It was on the suspect's person, and it contained the jewelry, with the exception of the watches. Do you recognize it as your property?"

"I recognize it as being exactly like the one in which our mystery gun was packaged. You're undoubtedly aware we unearthed a gun recently from our backyard garden, which was subsequently found to have human blood on it."

Chapter 17

Lyssa guessed she was as pale as the two officers at her announcement about the leather pouch.

"In that case, we will treat the pouch as part of the investigation," the woman officer said, her voice shaky. "Dansko, did you get everything Mrs. Pennington said?"

"Got it," Dansko said. He exchanged a puzzled look with his partner. "Are there two leather pouches?"

Lyssa had the same question. She stilled her trembling hands by crossing her arms and gripping her forearms.

Manda used her phone to snap a picture of the pouch. "You okay?" she asked.

Lyssa nodded. "Let's go on. May I use this to point to items, then make a black check mark on the inventory each time? That way, I can discuss this with my husband." She held out the black marker for the policewoman's inspection.

"Agreed."

Manda slid behind Lyssa's shoulder and snapped photos of the items on the dresser.

The identification went quickly. All the cufflinks and tie tacks from the pouch matched items on the inventory, as did the watches. In addition, the pouch had held three of Kyle's rings and a platinum-and-gold-link bracelet Lyssa hadn't seen him wear since their honeymoon. She thought back to the dozen or more rings she'd seen, still in the jewelry box, last night. "The rings left behind had monograms or school crests," she said to herself.

"Say again?" the officer asked her as she gathered up the stolen items.

Lyssa explained and added, "That's why I didn't realize any rings had been taken."

"I understand. These items will be tagged as evidence until the case is closed. We're done here, Dansko."

"Kyle will not appreciate having his treasures in the hands of the police," Lyssa said quietly to her sister.

"No kidding," Manda said dryly. "When can my sister get back in her house?"

"We've finished with the scene, unless you think something else might be missing that you didn't report last night."

"I never checked the garage for Kyle's car. Can someone come with me right now to do that? If it's there, we're all set."

Officer Dansko accompanied Lyssa across the street and opened the side door to the garage with her keys. The Lexus was undisturbed. Dansko offered to come with her into the house, and Manda urged her to take him up on the offer.

Lyssa cringed at the fingerprint powder, starting at the French doors and continuing throughout the house. "Is there a cleaning service I can call?" she asked Dansko.

He gave her a name, and Manda noted it. "I'll call while you're checking the house," she offered.

Lyssa went room to room with Dansko, stopping only to reset the timers. She'd forgotten to do that the night before. That done, she grabbed her tall flowered rain boots from the coat closet and, on the way out, snagged the tin of tea they'd brought from Cornwall.

As she locked the French door to the patio, she thought to ask Dansko, "How did the thief get in?"

Lyssa explained to Joel half an hour later as she paced the Cushman's kitchen, "When they first investigated the break-in, I let them in the front door, which was locked. When we went back over with Dansko this morning to check the garage and recheck the house, I went to the patio door as I normally do, and I'm sure it was locked."

"Yes, it was," Manda said.

"And that's how he says the thief got into the house?" Joel asked. "Through the patio door?"

"Yes. We checked that all the windows were locked, and I remember seeing our thief go out the back. There's no secret door from the basement, and just tiny windows down there."

"So he had a key?" Joel's voice was incredulous.

"He must have," Lyssa said. "Dansko said there was no sign of tampering with the lock and, anyway, it's one of those claw locks"—she made her voice low and dramatic as she demonstrated by curling the fingers of one hand and pitching forward—"that grip into the sash." She tugged at her own wrist without its budging in any direction.

Joel smiled behind his hand until Manda let out a laugh, and he joined in.

Lyssa fisted her hands on her hips. "What? You don't like my advertisement for thief-proof glass doors?" She added her laugh to the mix.

Joel cleared his throat. "Who would have a key?"

"I know we don't have one," Manda said. "You didn't give one to a neighbor? To Gianessa?"

"No, and Kyle squawked when I asked if he'd given Nick a key, so I'm sure he hasn't given out any." She raised her hands in a hold-everything gesture. "I wonder if Estella did?"

"Who?"

"Estella Capellita, the woman who lived there before us."

"Wait," Joel said. "You never changed the locks?"

"What?"

Joel rolled his eyes while Manda said, "Lyssa, when you buy a house, you change the locks."

"Well, I didn't know that!" Lyssa stomped her foot. "Now you tell me. What do I know about buying houses, except the market value and trends and housing starts and mortgage fluctuations and all those money matters? What a fool I am."

Manda laughed. "Professors have no common sense."

Joel wrapped her in a hug. "We shouldn't have assumed. We're sorry, sis."

"Estella probably trusted sweet-talking Nick, like Kyle did. Bet you anything she gave him a key." She opened her phone and scrolled through her calls for the day after the gun's discovery, looking in vain for Estella's number. "Maybe we used Kyle's phone to talk with her. No matter. I've got her contact information on my spreadsheet."

Her phone rang, and she held it out, frowning at the Caller ID. "City of Tompkins Falls?"

"Police, maybe," Joel said.

"Hello," she answered with a suspicious tone.

"Officer Dansko," he identified himself. "We have a few questions for you, Mrs. Pennington, and we'd like you to come downtown."

"When you say 'come downtown,' what exactly do you mean, Officer Dansko?" she asked with a worried frown in Joel's direction.

Joel whipped out his phone and flew through his contacts.

While Officer Dansko explained a complication in their questioning of Nick Nunzio, Joel slipped out to the hallway, and they heard him say, "Harriet, Joel Cushman, Lyssa Pennington's brother-in-law. We need your support in a new development with the Pennington's gun."

Lyssa said to Dansko, her voice hard, "Nick is lying if he says I went to his house or contacted him in any way yesterday."

Manda stroked her arm.

"I will answer your questions with my lawyer present and my brother-in-law present to represent my husband, who as you know is in Europe on business. Will that be satisfactory?"

She made eye contact with Joel, who nodded and flashed open his hand, twice.

"Ten o'clock today, Officer?" she asked before glancing at the clock. After nine already.

Joel nodded again, and the officer agreed.

"Until then," Lyssa said and broke the connection. She held up a hand to Manda. "I will not bother Kyle with any of this nonsense until he's home again."

"You have to call him."

"No, Manda, not yet. He has very, very serious matters on his mind, and I need him to focus all his energy there. I'm a big girl, and I can deal with this, with your support. I'm just so sorry to have brought all this baggage with me into your home."

"Nonsense. That's what families do for each other." Joel held out his phone to her. "I need you to talk with Harriet right now, tell her *everything*"–his eyebrows lifted with emphasis–"about *all* your interactions with Nick, and answer *all* her questions."

Lyssa arrived at the police station with Joel on her right and attorney Harriet Feinstein on her left. Officer Dansko greeted them.

"Good morning, Officer Dansko," Lyssa said in her I'm-in-charge-here teacher voice.

The tone matched her carefully chosen mid-calf, beige linen skirt and navy cardigan over a navy shell, perfectly paired with mid-heel navy pumps. "This is Joel Cushman, my brother-in-law, and Harriet Feinstein, my attorney. I'm sure there's no issue with them participating in the session this morning. Will anyone else be joining us?"

Dansko was not only outnumbered, he was younger and shorter than the three citizens, but he didn't blink an eye. "Nice meeting everyone. The chief may join us at some point on a related matter. Come with me."

Joel and Lyssa exchanged a look, eyebrows raised. Lyssa mouthed, "The new chief."

Joel suppressed a smile. "It's one way to make connections," he whispered, his mouth close to her ear.

She allowed herself a silent laugh, and the knot in her stomach relaxed.

Dansko led them to a clean, spare, windowless room with the lingering odor of pine-scented cleaner. Nearly filling the space was a scrubbed gray table flanked by six armless chairs with minimally padded seats.

Harriet chose the chair at the head of the table, farthest from the door. Dansko, across from Lyssa, placed a recorder on the table and activated the device. After speaking the date, time, and purpose of the meeting, he asked each of them to identify themselves using their normal voices. They did.

"Mrs. Pennington, we've questioned your neighbor, Mr. Nicholas Nunzio, about the fact he had your husband's jewelry in his possession. He's insisting you gave him the jewelry."

"What?" Lyssa shrilled.

Joel pressed her forearm, and Harriet said, "Let's hear what he has to say, Lyssa, however outrageous it may be."

Glaring at Dansko, Lyssa said through clenched teeth, "Continue."

He read from notes on the screen of his tablet. "According to Nunzio, you'd been having an affair for six months, and he'd grown sick of it." Over Lyssa's *grrr*, he read on, "You'd given him gifts over that period of time, which he was unaware were from your husband's own jewelry."

"Lies." Lyssa gripped the edge of the table to keep herself from ripping Dansko's tablet from his hands.

"Last evening at approximately six o'clock, you came to his back door, telling him your husband was away and begging him to spend the night with you in your home. He obliged."

She shoved back her chair and shot to her feet. "He's a bloody liar," she said, both hands on her stomach, which was as outraged as she was.

"Later, the two of you argued, and he left your home to return to his, across the street. Mr. Nunzio claims that's when you called 911 and concocted the story about the burglary, fingering him as the suspect."

Harriet's quick action placed a wastebasket in Lyssa's hands just before she vomited her breakfast. When her stomach was empty, Harriet handed the bin to Dansko. "Officer, have this cleaned and the room freshened, please, and bring some water for Mrs. Pennington."

Joel braced Lyssa's shoulders, and she burst into tears. "Let's take a break, sis."

She walked beside Joel on shaky legs, grateful for the comfort of his arm around her shoulders. "I've never been so humiliated, Joel, even when I was stinking drunk in some alley in Austin."

"Why were you in an alley?"

"Chick fight on ladies night at the bar. They wouldn't let us go at it for long inside."

"Forget I asked that question. Nick's desperate. He knows you've got him."

In the unisex restroom, she splashed water on her face and rinsed out her mouth, then dug her tiny toothbrush and tube of paste from a side pocket of her tote. Finished with her cleanup, she gripped the edge of the sink with trembling hands. "Last time I was in a public restroom with a man, it was Kyle at the hospital after Richie Davis shot our neighbor. I had blood all over me. This isn't quite as bad."

Joel held out his phone to her. "You need to call Kyle."

"Not now. Not about this."

"Lyssa—"

"Joel, he's trying to salvage his business, which is important to us and our future. If I were to call him right now, he'd be on a plane back here. Wouldn't he?" At Joel's nod, she said, "I won't have that. I'm so grateful for your support and Harriet's. And please don't you or Manda call him either. I won't worry Kyle with this. Not now."

"He'll be angry that you've kept it from him."

"Yes, but by the time he finds out, Pennington Secure Networks will be back on solid footing, and that's more important."

A muscle jerked in Joel's cheek.

"Please, Joel, I don't need you to lecture me. I need you to help me think." She waved at the towel dispenser and tore off the paper. After blotting her face, she washed her hands and dried them while she said, "If Nick is capable of elaborate lies like this, and if the leather pouch he used to pilfer Kyle's jewelry is a match for the pouch the gun was buried in, chances are he was involved in whatever crime was committed with the gun."

"I hadn't thought of that." Joel leaned back against the door.

"And given that he's such a clever thief, he might even have stolen the gun from the Westover house during their fateful trip, or after, when the house was empty, and he might be solely responsible for its use after the Westovers were killed."

"Possible."

"Or maybe he did something horrible with the gun months before it was buried, then was invited to Vince and Patty's party, and took advantage of the newly planted tree to bury the gun."

"That one's far-fetched. There are easier ways to dispose of a gun. And why wait?"

"Right, good, and it doesn't explain the elaborate manner of burial, does it?"

"What do you mean?"

She explained about the lunchbox and bandanna. "I need to talk with Hank later today and run all this by him, starting with the burglary."

"That's fine, Lyssa, but right now, this minute, we have an opportunity to get the city police involved in the investigation of your gun. You can connect the dots for them. Let's give it a try. Find out what they're capable of. What do you say?"

"Brilliant. For that I'll need one of your killer cinnamon breath mints."

When they returned to the room for questioning, Lyssa noticed a muscular African-American man in conversation with Harriet. He had a buzz cut and sported a well-fitting suit.

He rose when they entered and seemed to fill the space, though he was shorter than Joel.

With his left hand still on Lyssa's back, Joel held out his right hand. "Don't crush," he warned. "It's been injured." He shook the man's hand and introduced himself and Lyssa.

"Chief Brian Smokes." The man gave Lyssa's hand a firm shake. His voice rumbled like Hank Moran's. "You own the Manse?" he asked Joel.

"I do, Chief."

"Family wedding there in February. Beautiful venue, excellent food."

"Thank you." Joel's smile was proud.

Lyssa parked herself beside Harriet, directly across from the chief. Dansko restarted the recorder, and they repeated the opening ritual.

Harriet preempted. "My client insists on receiving a written transcript of Mr. Nunzio's allegations. We reserve the right to use it in a libel suit in the future."

The chief voiced his consent.

Lyssa thanked them both. She'd ask Harriet later what that was about. "Chief Smokes, thank you for joining us. My stomach is now completely empty, so it's safe to resume. I've been accused of lying to 911, of giving away my husband's jewelry, and of having an affair with Mr. Nunzio for the past six months. Those are false accusations.

"First, I value the 911 service in our community, and I would never waste their time, any more than I would pull a fire alarm without cause.

"Second, I have lived on Seneca Street since mid-January, not the six months that Nick Nunzio is alleging, and my husband and I just met the man last week.

"Third, I have never"—she closed her eyes and inhaled sharply, then let out a calming, cinnamon-scented breath—"never engaged in any relationship with that vile man. Kyle and I met him for the first time the day after the gun was unearthed in our backyard. I believe you're aware of that incident?" Her gaze bore into the chief's. "The gun with human blood on it?"

He shifted his bulk and cleared his throat. "I am, and I understand Hank Moran of the state police has some interest in the matter as well."

"Although your department *emphatically* has no interest in the gun's history." Lyssa let the phrase and her accusatory tone hang in the air for a moment. "When we identified my husband's stolen jewelry in Mr. Nunzio's bedroom, I pointed out to the officers that the pouch Nick used to conceal my husband's cuff links and other jewelry was similar to the pouch used in the burial of the gun in our backyard garden, on May 20th five years ago. May I know where my husband's jewelry is being held and where *both* pouches currently reside?" She sat back and folded her hands on the table.

"The jewels and the pouch found on Mr. Nunzio's person are in our evidence room, tagged with the identification of the larceny case under review here and now. The pouch associated with the shooting in your backyard is tagged in association with the shooting last week. That was verified this morning when I personally examined the two pouches side-by-side."

Lyssa and Joel exchanged a look, eyebrows raised. They'd connected the dots. "And?"

"Allowing for wear and soil stain, I would deem them identical. We've asked Mr. Nunzio to tell us what he knows about both pouches. Let's leave that matter for the moment. Officer Dansko will continue now with the questions about the robbery, from your earlier interrupted meeting."

Lyssa nodded and glanced at Harriet, who was busy taking notes on her iPad.

"Mrs. Pennington, tell us where you were the afternoon and evening of the alleged burglary?" Dansko asked.

"Alleged," she said under her breath. "I am an economics professor at Tompkins College. In anticipation of final exams, I have initiated regular review sessions, starting last week. Those sessions immediately follow my Monday, Wednesday, and Friday classes, through the end of the semester. My classes end at five-forty. The review sessions last as long as students want.

"This Monday's session went very long, until . . ." She scrolled through the log of calls on her iPhone. "I called my sister Manda at eight-twenty-five as I left campus and asked her to meet me at the house. So the review session formally finished at about eight-fifteen.

"I answered student questions on my way out of the building and continued to my car. If you need proof, I do take attendance at every class, and I have my students sign in and out of review sessions. I'm sure they'd respond to your questions in a timely way."

She raced on, "At eight-twenty-five, when Manda did not answer her phone, I left a voicemail, asking her to meet me at my home. I parked on the street opposite the house and saw that, indeed, our timers had been unset by the power failure the night before. That had been my main concern in visiting the house."

"When you say 'visiting,' you're not living in the house?"

"No."

Dansko gave her a puzzled look. "And you weren't willing to enter the house alone?"

"Correct. My husband left on business Saturday, and, given the danger we perceive ourselves to be in"—she paused to let the words sink in and fixed the chief with a stony stare—"in connection with the gun unearthed in our backyard, which no one but us cares to investigate, my husband insisted I stay with my sister and brother-in-law." She nodded across the table to Joel. "They've been extremely supportive through this ordeal."

"Mrs.— "

"Apparently, Kyle did not tell the police the house was unoccupied, nor did I. We did tell our next-door neighbor, Toffee Winkel, the one who was shot by the gun unearthed in our backyard, who is now thankfully recovering at home.

And Kyle told me he'd informed Nick Nunzio we'd be away." She rolled her eyes. "We agree that was a mistake."

"And did your husband provide a key to either or both neighbors?"

"He did not. And I did not. Ever. Neither of us has ever given a key to anyone, not even to Joel and Manda. Nor did we have the good sense to change the locks when we moved in. It's possible Estella Capellita, who owned the house before us and who installed the patio and the French door through which Mr. Nunzio *allegedly* entered and left the house, might have given Nick a key." She passed a sticky note across the table to Officer Dansko and sat back. "That's Mrs. Capellita's phone number."

Joel drummed his fingers on the table. The chief shifted in his chair. Harriet keyed in notes. Lyssa breathed.

"Thank you, Mrs. Pennington," Officer Dansko said. "I understand from the 911 log that your sister, Manda Cushman, arrived approximately the same time as the police cruiser at eight-fifty-two. I also understand, before that, you attempted to video record the burglar as he ran from your driveway to Mr. Nunzio's driveway. May we see that recording?"

"I'd forgotten, yes." Lyssa dove for her tote. She drew out her iPad and navigated to the video. "I've no idea what it looks like, but let's play it. Harriet, since you're at the head of the table, would you hold this for us to see?"

The video was darker than she might like, but she'd held the device steady enough during the recording. The film showed a man darting across the street. For a moment, he'd looked directly at the camera, stiffened, and nearly lost his footing. Then he continued his dash down the driveway of Nick's house.

"Dansko, rewind to the full-face view and freeze it." Chief Smokes ordered.

The man in the freeze frame was clearly Nick Nunzio, and his right fist held a bulging dark object just inside his jacket. The leather pouch.

"Thank you, Mrs. Pennington. May I see the device?" The chief wiggled his fingers at Harriet, and she passed it to him. He checked the information associated with the video. "Recorded at eight-fifty on the night of the alleged burglary," he said with a question in his eyes for Dansko.

"Sir, that precedes the arrival of the cruiser by approximately two minutes."

"You'll send this to us now, so we don't have to confiscate the device?" It was a command, not a suggestion.

Lyssa reached for the iPad, emailed the file to the address he gave her, and tucked the device into her tote.

"Mrs. Pennington," the chief asked, "is there anything else you wish to tell us at this time concerning Mr. Nunzio's allegations of how he came to be in possession of your husband's jewelry or the nature of your relationship with Mr. Nunzio?"

Lyssa pressed a finger to the spot where her eyebrows met, a trick Gianessa had taught her to usher in calm. "Aside from the fact that all his allegations are monstrous lies, I have nothing to add at this time." Her gaze shifted to Harriet.

Harriet told Chief Smokes, "There is another matter we'd like to discuss that has bearing on Mr. Nunzio's conduct. However, I think that's best left for a separate discussion with you. Soon."

"Very well. Dansko, more questions?"

"No, sir."

"Thank you, everyone. Mrs. Pennington, you're best reached by cell phone, correct?"

"That's right. I do turn it off during my classes, in which case you'd want to leave a message."

"And you're not residing at your home at this time?"

"Correct. I'm not sure Kyle and I will ever reside there again." She said a silent prayer that his week was going better than hers.

Chapter 18

Kyle had made steady, if painful, progress in Europe. He'd worked several hours on Monday morning with the tech person in Bern. The tech had encountered an unforeseen glitch that none of Kyle's engineers had been able to fix, although his lead engineer should have been able to handle it. A quick call to London informed him the lad had quit two weeks ago after a go-round with Geoffrey.

That clarified the problem with tech support in London, and it gave him one more reason to sack Geoffrey. Not only should Kyle have been informed immediately of any change in personnel, Geoffrey had known better than to alienate anyone on the technical side of the business.

Once Kyle took care of the glitch, he engaged his engineers in London via video conference to explain what he'd found and how he'd fixed it. Each gave him their assurance they would not quit, at least not before he saw them in person at week's end. He was certain he'd given plenty of hints at why he was coming and who was in jeopardy.

His presence in Bern and the resolution of the glitch appeased his client, the Bern CEO, Rudolf. He and Rudolf spent the balance of Monday hashing over Rudolf's long list of grievances and exacting promises from Kyle that none of

Rudolf's complaints would ever happen again. More strikes against Geoffrey and more items for his To Be Fixed list.

Tuesday morning, he met at length with Hubert in Munich and with his tech staff that afternoon. Assured that parties in Bern and Munich were once again satisfied with Pennington Secure Networks, he departed for London on a commuter flight, retrieved his Jaguar from the garage at his loft, and drove straight through to Cornwall, grateful for the longer twilight in the UK.

He'd promised himself a full day to regroup before dealing with Geoffrey and his damaged company. Lyssa had advised letting Geoffrey stew, and he agreed, but he wasn't foolish enough leave Geoffrey unwatched. He activated a long-standing agreement with one of his security guards, a retired intelligence officer, to shadow Geoffrey and keep a close watch on his phone use. The measures gave him more ammunition for the dismissal, which Kyle now had on his calendar for Thursday afternoon.

That gave him Wednesday and early morning Thursday to himself. First on his personal agenda was a matter that would not wait. A phone call at first light Wednesday to his old boarding school in Somerset, Mullett Academy, told him his favorite teacher was still on staff. Mr. Bullock remained Kyle's finest mathematics teacher, bar none.

Bullock welcomed him to his office in the schoolhouse, one of half a dozen hamstone buildings that surrounded three flagpoles, the tallest the Union Jack, next the Somerset red dragon, and finally the Mullett coat of arms. Bullock wasted no time. "You have a burning question for me, do you, Pennington?"

"Yes, sir. Any chance you recall my classmate Wollings?"

"I suspected that's what this visit was about. I do, indeed, remember him. How could I forget his brief and tragic time here? You have some unfinished business with Wollings, eh?"

"I have, sir."

"I'm quite sure Wollings would disagree with you on that, Pennington, but the truth of it is, he's passed."

"He died? When, sir?"

"Lived a full life in his short years. Did his advanced study in geothermal energy, fascinated by the sorts of energy produced by seismic activity. Worked up until his death at the geoenergy research center not far from Newcastle. Married a widow and raised her two lads."

"I'm glad for that, sir. When—?"

"He died last year. Heart."

Kyle did the math. Thirty-nine years old.

"They said his condition, the paralysis, exerted a constant strain on the heart, which simply stopped beating one day.

"Sir, would it be appropriate for me to send the wife a note or make a contribution somewhere?"

"You might look up the obit and see if they specified a charity or a scholarship fund for the boys. June, I think it was, made the *London Times*. He was revered in the scientific community. As for a note to the wife, no, too much time has passed." He sat forward, hands on his knees and said in a chipper voice, "However, I think Wollings himself would like a visit from you, Pennington."

Kyle shook his head to clear it. "Beg pardon, sir?"

"No, I'm not senile. As I recall, you stayed with Wollings through his darkest hour out there on those logs. You're the reason Wollings didn't perish from shock and wasn't swept away with the swollen stream surging inches below your perch. I suspect he'd like to thank you for that. I'll send you directions to the grave, shall I?"

Kyle wanted to scream, "Bloody hell, no!" Instead he nodded and mumbled something about taking a drive there this summer with Lyssa.

"Unlike others, you stayed true to your moral compass through the trials of your schooling here, Pennington. As true as any of us can under the circumstances, if you know what I mean."

"I believe I do, sir. Thank you for saying that."

They chatted a few minutes more about Kyle's work, which Bullock praised. For the first time in many months, Kyle felt a swell of pride for the ground-breaking technology he'd built into a thriving business.

"You're a good man, Pennington." Bullock's parting words brought tears to Kyle's eyes.

When the Jaguar crossed the Tamar, he sent a text to Lyssa, *Back in Cornwall, my love. Miss you.* Later when Bodmin Moor gave way to the green fields of home, he felt his soul come to life.

Bullock had said he'd stayed true to his moral compass. Could the same be said of the missing lads from the Tompkins Falls neighborhood?

When Nate Westover was denied a placement for student teaching, he'd chosen to complete his courses and start over somewhere else. He'd stayed true to his passion to teach. *So, where is he?* Why was Nate all but invisible, except to his mutual fund company? Was Nate really the person using the account? Or was he the victim of his father's gun, and Vince Tuttle and Nick Nunzio were exploiting the funds for their own gain?

Kyle was less sure about Vince Tuttle's moral choices. Vince had fought with his parents over his bride and had left home to start married life with her. But why had he never talked with his family again? Worse, he'd ignored his father's obituary, which his mother had sent to his school in Green Bay. Kyle wanted to know what Vince had to say about that.

"Let's hear what you have to say about Nick Nunzio," the chief said to Lyssa at seven o'clock Wednesday morning.

Lyssa set her hot pink folder on the table and faced Chief Smokes and Officer Dansko across the now-familiar conference table at police headquarters. Harriet, who had convened the meeting, sat on Lyssa's right. Hank Moran was on her left.

Lyssa described her meeting with Nick Nunzio at the Manse Lounge.

"What was your purpose?" the chief asked, his voice hard.

"We hoped Nick would know something about Vince Tuttle and Nate Westover's whereabouts since graduating. In particular, I wanted to follow their money stories—"

"Explain."

"A money story is popular tool I teach my students, a way for them to understand their values and priorities and ethics by tracking how and why they spend their money. It's generally used for self-knowledge, preparatory to making changes to spending-and-saving habits in order to meet one's life goals. You're probably wondering why I care about Vince and Nate's money stories?"

The chief nodded.

"During our investigation into the ownership and history of the gun, Kyle and I encountered significant discrepancies having to do with money. For example, why did Vince Tuttle buy a luxury condo on the waterfront in Green Bay? Vince was a hardworking young man from a hardworking family, and he did not receive a windfall ever in his life.

"Yet he bought a luxury condo in a high-end location for about half a million dollars, before he even started his teaching job. It was out of character and out of budget for him. Where did the money come from for the purchase? And was it simply coincidence the purchase closely followed the burial of the gun under the tree in Vince's backyard in Tompkins Falls?"

Chief Smokes nodded for her to continue.

"We also found that Vince's lifelong friend Nate Westover had a lot of money at his disposal. His portfolio is currently valued at approximately twenty million dollars. While it's conceivable Nate bankrolled Vince's condo, Kyle and I assumed the two young men were at odds by the time Vince left for Green Bay.

"I say that because Vince had won over Nate's girlfriend Patty Beck and, on May 19th five years ago, the day before the gun was buried, Vince brought Patty home to meet his parents. That suggests Vince and Patty planned to marry. Given that, it didn't make sense that Nate, the rejected suitor, would bankroll Vince and Patty's luxury home on the bay.

"I set about understanding Vince and Nate's money stories to try to make sense of their choices and their whereabouts." She looked at the two faces across from her. Both men looked intently at her. "It stood to reason Nick

Nunzio, their teacher and neighbor, had some of the answers. Hence the meeting with Nick at the Manse Lounge."

"Lyssa, please tell the police what's in your folder and share the documents with them," Harriet directed.

"Yes." The chief slid the folder toward him and opened the cover.

"First." Lyssa placed her hand on top of the papers and told them about the unexpected opportunity Nick Nunzio handed her as she and Bree talked with him at the Manse Lounge, concluding, "These are screenshots I took of Nate Westover's investment portfolio, mostly his money market account, which he apparently uses for periodic and one-off withdrawals."

She paged through the images and explained what they were seeing. The documents passed from Smokes to Dansko to Hank Moran. "As I've pointed out, many of the withdrawals are tagged NJN, which by his own admission refers to Nicholas Joseph Nunzio. Or VTT, which we assume refers to Vincent Thomas Tuttle."

She responded to questions. They asked for proof she hadn't helped herself to some of Nate's money. As the morning wore on, Lyssa shook with the aftereffects of her initial adrenaline rush. Her mouth grew dry.

When the chief asked, "What was your point in bringing this to us?" she buried her face in her hands.

Hank rested his hand on her shoulder.

Harriet drew in a deep breath, held it, and let it out again. "This is a follow-up to our meeting regarding the burglary, Chief Smokes, the related matter I mentioned at the conclusion of that meeting. You and I have since discussed that my client had visual evidence obtained during a discussion with Mr. Nunzio concerning his ongoing access to a large store of money, not his own, possibly dating from the time the gun was planted in the Pennington backyard."

Harriet looked directly at the chief. "You agreed to the meeting and specifically asked to see the folder."

The chief stood, made a quarter turn to his officer, and ordered. "Dansko, confiscate the documents." To Harriet and Lyssa he said, "Thank you. That will be all."

Hank pressed Lyssa's forearm and quietly told her, "Harriet and I will see these get the attention they merit. You've done everything you can."

When Hank Moran reached him, Kyle had been hiking alone most of the afternoon on the coast path. He was twenty minutes, via the cliff path, from Pennington House, and a squall was just visible on the horizon. He'd need to pick up the pace if he wanted to make it home dry.

"I've got an update on your burglary, Kyle."

"Good, let's hear it, Hank."

"First, your wife did a heroic job this morning telling the police about Nunzio's withdrawals from the Westover account. Since then, I've learned more about the investigation by the Tompkins Falls Police Department into Nunzio's career as a burglar. Turns out our friend had a whole stash of those leather pouches that he used for all the burglaries he perpetrated in the College Heights neighborhood, and beyond, over the years. He had a sweet deal for himself. He was a popular and trusted teacher who knew all about his students and their parents' lifestyles. No one suspected his evening walks were missions to set up for the next robbery."

Kyle exhaled his disbelief. "But he couldn't have walked around wearing people's jewelry, could he?"

"He was careful. Judging from what he said, he'd have worn men's jewelry, like your cufflinks and bracelets, only on weekend trips to impress his date and the first-class establishments he frequented. Most of what he stole was women's jewelry, and he sold most of it or gave it as gifts to women he knew."

"Did it pay enough to justify the risk, do you think?"

"He claims his Mercedes came from profits of those sales. The guy was so busy boasting he didn't realize he'd accused himself of grand larceny, not even counting what he'd taken from you this week."

"I wondered how he afforded the car but, until Lyssa called Monday night after our burglary, I never suspected he was a thief. He was very convincing about neighbors watching out for each other."

"Well, he fooled a lot of people for a couple of decades."

"Makes you wonder what else he's been up to that no one knows about."

Hank snorted. "For one thing, Nunzio admitted he's the one who stole the gun from the Westover home while the house stood empty after the rockslide."

"Ah, that's how the gun came to be in a leather pouch. Did Nick admit he buried it under our tree?"

"No. And I think he's telling the truth about that."

Kyle brayed a laugh. "Sure about that, Hank?"

"He says Nate returned home from the trip out West and went looking for the gun. He wanted it for his girlfriend, but he came up empty. Mrs. Westover's jewelry was missing, too, and so were some other things of value. Nate immediately thought of Nunzio."

"You're saying Nate knew about Nunzio's criminal habits?"

"According to Nunzio, Westover had followed him a few times and figured out what he was up to. To hear Nunzio tell it, Westover really looked up to him for his skill and admired him for going undetected all those years. Take that with a grain of salt."

"Right, it's Nunzio boasting about himself." But was that all? Did Nate Westover want in on the action? Or did he want something else from Mr. Nunzio, the respected teacher?

"He says he became a sort of replacement father for Nate Westover after Bill Westover's death. Whenever Nate got into trouble in Tompkins Falls or in Geneseo, Nunzio bailed him out."

"So Nate Westover was not an upstanding citizen?"

Kyle had arrived at a vantage point. He waded through wildflowers up to a rocky outcropping. The Atlantic spread before him, waves building ahead of the approaching squall. The wind knocked him sideways, and he dropped his phone.

"Hold on, Hank," he shouted. Phone in hand once more, he stepped back down to the coast path and paused to check landmarks. He was just yards from the turnoff that cut across the cliff top and gave him access to a rutted track down to the road. It was the only safe choice in this weather.

"Sorry, Hank. Bit of weather up here. Go on."

Hank continued, "Nunzio claims he knew very little about Vince Tuttle."

"Yes, he told us he never had Vince in class. And our general impression was Vince didn't have time on his hands. He was a hard worker, had after-school jobs, and worked summers at the library in the children's reading program."

"Interesting. My general impression is Nate Westover was shrewd. Nunzio said he pumped him for all his wisdom. Whether he meant his skill as a teacher or as a thief is not clear. What is clear is Westover wanted Nunzio to help him get certified as a teacher."

"So that's what he was after? Makes perfect sense."

"If Nunzio delivered, he'd get a cut of the settlement from the lawsuit."

"That tracks. Nate was tenacious about becoming a teacher, we know that." The wind blew so hard from behind as he crossed the cliff top, he had to run to stay in control. At the edge, he scrambled down the bank to the sheltered track and paused, out of breath.

Hank was saying, "Lyssa showed me the screenshots of Nate's accounts, so we know he's helping himself to Nate's money every month. The guy's a real operator."

"He is that." Kyle watched his footing. He might not beat the squall, but he'd sooner arrive without a sprained ankle or twisted knee.

"The point is, Kyle, he must have found a way to get Nate certified. Any idea where Nate is teaching?"

"You've got his address on one of those screenshots, and Lyssa asked our librarian, but she didn't find him at any of the area schools." He skidded on loose stones and went down. His phone flew ahead a few feet. He brushed himself off and retrieved the phone. "I need both hands here, Hank," he said before noticing the phone was dead.

Chapter 19

Lyssa asked for a brief meeting with Harriet before leaving the police station.

Harriet asked with a twinkle in her eye, "For what purpose?" They laughed.

"To keep me from storming into Nick Nunzio's house and ripping his throat out. I need your strongest and best advice about how to handle defamation of character. My character."

"You're always going to find people who use slander, rumors, blackmail, and other dirty tricks to get what they want. And Nick wants a get out of jail free card."

Lyssa gave her a puzzled frown. "Not sure I understand that. I also don't get why you brought up a libel suit? Should we consider it?"

"I meant it as a threat, to let Nick know he can't push us around. And to apply pressure to the police investigation."

"Okay."

"But let's not dismiss the idea of a lawsuit quite yet. I want to keep our Mr. Nunzio on edge. It wouldn't look good for a tenured English teacher to be charged with libel, any more than grand larceny."

Lyssa hit her forehead with the heel of her hand. "Which he will be facing unless he can discredit me. *Now* I get it. Nick can't afford the consequence of the crime he committed against Kyle, grand larceny, and he needs to make the charge disappear. By discrediting the witness."

"Exactly," Harriet said. "He didn't just let himself in with an old key someone else gave him and then claim to have the homeowner's best interest at heart. He got caught with the goods on his person, and the goods add up to substantially more than ten thousand, if we've done the math right. That puts this theft well into the scale of grand larceny."

"Thank you for explaining that. But honestly it makes me even more nervous to see it from that perspective."

"Good, because today you put the authorities onto the thousands he's taking from Nate Westover's accounts every year, which he's probably never reported to the IRS," Harriet said. "He's in hot water up to his eyebrows, and that means we can expect more dirty moves from him."

Lyssa blew out a shaky breath.

"In fact, it may be more than dirty moves," her lawyer said. "If he used the gun he stole from the Westover home, the one that was buried in your backyard, we need to consider him dangerous."

"And he lives right across the street from our house." Lyssa drummed her fingers on the table.

"We'll make sure he goes to jail, Lyssa," Harriet said.

"But he's not there at the moment, which is why I have a security company installing new locks and a security system as we speak."

"Good decision. Are you thinking about moving back to the house?"

Lyssa placed her hands flat on the table and opened her fingers wide. "The police have arranged an Order of Protection, which, realistically, I can only enforce if I'm living there. Since I will soon have adequate protection, I'm moving back Friday."

"Joel will say that's insane," Harriet pointed out.

"I will tell this to Joel and Manda, too, but please don't breathe a word to anyone else. I intend to slip quietly away for a spa weekend on Friday, coming back Sunday night, which should give you time to make sure Nick goes in jail and stays there."

When Lyssa's phone vibrated at the start of the Early Riser's meeting Thursday morning, she saw Kyle's number in the Caller ID. Grabbing the phone, she race-walked out of the back room of the Bagel Depot. "Hang on." It was also too noisy in the dining room for a conversation.

"Are you all right, my love?"

"Yes." She exited the building. "Sorry, I was in an AA meeting. I've been trying to reach you, and your phone seemed to be out of order."

"I dropped it on a stony patch. Turned out the battery had just shaken loose."

"How are you? Where are you?"

"I'm just getting in the car on my way to London. What's happening there?"

She kept her voice perfectly steady as she told him about the new security system at home, then about the spa weekend she had planned for herself just across the border into Canada. "I'm hoping Bree will go with me."

He affirmed she'd love Niagara-on-the-Lake. They talked about Kyle's mother and the housekeeper and gardener. "They wanted photos of your garden. I never thought to bring any."

"We've had a lot on our minds. We'll bring pictures of the house and the garden when we come this summer. That way they'll see the roses in bloom. You're on your way to sack Geoffrey?"

"Yes, no way around it. I've a pile of evidence. I won't bore you with it."

"Are things all right now in Bern?"

"I've got Bern and Munich back on track. You know, my love, the downside of letting Geoffrey go is I'll need to take the helm again."

Tears sprang to her eyes. She hated having him take on more work. *He needs to figure it out for himself.* "We can't have it both ways, can we? You need to take control and get everyone working together again and restore your client confidence and satisfaction."

"I'm grateful you understand. After I've seen to the staff, I'll need to have face-to-face visits with each of the clients."

"No way around it, I guess."

"I want you with me."

"Oh my gosh, don't bring that up right now, okay? She grabbed a fistful of hair." *Calm down.* "We'll talk about it when you're back."

"I may not be back for a while, you understand."

"What are you saying?" Her voice was shrill.

"I want to book as many client visits as I can next week and possibly the week after."

"You what?" Silence. "I can't believe you would just abandon me with this mess on my hands." *Joel's right, I should have told him all that was happening.*

"From all accounts, things are settling down. I'm very glad you're planning a break for yourself, my love. Things will look better after your spa weekend, I'm sure of it."

She stood with her mouth open. *That's what I get for keeping it from him.*

"I need to pay attention to the road, sweetheart. Enjoy your spa weekend and give me a call when you're back."

With that, he ended the connection.

Anger swelled in her chest. She stormed across the parking lot of the Bagel Depot and jabbed at the pedestrian crossing light for the four-lane bypass. Her destination was the willow path along the lakeshore. She couldn't call Gianessa. Her sponsor would get the truth out of her.

By the time she'd hit her stride on the gravel path, she pictured flames shooting from her nostrils. *God, I don't want to drink or drug, but I'm so mad.*

Her phone vibrated in her pocket.

"Thank God you answered your phone. Lyssa, I am worried about you." Bree's voice quavered with emotion. "I saw you fly out of the Early Risers meeting. What's going on?"

"I didn't see you. I didn't realize you're working this morning."

"Spill, already. I've got five minutes."

Lyssa blurted the whole story—her decision not to let Kyle know what was happening with Nick, Kyle's decision to stay in Europe another week or more, her obsession with going to Green Bay to meet with Vince and Nate. She had to get to Green Bay. She had to know the two young men were all right.

As she talked, her steps slowed.

Bree told her, "I drove by your house yesterday and security guys were crawling all over it. Then Hank told me why you weren't staying there."

"I've been at Joel and Manda's, but I'm moving my things back to the house first thing tomorrow morning. I don't want them to know I'm going to Green Bay. I need to prove to myself I'm strong and capable."

"Which you are."

"Thank you. Is there any way you can go with me this weekend?"

"Oh my gosh, I'm sorry. I've got work and a paper due and a big exam on Monday."

Lyssa held her breath and took the plunge. "You don't have to do this, but I want Kyle and everybody to think I'm doing a girlfriends' getaway. You know, spa and shopping and a play or something. Kyle's always talking about driving up to Niagara-on-the-Lake, in Canada, just past Niagara Falls."

"And you're really going to Green Bay and not telling them?"

"Exactly. Chief Barker says talking face-to-face with Nate and Vince is the only way to learn the truth about the gun and what happened that weekend. The police aren't going to do it, and so far they think Nick Nunzio is just a thief. Nick's also involved in whatever happened with the gun, I'm sure of it. You remember the pouch the gun was buried in?"

"The leather one with the drawstring?"

"Right. When Nick stole Kyle's jewelry, he used a pouch that's identical. Identical. Even the new chief says so. Nick's involved, no question in my mind, and I pray they get the truth out of him. I've thought hard about this, and I need to know that both Nate and Vince are alive and well. I don't care what they did or why. I just have to confirm for myself they're not dead. And I need to understand what these nightmares are about."

"I'd go with you if I possibly could, but I just can't, Lyssa."

"I totally understand, Bree. So I'm going alone. I'll tell people I hoped you could come, but you couldn't. I'll rave about Niagara-on-the-Lake and all the amenities at the best hotels and the plays and the shops, until they want to shut me up."

Bree was laughing. "And if anyone asks where you are, I'll cover for you. I'll check out the website as soon as I can so we sound like we're on the same page."

"I owe you, Bree." Lyssa felt relief course through her whole body. "Really, I owe you big time."

"So, we'll go to Niagara-on-the-Lake for real when I get my bachelor's in December, okay?"

"Absolutely. My treat."

"But you have to stay in touch this weekend. The whole weekend. You have to tell me where you are and how it's going."

"I promise."

"Wear that scarf like the one you brought me for good luck."

"Good idea." *God, it's you and me, and one of us is scared.*

Friday after work, Kyle walked purposefully from his office to his and Lyssa's favorite bistro on the Thames. His choices were to wait an hour for a table or take a seat at the bar. He chose food over comfort, deafening noise over the chance of a quiet phone conversation with the love of his life. With a brandy and a salmon steak dinner in him, he took the underground to his loft and let himself in. The silence was oppressive.

He'd tried twice on the Underground to phone Lyssa, but his call went to voicemail each time. It wasn't like her to shut off her phone unless she was in class, and, allowing for the five-hour time difference, her next class wasn't for another hour or more.

He tried her number one more time and left a message this time. "Hello, my love. Hope all is well. Give me a call if you can, don't worry about waking me. It was a nightmare firing Geoffrey yesterday, but the good news is the energy throughout the company improved the moment he was escorted out the door. I've talked with each of the groups today, and on the whole we're in reasonably good shape. Senior staff have agreed to come in tomorrow to set new direction."

He paused, thinking about how she might respond. "As you would say, one day at a time. I love you, Lyssa, and I miss you and I wish we were together. Please call as soon as you get this."

Friday night, just after nine o'clock Central Daylight Time, Lyssa was enjoying her private balcony overlooking moonlit Sturgeon Bay, bundled in a sweater and jacket, wearing two pairs of socks and the blue silk scarf from Myrtle Beach. As Bree had requested, she'd wrapped it around her neck before leaving the house that morning. It held both her scent and Kyle's. It had brought her luck so far, and she intended to wear it nonstop on her mission.

She had emailed all her students Wednesday morning with a proposal. She'd cancel her Friday afternoon classes and the Friday review session if they would attend the

Wednesday review session for one hour. They agreed. To the few who blew off the Wednesday review class, she sent follow-up messages inviting them to see her with questions or concerns.

Thursday morning, she'd booked the early Friday afternoon flight to Green Bay via Detroit and chosen a suite at a resort on the Door Peninsula for two nights, checking out Sunday morning. If everything went according to plan, she'd arrive at the resort in time to get a massage before the local AA meeting, track down Nate on Saturday, drive back to Green Bay Sunday morning, and find Vince in the few hours before her return flight to Rochester, via Detroit.

From her perch overlooking the bay, she told Bree, "So far, so good. This place is serene. Evergreens everywhere, and the water is magical. I keep expecting the fish to put on a show for me. Did you know sturgeons are fish?"

"Hey, girlfriend, did you go to an AA meeting or did you get yourself some pot instead?"

Lyssa laughed. "No pot, no booze. I'm just a little edgy. This feels like do or die. Like I have ten hours to change my mind and head back to Tompkins Falls."

"You won't. How are you going to find Nate?"

"I figured I'll start at the post office and see if I can get someone to take pity on me."

"Yeah, right. Or maybe he'll happen to walk in to pick up his mail." Bree snorted.

"I do have his photo and his phone number. And I'm good at getting people to tell me things."

"What do you think he's like?" Bree asked.

"I think he's an outdoorsy kind of guy who keeps to himself except when he's teaching little kids."

"Did the librarian, Kathy Regis, ever find him listed with a school?"

"No. To be honest, that makes me uneasy." Lyssa propped her feet on the railing.

"Maybe he stopped teaching?"

"I really don't think so. I think teaching became the most important thing in his life after he lost his parents. I mean, think about it. Even after he botched his chances at certification in New York, he kept on taking courses."

"So, what, you think he moved to Wisconsin, transferred in his courses, and did the rest at one of their colleges?"

"Maybe, but I'm pretty sure he and his buddy, Nick Nunzio, had a scheme all figured out. Remember Nick boasting about helping Nate?"

"Right, and that's how he was given access to Nate's money. But how could they pull it off?"

"I don't know, but Nick's pretty devious."

"Maybe Nate's devious, too."

"I hope not. I hope he's a good guy. After all he's been through, I want him to be all right." She blew out a breath and watched it form into a cloud of vapor. *Chilly night ahead.* "I'm scared for him, I don't know why."

Chapter 20

While Lyssa tanked up with a full breakfast in the dining room at the resort, she kept an eye out for a busybody. Someone here might know Nate or have some tips for her about how to locate him. Like the woman approaching her with a carafe in hand.

"More coffee?" the waitress asked.

"Yes, please. And I have a question, when you have a second."

"I'll be back." The woman continued her rounds of the nearby tables, dispensing regular and decaf, milk or cream, sugar or sugar substitute. Finished with that, she cocked a hip next to Lyssa's table. "Shoot."

"Have you seen him around? He'd be five years older now." She set Nate's yearbook picture, blown up to twice the size, on the table.

"Looks a little familiar. Not from the resort, though. Yeah, I think I've seen him. My boyfriend and I hike on the Lake Michigan shore out near Whitefish Dunes. Seems like I've seen him there with an old geezer."

Lyssa laughed. "How old is this geezer?"

"Old enough to walk pretty slow in the sand."

"Trudy, order up!" rang across the dining room.

"Gotta go. Can I have this and show my boyfriend later?"

"Sure. Thanks." She'd made copies. "I'm checking out after breakfast tomorrow."

"Catch you then," Trudy called over her shoulder.

Lyssa made a fist pump. *Good start.* She consulted her iPad for the location of Whitefish Dunes, which she found on the Lake Michigan side of the peninsula, as Trudy had said. It was a big area. She'd have to do better than sit on a dune and wait for Nate to show up with or without an old geezer, especially when the weather report promised afternoon showers.

Her phone rang. Kyle from London at three in the morning? "Hi, you're up early," she said breezily. "Are you at the office today or are you in Cornwall?"

"Office today. Staff's coming at six. We're going over the books and working out a staffing plan with HR. I was worried when you didn't call last night."

"I was exhausted when I got here and just fell into bed." *I will not say I'm sorry.*

Silence.

She caved first. "I've just finished a delicious breakfast and am feeling some energy again."

"Seeing some plays today?"

"Possibly. Right now I just want to walk and window-shop. Look, I know you're busy and I don't want to keep you from your work." Was her tone really as frosty as it sounded to her?

"Is everything all right, Lyssa?"

"Yes, of course. Good luck with everything today, darling." She ended the connection, held the phone for a moment, and then dropped it in her tote. After signing the check, she gathered her jacket and headed into the village of Sturgeon Bay.

~ ~ ~

Kyle pressed Joel's number and got him after four rings. "Good morning," he remembered to say first. "What's been going on there that no one's telling me and that's got Lyssa so upset?"

Lyssa's first stop was the post office. Nate's postal box was the smallest available to customers. What did that tell her? He didn't get much mail? He had packages shipped directly to his house? Not very revealing.

She found a quiet spot out of the flow of customers and eyed the steady lines at the windows. Someone here knew Nate, she could sense it. She rejected the idea of showing his picture to every person who came by. If she did that, they'd have the cops on her, she was sure. Lurking by the postal boxes was not much better, as strategies went.

After forty minutes of shifting from one foot to the other, the lines were shorter and fewer people were hitting up the postal boxes. One of the window clerks had been eyeing her, and now he posted a Closed sign in front of him.

She started toward him and, to her surprise, he started toward her.

"Something I can help you with, miss?" His tone was more threatening than solicitous.

"Yes, I hope so," she told him. "Oh." He looked familiar.

He was her height, wiry and dark-haired, and he could be any age from thirty to fifty. When he gave Lyssa a smile, his flattened nose and smudged eyeglasses projected a well-worn, comfortable look. And memorable.

"Oh my gosh, you were at the meeting last night," Lyssa said without thinking. She clapped her hand over her mouth.

"You're a friend of Bill W?" he asked.

"Yes, two years now. My name is Lyssa." She stuck out her hand.

"Tucker." He gave her hand a firm shake. "Now I remember. You're hoping to connect with someone from your hometown, right? And I'll just bet he's got one of the small boxes over there?"

"You're a good detective, Tucker." She gave him a sunny smile.

"Figured there was some reason you were hanging out. Box number?"

Lyssa showed him Nate's address and phone number and photo. "My husband and I live two doors down from his childhood home. I don't suppose you can tell me where he lives now? Someone thought his house was over near Whitefish Dunes."

"Sorry, I'd be fired and my family would starve." His hand shook as he handed back the photo.

"But you recognize him, don't you?" she asked.

Tucker averted his face.

"If you can give me one tiny hint," she said, her hands clasped in prayer. "I'll keep putting the clues together as I gather them."

Tucker swallowed. "Walk out with me." He opened a section of counter and led them through mail bins. Just outside the back door, he lit a cigarette.

"Am I in trouble?"

He shook his head. "Just going to tell you the special place I go fishing about every other weekend. You want to take Route 57 that way." He pointed farther out the peninsula. "Make a right onto Whitefish Bay Road. Take that all the way to the end, and then turn left. Keep your eyes open." He winked. "You're at the right spot for fishing when you see a big log-and-glass home, set up high on your left. If you run out of road, you've gone too far."

She repeated the directions until she got it right. "Is this one of the weekends?"

Tucker shook his head. "But you never know. Sometimes we miss a week fishing, sometimes we go two in a row. Sometimes, around the holidays, it's a whole week."

Her blood raced with excitement. "I can't tell you how much this means to me."

He shrugged. "I figure, if you hadn't met me, you'd talk somebody else into telling you. Nate's a good guy, keeps to himself, loves the outdoors. Never talks about what he does when he's not out here."

"You mean he doesn't work around here?"

"Nope. Don't know where he lives or what he does when he's not here. I've asked him a few times, too. Sometimes you've just got to respect a guy's privacy."

"Does he ever bring anyone with him?"

"Strictly solo. Sometimes in summer he stays a few weeks, usually just the weekend."

"The person who mentioned Whitefish Dunes said he's usually with some old geezer. You definitely don't fit that description."

"Maybe somebody he hangs with on Sunday. Probably hikes that day. Fishing's always Saturday." He waved as he reentered the post office.

Kyle paced his office, twiddling his pencil, muttering. It had taken fifteen full minutes to get the truth out of Joel.

If he hadn't been so bloody focused on saving his business, he'd have seen right from the start Lyssa was far too cheerful about the burglary, and when she got more and more stressed each day it was because Nick Nunzio, the rotter, was hell-bent on discrediting her.

Joel was a gentleman, but if he'd been there he'd have slammed Nunzio into the wall and choked him within a millimeter of his life.

The pencil snapped.

Lyssa shielded her eyes as she lifted her gaze to the soaring peak of Nate Westover's cedar log home just back from the road on the shore of Lake Michigan. Why wouldn't Nate spend every moment here? He had enough money he didn't have to work.

But of course he worked. He'd had money back when obstacles had been thrown in his way toward becoming a teacher and he'd persevered. His passion had carried him forward. So he must be teaching.

Just not nearby.

She switched on her phone and left a message for Bree. "Hi, I'm in the driveway of Nate Westover's log-and-glass home near Whitefish Dunes in Sturgeon Bay. Can you follow up with Kathy Regis and see if she's learned anything new about the school where Nate's teaching? He's definitely not working in this area, just comes alternate weekends and school vacations. Also, I'm pretty sure there are ferries coming to the peninsula. I saw a ferry sign in Sturgeon Bay, and there are others that come across Lake Michigan to cities down the coast. Can you see where those ferries come from and if he's teaching near one of the departure cities? Thanks a million."

She'd check the ferry terminal in town later to see if they recognized him.

Did she dare knock on the door to Nate's house? From what Tucker had said, he probably wasn't here this weekend, but it was worth a try. She drove up his driveway and parked by the walk. What was her story if he answered? And if he didn't answer, but someone got suspicious of her car and called the police?

She continued up the drive and parked behind the house, out of sight of the road and neighboring houses. As she shut the driver's door she shivered, though it wasn't cold today. The property had an empty feel. While there were signs of life—a plow blade parked by the shed, a bucket under the spigot by the back door—nothing stirred.

A cluster of yellow crocuses bloomed in a sunny spot by the back door. She smiled, thinking of Kyle and the one yellow crocus he'd spotted in Tompkins Falls.

She looked up at the clouds and guessed the rain would hold off for a bit. A path led her into the woods of evergreens and hardwoods. Rattling brown oak leaves still clung to many of the trees, and there were only the tiniest buds on the maples. Because the path, thick with needles, muffled her steps, she surprised three deer feeding on emerging shoots. They might be the reason Nate didn't plant much. That, or he wasn't interested.

The deer stared at her. She stared at them. A scurrying behind her made her whirl with fright.

She patted her hand over her thumping heart. *Squirrel chase.* When she turned back, the deer had vanished.

She walked on to a clearing stacked shoulder high with firewood. Although she had no frame of reference, she thought it might be enough fuel to heat the house through the winter, though she doubted wood was Nate's main source of heat. Nick had said the house was luxurious.

A branching path called to her, and she followed it for a quarter of a mile until it veered deeper into the woods. She'd seen enough to think there were no marijuana plants out here, no meth lab, no Druidic circle where maidens were sacrificed. Just a lovely wood that supported deer and other wildlife and furnished the house with firewood.

On the return she noticed, behind the shed, a small orchard on a rise that gave the four fruit trees good drainage and nearly full sun. Young trees. Well tended, free of suckers, no saplings or vines within ten feet. It had been years since she and Manda had raided Billy Adams parents' orchard, but she thought these trees were apple and cherry. Was Nate in residence often enough to pick his crop before the birds got them? One half-bushel basket and one swing-handled berry basket hunkered behind the shed under a waist-high slab of wood that probably served as a workbench.

She'd been on the property long enough that anyone in residence would be aware of her presence. From behind the shed, she listened for approaching footsteps, but there were none. She peeked around the shed toward the house. No one looked back at her from a window. No one stood with a rifle.

Pressing her face against the window of the shed door, she spied a riding mower, a snowblower, and assorted tools carefully positioned on a pegboard above an indoor workbench that was bare of projects. She tried the doorknob and shoved against the door. Just inside, a few concrete blocks littered the dirt floor, and ropes of various thicknesses hung from hooks. Next to them were a soiled rain slicker and a stained puffy jacket.

She pulled the door shut behind her as she left. Still no sign of life in the house.

She climbed the few stairs to the back porch, where two heavy wooden chairs sat side by side with a round log table between them. Half the tabletop was scarred with cigarette burns. Spent matches and used butts littered the ground on that side of the porch.

She put her hand on the doorknob and withdrew it. While it hadn't given her an evil vibe, she thought it prudent first to walk the length of the porch and peer through windows, alert to any sign of a security system.

Seeing none, she tried the knob and opened the back door.

Kyle gathered his senior staff at half past four Saturday afternoon to thank them for giving up their day. They'd given him a state-of-the-company report, and together they'd brainstormed a strategy for the months ahead. They'd identified holes in staffing and laid out a recruiting plan. They'd characterized the level of satisfaction of the various clients and made a prioritized list of action items.

"I see our list of measures to address client satisfaction are chiefly, 'Kyle to visit So-and-So'," he joked, and they all laughed. "Which I will do over the next few months, assuming the CEOs are not all vacationing the entire summer."

One of his engineers said, "They'll want to talk to you, no question. Not to speak ill of the dead, but Geoffrey spread the word our technology is outdated and full of holes."

"Interesting. Do you think is it?" Kyle waited respectfully for the answer. Everyone sat straighter.

"No," another engineer said. Heads turned to him. "There might be a few more glitches like the one you found in Bern, but nothing that can't be fixed. If you ask me, he wanted to start his own company and lure away our clients."

Kyle thought so too, but he hadn't realized the tech team was onto it. "Yes, well, I've taken steps to disable anything he might have removed. I want to assure you, no one at Pennington Secure Networks need fear losing their job– well, no one else." That got a few chuckles, but mostly he saw his people drawing in deep breaths and relaxing brows that had started the day deeply lined. "You've alerted me to a few seriously disgruntled employees, and I thank you for that. HR and I will address those in the coming week."

He called for as-yet-unspoken concerns, waited a few beats, and closed with, "I'd say let's have dinner together somewhere amazing, but we all need a break from this. Each of you will find in your mailbox an envelope with a few pounds that should cover dinner for you and a loved one at whatever restaurant you fancy. Good work, everyone. Enjoy what's left of the weekend."

With that, he left the building, pulled on his jacket against the downpour, and walked the ten blocks to his loft.

Chapter 21

Once inside Nate's lakeside home, Lyssa's heart raced with anxiety. *What's got me spooked? No one's here.*

At the same time, she was enveloped in sadness, though she couldn't readily connect sadness with Nate's magnificent home on the shore. Or the fishing he did here with Tucker or the hiking with the old geezer.

She wanted her emotions to settle before going deeper into the house. Besides, the kitchen, where she stood, had revelations of its own, like a big empty space where a roomy table and six chairs might have stood. And there were just bar stools at the island, all but one tucked under. The cupboards held china service for eight—matching large and small plates, bowls, cups and saucers. The set might have come from his parents' house, as it was a pattern popular with her parents' generation. She doubted it was ever used. A few stoneware pieces were handy on the lowest shelf.

The refrigerator was squeaky clean, populated by a big hunk of butter, rounds of cheeses, and a half carton of eggs with BROWN stamped on the cover, no company name, probably from a local farm. The freezer was crammed with labeled packages. Trout, lasagna, stew, and Cowboy Cookies.

Her stomach grumbled with hunger, and she checked the clock. Noon. She popped a package of Cowboy Cookies in the microwave and helped herself to a cookie. Delicious. She'd have to get the recipe from Toffee Winkel.

She carried the package with her to her next stop. The pantry had no beer, wine, or liquor, and its wine refrigerator was empty. Maybe Nate was sober now. Maybe that's how he'd met Tucker.

The shelves were stocked with boxes of pasta, jars of sauce, canned vegetables and fruits, salsa, chips, oils, and vinegars, all of it pricey and very selective. No cigarettes or bags of pot, no sign of other drugs. No baking supplies. Where does he make the Cowboy Cookies?

As she crossed the threshold to the living room, a sudden ray of sun shone through the wall of windows. *Did you do that, God?* The shaft of sun rested above the fireplace, highlighting a framed photo of snow-covered mountain peaks reflected in a deep blue lake surrounded by evergreens. She read the label. Saint Mary Lake, Glacier National Park, E.B. Jones, 2003. As she admired the scene, the anxiety she'd felt earlier vanished. Maybe Nate's did, too, when he looked up at the scene.

She did a one-eighty and stood a moment, mesmerized by the soaring, cedar-paneled room. The window wall faced south, as the transient ray of sun had demonstrated. She tried to imagine moonlight pouring in. While she was sure it did from time to time, she thought Nate did not care. This wasn't a room for romance. Nate was alone here.

She knew that because the leather sofa had no indentations, nor did the Morris-style armchairs. All the pillows were perfectly centered, and the throws draped on the arms had no signs of use. Maybe a designer had positioned them sometime in the past, and they hadn't been touched since. Did Nate have a housekeeper? She didn't think so. He was too private a person to let a housekeeper touch his space. More than likely, he'd bought the house furnished and used only what he needed.

He clearly used one chair, the one near the fireplace with a footstool drawn up and a side table loaded with books, whose titles covered fishing and hiking.

In the near corner of the room stood a desk barely large enough to pay bills or write a letter. The single drawer was locked. She started a halfhearted search for a key but decided that was one boundary she wouldn't cross. When she analyzed the choice, she saw it was fear from having opened the lunchbox he'd planted in her garden and finding a gun inside.

Wait. Was she certain now that Nate was the one who'd buried the gun? Yes. So the oilcloth and bandanna must be artifacts from his outdoor vacations with his parents, maybe from the final trip with them out West.

The sadness that had greeted her at the back door intensified. She turned her footsteps to a staircase that rose from the front of the room. Climbing just high enough to see the space above, she noted a well-furnished loft, apparently unused, if the thick layer of dust over everything was any indication. Lit by four large skylights, it was the kind of space that would host many children at one time. Six unmade twin beds, each with a stack of bedding and blankets and pillows, and a low chest of drawers with a lamp between every two beds. Could she trust her intuition, that Nate had longed for children of his own and had given up the idea?

She shook off the sadness. It was Nate's emotion, not hers.

Retracing her steps, unconcerned about the footprints she'd left on the stairs, she looked for a master bedroom. Probably the room behind the door under the stairs.

She turned the knob and toed open the door of a sumptuous master suite. A king-size bed against a cedar-paneled wall afforded a view of sunrise through tall undressed east-facing windows. Layers of alpaca, silk, and cashmere covered the bed, and six pillows of assorted sizes, each covered with some deep-colored design, were propped against a headboard of dark leather edged with brass nailheads.

A single framed photo stood on the only dresser. Nate with his parents, the Vermillion Cliffs spread out behind them. She shuddered, sure it had been taken the morning of their fatal hike. She refrained from touching the frame of gleaming polished silver, noting the glass was marred by fingerprints in just two places, one beside his mother's face and one over his father's hand. It must be a treasured memory, and it made her think Nate was trying to go back in time to the moment before his family was eradicated.

She sat on his bed and opened the single drawer of the only bedside table. A thin, cloth-covered book lay atop four others like it, each with a different-colored cover. She riffled through the pages of what was apparently this year's journal. Entries followed one another, with no page breaks, each starting with the date.

The previous weekend, Nate had fished alone from the shore Saturday morning and again with Tucker that afternoon, from Tucker's boat. The next day he'd hiked all day in the adjacent state park with someone named Montana. If she wasn't mistaken, Glacier National Park was in Montana. Maybe E.B. Jones, whose work hung over the mantel, was a photographer friend nicknamed Montana who looked like an old geezer. *Possible.*

The journal entry finished, as all the others did, with the words, 'Rest in peace, Mom and Dad.'

Her heart ached for the young man who still mourned his loss and honored his parents' memory. She lifted out the other four journals and opened the earliest.

He'd been keeping them, evidently, since Memorial Day weekend five years earlier, a week after the gun was buried under Rikki Tuttle's newly planted tree. With a shiver, she read the first entry, which began, "Here I can be myself." She puzzled on that as she leafed through the book, but she found no startling revelations.

How different this journal is from Kyle's.

As she set the book aside and started through another, her phone vibrated in the pocket of her chinos. *Kyle.*

"Hello darling. I'm so glad you called." The words came from her heart.

"Where are you, my love? You sound like you've been crying."

She brushed at a tear, unaware. "Just reading something sad. I shouldn't be doing that on my spa weekend, should I? How are things going there?"

"The staff are relieved to be rid of Geoffrey and are pulling together to repair the damage that's been done. Lyssa, I called Joel after we talked last. I sensed all was not right between you and me and that you were keeping something from me, some burden you were carrying."

"Did you?"

"I browbeat him into coming clean about the ordeal you've endured because of Nick Nunzio. Sweetheart, I'm so sorry. I'm deeply ashamed I wasn't any help to you. And that

I carried on about staying away indefinitely while you were immersed in such a—"

"I didn't give you the chance to help, did I? And I came to realize that was a mistake. Joel warned me it was, and I didn't listen. For that I'm sorry." They were silent for a beat. "You're planning to meet with more clients?"

"Soon, yes, but perhaps I'll come home first. Would you like that?'

"Yes." She covered her mouth, but a sob escaped. "Yes, very much." She snuffled and got her voice under control. "And I've been thinking, Kyle, when you meet with each client, you could frame it not as groveling, but as a session to look ahead and bring them up to date on your newest technology."

"Brilliant. And while I would like you to come on some of those trips with me, I know it's not fair to throw you into that role all at once. Particularly when you have so many responsibilities already."

"That helps. Why don't we talk more when you're back?"

"I'll keep you posted on my travel plans. How are the plays?"

"Actually, I haven't been to any. I'd rather go to plays with you. Let's do that together."

"Yes, let's."

"I'll see you soon. Safe travel."

"You as well, my love."

She held the phone to her heart long after they'd ended the connection.

Spatters of rain against the east windows reminded her where she was and why she'd come. *None of which I've told my husband.*

She returned Nate's journals to the bedside table, straightened the bedcovers where she'd sat and closed the bedroom door behind her.

Why is he completely alone here? What about the rest of his time?

Her only sense of anyone's presence, other than Nate, was the burn-marked table she'd seen on the back porch, and she'd bet that was Tucker's signature. Maybe Montana's signature was the stunning photograph above the mantel.

On her return to the back door, she picked up her cookie crumbs and pilfered one more package of Cowboy Cookies for the road.

After a quiet supper at the bistro, Kyle parked his Jaguar in the garage beneath his flat in London and dragged himself out of the driver's seat. He felt no lingering doubt at having sacked Geoffrey. The sessions today with the senior staff satisfied him he'd done the right thing.

What still bothered him was he'd groomed Geoffrey and trusted him. The error in judgment had cost all of them at Pennington Secure Networks. *Lord, help me to see what I missed so I don't make that egregious error ever again.*

What would Lyssa tell him? Look at what's going good. No question, the upside was the staff were brighter and more energetic now the source of their woes, Geoffrey, had been removed. Well done. Move on. He locked the car and looked forward to a brandy and a good talk with the love of his life.

Before he reached the elevator, though, his phone chirped. Hank Moran.

"What is it, Hank?"

"Kyle, we have a match for the blood on your gun."

He felt light-headed at the news. "Tell me."

"A body was found in Pennsylvania five years ago, believe to have been killed within the time frame your gun was buried."

His heart quickened. He couldn't make himself ask the question.

"Are you there?"

"Yes," he croaked. "Whose body?"

"I was convinced your victim was Nate Westover, and the two others—Vince Tuttle and Nick Nunzio—were milking his accounts for their own purposes. But the photos of the victim, which was well preserved on discovery, show a prominent nose. Per procedure, the state police have requested dental records from the Tuttles' dentist, but I'm betting they'll simply confirm it's Vince Tuttle."

"Lord," Kyle whispered. His throat closed and tears filled his eyes.

"I tried to reach Lyssa but got no answer and didn't want to leave a message with that kind of news."

"She's in Canada for the weekend, taking a spa break. She has international coverage for her phone, and in fact, I talked to her an hour or so ago."

"I'll check with border patrol as to her destination."

"Niagara-on-the-Lake, she said, but I don't know which hotel. One of the big ones with a spa and indoor pool, I'd guess."

"Kyle, there's more. They've asked the only living relative, Janet Tuttle, to identify the body. She'll do it, but only if you accompany her." Hank paused for a reply and then offered, "I can try to recruit Lyssa instead."

"No. No, I'll come. I don't want Lyssa doing that, especially not with a drunk like Janet. Sorry to be so frank. What is my destination?"

Chapter 22

The instructions on the electronic directory of Vince Tuttle's luxury bayside condo complex told Lyssa to scroll to the resident's last name and press in the code to contact the resident's unit.

She found Patty Beck under B and Vince Tuttle under T, and they both had the same code. No surprise.

She laughed, thinking of the Facebook entry Bree had described last night of a "trampy-looking Patty Beck who bartends at a casino. Blond with gobs of makeup, pouring a nozzle-snout bottle of something red into a stainless cocktail shaker."

Wish you were here, Bree. She pressed in the code for the Beck-Tuttle unit. After four rings, Lyssa tapped her foot impatiently. After six rings without a response, she cancelled the call. Since the directory didn't tell the unit number for the resident, maybe that meant there was a security guard or doorman she could ask.

Planning to make friends with the doorman, she rounded the corner to the front of the building. At the sight of glass and steel rising five floors to a rooftop garden she slowed her steps. Not what she imagined Vince choosing as his home. Probably it was Patty's taste.

She still hadn't decided if Vince was the bad guy Janet and Vince's parents said he'd become, or if he was the good guy he'd always been. In the beginning she'd seen Vince as the one who'd knocked off Nate for trying to choke Patty. But after Nick Nunzio had shown his true colors, she wanted to believe Nick was the only bad guy in the mix.

One bad guy was enough and, as Kyle had said, the crime committed with the gun needn't have been murder. Nick might have shot up someone's property during a burglary and needed to hide the gun. Or he might have shot a person, causing injury but not death. Whatever he did, the police would eventually get it out of him.

First things first. While she didn't look forward to meeting Patty and still couldn't understand why Vince had married her, she wanted to see for herself that Vince was alive and well.

Then she could get on the plane back to Tompkins Falls and get on with her life, her teaching, her students, and her husband, who was far less perfect than she'd previously thought but still a good guy.

"Help you, ma'am?" a doughy young man in a dark blue uniform asked her. Textbooks open on the desk told her he was a student taking advantage of a boring desk job.

"Yes, hello. I'm hoping to talk for a few minutes with one of your residents who grew up in the house my husband and I bought this year in Tompkins Falls, New York."

"Unit number?"

"Don't know."

At the security guard's sneer, she laughed. "I don't have a clever story for you. The fact is, when my neighbors and the Alumni Office at the college where I work heard I was coming to Green Bay and staying at a resort in Sturgeon Bay, they asked me to look up two young men from our neighborhood who graduated from Tompkins College, where I'm an economics professor, six years ago. That didn't sound right. They graduated six years ago, I currently teach there. I did succeed in finding one of the gentlemen, Nate Westover, in Sturgeon Bay, and I know the other, Vince Tuttle, lives here and was at one time on the board."

"So why don't you call him, lady?"

"Because I don't have his personal phone number, just the number at the school where he's an award-winning primary grades teacher."

"You try him at school?"

"If I hadn't been having so much fun on the Door Peninsula, I'd have thought of that during the week." She gave him an exaggerated frowny face. "But I was having fun, and I didn't. Now I'm at your mercy." She squinted at his nametag. "Brian."

He looked her up and down before jerking his head to the left. "He's in the park walking Butch and Sundance. Do me a favor. Don't tell him I'm the one that told you. That way, you won't get me in trouble and I won't say anything to Patty about someone looking for Vince."

"Patty Beck? Does she keep him on a tight leash?"

"Funny." He laughed drily. "She's not in control where Vince is concerned. It's just that you don't want to be in Patty's sights. Take my word for it."

"I totally agree, Brian. I won't reveal my source. And Butch and Sundance?" She squinted again. "They are Patty's poodles?"

"Rottweilers."

"Seriously?" That didn't sound good. She thumbed the name of the breed into her phone's search engine. "Hardworking and loyal. No mention of vicious. No reason to be afraid, right, Brian?"

"If Patty were holding the leash, you'd want to take a pass. Vince?" He shook his head. "Verdict's out on him. I can't see someone with his personality teaching little kids, but the school loves him, like you said."

She hadn't seen that coming. Everyone had said he was meant for teaching. What did he mean by Vince's personality? "Okay. So, I go left out the building?"

"And across the four-lane street. Do yourself a favor and cross at the light. Everything after that is the park. Just look for the dark-haired guy walking two Rotties."

"Wish me luck, Brian."

He guffawed. "You'll need it, lady."

The park was heavily treed, and paths went in all directions. She headed on the diagonal that would take her to the center and kept an eye out for two big mean-looking dogs with a tall dark-haired man.

Her path entered a tunnel of evergreens. *God, I am seriously spooked. You're with me, right?*

When it emerged into a broad rolling green space dotted with century-old oaks, laughter drew her attention to the eastern edge of the green. Half a dozen children on shiny yellow-and-green playground equipment climbed ladders, crawled into giant tubes, and slid down an assortment of slides, shrieking and laughing. They reminded her of sitting on the kitchen island with Kyle, swinging their legs. *Moms wouldn't bring their kids here if this were a dangerous place.*

On the north edge of the green, probably fifty yards from her, the trio she sought came into view from behind a massive oak. Two spirited Rottweilers in the lead and a man who leaned his weight back, holding tight to their leashes.

She amended her assessment. The park was safe except for the man-eating dogs.

Vince and the dogs continued toward her on a path that intersected hers, and she moved forward, head high, sunny smile in place. He gave her a curious once-over when she stopped in the intersection of their paths. She now presented an obstacle in his path, and she was obviously checking him out. He slowed his steps.

Something about him didn't match her image of Vince. Gone was the creative child standing proudly with Tommy Tuttle under the portrait he'd painted of his dad. The frown that seemed grooved in this man's face was at odds with the smiling young man in the Geneseo poster. Gone, too, was the prominent nose evident in Vince's college yearbook picture. Janet had said Vince hated the Tuttle nose as much as she had. He'd evidently had it fixed.

Maybe because he had a deep tan for someone who'd been teaching all winter and because he seemed very fit—strong enough to handle the two massive energetic Rottweilers—she kept picturing him on the shore of Lake Michigan, hiking on the dunes or casting from the shore.

Possibly he and Nate were still friends. It was the outcome she'd always wanted. Maybe he spent time with Nate the weekends Tucker didn't see him. But, no, the journal entries would have said so. It was time to let go of her wish that Vince and Nate had remained friends.

As soon as she did, hackles rose on the back of her neck.

She checked that the children were still shouting and squealing with joy. They were, and their moms were still chatting on the nearby benches. No one but her was afraid.

"Hi, Vince," she said, loud enough for the mothers at the playground to hear.

He commanded the dogs to stay, and the trio halted twenty feet short of her. "You're not one of my first-graders' parents," he said in a strong baritone.

Janet had told them Vince was a tenor, like his dad. Had he picked up smoking? She thought of the cigarette butts beside Nate's back porch. No, those were Tucker's, she was sure.

"No, I'm not one of the parents," she said, making her voice strong and cheerful.

His eyes narrowed. "What do you want?"

"My name is Lyssa, and I live at your old house, at 57 Seneca Street, in Tompkins Falls, New York."

"So?" The dogs tugged at their leashes. He gave a jerk, and they snapped to attention.

She took an involuntary step backward and chastised herself for showing her fear of them. One growled low in its throat.

She lifted her head high. "You don't know me, Vince, but two of your old neighbors wanted me to look you up while I was in Green Bay. Maybe you remember Toffee Winkel and Becca Farnsworth? Toffee lived next door, and Becca taught Sunday School."

His face softened. So did his grip. The dogs surged forward. He snapped the leashes. "Stay!"

God, protect me. Her insides trembled, but her sunny appearance held up. "I hear you're an award-winning teacher."

That brought a wistful smile to his face, but he didn't meet her gaze.

"When my husband and I bought the house at 57 Seneca Street, your mother's rose garden was a sorry sight. I decided to restore it."

His face hardened, and some dark emotion flashed in his eyes.

She swallowed her fear. "The garden is finished, and it's quite lovely." *Do not mention the gun.* She didn't know where the thought came from, but she cooperated with it. That meant she had to scramble for a reason for bringing up the garden. "I just thought you'd want to know that. Apparently, it meant a great deal to your mother."

"Yes, it did. Thank you." Despite the kind words, his voice was hard.

"Do you remember—" She'd been about to ask if he remembered Nick Nunzio when her phone rang. "Just a sec."

She glanced at the screen, It was a text from Hank Moran's number.

Kyle en rte PA, mtg JT to ID body of VTT. Where r u?

Pennsylvania, Janet Tuttle, body of . . . Icy cold enveloped her. *God help me.*

She struggled to breathe, forced herself to meet Vince's eyes.

He was watching her warily. The dogs whined and strained at their leashes.

Tears threatened. *God, tell me what to do.*

"I–I have to go." The words poured from her mouth. "My husband's traveling, and something's happened. I'll tell everyone at home you're well."

She pivoted to face the playground, where the children continued their play. She sidestepped across a strip of grass to a path that led directly to the play equipment. "Nice talking with you, Vince," she said over her shoulder and race-walked toward the yellow swings.

As she passed the playground, Lyssa smiled at the young mothers and nodded hello, then glanced at the intersecting paths behind them.

Vince remained at the intersection where they'd talked, watching her. Though the dogs yelped and strained at their leashes, he held them in check with one hand. With the other, he held a phone to his ear.

Who's he calling? She broke into a run, reached the pedestrian light, jabbed at the crosswalk button, and leapt forward as soon as the light turned.

God, I need a plan.

Kyle would say, "God's got our back, but we have to do the footwork."

So, Plan B. Start driving, and make it up as you go.

Kyle's plane had flown against a headwind through the night into JFK. He'd nearly missed his connection to Pittsburgh. He approached a nondescript man holding a sign with PENNINGTON. The man insisted on seeing his passport.

Kyle supposed he looked like a vagrant, and he was sure his breath could fell an army. Having verified his identity, the man wordlessly handed over a manila envelope.

He forgot to breathe for ten seconds as he felt the import of the still-sealed contents.

Their gun *had* killed someone.

The hand rising from the garden was Vince Tuttle's.

Nate Westover had gotten away with murder for five years.

No one would have known if he and Lyssa hadn't done what they'd done.

Where was Lyssa?

When he looked up, the courier had vanished. He supposed he ought not stand in the middle of the Pittsburgh airport with an official envelope in his hands, one that spoke of the death of a young man who'd wanted to be a teacher and never gotten the chance. And, he knew, if he stayed where he was a moment longer, he would weep.

Next steps? Prepare to meet Janet and show up at the morgue. How Hank had arranged to for them to view the photos of the body on a Sunday he'd never know. And didn't need to.

Lord, I'm a mess. He glanced at his watch, shook his head, and sought a clock with local time. He had one hour until Janet's plane was due to land. He needed to shower and shave if he and Janet were to lay Vince to rest today.

He shoved the still-sealed envelope in the outside pocket of his carry-on, his only bag, and went in search of the airline's elite passenger lounge. After showering away the kinks and aches and grunge of travel, he brushed and flossed his teeth, and styled his hair the best he could.

Lord, let this be over soon. Lyssa's nightmares, too. How was he going to tell her? He'd given Hank permission to prepare her. Maybe Hank had reached her, maybe not.

She'd be waiting for him at home tonight, regardless. That motivated him to don clean clothes from his carry-on— chinos and a decent shirt. His suit jacket had shed some of its wrinkles in the steam of the shower. Decent enough for viewing the body of a young man dead five years and abandoned beside a highway in Pennsylvania. With a shuddering exhale, he accepted it was the best he could do.

A check of the arrivals board told him Janet's flight from Charlotte was on time. That left him twenty minutes to eat something. A twenty-dollar bill persuaded the clerk at the salad stand to slice a firm red apple and a chunk of cheddar for him, and he poured a large iced tea from the crock they'd just brought out.

As he munched, he perused the documents from his manila envelope. First was a map and set of directions to the morgue, next a single sheet with do's and don'ts. No pets or children, no surprise there. It eased his mind to know they'd not be seeing a corpse so much as photos taken at the time of the body's discovery and subsequent autopsy. Grisly just the same.

While he sipped his tea, he scanned the remaining information about the particular body they'd be seeing and where it had been found.

Single gunshot to the heart. *Wouldn't there have been a lot of blood?*

Death had been immediate. *Or did bleeding stop when the heart stopped?*

The body had been dumped sometime in late May, naked, into a ravine near the city of Latrobe. *Why was he naked?*

As determined by the condition of the body, it was discovered within two to three days after death, by teenagers looking for a place to drink their six-pack. May 22.

His watch alarm sounded. Time to meet Janet's plane and lay to rest the young man killed in their guest room. *Lord, have mercy.*

"Green Bay just sold the last seat on the earlier flight," Bree told her. "Milwaukee has no availability on any flights until tomorrow evening."

"Not any?" Lyssa cringed as another semi screamed past on her right. She pushed her speed to seventy-five.

"No."

"Not even to–"

"Not anywhere."

"Wait." She pointed to an electronic billboard Bree couldn't see a time zone away. "There's a sign saying the fast ferry is back in service as of yesterday. The Lake Express. Where does that go?"

"Hold on." Bree's anxious breathing on the line was loud enough for Lyssa to hear even with three lanes of fast-moving traffic on I-43. "To Michigan. There's an interstate from there over to Detroit. Isn't Detroit where your second flight is leaving from?"

"Perfect. How do I get to the ferry?"

"The Lake Express leaves from Milwaukee. You're about halfway to Milwaukee. What's that beep?"

"Low battery. My phone charger is in the trunk in my duffel. I don't dare stop. I'll call you back as I get closer to Milwaukee. I need you to figure out which exit to take and what time the ferry leaves, okay?" She ended the connection.

Forty minutes later, just as the highway signs with the overview of the Milwaukee exits popped up on her right, she called Bree.

"What exit are you near?"

"I'm already at exit 85."

"Which is the same as mile 85. Around exit 73, which is coming up fast, you need to pick up I-94 east. It might be called I-794. It's real short and it ends at the ferry."

"Thank you. When–?"

"Leaves at half past noon."

"That's twenty minutes. I can do this. Love you, bye."

She studied every upcoming sign and memorized the icon for the ferry. *Which lane should I be in?* She guessed wrong. With a quick check of her rearview mirror and her blind spot, she shot across three lanes to a blare of horns, and careened down the ramp to I-794.

In a few minutes, the ferry icon made its appearance and guided her directly to the departure pier. *Thank you, God. And Bree.*

The Lake Express, just starting its season, was happy to book her and her rental car on the twelve-thirty to Michigan. "Muskegon," Lyssa said. At the ticket-seller's nod, she asked, "And do you sell a map of Michigan?"

He pointed to a rack of postcards and maps. She bought a roadmap, got back in her car, and rolled onto the ferry. Before heading to the passenger deck, she dug out her charger, tucked it and the map into her tote, and joined the flow of passengers on the stairway.

Grabbing a seat next to a charging station, she plugged in her phone and spread open the map. And breathed.

With one finger on Muskegon, she traced the interstate through Grand Rapids and Lansing to Detroit. Two hundred miles, which would put her there . . . The ferry was due in at four o'clock, then three hours driving, she'd get to Detroit around seven, best case. She brought up her flight information. Her connecting flight from Detroit to Rochester would depart at eight-fifteen.

What if they declare me a no-show in Green Bay and give away my seat?

Chapter 23

A dear friend came with me as far as Charlotte," Janet told Kyle. "She'll stay in the city overnight, you know, and shop. So it's not a burden to her. I'll fly back to Charlotte in the morning and meet up with her. Unless . . ."

Kyle patted her hand. "We'll take it one step at a time, shall we, Janet?"

"You're a dear for meeting me, Kyle. Even with the tranquilizer my doctor ordered, I know I couldn't do this alone."

"Nor should you do this alone. No one should." *That explains why she's not reeking of alcohol.* He caught himself. *Lord, give me compassion.* This was immeasurably harder for Janet than for him.

The taxi deposited them at Janet's hotel and agreed to wait fifteen minutes, with the meter running. While Janet checked into her room, Kyle generously persuaded the desk clerk to hold his own carry-on for a few hours until his grim duty was done. He inquired about a rental car, and the clerk agreed to have one on site for him when he returned.

He tried Lyssa's phone again and left a voicemail that he'd just met Janet Tuttle and they were on their way to identify Vince's body. As he pressed Send, he remembered Lyssa might not have gotten Hank's message. She'd be confused, even horrified by what he'd just said. Blast.

The taxi drove them to the front entry of a nondescript office building. Other than an official-looking seal on the glass door that might signify a city, county, or state, there was no wording to identify the facility. Kyle checked the address on the building against his instructions and handed his credit card to the driver along with a twenty-dollar tip.

"That's too much, Kyle, and I should be paying for this," Janet said.

"Let me worry about all this, Janet. You've quite enough on your mind."

With his arm protectively around her shoulders, he approached the information desk. He introduced them and handed over the paper he'd been given, labeled "Vincent Thomas Tuttle."

While they waited for their escort, he examined Janet's face. Deep lines dragged at her mouth, and she breathed shallowly through parted lips. "You're being very brave, Janet. I'll be right beside you."

"You'll be with me for . . ."

"Yes, of course."

A woman in uniform approached them.

"Here's our escort."

"She looks kind, doesn't she, Kyle?"

"Indeed."

The woman, who introduced herself as an officer with the Pennsylvania State Police, shook their hands and explained the procedure Kyle had already read about in his manila envelope.

"After the viewing, I'll need to ask Mrs. Tuttle some questions. It won't take long."

Janet asked, "Is–has the body been buried already?"

The office told her the remains had been cremated. Should she want the ashes, they could furnish them to her today.

"Yes, please, if this is really Vince." Her own words shocked her, and she gripped Kyle's arm as she fought for control.

Kyle asked if she was all right, and she nodded.

"That's fine, Mrs. Tuttle," the officer said. "Let's proceed."

With each doorway they encountered, Kyle's heart beat faster. Soon it thudded in his chest, and his breathing was as shallow as Janet's. *Stop thinking. Breathe. Do your job.*

In the viewing room, Janet took one look at the photo of the dead man's face and screamed, "Vince! Our Vince." She collapsed against Kyle, sobbing into his chest. "Oh God, forgive me, I've been so wrong."

She beat on Kyle's chest, and he braced her. "We were so wrong, Tommy," she sobbed.

Lyssa and I had it wrong, too.

As Kyle held Janet's trembling body, his mind sorted through the data they'd unearthed, trying to fit it together with Vince as the victim at the center of it all. Who killed this man? His lifelong friend? It was impossible to compute, here in this place, with a traumatized woman in his arms. There was no making sense of it. Who would want to kill Vince Tuttle?

Just do your job.

"Is that sufficient for identification of the body, Officer?" Kyle asked.

With a nod, the officer spoke into a tiny lapel microphone. "Mrs. Janet Tuttle has positively identified the body as that of her nephew, Vincent Thomas Tuttle."

"Let's get her some water, shall we?" Kyle said. "I doubt if she can answer any questions, but I may be able to fill in what I know of the circumstances surrounding Vince's death."

While the staff assisted Janet with signing the official papers, Kyle was escorted to a conference room. A TV monitor came to life, and he spotted someone seated at a control panel and wearing headphones. He returned his attention to the screen to see Hank Moran and Harriet Feinstein blinking at him. He lifted a hand to them. "Did you reach Lyssa?" he asked.

Hank replied, "Texted her you were on your way here. Didn't hear back. Is it Vince Tuttle?"

Kyle nodded. "Janet is seeing to the paperwork."

"These proceedings are being recorded," the woman officer told them in a voice that shut down their personal exchange. Following introductions, she made a formal statement that the body had been identified, by next of kin, as that of Vincent Thomas Tuttle, whose last known address was 57 Seneca Street in Tompkins Falls, New York.

Kyle related everything he knew about Vince's death from his and Lyssa's investigation. He added, "I don't know who killed him. It's my understanding someone using his name has been residing in a bayfront condo in Green Bay, Wisconsin, and is a schoolteacher in that city and has received awards for excellence in teaching." He lifted his eyes to the image of Hank Moran, who appeared to be as shell-shocked as Kyle felt. "Exactly who is the Vince Tuttle teaching little children in Green Bay, Wisconsin, Officers?" He rose to his feet, pounded the table, and yelled, "Isn't it time someone found out?"

"Easy, Kyle," Harriet said sharply. "Let's let the state police work together on this."

"They'd bloody well better," Kyle shouted. "Heaven help those children. And until someone apprehends him, my wife and I are in danger of ending up like that poor boy on a slab in a morgue. Hank, you talked with border patrol. Where is my wife?"

Lyssa had confirmed with the airline to hold her seat on the flight from Detroit to Rochester. She'd given the rental car company a heads-up that she'd had to drive into another state to make her flight, and they reprimanded her for violating her rental agreement. She argued for half an hour and, finally, the company agreed to levy a surcharge, which she gladly paid.

She then left a message for Kyle that she was en route but had just encountered heavy traffic. Unfortunately, that was true.

As she ended the connection, the images flashed through her mind, as intrusively as the cars passing and weaving on Michigan's I-96: the dirt-caked lunchbox buried under the dead tree in her garden, blood pulsing from Toffee Winkel's arm, two growling Rottweilers straining at the leash, Nate Westover glaring after her with the phone to his ear.

Had Nate booked the last seat on the early flight out of Green Bay? Or was he in full flight, packing up his treasures from the house on the shore and heading for the Canadian border?

She needed to call Hank Moran to tell him everything she'd learned in the past two days, but she couldn't do it while the horrible memories, mixed with scenes from her nightmares, whirled through her mind with the frequency of the passing semis.

She'd felt compelled to learn the truth about the gun, and now she knew. Nate had killed his friend Vince, because Vince had stolen his girlfriend, Patty, and that loss came on top of losing his parents to the rockslide. Was it his best friend's betrayal that had made him snap?

"No, that's not it," she said to the dashboard. Something was off in that scenario.

A horn blared. She gripped the wheel and centered her car in her lane. *Just drive the car.*

Once she passed Lansing, she tried again, starting with the body, which they now knew was Vince's. Her heart ached. She hadn't wanted either boy to be the victim. Nor had she wanted either of them to be a murderer. She tried to fit the pieces together right this time. Nate had killed Vince in his own bedroom and hidden the gun in the garden. Nate and Patty had dumped the body somewhere in Pennsylvania, on their way to Green Bay. So far, the scenario felt solid, but where did Nick fit in?

And what about Nate's truck? Did they roll the truck into the ravine with the body in it? No, the truck would have been discovered, and it would have led back to Nate.

So, what, they dumped the body, kept going, stopped to file off the vehicle ID number and strip the plates before abandoning the truck in a parking lot or a field somewhere? That way, someone could have helped himself to the truck and, for self-protection, kept its origin secret. That would work.

So Patty and Nate were driving separately until they abandoned the truck, which came sometime after they dumped the body. Then they continued in Vince's old

Honda, similarly abandoned that car, and bought themselves new cars in Green Bay. No messy purchase of Wisconsin plates for the old car, which would have required proof of ownership, which Nate likely hadn't thought of beforehand.

No one could connect Nate or Patty to the body, the truck, or the old Honda. All that was left for the plan to work was for Nate to spread the story to his new school that he'd decided to get his nose fixed. Maybe he'd even started the rumor before ending Vince's life and assuming his identity. He was good at planning ahead. After all, he'd bought his log-and-glass house on the shore ten days ahead of the killing.

"Premeditated murder," she said out loud. But where did Nick fit? Wouldn't it take two strong men to maneuver Vince's dead body down the stairs and into Nate's truck? And why take time to ceremonially bury the gun the way Nate had?

It was dark by the time Kyle left Pittsburgh and pointed his rental car in the direction of Tompkins Falls. He'd had a meal with Janet and tipped the person on the desk to look after her needs tonight and make sure she got to the airport in time for her flight to Charlotte.

He supposed a good caretaker would have stayed the night in Pittsburgh and put Janet on the plane in the morning, but he'd done enough. Or maybe he'd just *had* enough. Either way, he needed to see Lyssa and know she was all right. He needed to sleep in his own bed with his wife.

The GPS told him it was a five-hour trip on the interstate, north to Erie and then east to the Canandaigua exit of the New York State Thruway. Pittsburgh's classical music station faded within an hour, and he snapped off the radio. The highway and surrounding countryside were devoid of light, except the occasional farm or petrol station.

Lyssa's voicemail had assured him she was all right, though heaven only knew where she was. Hank still hadn't heard anything from border patrol about her crossing into or out of Canada. The hotels in Niagara-on-the-Lake refused to tell him if his wife was a guest. Her spa getaway came with too many unknowns.

He hoped she'd booked into one of the larger hotels, one with a spa and an indoor saltwater pool. He pictured her having a massage, dining on nouveau cuisine, shopping along the flower-lined main street. If she'd seen an evening play and then tackled the border crossing along with everyone else returning from a weekend in Canada, she might even be later than he.

Now that presented a problem. He didn't have the new key or the code to the new security system. He supposed he could call on Joel and Manda for assistance. *Stop thinking. Drive the car.*

He tried fantasizing about a trip with Lyssa. Soon, next weekend perhaps? But his mind's eye kept coming back to the photo of Vince's white, waxen face, the look of surprise he'd worn at the end, killed by his good friend Nate, in his own home. The same friend who'd choked Mrs. Tuttle at her own dining room table. The same friend he'd defended when Nate faced an assault charge, lest he be denied a teaching position.

That same friend was now teaching in Vince's name and winning accolades for the job as Vince Tuttle? He couldn't get his head around it. What had happened to Nate

Westover's love for his lifelong friend? What had happened to his sense of decency, his moral compass?

Ah, that's why Wollings' accident hit me in the face early in this investigation. Twenty years ago, the night Wollings was hurt, Kyle had followed his own moral compass. Five years ago, maybe six, something had gone awry with Nate Westover's moral compass.

Or had it?

No one doubted the body recovered from the ravine, the body Janet identified, was Vince Tuttle's. And, according to Hank Moran, the dental records kept by the Tuttle's dentist in Tompkins Falls had matched the dentition of the corpse. Kyle could accept that.

But it didn't compute that Nate Westover was the murderer. Was Nick the murderer? Hank didn't think so.

As the car transitioned from I-79 north to I-90 east, he thought back to the evening Lyssa and Bree had talked with Nick Nunzio at the Manse Lounge. Nick had told Lyssa he and Nate were still in touch. Did Nick know his former student was impersonating Vince?

"Wait a minute," Kyle said to the deer alongside the road. Did Nick even know Vince was dead?

Once Lyssa turned onto Seneca Street, she called Bree to let her know she was almost home. "No, wait." She stopped the car in front of her house. "Bree, there's a light on at Nick's, and I can tell someone's walking around inside. Did your brother, Peter, say anything about Nick being out of jail?"

"No, nothing. That's not good, Lyssa. If he's there and sees you at your house, who knows what he'll do?"

"I can't believe this. I am too tired to deal with him. Maybe I'll leave my car on the street, dash inside, and set the security system behind me."

"Why don't you just come to my place?"

"I would, but Kyle's coming home. His voicemail said he'd get here not long after midnight. It's only eleven now, and he doesn't have a key, remember?"

"I'm not leaving you alone with a pervert across the street, girlfriend."

"I won't turn on any lights, okay? I'll run upstairs and light a candle and hop in the shower and wait by the window for Kyle to get here."

Bree laughed. "That's pathetic. I'm calling Peter to see if Nick's been released, and if he has, I'm coming over."

"Deal."

She parked the VW on the street, dragged her duffel and tote with her, and stayed in the shadows as she slunk down the lawn on Toffee's side of the house. Using only the penlight on her keychain, it took all her concentration to open the French door into the kitchen and disarm the security system.

She tossed her duffel and tote on the kitchen island, added her jacket to the pile, and drank a full glass of water at the sink. *Home again.*

Still thirsty, she poured another glass of water and raised it in a toast to a safe journey. "Thank you, God," she said and tipped back the glass.

It shattered in her hand. "What?" She dropped to the floor behind the island before knowing why. A second shot shattered the window over the sink. The overhead lights flashed on.

"Me, when I get home from a trip, the last thing I think about is water," a grating female voice said. "I pop a beer."

God help me. She forced herself to act the part of someone who routinely encountered murderers in her kitchen. "So it wasn't Nate who bought the last seat on the early flight out of Green Bay, was it, Patty?"

Though her right hand had a few superficial cuts, the left had a gash on the pad below her thumb issuing a steady flow of blood. She opened the bottom drawer next to the sink a few inches and snagged a clean cloth. With the cloth folded against the cut, she wrapped her hand tight with the blue silk scarf, the one she'd worn the whole trip. It had brought her luck so far, and Heaven knew she needed luck now.

Gritting her teeth at the needles of pain in her hand, she quietly opened another cabinet door and drew out the heavy sauté pan. Excellent weapon. Broad surface, plenty of heft, nice sharp edge to crack someone's skull.

Staying low, she scooted backward to the end of the island closest to the outside door, but she projected her voice to the cupboards where she'd been standing, to the left of the sink. "You're Patty Beck, right?"

She peeked around the island and caught a glimpse of Patty near the French door to the patio. *Darn, that's my escape route.*

"Got it in one, honey," Patty said with a smirk, her shimmering dark red lipstick making her smile grotesque. Bree was right. Patty wore heavy makeup. Her platinum blond hair was skinned back from her face into a tight ponytail.

It could be fun jerking her around by that tail. Lyssa covered her mouth to suppress a hysterical laugh. Who knew her Austin, Texas, chick fights would come in useful as a sober married woman?

"Nice to meet you, Patty." *Keep her talking.* "How did you get a gun through airport security?"

"This belongs to my buddy Nick," Patty said. A dozen bracelets rattled on her bare forearm as she brandished the gun. Her arm straightened and she took aim at the glass-fronted cabinet to the left of the sink.

No, please, not the Waterford. Two shots in quick succession destroyed the two shelves of glassware Joel and Manda had given them as wedding gifts. Patty was a crack shot, Lyssa had to admit. Was that four bullets gone? Could she rely on there being only six? Even if she could see the gun, she'd have no idea what kind it was.

"So where is Nick tonight?" she asked Patty.

"I don't know. His house was empty when I got here."

"How'd you get in?"

"I've had a key forever. Nate gave it to me when we first dated. You ought to try Nick sometime. He's pretty good in the sack."

"No thanks." She breathed deeply against sudden nausea.

"Bet you didn't know Nate gave me the other gun."

"The one that killed Vince? Actually, I did know that. Nick told us about it. He'd stolen Bill Westover's gun and Margie's jewelry from Nate's parents' house, and Nate wanted the gun back for his girlfriend. That was you, right?"

Patty's gaze was still trained on the far end of the island, as if she thought that's where Lyssa was. "See, that's your problem, bitch. You know too much."

Lyssa drew a lid for a small saucepan out of the cabinet and set down the skillet for later retrieval. She couldn't risk giving away her real position. Patty would be on her in a flash with a bullet to the brain. *I will not let Kyle come home to my brains splattered on the floor.*

She crawled toward the far end of the island. Glass slivers littered the area beyond the sink, but she'd gone far enough to toss the lid in the air without it arcing.

First, though, she wanted more information. "Patty, I'd love to know who all was in on the plan to kill Vince."

"That was all my idea. Nick had a different plan to get Nate certified. In fact, they were across the street working out the details when I shot Vince." She gave a sharp laugh. "Vince and I made love for the last time, me on top, one shot to the heart. But do you know how heavy a dead body is? Impossible to move. So I called Nick, and the two of them came over. We put the body in Nate's truck and I made them swear they'd never tell a soul. I took off in the truck, and Nate stayed to get rid of the gun."

Lyssa couldn't listen to any more. She flipped the lid like a Frisbee, and it sailed straight up to the ceiling. A shot rang out. Patty nailed the lid on its way down, and it crashed with a bullet hole close to its center. *God, help me, she's good.*

One bullet left?

She scurried back to her end of the island and noticed Patty had moved away from the outside door. Before she could make a run for the door, though, her phone rang in her tote bag on top of the island. She pressed the back of her hand to her mouth to keep silent, wishing she could tell the caller to send help, wishing it were Kyle and she could tell him she loved him.

Focus.

A scrabbling sound above her sent Lyssa cowering as close to the island as she could. What was Patty doing?

Coming over the island to get to her? She wanted to protect her head with the sauté pan, but it was now out of reach.

The phone rang a second time, louder now.

With no warning, the phone whizzed toward the patio door, ricocheted off the glass pane, and broke in pieces on the stone tiles. Lyssa's heart thudded. *Keep your head.* If she ran now, Patty would put a bullet in her back and she'd be dead.

She peeked around the corner of the island and couldn't see Patty. She shifted into a crouch, crept along the side of the island, and peered through the legs of the first bar stool. Patty was sneaking around the other end, the gun pointed ahead and down.

Lyssa half rose, her body hidden by the bar stool. She grabbed onto the back legs and raised it to protect her core and her head. Should she throw it with all her might? Or move backward to the door using it as a shield? But if Patty had locked the door behind her, Lyssa would lose too much time fumbling with the lock with her good hand, and possibly lose her grip on the stool with the injured hand. *Forget that.*

She lifted the stool just a bit, testing for its center of gravity, planning to hurl it. The movement was enough to catch Patty's eye. Patty swung around, aimed for Lyssa's heart, and fired.

It was pure luck that, when Lyssa jumped reflexively, one leg of the stool deflected the bullet so it pierced her body two inches above and to the left of her heart. She screamed as searing pain ripped through her shoulder.

Last bullet? She hoped so. She was barely able to stand. Setting the stool square on the floor, she leaned over its back to get her breath. Judging by the level of pain, she was very much alive. Blood was soaking her T-shirt but wasn't pulsing. *I can do this.* She straightened and faced Patty.

"And I was just starting to like you," Patty said with a cruel laugh. She pressed the trigger, but the only result was a feeble click. And another.

Patty hurled the gun at Lyssa and stormed around the island toward her. Adrenaline fueled Lyssa as she hefted the stool with a growl of rage. She smashed it into Patty's face as the blond advanced on her. Patty went down without a sound, and her head cracked against the tile floor.

The stool's momentum carried Lyssa to the floor by the small dining table near the French windows. She thought of Tommy Tuttle using a heavy candlestick on Nate when he'd attacked Rikki Tuttle in their dining room. Breathing hard, she struggled to her feet and grabbed for one of the leaded-glass Waterford candlesticks on the tabletop.

She approached Patty's inert body with caution. No movement, not even the twitch of an eyelid. With her good right hand, she raised the candlestick overhead and slammed its base into Patty's cheek. Blood flowed from the gash. "That was for killing Vince Tuttle."

She raised the candlestick again and yelled, "This is for the mean tricks you played on Rikki Tuttle." She didn't recognize her voice, which dripped with venom.

Why wouldn't her arm move? Someone had a hold on it and was shouting at her, "I said put down the weapon."

Lyssa looked into the face of Officer Peter Shaughnessy. "You came, Peter." Her hand lost its grip. The heavy crystal weapon dropped to the stone tile and shattered. The blood drained from Lyssa face, and she spiraled into unconsciousness.

Chapter 24

The beep tormented her. Every second, like clockwork. Who would invent a clock whose big hand beeped every time it jumped to the next second? "Relentless," Lyssa said, her voice a croaky whisper.

"What's relentless, sweetheart?"

"That beep."

Kyle folded her bandaged hand in his and kissed her fingertips. "That's your heartbeat, my love. We don't want that to stop, do we?"

"Why is my heart beeping?"

"You're hooked up to a monitor. Can you open your eyes?"

She lifted her eyelids halfway. The room was shadowy with a green glow to her right. The monitor. Her left shoulder was bandaged and heavy. "What did I do to my shoulder?"

"You remember."

Her eyes opened wide, her stomach pitched, and she sucked in a sharp breath. "Oh." She rolled her head to the left and met his gaze. "Are you angry with me for going to Green Bay?"

"I am, yes."

She swallowed. "How did the police know to come?"

"Bree tried to reach you and you didn't answer. She called it in. Toffee heard the gunshots. She called it in."

"I fainted, did I?"

"Collapsed, they said. You were dehydrated and exhausted and you'd lost blood. The bullet went straight through, and they've patched you up. They were worried about shock, too, and they're making you stay the night."

Lyssa held his gaze. "Kyle, I wanted very badly to kill Patty Beck."

"I would have, too, my love."

"Do you mean it?"

"Yes, though I don't like admitting it."

"I think I would have done it, if the police hadn't shown up and made me stop. She isn't dead, is she?"

"No. The police arrested her for first-degree murder and transported her to Rochester for surgery to her face. She's about to make a name for herself, here and in Geneseo. Probably in her home town in Pennsylvania, too."

"And Nate? Has he been arrested?"

"He's vanished. Hank wants to talk with you as soon as you're able."

She nodded and searched her husband's face. *He's exhausted.*

"What is Nate like?" he asked.

"Dark. Living two lives. He's himself at the house on the Door Peninsula. His fishing buddy, Tucker, says he's a good guy. No alcohol in the place, no drugs, no weapons, just fishing rods and berry baskets.

"He's so alone there, Kyle. When you called and I was sad from something I'd read?" At his nod, she continued, "It was his journals. He records every day he spends there, the fishing with Tucker, the hiking with Montana. And he ends every entry with, 'Rest in peace, Mom and Dad.'

"He's never told Tucker where he comes from or what he does the rest of the time. Yet he's just miles away, being someone else."

"Being Vince Tuttle, award-winning teacher," Kyle said with bitterness. "How could no one know he's not who he claims to be?"

"He's clever. But what kind of life is that, shacked up in a bayview condo with that slut Patty Beck?"

A smile tugged at Kyle's mouth.

"She is, you know. She said as much." Lyssa plucked at the almost-white sheet and blanket. "Nate's her dog walker."

"Toy poodles, I suppose?"

"Rottweilers. Butch and Cassidy."

"You mean Sundance."

"I suppose so. Outlaws all of them."

He lay his head on the mattress by her side. His eyelids lowered.

She caressed his face, the forehead creased with worry and fatigue, the stubble that showed how haphazardly he'd shaved, the mouth devoid of expression.

"I love you so much, my darling." He didn't respond. "May I use your phone?"

He drew it from his pocket.

"I'm asking Justin to pick you up and take you home with him." She pressed in the number.

"Thank you, my love," he said.

It was dawn when Hank Moran pushed open the door to Lyssa's hospital room. "Sorry to wake you," Hank said in his deep voice. He opened the blinds, letting the rosy glow of sunrise into the room.

Lyssa rolled her head toward the window, away from the green light of the monitors. "You're not sorry at all." Her voice was croaky, and she welcomed the glass of water he held out.

"Use the straw. Take little sips. Are you up for some questions? I heard you're refusing drugs."

"Honestly, it's not so bad."

He puffed out his breath. "This is on the record," he told her.

While he set up the recorder, an aide raised the head of Lyssa's bed, fluffed her pillows, and checked her pulse and blood pressure.

She recounted for Hank and for the record how she'd found Nate's house and what little she'd learned from her time on his property. She told about Nate's pattern of fishing on Saturday with Tucker, the postal clerk, and hiking on Sunday with Montana. "I think he might be the photographer, E.B. Jones, who took the photo in Nate's living room. Otherwise no one has any idea."

"Any idea how the two met?"

"He's not from the Door Peninsula. People had seen him but no one knew him or recognized the name Montana. He has to be someone Nate trusts completely. My guess is he's a teacher with Nate at the same school or maybe in his literacy program. Probably from Montana. He might be retired already." She told Hank about the waitress at the resort who said he was an old geezer who had difficulty walking in the dunes.

"We believe Nate had a plan for himself, and I want to hear your thoughts about what that might be."

"I remember thinking he was either in that last seat out of Green Bay, which he wasn't, or on his way to Canada. Twenty million can go a long way toward establishing a new identity and a new life."

"Good thought. However, what we found at his house on the Door Peninsula didn't match that theory. We've since learned that Nate visited his bank immediately after meeting you in the park.

"There, he accessed his safe deposit box and used the bank's computer to access his investment accounts, simply to change his password. The balance is still over twenty million. He did not make a withdrawal. Evidently, his intention was to lock out others who knew the previous password."

"Nick and—just Nick, I guess. What did you find at his house?"

"His journals were gone, and his last will and testament was on top of the desk in the living room."

"Does that mean he's planning to kill himself?" Lyssa asked. "Or just make it look that way?"

"The will wouldn't stand without a body," Hank said. "And the will gives away all the money in his accounts. In fact, all his assets."

"Can you share the specifics? Maybe there's a clue."

"I can tell you it was drafted earlier this year on his 27th birthday."

"Oh my gosh, he's my age." Lyssa jerked forward without thinking, and fell back with a cry as pain stabbed her shoulder. "Stupid. They warned me not to move suddenly."

"Do you need a nurse?" Hank asked.

"No, I'm okay, it's just pain."

Hank snorted. "There's such a thing as too tough for your own good."

"I'm flattered you think I'm tough. Let's go on."

"Nate left the house and land on the Door Peninsula to Tucker, along with one-fourth of his investment portfolio. The condo in Green Bay, his SUV, and one-fourth of his investments go to Montana. And one-fourth each to Nick Nunzio and Tompkins College, an unrestricted gift."

"Nothing to Patty?" she asked.

"Her car and the dogs."

"He had her number, after all," she muttered.

"How would you go about finding Montana?"

"Like I said, he's not from the Door. The waitress was sure of that when I talked with her again Sunday at breakfast. If he's a fellow teacher, Nate had to trust him enough to see both identities."

"That's heavy."

"Except with Montana, he kept those two identities very separate," she said. "I'd start with the roster of teachers at his school, back to the date Nate started teaching there, narrowing to older male teachers, and seeing who's from Montana. Possible name E.B. Jones."

Kyle slept until midafternoon, when Gianessa knocked at the guest suite on the lowest level of the Cushman home. "Manda just called from the hospital. Your wife is being discharged in an hour, and she wants you to take her to Lynnie's for a very late breakfast. What do you say?"

He wrapped himself in his travel robe and opened the door a crack. "Absolutely, yes. Just need a shower and a shave."

She pinched her nostrils and gave him a dazzling smile. "A very long shower, please. I'll bring one of Justin's robes for you, and you leave your bags outside the door. We'll do your laundry while you're gone."

"So sorry. I'll throw open the patio door, shall I?"

"Please." With a finger wave, she bounded up the stairs.

One look in the mirror confirmed he looked a fright. The shower revived him. With a steady hand and a fresh blade, he made short work of the patchy stubble on his face. Then two passes with the toothbrush, and a full minute with the mouthwash someone had thoughtfully included in the guest basket. Eye drops, dug from his carry-on bag, didn't go far enough to remove the redness, and he suspected nothing less than a week of extra sleep would erase the bags from under his eyes.

It will have to do.

Dressed in the only clean item from his bag, a pair of blue jeans, he padded barefoot up two flights to the kitchen. "I don't suppose Justin would lend me a shirt and some socks?" he asked Gianessa as he grabbed onto the mug she held out to him.

"He's feeling generous today. He's even teaching Lyssa's afternoon classes. I'm sure he'll spare you a shirt and socks."

"That's brave of him teaching a class."

"He's a ham. He loves being in the classroom."

While she fetched the clothing, Kyle stood at the window, sipping his coffee and gazing at the lake. The water was turbulent in the stiff south wind, and gray under the ominous overcast. *How does it always know my mood?*

Gianessa was back with a Henley shirt and coordinated socks by the time he'd drained the cup.

"I don't know how you manage to make the world's best cup of coffee," he said.

"Magic. Be gentle with each other, Kyle. I could feel your anger from across the room."

"Good advice. We'll get some food in us before we get into it."

They'd consumed their eggs and potatoes, drunk the juice, emptied the carafe Lynnie had left them, and requested another before he and Lyssa talked about the previous week.

"First, can you tell me about your time with Janet at the morgue?" Lyssa asked.

He gave her the facts and said, "Apparently, they'd cremated the remains long before, which stands to reason." He swallowed hard and looked away for a time, until Lyssa caressed the back of hand. He nodded. "Janet asked that I bring the ashes to Tompkins Falls and work them into the rose garden. I declined, saying I didn't know the health regulations and, in any event, wouldn't spring that on you without talking it over first."

He dared to look at her face.

She had closed her eyes and was holding her breath. "Thank you," she whispered and cleared her throat. "Maybe we can make a small plaque for the garden, in memoriam. You've been run ragged helping her, and I was on the verge of drinking her wine when she lunged for my throat in Myrtle Beach. I say we've done enough for her. Personally, I think Vince's remains belong with his parents, reunited at last."

"That makes two of us, my love."

She exhaled a soft laugh and caressed his face.

He took her hand and kissed the palm. "I blasted out of her hotel after dinner, knowing the right thing was to see her onto the plane in the morning, but I had not a drop of energy left. It was all I could do to drive home."

"And what a horrible greeting awaited you. I'm to blame, no one else. I'm so very sorry for putting you through that."

"It sent me over the edge, just as you were before we went to Myrtle Beach."

"Will we be all right?" Her sapphire eyes beseeched him.

"I'm still very angry," he said, his voice so hard he didn't recognize it. "I thought I'd lost you, too. I thought I was coming home to your dead body in our kitchen."

He buried his face in his hands and fought for control. Silence at the neighboring tables gave way to quiet conversation, the snap of a newspaper, the clink of tableware.

Lyssa pressed a fistful of napkins into his hand, and he dried his eyes and saw to his nose. "Let's leave all that aside for now, do our jobs, and get ourselves back to Cornwall as soon as we can. Will that work?"

The joy that lit her face was his answer.

Chapter 25

Patty pulled the trigger, then enlisted Nick and Nate to move the body, but otherwise the two men had nothing to do with Vince's murder, is that what I'm hearing?" Lyssa asked. They were gathered at Manda and Joel's for steak dinner–the Cushmans, the Shaughnessys, the Penningtons, and the Morans, assuming Hank arrived before the steaks burned.

Peter Shaughnessy nodded and handed a glass of iced tea to his sister, Bree. "That's the official conclusion. He stole the gun and Margie Westover's jewelry after the Westovers were reported dead. Nate eventually went looking for the gun to give it to his girlfriend, Patty Beck, for her protection. He knew Nick was a habitual thief, and confronted him. Nick had kept the gun in the pouch, the same kind he used for all his thefts.

"When Nick returned the gun, he struck a deal. He'd get Nate certified one way or another, if Nate would exonerate him of any blame if he had to do anything illegal for the certification. Nate went even farther. He latched onto Nick as a father figure and offered to share some of his fortune, in exchange for certification and mentoring."

"Strange choice for a mentor, eh?" Kyle asked.

"Nick didn't made good on his offer to get Nate certified, simply because Patty beat him to it with her own solution," Lyssa said. "Which was to kill Vince and have Nate impersonate him."

"So, what's Nick status now?" Kyle asked.

"He admitted he stole more than three thousand dollars worth of Kyle's things, which is the threshold for third-degree grand larceny," Peter said.

All eyes were on Kyle now, and the room was quiet.

"I suppose you're all wondering if I know about Nick's outrageous lies about my wife? Yes, I do, and we are going forward with a libel suit, with Harriet's help."

"Will Nick go to prison?" Lyssa asked.

"For sure he'll lose his job," Peter said. "That's already happened. He was caught red-handed with Kyle's jewelry, which is a felony offense. As for the rest, that's up to a judge and jury."

"Okay, people," Joel said. "Hank and his wife have arrived. Steaks are done. The table is groaning with salads and baked potatoes and fixings. And we have much to be grateful for. Let's eat."

On Thursday afternoon, Lyssa and Bree sat on the brick patio at 57 Seneca Street, drinking iced tea, and waiting for Hank Moran to arrive.

"How is it for you and Kyle living in your house, knowing what happened?" Bree asked.

"We're okay here for now. We talked about staying in one of the apartments at Lakeside Terrace, where I lived last fall, but we decided to stick it out here, at least until we leave for Cornwall."

"What do you think Hank's going to tell us?"

"He said he wanted both of us here because we were together at the start, when the gun was unearthed. I think it's about Nate, and I don't think it's good."

"I'm with you. Help me with something." Bree held up her camera for both of them to see the photo of the rusty lunchbox stuffed with dirty plastic. She clicked to the next slide, which showed the layer of red-and-white-check oilcloth, followed by the navy-and-white bandanna. And the leather pouch. Finally, the gun. Then she played the show backward. And forward.

"Why?" Bree asked. "Why did he bury the gun the way he did? Why didn't he just stuff it under the tree or pitch it in the lake?"

"After all we've learned, we still don't know," Lyssa said.

"I don't think Patty had anything to do with it, and we know Nick didn't."

"I'm sure Nate's the one who planted it in our garden. He used his father's lunchbox, and wrapped the gun in items from their outdoor adventures." She scrolled backward through the photos, starting with the gun. "The pouch protected the gun. The bandanna and the oilcloth protected the pouch."

"I don't get it," Bree said.

"All I know is Patty pulled the trigger, and Nate made sure the gun would never be used again."

"I think you were right before, when you thought he was laying to rest his parents, remember? They never recovered their bodies, and he needed closure."

"Maybe, but I saw his journals. He never did get closure. As Nate Westover, he had a shrine to them on his dresser. And he wrote to them every day when he was on the Door

Peninsula, where he could be himself. He always signed off with—"

A car door slammed on the street and footsteps sounded on the driveway. "Hank's here," Bree said. She went to greet him, while Lyssa poured iced tea for him.

He sat between them for a few minutes, sipping his tea and gazing at the budding roses.

"Kyle and I are having a plaque made up for the garden, in Vince's memory," Lyssa said. "Beloved son, that kind of thing. Janet's sending the ashes to be buried with Vince's parents."

Hank nodded. "Very fitting." He finished his drink.

"More?"

"Yes."

Bree poured.

Lyssa asked him, "Why are you looking at me that way?"

"There's something you were never satisfied about, and we found the answer yesterday when I sat in on another interrogation of Patty Beck."

"What do you mean?"

"You said Nick was on the verge of getting Nate certified as a teacher, which made you wonder why Patty went through with her plan to kill Vince and have Nate assume his identity."

"Right. Do you know?"

"She gave us her reasons, for the record. Vince was disrespectful to her when they first met. He treated her like a trashy waitress until he realized she was Nate's girlfriend. And, on top of that, Vince's parents called her trash to her face and forbade Vince to marry her or even bring her to their home. She hated them all. She loved Nate and believed she had to be indispensable to him or he wouldn't keep her in his life. She wanted to be his hero, but Nick was motivated by the money Nate had promised, and he pulled ahead in the competition to get Nate certified."

"Did she know about the money?" Lyssa said.

"Nope. Nate never told her he had millions. When it looked like Nate was ready to sign onto Nick's plan, Patty executed her plan first. She killed Vince and recruited them to move the body to Nate's truck, thus buying their silence."

"Was Nick in on the plan before that?"

"She says he knew about her plan. Nick denies it."

"But Nate must have stopped seeing Vince as his friend. Otherwise how could be do what he did?" Lyssa asked.

"You mean, assume Vince's identity? According to Patty, he saw himself as a better teacher than Vince," Hank answered. "In fact, it was Nate who talked Vince into becoming a teacher back when they worked at the Tompkins Falls Library helping kids learn to read. Until then, Vince had been planning a career in corporate communications and graphic design. Nate hooked him on teaching. Vince started getting kudos for his classroom style. Then the faculty at Geneseo raved about Vince and featured him in their promotional materials. Nate couldn't stand to have Vince beat him. That jealousy was the hook Patty used to string him along when she was dating Vince."

Lyssa's gaze dropped to the patio. A few tears fell on the bricks. Hank covered her hand.

"So it was her plan?" Bree asked.

"Yes. She said she'd have killed Vince's parents, too, if they hadn't gone away for the weekend."

"Oh my gosh," Lyssa said in a whisper.

Bree said, "And she came to Tompkins Falls this time to kill Lyssa?"

"No question," Hank said. "She had to protect her life with Nate, which meant getting rid of anyone who knew Nate had taken Vince identity after she'd murdered Vince."

"Her pathetic life with Nate," Bree said. "It's so twisted, Hank."

"What else did you come to tell us?" Lyssa lifted a tear-stained face. "Where is Nate, Hank?"

Hank set down his glass and leaned forward, his hands clasped between his knees. "Thanks to Lyssa, we found Montana," Hank told them. "He was the one teacher at the school Nate trusted. Apparently, Nate had told Montana he was part of the Witness Protection Program and had inherited a lot of money when his parents were killed."

Bree laughed and then thought about it. "Well, he witnessed his parents' deaths in a senseless accident, I'll give him that. Did he have a psychotic break or something?"

Lyssa drew up her knees and rested her head on them for a moment. "It was more than PTSD, wasn't it?"

"It's a moot point," Hank answered.

"What did you come to tell us, Hank?" Lyssa asked again.

"Montana had been forced to retire for health reasons a couple of years ago and struggled to pay for the medication and procedures required by his heart condition. The two of them, Nate and Montana, whose real name I can't officially say, though Lyssa knows it, loved to hike together, and they continued to, in spite of Montana's illness."

"Montana was also a talented amateur photographer," Lyssa said to Bree.

Hank nodded. "He grew up around Whitefish, Montana, which is near Glacier National Park."

"Whitefish?" Lyssa smiled. "Like Whitefish Dunes State Park? I'll bet that's not coincidence."

"And you'd win that bet," Hank said. "He and his college friends spent one summer working on the Door, and he was curious about Whitefish Dunes. He loved it so much he applied to schools around Green Bay. That was about thirty-five years ago. He married and divorced. There were no children. He and Nate struck up a friendship when Nate first started teaching, based on their shared love of hiking."

"If my math is correct, he was about thirty years older than Nate. So he was like a father to him?" Lyssa asked.

"Could be." Hank shrugged. "For the past two years, since Montana retired, Nate had been paying Montana's medical bills, which are astronomical. And, coming from a wild, remote area, Montana knew about people on the run, people in hiding, so he kept Nate's secret. The one about his dual identity."

"What aren't you saying, Hank?" Lyssa's voice quavered.

"I'm saying all this so you have the background when I tell you how Nate died."

Lyssa's stomach plummeted, and she struggled with her next breath. "I'm glad he died, Hank. He could not have survived incarceration."

"Probably Nate would have been in a psychiatric setting, on a forensics unit. But I have to agree with you."

"His heart and soul were in the outdoors," Lyssa said, "except when he was teaching."

"How did he die?" Bree asked.

"You already know that he went directly to his log home on the Door after he met Lyssa in the park, after a stop at his bank. He placed his will on the desktop, took some small books with him that were found on his person–"

"His journals," Lyssa said. "And then?"

"He drove to Montana's townhouse in Green Bay, and the two of them drove to a cabin that Montana owned, over near Appleton. Nate had a concrete block in the back of his SUV, and a length of rope."

"I saw the block and rope in the shed," Lyssa said. "They were right by the door. He was ready."

"He may have known all along the day would come when he'd need to end everything," Hank said. "He was pretty young to have a will all made up."

"How did he die?"

"Evidently during the night, while Montana slept, Nate hauled the block and the rope to a skiff tied up at Montana's dock, secured the rope to the block and to his own neck, rowed out to the center of the lake, threw the block and himself overboard."

"He drowned," Lyssa said, her gaze intent on Hank's face.

He gave her a tight-lipped nod.

Bree drained her glass and gripped it, as though she planned to smash it. Instead, she tossed it from one hand to the other and set it on the brick patio.

"The next morning, Montana saw the rowboat floating aimlessly on the water, way out from shore, and Nate was missing. He called 911. Divers found Nate's body on the bottom, in the deepest part of the lake."

"May he rest in peace." Lyssa choked on the words.

Hank touched her arm. "Amen." He chugged the rest of his iced tea and distributed what remained in the pitcher equally among their glasses.

They drank silently, watching the flow of water from the fountain at the center of the rose garden.

"Hank, will the state honor his will?" Lyssa asked.

"We think so, since none of his investments came from illegal sources or activities. Even Nate's salary as Vince Tuttle went directly to a checking account in Patty's name and not a penny of it crossed into his investment accounts. He was a shrewd young man. Montana will get the SUV and the condo. It's one level, which he needs for medical reasons. And he'll get one fourth of Nate's portfolio, which will go a long way toward paying his medical bills for as long as he lives. He may just have a few more years."

"And Nick gets a fourth," Lyssa said with an ironic chuckle. "That might buy a sharp lawyer who'll keep him out of prison."

"Maybe he'll move to Florida with his brother. He loved that lifestyle," Bree said.

"As long as he's not living across the street from me, I don't care."

"Good riddance," Hank said.

"And Tucker gets the log home and a bundle of money to put his kids through college," Lyssa said. "He'll do something good with the rest, I think."

"What about Tompkins College?" Hank asked. "Lyssa, have you heard what they're planning to do with their five million plus or minus?"

"Justin wants to establish a counseling center, with an arm in the community, for troubled youth."

"Chief Smokes and my sister-in-law, Gwen, are talking with him," Bree said. "They want to make sure no one falls through the cracks the way Nate did."

A car sounded on the driveway. "That's Kyle, home for supper. Will you join us?"

"No way, girlfriend."

"I wouldn't dream of it," Hank said.

Lyssa followed them through the house to the front door. "Lyssa, you'll tell Kyle what we've talked about?" Hank asked.

She nodded and gave them a little wave. She took a few seconds to splash cold water on her face and to remove the salad from the refrigerator and place it on the table for their dinner, before she joined Kyle on their brick patio. "Hello, darling."

He drew his gaze from the budding roses to his wife's slender beauty. Her sunny smile warmed him, and her intense blue eyes sparkled with love.

And some recent tears. "They've found Nate?"

She came into his arms, and her fragrance of roses and lily of the valley expelled the shadows that had haunted him the past few weeks, since they'd unearthed the gun.

"They've found Nate's body." She wrapped her arms around his waist. "Suicide."

He kissed her temple. "It's better than any of the alternatives, don't you think?"

"Yes."

The afternoon sun shone brighter as it glanced off her red-gold hair, dancing in the fickle wind.

"Both boys can rest in peace now," she said as she rested her head against his shoulder.

"And you and I can sleep in peace, my love."

Her arms tightened around him.

Eyes on the rose garden, he watched the water bubble from the center of the fountain, track through the channels in the granite, and spill over the side, back into the earth.

THE END

Relatives who are friends are treasures.
To Anne, Martha, and Kathy
for their unfailing support
on this writer's journey.

iv

The author gratefully acknowledges the following persons. Lourdes Venard, editor. Authors who critiqued early drafts: Kat Drennan, Chris Roeder, Christine Chianti. The Lilac City Rochester Writers group and the Canandaigua Writers Group. The generous experts at crimescenewriters.com. And the Guppies Chapter of Sisters in Crime.

Chapter 1

D one. They're safe." Lyssa Pennington ran the back of her hand across her sweaty forehead as she surveyed the seventeen rose bushes, each in its own pot, out of harm's way on the brick patio. She and her friend Bree Shaughnessy had reduced the Penningtons' weed-choked backyard garden to a pit of pockmarked soil with a dead miniature tree in the center. "Can you believe this was once a prize-winning rose garden?"

"No way." Bree rocked back on her heels and stood. "When is your tree removal person coming?"

"Any minute. I want him out of here before Kyle gets home. You're joining us for lunch, right?"

Bree was massaging her lower back. "If your handsome Brit is in, I'm in."

Lyssa blushed. Her husband still made her heart flutter.

"Do you care that you have dirt on your chin and your left cheek?" Bree screwed up her face and ran two fingers down her cheek to her chin. "Forehead, too."

Laughing at Bree's primitive warrior act, Lyssa took off her gardening gloves and apron and scrubbed her face with the towel Bree held out. "Presentable?"

"Good enough. Why do you think the tree died?"

"I guess it was dying when the last owner bought the house. They ignored the garden while they renovated the kitchen and added on a family room and patio." Lyssa fingered the few remaining buds of the miniature Japanese maple. "Poor tree."

"Look up."

Lyssa posed as Bree snapped a picture of her holding the branch. "I've been immortalized with a dead tree. Why exactly?"

"In case anyone asks why you got rid of the tree."

"Like the nosy garden club, right?" The real estate agent had warned them people would be watching what they did with the rose garden.

A steady beep-beep from the driveway signaled an arriving vehicle.

"Right on time." She fluffed her wavy red hair. Not that Davis Landscaping cared.

A pickup truck backed along the driveway between the Pennington house and the neighbor's fence and parked just short of the detached garage. A college-age male gave a cool wave from the passenger side.

The driver swung out of the cab and came around the truck. "Dick Davis." He held out a calloused hand to Lyssa.

She introduced herself and Bree.

"And my son, Richie, home for spring break and earning a few bucks. Son, bring two spades from the truck," Dick directed. "I'm glad you decided to salvage the roses. Shame about the tree." He appraised it with a frown. "This won't take any time at all."

"Sounds good. My husband will be home for lunch in an hour. Dick, will this be really noisy?" Lyssa tipped her head toward the barberry bushes lining the far side of the yard. Beyond the hedge, Mrs. Winkel's clothesline dipped and rose, her hands and white hair visible as she clipped another pillowcase to the line. "Our green neighbor"—Lyssa gestured with her thumb and lowered her voice—"has been watching every move."

"No chain saw, if that's what you're worried about. For a miniature tree like this, we can do the job with sharp spades and a lot of muscle. Any roots the spade misses under the tree, we'll cut with clippers. That's it, except for wrestling it onto the truck."

"Sounds like a plan," Lyssa told him. To Bree she muttered, "We could have done that ourselves."

Bree poked her with an elbow. "Stop being such a penny-pincher. Kyle can afford it." She snapped a picture of the men as their spades sliced the earth.

"Are you seriously documenting the whole procedure?" Lyssa asked.

"Like I told you, I know nothing about gardening. This is a cool way to learn."

Lyssa laughed and waved a hand. "Have fun while I clean up and fix our salad." She finished preparing the Salad Niçoise in the time it took Dick and his son to separate the tree from the surrounding soil, then returned to the patio with a pitcher of lemonade and tall glasses.

Dick leaned on his spade and dragged a red bandanna over his face to wipe away the sweat. "Good job, son."

Richie used the fabric of his Geneseo State T-shirt to blot his face. "What now, Dad?"

"Need lemonade?" Lyssa called to them. "It's all ready for you."

"As soon as we drag the tree onto the truck," Dick said. He wiggled the tree and gave it a tug. "Son, get down there and snip the last few roots."

Richie knelt with the clippers beside the root ball. Dick braced his feet in the dug-up soil and gripped the trunk with both hands.

The tree resisted for several minutes, measured in grunts and cuss words. *Glad I pointed out Mrs. Winkel.* Their neighbor would not have appreciated hearing an f-bomb.

Richie severed the last root. Breathing hard, Dick dragged the lifeless tree toward the pickup, but his son stayed behind, poking at the tangle of root ends sticking up from the soil.

"There's something buried here." Richie's voice warbled with excitement.

"Please leave it, Richie," Lyssa said, more sharply than she intended, but she wanted them to wrap up and depart.

"I see it." Bree squatted near him and snapped a picture. "What do you think it is?"

"Some kind of box. It's all rusty." He wrestled the object away from the clutching roots.

"It's an old tin lunchbox," Bree said. She snapped pictures as Richie examined it from all sides.

God, give me patience. Lyssa took a deep yoga breath.

"How can you tell?"

"That simple latch, and you can see where a handle used to be. My friends and I used to carry ours with one finger holding the lid closed, because the latches were always popping open. But this is bigger than ours. Probably for a grown-up."

"I'll bet it's a time capsule," Richie said.

"Sweet." Bree gave him a knuckle-bump.

Dick Davis rejoined them just as the latch snapped off the lunchbox.

Lyssa needed an ally. She quietly asked Dick to finish up before her husband blocked him in the driveway. With only a curt nod, he made for the pitcher of lemonade, poured himself a glass, chugged it, and set it down.

Richie had drawn a penknife from his pocket to work on the rusted lid. When it gave with a scratchy metallic groan, he shouted, "Got it!"

"That's far enough, Richie," Dick said and wiped his mouth with the back of his hand. "That's the Penningtons' property. Give it to Mrs. Pennington and get your butt out of the garden."

"Seriously?"

"You heard me."

Grumbling, Richie passed the box to Lyssa.

Her hand tingled at first touch, as though she'd picked up dry ice cubes. *What's up with that?* She tugged down the long sleeves of her t-shirt to protect her hands.

"Thanks for your hard work, Richie" she told him. To Bree she muttered, "Please do not encourage him."

Richie gave her a sour smile and dragged himself with exaggerated slowness out of the hole.

"Come on, son, let's get the tree onto the truck."

"Spoilsport," Bree chided Lyssa.

Lyssa opened her mouth to reply, but Bree spoke first. "Uh-oh. Neighbor alert."

Mrs. Winkel peered over the hedge, a clothespin in one hand and a wet towel in the other.

"Sorry about all the commotion, Mrs. Winkel." Lyssa strolled to the hedge. "We've removed the dead tree from the rose garden so Kyle and I can install a new water feature. Then I'll replant the beautiful roses, and it will be lovely."

"Oh dear, a fountain will keep me awake all night."

One more mistake. "We couldn't stand splashing and gurgling either, Mrs. Winkel. This won't be a fountain. I promise it will be silent."

"We'll see." Mrs. Winkel's usually sweet voice held a warning as she returned to hanging her blouses and kitchen towels on the old-fashioned clothesline.

"That went well. Not."

"Lyssa, seriously." Bree motioned Lyssa back to the patio. "Give us all a peek at your time capsule."

Lyssa's sank down onto one of the Adirondack chairs. She rested the lunchbox on her knees and ran her hands on her pants to rub off the tingling sensation. "Honestly, Bree, I don't want to do this."

"Humor me, okay? These guys have sweat for an hour, and this is something really cool you can do for them."

"You are totally right." She wiggled into a more comfortable position.

"That's the spirit. They're coming. Just pop the lid off. What have you got to lose?" Bree handed glasses of lemonade to Dick and Richie and motioned them to gather around Lyssa. "Ready for the grand opening, guys?"

Lyssa flashed a smile and hinged back the lid. Inside was a tattered plastic-wrapped bundle that filled the box. "Yuck."

"You are such a girl," Bree teased.

"Thank you." Lyssa sounded a playful screech as she yanked out the filthy package and set the lunchbox box aside.

With the three of them crowding around her, Lyssa cut into the tattered plastic and tossed it away, revealing an inner wrapping of red-checkered oilcloth that might have been a scrap of picnic tablecloth. Her heart raced as she unwrapped the oilcloth. Inside, another layer, a navy-and-white bandanna, protected a lumpy leather pouch about eight inches long and five inches across. Both were splotchy with dirt that had worked through the plastic and oilcloth during the time underground.

As she fingered the pouch's drawstring, her heart thudded. She met Bree's gaze. "Something's off about this." A tremor rocked her body. She didn't understand it, but she knew they had to stop.

"What's wrong?" Bree asked.

"I don't know. But back me up, okay?"

"Let me see." Richie reached for it. His father held him back.

"Richie," Lyssa said firmly, "I prefer to leave it until my husband comes home. I'm sorry to disappoint you. If it turns out to be something interesting, I'll give you and your dad a shout, okay?"

Father and son groaned and looked at each other, eyebrows lifted. They might as well have said "Chicken."

"It can't be anything bad, Lyssa." Bree's voice cajoled her. "Want me to look?"

"Give me a break." Lyssa squeezed her eyes shut for a second.

"You're being a ninny."

She was probably just hungry, maybe a little dehydrated. "All right." Her fingers trembled as she worked out the knot. She loosened the drawstring half an inch, but a sense of impending doom stopped her. This wasn't her usual panic attack. In fact, she hadn't one in months. *Enough.*

She handed Bree the bundle of cloth with the pouch nestled inside. "Your find. Your job. If it's something really awful, just end it, please." She rose from the chair and took a few steps outside the circle of eager faces.

"You mean like a dead mouse?" Bree chuckled.

Richie snorted, and Dick elbowed him with a grin.

Bree flipped the leather sack from one hand to the other and bounced it a few times. "It's too heavy for an animal or a body part."

Lyssa wrapped her arms around her middle and tapped her foot.

Bree explored the outside of the pouch with her fingers. "It feels hard, like metal." She fully loosened the drawstring and peered inside.

Her voice deepened. "Holy cannoli."

"What?" Lyssa asked.

"What is it?" Dick said.

"What'd they bury?" Richie's eager voice asked.

Bree drew out a handgun, gripping the wood handle with her thumb and two fingers.

"Oh my gosh." Lyssa's head and heart pounded. "Put it back. We're done with this." She started toward Bree, but Dick shifted on his feet and tightened the circle, blocking her access.

"Revolver," Dick said. "It's in good shape for something that's been buried as long as that tree's been there. Look at the gleam on parts of the barrel. Someone shined it up before they buried it."

"Buried is right," Bree said with a short laugh. "It was wrapped in—what? —three layers like a mummy inside that metal box."

Lyssa shivered and sank onto the arm of the nearest chair. "How can you joke?"

"This is an old Smith and Wesson with a wooden grip," Dick said. "My aunt lived way out in the country and got a gun like this for protection after her husband died."

"Can I see, Dad?"

"Ask Mrs. Pennington."

Dick and his son looked her way.

"No." Lyssa scowled at Dick.

"I've shown Richie how to handle a firearm, and we've shot together at the rifle range."

"Come *on*, Lyssa." Bree rose to her feet and struck a pose, one fist on her hip, the gun resting on her other palm. "You'll be very careful, right, Richie?"

"No worries." Richie took the gun reverently from Bree, his eyes bright with curiosity.

"Son, remember it might be loaded. The barrel could have dirt in it. If it went off in your hands, it could explode and you'd be badly hurt. Just look it over and give it back to its owner."

Richie nodded and moved apart from the group, cradling the gun in his hands.

"Who would bury a gun under a tree?" Dick sat back in his chair and stretched out his legs.

"Somebody who committed a crime with it?" Bree said.

"Stop it, Bree," Lyssa said sharply. "If you really believed that you wouldn't have put your fingerprints all over it, would you?"

"Honestly, I have no clue. Why do *you* think someone put it in your garden?"

"I don't know, but I'm going to give it to the police." Skirting the garden, Lyssa hustled toward Richie, who was examining the gun from all angles. "Give it back now, Richie," she told him in her strong teacher voice.

"Sure, just a sec."

"Now." She held out her hand.

"Why do you want to take it to the police?" Bree called.

Lyssa glanced back at her. "I can't help thinking someone buried it like that because they'd used for some evil purpose."

At Bree's sudden alarm, Lyssa followed her line of sight.

Richie was fingering the trigger.

"Richie, stop! Set the gun on the ground," Lyssa shouted.

He straightened his arm, pointing the gun at the hedge.

Lyssa shied to her right. "Put. It. Down."

"Son!"

The weapon fired.

The explosive report echoed though the quiet neighborhood, and the recoil knocked Richie onto his backside.

Beyond the hedge, Mrs. Winkel screamed.

Lyssa spun halfway around and watched in horror as her neighbor crumpled out of sight. "My neighbor's shot," she yelled. "Bree, call an ambulance." She raced the full length of the prickly hedge and around it.

"Hurry," she shrilled as she spotted her neighbor collapsed on the lawn. Mrs. Winkel's right hand gripped her upper arm, where blood poured from a wound. "She's losing blood fast."

Through gaps in the hedge, Lyssa saw Richie, still sprawled on his butt, gawking in her direction while Dick Davis stormed to his son's side.

"What the crap were you thinking?" he roared. "You're lucky you weren't killed."

Lyssa yanked a pillowcase off the clothesline, tore into it with her teeth, and ripped it into wide strips.

Bree shouted, "The ambulance needs to know the Winkel's house number."

"Fifty-nine Seneca, and make them hurry!" She knelt beside her neighbor. "The ambulance is on its way, Mrs. Winkel. I'm going to stop the bleeding the best I can." When she lifted Mrs. Winkel's right hand away from her left arm, blood pulsed from the wound.

God, help us. Back in Girl Scouts she'd learned to make a tourniquet. With shaking fingers, she wrapped strip of cloth tight around the wound. Hands slippery with blood, she wiped them on her shirt, then twisted another strip of pillowcase to make a tourniquet and tightened it with a clothespin.

What am I forgetting? "Bree," she yelled, "I've got a tourniquet on the wound, and I can't let go of it. What else do I need to do?" She brushed angrily at a tear with the back of her wrist.

"Right beside you." Bree squatted next to her. "She'll need her insurance card and doctor's name, and they want me out front to meet the ambulance."

"In my purse," Mrs. Winkel gasped. "Hallway table."

"I'll get it."

"I want to go with her to the hospital," Lyssa said.

"Then take my car and follow them, but don't let the police see you, or they'll make you stay here to answer questions."

"Evade the police?" *Keep it together, Lyssa.* She switched hands and brushed her hair out of her eyes. "Mrs. Winkel, once the ambulance arrives—"

"Stay with me." Her neighbor's voice quavered.

"I will. I promise."

Mrs. Winkel's bloodied right hand grabbed at Lyssa's T-shirt. "Call Mary. My sister." She groaned, her grip loosened, and her arm dropped heavily.

"I will," Lyssa promised.

Mrs. Winkel's eyelids fluttered and her head rolled to the side.

Chapter 2

"H aving a good morning?" Kyle Pennington asked his bosses as he breezed past them in the hallway of the Tompkins College administration building.

"How is the search going for your replacement?" President Justin Cushman asked him.

Kyle paused but didn't walk back to them, not when lunch and kisses with the beautiful Lyssa awaited him.

"The committee will finish interviews this week and have a recommendation for you by week's end." He smiled his reassurance at the provost, who would ultimately generate the job offer. "I predict it will come down to one internal candidate everyone likes and an external candidate we've yet to interview."

"You're not going to change your mind and stay with us?" The provost, Miriam Sekora, looked at him above the rim of her glasses.

"Most definitely not." It was an effort to hang onto the smile. "Pleasure working for you both, but I'm negligent with my responsibilities in Cornwall, and that can't wait any longer. As I've said, I'm happy to be available in a consulting role on network security issues."

The provost transferred her gaze to the president. "He's a broken record, Justin." Her voice held a note of fondness for her departing chief information officer. "But he's agreed

14

he won't force Lyssa to move to Cornwall until her grant is finished two years from now."

"He'd better not." The president softened his gruff delivery with a wink for Kyle.

This time Kyle's grin was genuine. "Forcing Lyssa to leave prematurely wouldn't do at all. She loves her teaching and her students."

"I hope she's using the break to relax and get away?" Miriam asked.

"Neither. She's going great guns with a backyard project, trying to restore the prize-winning rose garden left to perish by the previous owner. Today she has someone digging out the dead tree in the middle so we can install a Zen water feature. I've no idea what that is, but I do know I'm late for lunch with the lady in question. Must dash." Without a backward glance, he exited the building, flew down the granite steps, and jogged across the quad to the parking lot.

He slid into the driver's seat, checked his voicemail, and noticed five messages from Lyssa in the past half hour. Whatever it was, he'd see her in three minutes.

When he swung the car onto Seneca Street, though, an ambulance with its siren blaring raced away from his neighbor's house. The redhead driving the blue mini on its tail looked like Lyssa. *Can't be.*

Emergency vehicles, light bars pulsing, remained outside his home. *What on earth?*

He deduced, from the lumpy, ten foot-wide hole in the backyard, that the landscaper had excised their dead Japanese maple and Lyssa had removed the rose bushes. But where was she? Why were men in blue swarming his backyard and that of that of the neighbor?

He danced aside as two officers strong-armed a white-faced teenage boy to their cruiser. A middle-aged man darted around them, shouting, "Don't hurt my boy. He's stupid, not a criminal. Don't hurt him."

"Where's Lyssa?" Kyle thundered. No one paid him any mind, but a second officer eyed Kyle's sedan blocking the driveway.

Before the officer could issue a command, Bree rushed at Kyle with a tote bag in one hand and two purses swinging from the other. "Lyssa drove my car to the hospital. Let's go."

"Is she hurt?"

Bree shook her head. "Come on." She grabbed him by the arm and hustled him to his car. "We're taking your car. You need to call a lawyer right away."

"But—"

"Get in. Drive."

Kyle backed over the curb, and Bree lurched as she clicked her seatbelt. The tires squealed as he took off in the direction Bree pointed.

"Who is hurt? Is it Lyssa?"

"Go right at the stop sign. Lyssa's not hurt, but your neighbor was shot with a gun we dug up. The police are not happy Lyssa snuck away behind the ambulance. They just sent someone to question her at the hospital, so call your lawyer right now. Then I'll tell you the rest."

"Were you hurt, Bree?" He switched on his Bluetooth connection.

"No."

Kyle called his solicitor and left an urgent message. "Where did the bloody gun come from, and who fired it?"

"It wasn't bloody, I don't think," Bree answered. "The kid they were taking into custody fired it. He's the landscaper's son."

Kyle allowed himself a smile. "Beg pardon, Bree. 'Bloody' is a British swearword. Terrible choice. My fault."

"What's weird is it was wrapped up in layers and buried in a lunchbox, like a time capsule. The roots had grown around the box and it was all rusted. The box, not the gun."

"What?" He couldn't make sense of it.

"I have pictures." She waved her phone.

"What was a gun doing buried under our dead tree?"

"Who knows? But, technically, it's your weapon."

"But—"

"Let's hope your neighbor doesn't die."

Kyle's fists thudded on the edge of the information desk in the emergency department. "Where's Lyssa Pennington? She came in with our neighbor who's been shot."

"Name of the person shot?" the attendant asked.

"Oh good Lord. Twinkle or something. Winkel, that's it." He spelled it.

"Mrs. Winkel is in surgery. Your wife's the redhead?" At Kyle's nod, she said, "She followed the gurney. She's probably in the surgical waiting room." She pointed toward the depths of the hospital. "Along with the police. An officer arrived a minute ago looking for her."

"How do we—?"

Bree tugged his elbow. "Come on." She pointed to the signs overhead and the colored stripes on the floor.

"You can make sense of that?"

"I made a lot of hospital visits with my old druggie friends." A few turns later, they reached a half-filled waiting area. Faces turned toward them. A young woman about Lyssa's age removed one earplug and asked, "Are you looking for the woman the police are talking to?"

At Kyle's nod, she pointed and said, "That little room next to the vending. Just to warn you, she's got a lot of blood on her."

Kyle rocked back on his heels. *Lord, help me. This has to be a nightmare.*

Bree squeezed his shoulder. "It's not Lyssa's blood. Remember that." She thrust the tote bag into his hands. "Clean clothes, washcloth, towel, and here's her purse." She shoved him toward the closed door. "Make them give her a break to get cleaned up, then hold off until your lawyer gets here."

He drew in a ragged breath. "Right," he said, crisply this time, and tugged down the sleeves of his suit jacket.

With a forceful rap at the door, he barged into the ten-by-ten room. The love of his life perched on the edge of a hard chair across the table from a middle-aged policewoman. A recording device sat between them on the table.

Shaking, Lyssa clutched a worn cotton blanket around herself, her face smeared with something he knew wasn't dirt. "Kyle," she cried and rose from the chair.

Disturbed by the fear and pleading in her eyes, he enfolded her trembling body and pressed his cheek to hers. "It's all right, sweetheart." *It has to be all right.*

To the policewoman he said, "Unless my wife is under arrest, she'll take a break now to clean up a bit. I'm sure her statement will be more coherent after that." He ignored the officer's protest and ushered Lyssa out.

"We'll commandeer a sink," he told Lyssa, his arm sheltering her as they dashed down the hall in the direction Bree pointed. "Bree, can you find us some hot, sweet tea?"

"You got it."

Lyssa told him, her voice an octave higher than usual, "I'm so afraid."

"We've a lawyer coming, and you needn't say another word until then."

"No, I'm afraid Mrs. Winkel is going to *die*."

That stopped him for a beat. "We'll let the doctors do their job, eh?" He pushed open the door of the handicap-accessible restroom on their left.

The space barely held the two of them. Lyssa sank down on the edge of the toilet seat and drew in a deep breath.

"Bree knew you would need this." He handed her a washcloth from the tote.

She gripped the cloth in one hand and shrugged aside the blanket.

Kyle gasped at the sight of her bloodstained clothing and her hands and arms smeared with more of the reddish brown. *Lord, what has she been through?*

He kept his voice light as he sorted through the bag. "She's made you a care package." With nowhere to lay out the contents, he draped the bath towel over his shoulder and tucked the clean blue jeans and Tompkins College sweatshirt under his arm. Lyssa's purse he hung from the door handle.

She had peeled off her bloodied T-shirt and gardening pants and stood at the sink, washing her neck and arms and hands with long, sure strokes of the soapy cloth. Her eyes were wide with remembered horror. "So much blood, Kyle.

They said the bullet nicked the artery in her arm. I was afraid she would die right there, and it would be my fault."

"Stop, Lyssa. That's the kind of statement that could land us in a lot of trouble if Mrs. Winkel were to file suit."

"Oh my gosh, I never thought of that. What am I doing?"

"You're just getting cleaned up right now, nothing more. The lawyer will coach us with our statements."

She rinsed out the cloth, squeezed on more soap, and checked her body for blood.

Kyle didn't see any on her torso or legs. "Good job. It's just your face and hair now. Then we'll drink that hot tea Bree's getting us. That will help with the shakes." *Yours and mine.*

She lifted her gaze to the mirror and made a strangled noise in her throat. Her eyes met Kyle's for a second, and he gave her an encouraging smile.

"Shall I do it for you, sweetheart?"

"I'm okay." She dabbed at her cheek with the cloth, frowning at two slashes of blood across her forehead.

"I was trying to keep my hair out of my eyes, I guess." The dark smudges continued into her hair and scalp. She cleaned her brow and dropped the washcloth to the floor with her ruined clothes. Then, with a shudder, she bent her face to the basin and positioned her matted hair in the stream of water running from the tall, rounded faucet. "Tell me when it runs clear," she said, her voice muffled.

Kyle sucked in a breath as he watched red water swirl into the basin. Gradually the water changed to pink and, finally, clear. "That's good now."

She groped for the towel on his shoulder. After drying herself, she stood clutching the bath towel around her shoulders, eyes closed.

"Are you chilled?" he asked, but she shook her head.

Tears spilled down her face, and he gave her a quick hug.

"Let's get you into warm, dry clothes." He handed her the sweatshirt first and then the jeans. "Bree will have got us that hot tea by now."

"I shouldn't have let him touch the gun." Her gaze met his, her eyes pleading.

"It will be all right, Lyssa."

But the pile of bloodied clothing at their feet told him it wasn't all right and wouldn't be any time soon.

Chapter 3

Unable to face being in the house alone, Lyssa called her AA sponsor from the hospital and accepted an invitation to spend the afternoon at the Cushmans' lakeside home. Kyle dropped her there on his way back to work. Gianessa welcomed her with a dazzling smile and a warm hug.

Halfway through playtime in the park with the Cushmans' twins, Lyssa let out a laugh at their antics. *Thank you, God, for restoring my sense of humor.* After they went down for their nap, Gianessa drew her onto the sunny porch.

"Now let's have the whole story," her sponsor said. "The gun, the shooting, the lawyer, and the police."

Lyssa hugged her knees and rested her chin on them. When her long tale of awfulness was finished, she let her gaze wander to the calming view of Chestnut Lake, a slender twenty-mile-long finger of dark blue water, its surface ruffled this afternoon by a fickle wind. "No wonder I was an emotional wreck."

"I wouldn't say that." Gianessa shifted her chair and adjusted the umbrella.

"How do you see it?" Lyssa stretched her legs into the newly created shady patch.

"You responded to trauma—your neighbor being shot— with swift action and you saved her life. Did you feel any emotion while you were doing it?"

"Mostly not. I was a little busy."

Gianessa laughed.

"Okay, I felt horror and self-doubt."

"Horror I get. Why self-doubt?"

"It's been forever since I took that first-aid class in Girl Scouts."

"So, what, you gave up?"

"Of course not. I grabbed something cotton and thin and clean, and tore it into strips and made a tourniquet."

Gianessa raised her glass of iced tea. "Brava for taking charge and for being resourceful."

Lyssa popped up from her chair. "But before the gun went off, I was furious that I couldn't make myself heard." She stomped to the edge of the deck and slapped her hands on the railing. "It was my own backyard, and I was firm and loud with Richie, but he wouldn't put the gun down. And before that I was clear with Bree and Richie's dad that I didn't want to open the freaking lunchbox, but none of them listened. And look what happened." She twisted to face Gianessa. "Why couldn't I get them to listen?"

Gianessa opened her hands and shrugged. "They were having too much fun. They united against you. Short of taking the box into the house and stuffing it in some closet, you weren't going to get your way."

"Which would have been juvenile, but I wish I'd done it." Lyssa leaned back against the railing. "I had the weirdest vibes from the box. I remember thinking the gun carried some evil." She shook her head. "Too bizarre."

Gianessa sat up straighter. "Tell me more."

"It's crazy. I had horrible tingles when I first took the box from Richie. You know that feeling when you pick up an ice cube fresh out of the freezer?"

"It sticks to your skin and you can't get it off?"

"Exactly like that. And my heart was racing." She pounded her hand over her heart. "And then it started thudding. Ka-thump, ka-thump. I totally stopped then and handed the whole thing to Bree. She thought it was a game."

"She wasn't getting the same sensations." Gianessa curled her legs under her. "Do you think all that was one of your panic attacks?"

"No, it was nothing like that, and I haven't had one in a long time. What was going on? Why did I get those weird feelings?"

"Not feelings. Sensations, which are physical responses. Some people can sense an aura around certain objects. You sensed evil."

"Aura? Don't tell me I'm psychic." She waved her hands in dismissal. "I've got enough to deal with being a recovering pothead and drunk."

"I see psychic ability as a gift."

Lyssa grabbed her head with both hands. "I really don't want to talk about this."

Two hours later, in the quiet of their kitchen, Kyle was shoveling crisp scallops onto a warming plate, preparing to add fresh spinach to the pan, when he felt Lyssa's gentle touch on his elbow. "What is it, my love?"

"Cinnamon on your grapefruit?" she asked him.

"Not for me, thanks. Mind if I pour myself a brandy with dinner? I won't if you're the least bit uncomfortable."

"No problem."

He paused to watch her sprinkle cinnamon on her half grapefruit and set the two halves aside. The whistle of the teakettle confirmed she was fixing a pot of tea for herself, probably the good black tea they'd brought back from Cornwall after the holidays.

In a few minutes they converged on the table, he with steaming dinner plates brimming with scallops and spinach, she with an aromatic basket of warm garlic bread.

"Cheers," Kyle said, holding up his brandy snifter with a smile.

"Cheers." Lyssa clinked his glass with her bone china cup. Her gaze slid to the gaping hole in the backyard.

Which should be invisible in the darkness. "When did you switch on the floodlights?" he asked her.

"I believe you were smokin' hot with the scallops at the time." She gave him a flirtatious smile, but her body was tense.

Something's not right. "And why did you feel the need to illuminate the scene of the crime?"

The smile dimmed. "It's silly." Her hands shook, and she had to concentrate to get a forkful of spinach to her mouth.

"I don't think so. Something's got you very frightened."

She sliced a scallop in two without answering.

"Mrs. Winkel will recover, we both know that. Why are you afraid, my love?" He slid his hand close to hers on the table but didn't touch.

She blinked and set down the knife. "All right. I expect some hand to reach up out of the dirt groping for something." She glanced at him and away again. "For vengeance or justice."

"And whose hand might that be?" He touched her fingers, and she let him wrap her hand in his.

When his thumb caressed her wedding ring, she smiled. "The person killed by the gun," she answered.

"Perhaps no one was killed with our gun." He played a nervous trill with the fingers of his left hand on the tabletop. "Sweetheart, it could simply be that years ago the woman of the house hated having a gun on the premises and buried it when the tree was planted." He shrugged. "Hers was a snap decision and the tree was a good cover."

"Perhaps. Actually, I'd like to think so." She gave him a nod and a weak smile.

Kyle squeezed her hand and let go.

She wasn't finished. "But the gun looked like it had been cleaned before it was wrapped in layers of stuff that must have had some significance to the person who buried it. And don't forget the first layer of protection was a leather pouch. Does that fit your scenario?"

Kyle picked up his fork and stabbed a scallop. Beyond exhausted after a day of overwork interrupted by her crisis, he sent up a prayer. *Lord, don't let me snap at this woman whom I love more than life itself.* "Okay, yes, it fits. The gun was clean, either because it had never been dirtied, or it had been kept in pristine condition. And the wife felt a little guilty and left open the possibility of retrieving it, by wrapping it up. That way it wouldn't be ruined by the soil and fertilizer and water."

Lyssa speared half of a fat crispy scallop. "Perfectly cooked." She gave him another flirtatious smile, this one a little too tight to be real.

Now I've shut her down. He knew from experience they could not have a serious conversation until they'd had a meal, and he was pretty sure neither of them had had a proper lunch, so he put the next question on hold.

As they cleaned up from their dinner, he asked, "My love, are you still thinking the gun was used to commit a crime before it was deposited in our garden?"

"It was used as a weapon, Kyle, I'm sure of it. It wasn't just tossed in the garden. It was buried so the growing roots would swallow it up from view. Why would someone do that, unless they'd committed some awful crime with it?"

How had he missed that her main worry, Mrs. Winkel aside, was why the gun had been hidden in the first place?

"I sensed it when I held the pouch in my hands. Some evil was deposited in that pouch and buried under our tree."

Evil planted along with the tree?

"Do you get what I'm saying?"

He cleared his throat. "If you're right, and you may be, I would expect the police to be investigating the gun right now, matching its ballistics to their database of unsolved crimes, or whatever it is they do."

Lyssa's gaze darted to the hole and back again. "I hope they are."

"Let's let them sort it out. It's important that we talk about our lawyer's advice. She wants us to appease the neighbors for all the noise today and apologize for Mrs. Winkel being shot and nearly killed."

"I'd forgotten that. She's worried about lawsuits, too, isn't she?"

So am I. He paused with a rinsed plate in his hand. Droplets plopped on the floor.

"It's really serious, isn't it?"

"It is, yes. When someone's wealthy, as I am, and an innocent person's shot, there's potential for legal action by any and all aggrieved parties. Mrs. Winkel for one. Dick Davis for another."

"I can understand Mrs. Winkel, but why do you think Dick Davis would sue?"

"When I arrived at the house, the police had handcuffed his son and were depositing him in the back of a cruiser. The son was terrified, and the father was in a state. It's human nature for them to look for someone to pay for their anguish."

"But Richie had no business fingering the trigger. His father warned him. We all did."

"Someone could just as easily say we had no business hiding a gun under the very tree they were digging up."

"That doesn't make sense." Lyssa set the plate in the dishwasher and reached for another.

"It's not rational, I grant you. However, where there's wealth, there's an increased likelihood of suit being brought."

"And that's why Harriet Feinstein wants us to talk with everyone on the block to apologize?"

"Yes. Our job is easier now Mrs. Winkel survived her surgery." He came beside her and gave her shoulders a squeeze.

"I wasn't thinking about lawsuits when I improvised a tourniquet from the contents of her clothesline." Lyssa looked at him sideways.

"Your mind's not geared that way, and for that I am grateful."

"Perhaps it should be, now that I'm married to your millions."

He grunted. "Probably this experience will sensitize you. Which is not a bad thing, as long as it doesn't make you cynical."

Lyssa met his gaze. "We need to lighten up." She flashed a smile.

"We need dessert. And while you're tending to the grapefruit, I'll put away our glassware and fine china."

"Thank you. Your hands are steadier than mine tonight."

He reached for a fresh linen towel and picked his brandy snifter from the dish drain. She slid the grapefruit under the broiler, the pan rattling as her hands trembled.

The glass and teacup safe on their shelf, he selected two small dishes from the cupboard while she checked the grapefruit.

"Done." She used tongs to transfer the bubbling fruit to the waiting dishes.

The aroma of tart citrus mixed with cinnamon on her half made him reach for the cinnamon shaker. They settled at the table and waited for the fruit to cool.

She's right. "Boggles the mind, doesn't it, how little regard Richie had for the weapon's destructive power?" he said.

"Exactly. That gun was a weapon meant for killing."

"And whoever buried it knew that."

"Are you agreeing with me?"

"If the police aren't already looking into the gun's criminal history, we need to make sure they do."

"How will we make that happen?" she asked.

"I will take responsibility for that, I promise you," he said. "Almost certainly, something happened here, possibly something terrible, that's been covered up for as long as that tree has been dying behind our house. Else why did the gun need to be buried?" He picked up his spoon. "Let's hope it's a simple answer." He bent to his grapefruit. "Mmm, refreshing."

Lyssa ate her grapefruit slowly, glancing between each bite at the hole in the backyard. "Kyle, you don't think there's a body buried out there, too, do you?"

Lyssa saved the six bulleted lines of text on her laptop and stood with frustration, eyes on the kitchen clock. Kyle would be home after his meeting to look over the script she was supposed to be writing for their neighborhood goodwill tour this afternoon. She'd gotten down their three main points—introduce themselves, apologize for disrupting the peace of the neighborhood, and assure the neighbors Mrs. Winkel was recovering.

To those, she'd added three questions: Did the neighbor know who had lived at their house in years past and how to contact them? Could they say when the dead tree was planted? And were they aware of another shooting or disturbance on the property in the past?

She couldn't get beyond that. Every time she looked up from her perch at the island, the roses looked back at her from their pots on the patio, begging for attention. If they were to survive, the plants had to be established in the soil before she and Kyle left for Cornwall in two months.

And they should have an irrigation system, or at least a sprinkler on a timer, to keep the roses alive for the two months they were away. It was fine for Bree to weed and deadhead weekly, as she'd agreed to do, but daily watering was too much to ask.

How long would it take to put in an irrigation system? Worse, how long would it take to dig for a body? Postponing the project meant the work would not be done on time and the roses would perish.

Plus, if they found a body, the roses would be stuck in pots indefinitely while the police investigated. Would she and Kyle even be allowed to leave the country until they found the murderer? If they couldn't spend the summer in Cornwall, Kyle would lose his mind.

Stop projecting. She took a deep breath, and the sun came from behind a cloud to warm the patio. When she'd first looked through the panes of the wraparound French windows to the darkened yard on a chilly night last November, she'd imagined breakfast on the patio with Kyle, sun warming their faces, birds flitting in and out of the barberry hedge. She opened the door now and inhaled the sweet spring air as she traversed the bricks.

She and Bree and Davis Landscaping had worked hard yesterday. With the dead tree and winter-bare rose bushes removed, her mental image of the garden restored to its prize-winning beauty came back to her. The next step was installing the yet-to-be-ordered Zen water feature. With the April breeze cool on her face, she could almost hear the near-silent movement of water bubbling over the edges of her natural stone fountain and smell the tantalizing aroma of roses in bloom.

A robin chirped from somewhere nearby, hopped into the yard, and cocked its head before tapping into the soil for a worm.

Lyssa squatted beside the potted rose bushes and stroked one emerging shoot, then another. Car doors slammed behind her, and she jumped, startled.

"Hey, girlfriend," Bree's cheerful voice sounded from the driveway. "Don't you dare plant those without me."

Lyssa welcomed Bree's hug. "Hi, Peter," she greeted Bree's brother. "Is this an official police visit, Officer Shaughnessy?" Although Peter was dressed in a Syracuse sweatshirt and blue jeans, the tall beefy stranger beside him was in uniform.

"Not exactly," Peter said. "This is my old buddy on the force, Hank Moran. Hank's a detective."

Gulp. Lyssa's hand trembled as she took the officer's outstretched hand. "Lyssa Pennington. Are you here because of our shooting, Detective Moran?"

"Because of your gun." His deep voice might have been reassuring in other circumstances, but this morning it revved up her anxiety.

"Bree had a rough night," Peter said. "A lot of nightmares about the gun. She tracked me down at Lynnie's, where Hank and I were having breakfast, and told us what she was worried about."

"Is any of that stuff still around?" Bree asked Lyssa. "The leather pouch and the material the gun was wrapped in?"

"Kyle and I didn't touch anything last night." The patio was empty, though, where the lunchbox and its contents had been. "I don't think Dick Davis took it," she told them. "Must be the police did. Isn't that what they do at a crime scene?" She turned questioning eyes on Peter and Hank. "Why do you want that stuff? Are you thinking, like Kyle and me, the gun was used in a crime before it was buried?"

"Unofficially," Hank said.

Her stomach did a dive. *So my instincts were right.*

The four of them peered into the lumpy pit and the deeper hole where the tree and the gun had been. Clawlike roots reached up from the bottom.

Lyssa shivered. "I've been making myself crazy, thinking we should dig deeper to see if there's a body."

"That's the other reason we came," Hank said.

Lyssa's heart sped up. "Seriously?"

"Bree's thinking that, too, and I couldn't convince her it's unlikely anyone's buried here," Peter said. "Hank, now that you see it, what do you think?"

"The hole right now is about three feet deep in the center. That's where the tree was, correct?"

"Yes, and the space around it was filled with those roses." Lyssa gestured to the pots banked on the patio.

Hank continued, "Let's assume the tree was planted around the time the crime was committed, making it a convenient hiding place."

Lyssa rubbed her arms. "That's exactly what Kyle and I decided last night. But one of the possibilities we talked about was that the woman who lived here might have hated having a gun in the house and just decided to get rid of it. Tossed it under the tree when it was planted."

"Good thought. However, I do have information that says that's very unlikely."

"What do you know? Something about the gun?"

Hank nodded, but all he said was, "I can't reveal my information at this time. I said what I did so you wouldn't get your hopes up about the easy out."

Lyssa's shoulders drooped with discouragement.

"Still, that doesn't mean the gun was used to kill someone or that there's a body buried here," Peter said. "Right, Hank?"

"Agreed," Hank said. "To bury a body undetected in the garden, someone would have to take out all the roses, remove the tree, and dig a trench deep enough for burial, the length and width of a person." He nodded to Peter. "Would you agree?"

"Yes."

"And to do all that digging overnight, without the neighbors hearing or seeing them, and then fill it in, stomp it all down, position the gun, replant the tree, and carefully replant the roses." Hank shook his head. "There's no way. That would be insanely risky."

"And no one could have pulled it off in a neighborhood like this," Peter said. "With the stony soil around here, a spade hits a rock, it's loud. That happens ten or fifteen times, the city police are on the scene."

Lyssa nodded. "Mrs. Winkel watched everything we did back here."

"Everything," Bree echoed with a laugh.

"Exactly my point, which is why I maintain there's no body here," Hank said.

"Hank's right." Peter's gaze swept the yard. "The same is true anywhere back here. If they buried a body in the backyard, they'd have to reseed, and the homeowners and neighbors couldn't miss that."

Lyssa felt the knot ease in her stomach. "Thank you, God," she said in a whisper.

"What do you think, Bree?" Peter asked, his voice upbeat.

"I'm good now. Thanks, guys."

Lyssa squinted at Hank and Peter. "So my garden project is no longer a crime scene?" *And Kyle and I can go to Cornwall as planned?*

"It was only a crime scene relative to Mrs. Winkel's shooting. The city police cleared it yesterday before I came on duty," Peter answered. "But, like we've said, this neighborhood is normally peaceful. You and Kyle are the new kids on the block. What are you doing to satisfy your neighbors after all that happened here yesterday?"

Chapter 4

R eady, Mr. Pennington?"
"Ready, Mrs. Pennington."

"I like being on your team," Lyssa said with a wink. Script and clipboard at the ready, they crossed Seneca Street to the first house on their block.

Kyle had his hand at her lower back, and she appreciated the feeling of protection. "Who's up first?" she asked when they arrived on the porch of house number 50.

"Allow me, my love."

She heaved a sigh of relief.

When his knock was answered, he covered their first three points and then asked about the prize-winning gardeners who once owned their home.

Instead of a name, Mr. Jonas's response was, "Damned garden of theirs! Cars parked on my lawn every summer for that fancy Tompkins Falls Garden Club Tour." His eyes narrowed to slits as he regarded his newest neighbors. "Wouldn't you think people who like gardens would know not to park on people's lawns? Damned nuisance."

Lyssa drew in a noisy breath and recovered her poise. She patted Kyle's hand, which had a death grip on her arm. "I assure you, Mr. Jonas, we have no intention of entering our little garden in the annual tour, this summer or any other summer. We just want to enjoy the lovely roses. Perhaps you'll join us on our patio for an iced tea one day this June when the roses are in bloom?"

Their neighbor with the long scowling face blinked twice. His mouth twitched in what might have been a smile. "I might do that. Rosa, my wife, would have liked that. Nice of you. What was the name again?"

Kyle thrust out his hand, even though he'd made the same gesture, unacknowledged, a few minutes earlier. "I'm Kyle Pennington, and this is my wife, Lyssa. We both work at the college."

"I was director of admissions," Mr. Jonas told them. "Retired more than a decade ago."

"I don't suppose you know the name of the people who owned our house when the garden tours still came to our street?" Lyssa asked with a bright smile.

He *harrumph*ed. "Tuttles. Lived there until about the time my Rosa passed. That's been four years."

"I'm very sorry for your loss. Did the Tuttles live there a long time?" A phone rang somewhere in the house. Lyssa held her breath, hoping he would answer her question first.

"Twenty years maybe." With a nod, he closed the door in their faces.

Kyle squeezed her shoulder as they returned to the sidewalk. "Nice save, sweetheart."

"We knew we'd get all kinds of responses." Lyssa removed the clipboard from under her arm, clicked her pen, and jotted notes in the first row of her spreadsheet. "We should add the garden club to our list of information sources."

"Good thought. Why aren't you doing all this on your iPad?"

"Too hard to type and walk at the same time."

"Remind me, and I'll show you how to voice record into your spreadsheet as you go. Did you notice, when we first asked questions, he didn't seem to know about the shooting yesterday or about Mrs. Winkel being in the hospital?"

"You're right. 'Stupid kid' was all we got on that topic."

"I think he probably wasn't home when it happened," Kyle said. "He'd have complained to us about the emergency vehicles, if he had been."

"Good thinking." She put a plus sign in the final column for 50 Seneca Street.

"Ah, a secret code. What does the plus sign mean? Clearly not 'warm and fuzzy.'"

"Hah. It stands for successful damage repair."

"Meaning, he doesn't hate us as new neighbors?"

"Exactly." She had penned 'Mr. Jonas' in the Name column, and 'Tuttle 20 years?' in the Notes column.

"Good work, Watson," Kyle teased.

"What Watson?" Lyssa elbowed him playfully. "Miss Marple, I'd say. Oh, I should add a comment that we've invited him for iced tea."

"But Jane Marple was solo. We're more like Nick and Nora, don't you think?"

"Weren't they sloshed a lot?" Lyssa said with a laugh. "I'm sober, don't forget."

"Right. Tommy and Tuppence perhaps?"

"Not sure. I'll have to reread those."

"Right, in your spare time. Do we happen to know any of our neighbors' names up front?"

"No, sadly. I probably could have learned that ahead of time at the library. Ah, there's another source. *Lots* of information." She jotted 'Library' in the Other Sources column and underlined it.

They crossed the street to number 51. A thirty-something woman with a no-nonsense hairstyle and a sharp-eyed gaze answered their knock. She slid back a deadbolt but kept the safety chain on until Kyle and Lyssa had both shown their driver's licenses. At that, she opened the door, introduced herself, and stood in the doorway, blocking their entry.

Kyle opened the interview with their Harriet Feinstein-approved statement. "Mrs. Klaus, we're deeply sorry for the shooting in our yard yesterday morning that has shocked the neighborhood and injured Mrs. Winkel. We assure you Mrs. Winkel is recovering, and her sister Mary is with her at the hospital."

As Kyle's British accent delivered the words, accompanied by his most charming Cornish smile, Mrs. Klaus relaxed. He embellished the main points by telling her how the shooting had happened and praising his wife's quick action in saving Mrs. Winkel's life.

"Must have been horrible." Mrs. Klaus shivered. "You'd think a college kid was old enough to know better. Where did the gun come from anyway?"

"That's the bizarre thing," Lyssa told her. "The gun was all wrapped in layers and buried in a lunchbox under the tree, snagged in the roots. It had probably been there since the tree was planted. That makes us curious about who planted the tree and when. I don't suppose you know anything about the old rose garden or its history?"

"Me? Why would I?"

"Have you lived here long, Mrs. Klaus?" Kyle asked.

"Ten years, about. Phil and I bought the house when I was pregnant with Ronnie, and he's nine." She went on to tell them she had three children, all in school. She had divorced Phil three years ago, had full custody of the children, and worked as an X-ray technician at the hospital.

Kyle smiled politely. "So you probably remember all the cars up and down the street when the annual garden tour rolled around each summer? Whoever owned our house at the time had a prize-winning rose garden featured on the tour. Was that the Tuttles, sweetheart?" he asked Lyssa.

He knows the answer. Why was he asking?

"Oh, I remember the Tuttles," Mrs. Klaus said.

Now I see.

"They were a nice couple. Their son was best friends with our neighbor's son." She motioned with her head to the next house, number 53. "Nice kids. Their parents made them shovel our driveway when I went into labor with Ronnie during a bad snowstorm."

"So the Tuttle boy and his friend next door to you were a lot older than your children?"

"Oh heavens, yes. They'd have been in college last time I saw them. They were inseparable." She shrugged. "Anything else I can tell you?"

"You wouldn't happen to know when the tree was planted in the Tuttles' garden?"

"No idea."

They thanked her and took their leave. Lyssa jotted notes as Kyle led them back across the street.

Number 52 Seneca was a prim pastel Painted Lady, not unlike the frail elderly woman who answered the doorbell. Mrs. Bischoff introduced herself and invited them in for a cup of tea.

"So kind of you, Mrs. Bischoff. Perhaps another time." Kyle launched into their standard apology.

"Oh dear, I hadn't realized it was that serious. Poor Toffee."

"Toffee?"

"Mrs. Winkel. Toffee was her husband's nickname for her. She's really Eleanor."

Kyle assured her Toffee was recovering. "Her sister Mary hopes to bring her home before long."

Mrs. Bischoff's hand patted her heart. "That's a good sign, isn't it?"

Lyssa asked, "Were you familiar with the garden next door to the Winkels? Mrs. Tuttle's roses?"

"Yes." Her eyes brightened.

"Kyle and I are trying to restore the garden, and we'd love to know what it looked like."

"I confess I never liked the tree, but before that the garden was glorious. Rikki had a green thumb with those roses."

Lyssa did an internal cartwheel. *She must know when it was planted and why.*

Kyle beat her to the question, "Tell us why she planted the tree at all, Mrs. Bischoff?"

"Because of the February ice storm. More than half her rose bushes perished. But nothing got Rikki down. Instead of giving up on the garden, she salvaged what she could, planted that miniature Japanese maple in the center, and arranged the healthy roses around it. The garden club had a fit about the tree, but Rikki told them to put a sock in it." Mrs. Bischoff chuckled.

Kyle politely joined in.

"She was spunky, that Rikki Tuttle," Mrs. Bischoff said with a decisive nod.

Lyssa fanned her face, hot with excitement. "Kyle and I weren't living in this area when the ice storm happened. Do you recall what year that was?"

"It was five or maybe six years ago. You'll find people around here are hardy. Our downtown shops went all out to commemorate the anniversary of the ice storm with a Friday night of refreshments and discounts. My niece has a dress shop just off Main Street, and she had me serve cookies. Sweet of her to involve me, wasn't it?" She placed her thumb on her chin and tapped her upper lip with her forefinger. "Now, was all that hoopla this past winter or the year before? I'm afraid my memory isn't what it used to be. I would call her to ask, but she's at Disney with her children this week. Spring break, you know."

"You've been so helpful, Mrs. Bischoff," Kyle told her. "If there's anything we can do for you, don't hesitate to let us know."

Her milky blue eyes fixed on his face. "Perhaps you'd bring me a rose this summer if they bloom for you."

"It will be our pleasure," Kyle said with a courtly bow.

They retraced their steps to the street.

"I've never seen you bow like that, Kyle."

"Yes, well, desperate times and all that. Another plus sign, wouldn't you say?"

"Three for three."

"What's that you're writing about me in the notes field?"

"Why are we crisscrossing the street? Is that only to give you time to write?"

"Partly. But I also don't want people to see us next door and try to avoid us. So far so good, don't you think?"

If there was logic in that, he failed to see it. "Frankly, I can't believe every house will have someone home on a weekday afternoon."

"Except it's spring break for the college and the schools. That's in our favor."

"Unless they're taking a vacation, which we should be." He hadn't given up hope.

"And we would be if you weren't working all week," she countered.

Blast, she was right. *I never should have taken the job.* "So, we'll catch as many neighbors as we can, shall we? What's our secret code for no one home?"

"Big zero."

As they crossed Seneca Street to number 53, Lyssa clutched Kyle's arm with excitement. "The library can tell us the year of the ice storm, and that will narrow things down to a month or two."

"Well, at least to the year the tree was planted."

"No, think about it. The ice storm was in February and the tour not until June. Rikki Tuttle must have entered her garden in the tour, so she planted the tree as soon as the ground thawed in the spring."

"Isn't that cutting it awfully short for a prize-winning garden that's completely replanted around a new tree?"

"But Rikki Tuttle had a green thumb, remember, and she told the garden club to put a sock in it."

"Point taken."

"We might even find out from the garden club what nursery delivered the tree and when. And if not, the library can give us a list of nurseries and I can call them. Then we can match the exact date to crimes reported in Tompkins Falls."

Kyle paused on the street.

Lyssa stopped her headlong rush. "What?" She faced him.

"You're turning into a madwoman before my eyes." His tone was stern.

"Am I?"

"Maybe it's just the thrill of the chase, but you sound obsessed with knowing who planted the gun, when, and for what nefarious purpose it was used beforehand. We really should let the police handle it."

"What if they won't?"

"Regardless, you're going to be swept up in our end-of-semester craziness first thing next week when the students come back from break. So am I."

She studied her pink sneakers on the macadam. "You're right about all of that, I suppose. But don't you want this over and done with so we can finish our semester and pack up for two blessed months at Pennington House? Time for you to attend to your responsibilities in Cornwall, spend time with your mum, and cherish all that beauty and quiet?"

"That needs to be our priority, yes, not this gun in our back garden," he said more harshly than he intended. She didn't respond, and he kicked himself for shutting down the conversation. "Else I shall lose my mind."

"So, big zero for 53 Seneca Street," Lyssa said, her voice filled with disappointment. They'd knocked and waited, noted the garage was empty, and concluded no one was home.

"Let's hope they're back soon. That's where the boy lived who was close friends with the Tuttles' son. If we can track him down, he's likely to have answers for us."

Lyssa put a star and "friends with Tuttle son" under Notes. "On to number 54 then?"

Kyle put his arm around her shoulders. "What say we stay on this side of the street and meet our next-door neighbors at 55? I saw a car drive in not five minutes ago."

"Brilliant."

Just home from her shift as a nurse at the hospital, Judy Pinkerton answered their knock. Like her engineer husband, Bob, she had been at work when yesterday's shooting took place. Judy had heard about it from the hospital grapevine.

She had known the Tuttles and the couple that bought from them, but only to say hello. Unaware the Tuttles had a rose garden, Judy looked puzzled when Kyle mentioned the cars lining the street in years past for the garden tour. A few more questions revealed only that the Pinkertons were both in their early fifties and had two children in college.

Kyle and Lyssa thanked Judy and crossed the street.

"Probably intent on paying tuition, building a retirement nest egg, and downsizing in ten years," Lyssa remarked. "They never look out the window."

"Agreed." He glanced back at the property. "Just two small windows upstairs on our side, both with the blinds pulled, probably bathrooms. And their wooden fence is my height, six feet, more or less."

"That explains why they didn't know about our horribly messy garden or Mrs. Tuttle's roses."

"Fancy a break, my love?"

"Soon, but let's try across the street first, number 54." *Great front door.*

~ ~ ~

Kyle appraised the house, a foursquare painted medium gray with sage-green shutters. "The color combination is a lot like ours, but I like our navy shutters better."

"Do you like the door?" Lyssa asked with a teasing sparkle in her eyes.

He laughed. "Your signature color."

She rapped with her knuckles on the shiny bright-pink paint.

A portly man who might be fifty opened it to them. "Yes?" His eyes shifted from Lyssa to Kyle and back.

Lyssa said, "We're Lyssa and Kyle Pennington, your neighbors across the street at number 57."

"Nick Nunzio. You two responsible for the sirens yesterday?"

She gave their canned apology with her prettiest smile. Kyle settled his hand on her waist, not caring for the way Nick's gaze traveled everywhere but her face.

"I teach at the high school, and I can't believe what goes on in their heads half the time," Nick said. "Who was the kid? He was probably one of my students." When they told him, he said, "I know Richie Davis. Good kid. Bad choice. This is going to be hell for him and his dad."

"We're concerned as well," Kyle said.

"You say the lady's going to be okay?"

"Mrs. Winkel is recovering," Lyssa said. "Nick, were you home when the shot was fired?"

"I was out back washing my car. I'm leaving for Florida in a few minutes. You just caught me."

"So you didn't hear the shot?"

"No, but I sure heard the sirens. Saw the ambulance take off with a little blue car on its tail." He glanced at his watch.

A classic Rolex. Kyle made a mental note.

"That was me in the blue car," Lyssa said. "Nick, can you tell us anything about the garden behind our house?"

Nick shifted impatiently on his feet. "You mean, the one where you found the gun?" he answered.

At Lyssa's nod, Nick told her, "All I know is the lady who lived there was really proud of those roses. The cars used to jam the street for the garden tour every June. My mother loved roses, and she and her friends always went. Just after Mom died, I snuck in without a ticket. Mrs. Tuttle just took my arm and told me I was welcome. She told me what every rose was named, and I told her about my mom. That's really all I know."

"I'm sorry about your mom, Nick," Lyssa said. "I love roses, too. What did the garden look like?"

"Beautiful mound, probably ten or twelve feet across, filled with all kinds of roses. Every color."

"Nothing in the center—no fountain or tree or statue?" she asked.

He squinted, his gaze far away. "No, just the roses. Dozens of them."

Kyle asked, "How long ago did your mother pass?"

"Seven years last month. I still miss her. Your folks still alive, Kyle?"

"My dad has passed, and my mum's still with us. She survived a bad bout with pneumonia this past winter. Lyssa and I will go back to Cornwall this summer to spend time with her."

"No kidding, Cornwall? I teach English, love those Arthurian legends. I'll keep an eye on your house while you're gone. People are like that in this neighborhood."

"That's grand. I'll take your cell number and call you this week if we see anything amiss over here," Kyle offered.

"Now you're talking." Nick scribbled his phone number on the corner of Lyssa's clipboard and smiled. "We all want the place to be safe and secure. Know what I mean?"

"Believe me, we want that, too," Lyssa said. "No more gunshots or sirens at our house."

They took a break from the neighborhood goodwill tour to regroup. Lyssa draped wool throws across the backs of the two Adirondack chairs on their brick patio. The carafe of hot coffee Kyle brought from the kitchen promised even more warmth on the cloudy fifty-degree day.

"Can you take these, my love?"

Lyssa rescued the mugs dangling from his pinky and held them out for him to pour.

After she'd wrapped herself in a throw and taken a sip, she said, "Did I tell you we've been cleared to proceed with the garden?"

"We're not digging for a body first?"

She shook her head. "Nor are the police." She told him about the visit from Bree and her brother and Detective Hank Moran.

"I'm glad to hear it but surprised a detective showed up. Was he in uniform?"

Lyssa waggled her hand as she blew across the steaming liquid in her mug.

"Meaning?"

"Hank was in uniform but he came unofficially, at Bree's request. She was freaked, the same as me, about a body buried in the garden. Hank and Peter wanted to see for themselves if it was possible."

"And they decided against?"

Lyssa nodded over a slurp of coffee. She repeated the scenarios Hank had talked through. "Oh, and when I told him your theory about the woman of the house wanting to hide the gun, he said they had reason to believe that was not the case. He wouldn't say anything more, even though I pushed on it a couple of times with a shamelessly pathetic look in my eyes."

Though she demonstrated the look for him, his mind was on something else. He played a trill with the fingers of his right hand. "Interesting. Harriet reported to me around ten this morning that the police had told her emphatically—she used that word—they were not interested in investigating the history of the gun."

Lyssa turned a puzzled face to him. "Maybe he's not with the city police. Now that I think of it, Hank's uniform was gray, not blue."

"Gray might be sheriff's department or state police or something else."

"Oh, wait a minute. I know something about this. Hank Moran is the guy who bought the big old white house on the east side of the lake that was Peter's wife's family home. Hank moved his family from Syracuse—parents, wife, and children."

"I'll bet he and Peter were on the force together in Syracuse," Kyle said.

"Yes, brilliant. Peter said 'old buddy on the force.'"

"We're amazing investigators." Kyle held up his hand for a high-five. "Judging by your spreadsheet I'd say we've learned a good amount, and I'm comfortable with the way it's going. You?"

"Yes, agreed."

"Yet you look puzzled."

"No, not about our neighborhood fact-finding. I'm still thinking about Hank buying that enormous lakeside property. I'm surprised he could afford it on his salary," Lyssa said.

"Ah, you're suspicious."

She squinted and tapped her fingernails on the arm of the chair. "She probably quoted him a figure below market value, since he was Peter's friend and she didn't need the money."

"That's my wife, always following the money story."

"He'll have enough of a challenge paying the taxes. Oh, and speaking of money . . ." She stopped to take a swallow of coffee.

"You've just put on your Savvy Spender persona." This time she responded to his teasing with a sunny laugh.

They had met when she was in London on a postdoctoral fellowship, living on a shoestring budget and making two public-television video series—the Savvy Spender and the Wise Woman Investor—about financial literacy for women.

"Have I done something that's horrified you, my love? You found out about the yacht and the chalet?"

Lyssa was dissolved in laughter.

"So, tell me. 'Speaking of money' what?"

She squared her shoulders and gave him her most disarming smile. "I spent time online before you got home and found the perfect Zen water feature. I really want it for our garden, but it's outrageously expensive."

"Define outrageous."

"So outrageous I thought about buying it without telling you."

"It costs thousands, does it?"

"One." She shifted her eyes and admitted, "And a half." When he didn't respond, she cocked her head expectantly.

"You know I'm not concerned about the money, but I would like to decide this purchase with you, because I'm going to have to look at the thing every day. Let's be sure I can live with it first."

"Then we'll get ourselves online after supper and take a look. I have a couple of runner-ups, too, in case you hate my absolutely perfect choice."

"Splendid. In fact," he said gently, "we need to get back in the habit of reserving twenty minutes every evening–after we've eaten, of course–for some serious discussion."

"Good, we did get sloppy about that. What made you think of it?"

"For one thing, I didn't know, until Harriet Feinstein brought it up this morning, that our house is in your name, not mine, not ours."

"Didn't I tell you? Do you object?"

"No and no." Kyle reached for her hand. "But that fact makes you liable for any lawsuit Mrs. Winkel or the Davises might entertain. You, my love, are the owner of the gun."

Lyssa blanched. "So," she said around the rock in her throat, "we'd better get back to our fact-finding."

When they backtracked to 53 Seneca Street, they found the owner just pulling in the driveway. Lyssa recognized the pretty woman from faculty meetings at Tompkins College. "I had no idea Professor Natalie Horowitz is our neighbor. I'm so glad for a chance to meet her."

"Let's hope she's friend rather than foe," Kyle said. College faculty were notorious for backbiting and undercutting, and Lyssa had started the academic year with more than her share of both.

Natalie welcomed them into her living room with what Lyssa thought was a genuine smile. After listening to their opening apology, Natalie thanked them for explaining the shooting and updating her on Mrs. Winkel's condition.

"How long have you lived here, Natalie?" Kyle asked.

"Four years now, and it finally feels like home," she said. "What a lot of work it's been."

"It's lovely," Lyssa said with an admiring glance around the room. Paintings, photos, and objects from around the world graced the walls and shelves, and the furnishings echoed the subtle colors of four serigraphs clustered above the mantel.

"You've traveled a great deal?" Kyle asked.

"I was an army brat, and my father and I both loved art, so we collected pieces wherever we lived. My folks had no room in their retirement condo for most of their pieces. Lucky me."

"Do you know anything about the family that lived here before you?" Lyssa asked. "We'd like to talk with them."

A tremor shook Natalie. She wrapped herself with her arms. "That won't be possible, I'm afraid. They died somehow, tragically, before I bought the house. That is, the parents died."

"How horrible. What happened?"

Natalie continued as if she hadn't heard the question. "I bought the house my first year at Tompkins College. No one had lived here for months, and the place needed a lot of work. The son sold it to me."

She told them about the tense negotiation over price and the cold atmosphere at the closing. "And he rushed out before the ink was dry, said he was a teacher and had to get back to wherever he lived."

They sat quietly, and Lyssa struggled for something more to ask or say.

"Sorry, I know you asked about the parents, but I can't recall how they died. Whatever it was, I've completely blocked it from my mind." Natalie's face puckered with an apologetic frown.

"I'm not sure we need to know, Natalie," Kyle told her, then put some cheer in his voice. "So, like us, you never knew the Tuttles, who owned our house when the garden was at its loveliest. But did you know the couple that bought our house from the Tuttles and later sold it to us?"

Natalie brightened at the change of subject. "Yes, the retired couple. Capellita was their name. He wasn't well, but she was a bundle of energy, determined to make the house their own. Estella and I were renovating at the same time, so we had lots to talk about."

"They gave our house a beautiful kitchen, and Lyssa adores the patio."

"They expected to enjoy it for years to come. When Mr. Capellita died, Estella was a lost soul. I'd pass her on the street when I was out with the dog. She'd just say a few words and continue on her walk.

"I wasn't surprised when she put the house up for sale last summer. She told me she was moving to Tucson to be near her daughter. She seemed happy about that. I got a card from her at the holidays, and she wrote a cheerful note about all the sunshine and being able to walk outdoors all winter."

"Is there any chance you saved the address?" Lyssa asked.

"Yes, let me get it from my office." Natalie left them and returned with a piece of paper.

"And that's her phone number, too. Just tell her you got it from me. I'm sure she'd like to know that a young couple is enjoying her patio. And please say hello from Natalie. I hope she's well."

Instead of crossing the street to their next stop, Kyle directed their steps to their own front porch. "I'm rattled by that interview," he said.

"I am, too. Let's talk about it." They sat side by side on the top step.

"We now know the couple that owned 53 Seneca died horribly, and the son sold the house to Natalie within a year or two of our tree being planted," he said. "Could there be a connection to our gun?"

"Hypothetically, the son could have killed the parents and hidden the gun in his good friend's backyard garden." Lyssa tapped a nervous staccato with her pen on her spreadsheet.

Kyle stilled her hand. "It sort of fits, but what motive might he have had?"

"Maybe they were abusive? Maybe he desperately needed money and killed them for their life insurance?" She shrugged.

"Why would he need money?"

"Gambling? Drugs? How old would he have been five or six years ago?"

"We don't know, do we?" Kyle scrubbed his face with his hands.

"Did Natalie say if she'd ever met him, the son? I was distracted, wondering about how the parents might have died."

"Yes. We know she met him the one time," he said. "At the closing."

"That's right, he couldn't wait to be done and get back to his teaching job."

"And she didn't say where that was?" he asked.

"No. I wonder if she'll remember anything more. She must have the family name somewhere and maybe even the address of the son." She started to tap the pen, stopped, and clipped it to the sheets of paper.

"Thank you, my love." He stroked her arm. "I'd hate to ask her, though. She was so disturbed about the parents' death."

"She was shaking. But if he killed the parents, he wasn't caught, because he's the one that sold the house to Natalie."

"True. We don't want to ask her again if we can find out what we need on our own. And we *can* find out, can't we? You're keen to ask the library for help, and they'll be able to track down the name of the former owners and what happened to the parents, don't you think?"

"Good. Yes." She wrote 'LIBRARY' in capital letters this time. "I don't think I'm right about the son killing the parents, but I can't help thinking their death is at the root of whatever happened with the gun."

"I don't follow."

"Nor should you." Her laugh was self-deprecating. "I'm being emotional and dramatic."

"That's understandable, as you did lose both your parents when you were a teen." Kyle patted her hand. "Do you want to talk more about that, sweetheart?"

"Not now, thanks." She smiled warmly. "Let's move on. We've got so little time to make our rounds, and I'm sure we'll find the facts we need by digging for them."

"We'll continue, then?"

The Richards had lived at 56 Seneca Street for almost forty years. "Our daughters were older than the Tuttle boy and the Westover boy, and we only knew the Tuttles to say hello. You'll have better luck with Becca next door."

"At number 58?" Kyle asked and received a nod in return. "The Westover boy lived at number 53, did he?"

Lyssa made a discreet fist pump behind her clipboard.

"Yes. Terrible what happened to the parents." A buzzer sounded from the back of the house.

"What did happen?" Kyle asked with urgency in his voice.

"Rockslide out West. If you'll excuse me," Mr. Richards said and closed the door.

"Brilliant, darling. Two big puzzle pieces. I'm relieved the son's not a psycho."

"And we've still one more neighbor to hit up for information," Kyle said.

"Becca, who allegedly knows more than the Richards."

The sixty-something woman who answered the door at the last house on their block introduced herself as Becca Farnsworth. "And this is Smudge," she said of the gray cat that slipped through the opening onto the porch.

Kyle took the lead with their standard apology, emphasizing Lyssa's heroic effort to save Mrs. Winkel's life.

Becca thanked them for their update and asked, "Is Toffee allowed visitors?"

Smudge wove around their feet and sniffed at Kyle's loafers.

"I don't know that, sorry, though she is out of intensive care now," Lyssa answered while Kyle made friends with the cat. "The hospital would be able to tell you. We hope she's well enough to come home before long."

"Dreadful thing to have happen. Who knew hanging clothes on the line could be so dangerous?"

When Lyssa blinked in surprise, Becca chuckled. "Sorry, you're not used to my wry humor. Toffee is *so* environmentally conscious. I'm always teasing her about it."

"We think of her as our green neighbor," Lyssa said with a smile.

"She would be tickled to hear you say that. She is a dear, dear friend of mine. You and your husband live in the house I'll always think of as the Tuttles, and Rikki Tuttle was another dear friend. I was sad when she sold and moved to Myrtle Beach with her sister-in law. She promised to stay in touch, but you know how these things go."

"I'm sure you miss her very much. Are you a gardener, Becca?"

"Not even a little bit."

"Kyle and I want to restore the Tuttles' rose garden. Rikki would be a wonderful resource for us."

"I know Rikki would love to talk with you about her garden. Would you like the phone number—hers and Janet's?"

"Absolutely." Lyssa gave her a sunny smile.

While Becca left them for the phone number, Lyssa squatted beside Kyle. "Why are you spending so much time with the cat? I didn't even know you liked them."

"I don't, and this one knows it. He's got designs on my new Italian leather loafers, and I'll be damned if I'll let him piss on them or take a bite out of them."

A laugh burst from her, and she gave in to a fit of giggles.

"You needed to laugh very badly, I think."

She brushed at a runaway tear as footsteps sounded in the hallway.

Becca was back with a phone number and address for Janet and Rikki Tuttle in Myrtle Beach. "Of course, I haven't heard from either of them for two years, so it may not be current, but give it a try. Rikki would be pleased that someone wants to preserve her roses."

"I'll let her know you gave me the number and that you were thinking of her."

Becca blinked and furrowed her brow. "Ask if they've heard from Vince, if you don't mind."

"Vince?"

"Rikki and Tommy Tuttle had one child, a son Vince. It was the saddest thing. He was a wonderful young man. As soon as he got his master's, he took a teaching job in Green Bay—you know, where that football team is—and married a girl Rikki didn't like. Vince never once came to visit after he left Tompkins Falls for the job. It broke Tommy's heart. I had Vince and the Westover boy in Sunday School, and they were such good boys. Such close friends for years and years."

"Really? Are you still in touch with the Westover boy? I've forgotten his first name already."

"Nathan. Nate. No, after he sold his parents' house we didn't see him in Tompkins Falls again."

"Do you know where he's teaching?"

"No idea."

"Is there anyone who might know how to reach him?"

"I can't think who would." She snapped her fingers. "Except Mr. Nunzio."

"Nick Nunzio, down the street?"

"Yes. He taught all the neighborhood children or, if he didn't, at least he knew them."

Becca glanced down at Kyle and her cat. "You're not thinking of taking my Smudge home with you, are you, Kyle?"

Chapter 5

Lyssa worked on the marked-up spreadsheet she'd tossed on the island while Kyle phoned Harriet Feinstein with a report of the goodwill tour. She was engrossed in jotting next steps when he touched her shoulder. His face was relaxed and a smile tugged at his mouth.

She set down her pencil. "Mission accomplished as far as Harriet's concerned?"

"Right. She's pleased."

"And you and I know lots and lots about the history of our neighborhood."

"More than we ever wanted to, yes," he said with a chuckle. "But we've not learned where the gun came from. What say we dig more into the Tuttles?" He picked up the linen towel he'd left crumpled on the counter, gave it a snap, and folded it over the handle of the oven door.

"And the Westovers," she said.

"Why the Westovers?"

"There's something off there. Natalie Horowitz could barely talk about them."

"True. And the Westover boy, Nathan, was best pals with the Tuttle boy, Vince. He's likely to know if Vince was mixed up with a gun."

She leaned against the counter. She'd love to know where Vince and Nate were now and what they were both doing. "Do you suppose they're still best friends?"

"I'm not sure why that matters." He returned the Belleek teacup and saucer to the glass-fronted cupboard.

"Just wondering if whatever happened with the gun changed anything between them."

"That's a curious investigative angle, Watson."

"Catch up, Kyle, we're not Sherlock and Holmes."

His shoulders shook with a silent laugh. "You mean Sherlock Holmes and Dr. Watson."

"I couldn't call you darling if we were those two."

"Silly of me."

"I've got it in my head Vince and Nate were college students when all this happened, and I'm thinking about my students, especially the ones who grew up here in Tompkins Falls. Those friendships are fiercely loyal."

He shrugged. "I'm more interested in that leather pouch the gun was buried in. That's not standard issue for a revolver, I shouldn't think."

"It was odd, wasn't it? We should ask Bree's brother the cop about that." She jotted his name on the spreadsheet. "He'd also know who in town is likely to be carrying a Smith and Wesson revolver, other than Dick Davis's aunt."

"Did Dick say all that about the gun?"

"Yes, that's how he recognized it."

"You don't want a gun in the house, do you?" When she shuddered, he said, "As I thought. Back to how we can learn more about the Tuttles and the Westovers."

"We have leads," she said, her finger jabbing her spreadsheet. "Besides the library, which is probably closed at this hour, we have phone numbers for Mrs. Capellita, who sold us our house, and for the former owner, Rikki Tuttle, whose rose garden started this whole thing. And Nick the teacher who's on the road to Florida." She looked up from her notes.

"I don't suppose it matters which one we call first?"

"I'm for Mrs. Capellita. She may not know much at all, but we'll get our blunders out of the way."

He barked a laugh. "Us? Make blunders?"

She poked him with her elbow. "Well, you might."

"That's war." He reached for her and tickled her middle.

She giggled and welcomed his arms around her. His kiss was deeply satisfying.

"Now I've got that out of my system . . ." He cleared his throat.

"I might want more of that later, you know," she said.

"I shan't forget you said that. What's our game plan with Mrs. Capellita, the lady who made the lovely improvements to our house?" He positioned the two bar stools side-by-side. "Shall I tell her how much you adore the soaking tub in our luxurious en suite?"

"That's a bit personal, definitely a blunder. But Natalie Horowitz said she'd be pleased to know that a young couple has bought the house and that we adore the kitchen and the patio."

"Good, there's our lead. Then we'll establish rapport, before hitting her with questions about the gun under the tree. Yes?"

Kyle nodded, pressed in the numbers, and pushed the speaker icon. A cheery voice answered on the fourth ring. "Hello?"

"Yes, hello, Kyle Pennington calling from Tompkins Falls, New York. My wife Lyssa and I are the new owners of

57 Seneca Street, and we're wanting to speak with Mrs. Estella Capellita. Is that you?"

The woman exhaled a chuckle. "Yes, but how did you ever get this number?"

Lyssa answered, "Our lovely neighbor Natalie Horowitz shared it with us and suggested we call. At the very least we wanted to tell you how much we're enjoying the beautiful kitchen and the patio you and your husband added to the house." When there was no answer, she winced.

Kyle patted her hand. "Mrs. Capellita, we realize we've caught you by surprise. Perhaps we should ring back another time?"

"Not a problem. To be honest, I was thrown by your accent, Kyle. It sounds just like Cornwall to me, where Tony and I spent some time early in our marriage."

"Aye, the Penningtons are from close by Padstow. Do you know where that is?"

"I do. We were in the Penzance area for the better part of a year. Tony was a videographer, and he worked with a movie company filming a swashbuckler. Smugglers and damsels in distress and all that."

"Smashing coincidence, isn't it? Tell me, how did you like Cornwall?"

"We loved it. We did a lot of hiking, which is how I know Padstow. I'm trying to think of the landmark nearby, the headland with the tower."

"Stepper Point, do you mean?"

"That's it!" Her breath came out in a laugh. "You've taken me right back there. Tell me, what brought you to Tompkins Falls, Kyle?"

"That's my doing," Lyssa said. "He and I met in London summer before last. When my fellowship came to an end, and I got an offer I couldn't refuse from Tompkins College, I moved here, which is where my sister Manda lives. Manda is married to Joel Cushman, who runs the Manse Inn and Spa."

"Oh, for heaven's sake."

"And I followed Lyssa here," Kyle added. He caressed her cheek. "That's what we do for love, isn't it?"

"Yes, it is. Tony would agree." After a pause, Mrs. Capellita added, "I can't help thinking there's another reason you called."

Lyssa jolted to attention. "Yes, there is, actually. We've made a shocking discovery in the old rose garden. Possibly, you can help us make sense of it. I've salvaged the roses and hope to replant the garden with a water feature where the dead tree was.

"However, when we had the tree removed yesterday, we discovered a gun underneath. Would you know anything about where it came from, Mrs. Capellita?"

"Where the tree came from?"

Lyssa frowned at the phone.

"No," Kyle broke in, "we're wondering how a gun, a Smith and Wesson revolver, came to be buried beneath the tree. Have you any idea?"

"You're saying there was a gun under the tree?"

Lyssa tried again. "Yes, exactly. I had a landscaper come yesterday to remove the tree, because it was completely dead. Once the tree was lifted from the ground, though, we found an old lunchbox snagged in the roots. Inside, wrapped in many layers, was a handgun. A revolver."

"I–I don't know what to say."

Kyle persisted. "The gardener's son thought the box might be a time capsule and wanted it opened. Unfortunately, when he saw it was a gun, he got too curious about how it worked. The gun went off, and our neighbor, Mrs. Winkel, was badly hurt."

"Toffee was shot?" Her shout made them both jump. "How horrible. Will she be all right?"

"Yes, we think so. But it's important for us to understand where the gun came from. Is there anything you know that might help us track down who owned it and why they hid it under the tree in our rose garden?"

"I can't imagine. That's shocking. Poor Toffee. Please tell her I'm praying for a quick recovery."

"It's not likely to be quick, Mrs. Capellita. She was very seriously hurt," Kyle said.

"Did you and your husband plant the tree?" Lyssa asked, although she knew the answer.

"No. You do mean the little tree in the center of the rose garden?"

"Yes, right."

"That tree was there when we bought the house. It was dying but still very pretty the first year, especially in the fall, when the leaves turned a dark pink. It was expensive, as we learned when Tony asked about replacing it. I'm sorry I can't be more help than that."

"Mrs. Capellita, did anyone else work on the garden or show an interest in it?"

She gave a sharp laugh. "One of the garden club ladies came by the second summer, just barged into the backyard and made a spectacle of herself, complaining about the state of the garden. I chased her off with a broom. Toffee was with me on the patio, and we laughed ourselves silly."

"You wouldn't remember the woman's name?"

"I didn't ask and she didn't say, just that she was with the garden club. The nerve of the woman."

"Was there ever any vandalism in your yard?"

"No, nothing at all. It was a very safe neighborhood. Very friendly. People watched out for each other."

"I see. Thanks very much, Mrs. Capellita," Kyle said. "We're grateful for your time."

Lyssa told her, "We'll be sure to give your regards to Mrs. Winkel."

"Yes, please do. And thank you for the memory of Cornwall, Kyle. It was a happy time for Tony and me."

They said goodbye.

"Fancy them hiking round Stepper Point?" His gaze was far away.

She rubbed his back. "We'll be there ourselves soon." *Please, God.*

"Yes, and this unpleasantness will be behind us," he said as he stood. "What's our next move?"

A stroll around the block to clear their heads made Kyle's worry increase, not decrease. Cornwall seemed very far away, and their timeline for departure was now jam-packed with distressing tasks, on top of their jobs. He wished for the tenth time they'd elected to take a vacation over spring break. *Damn the job.*

As they crossed the patio on their return, he thought of Mr. Jonas at number 50 shouting, "Damned garden of hers." He felt the same way about his wife's garden project, but it wouldn't do to say so. While she started water to boil for a pot of green tea, he fidgeted with his phone. "Is it too late to try Rikki and Janet Tuttle?"

"Not yet nine o'clock. Let's try."

A woman's voice answered their call with a clipped, "Yes?"

Kyle grimaced at the frosty tone. It didn't match his idea of master gardener Rikki Tuttle. He scribbled "Janet?" on a notepad between them.

Lyssa nodded and took the lead. "Ms. Tuttle, my name is Lyssa Pennington, and I'm calling from Tompkins Falls, New York. Your phone number was given to me by our neighbor at the end of the block, Becca Farnsworth." When there was no response, she forged ahead. "My husband Kyle and I are the new owners of 57 Seneca Street, and we understand Rikki Tuttle lived here until a few years ago. Kyle and I are trying to restore the Tuttles' rose garden, and we have some questions for Rikki Tuttle."

The woman cleared her throat. "I'm sorry to say my sister-in-law passed away within the year. Rikki was married to my brother Tommy. You're speaking with Janet Tuttle."

"We're sorry for your loss, Janet," Kyle said. *You don't know how sorry.*

"I doubt if I can answer your questions, but I'll try," Janet offered. "Rikki and Tommy both loved their garden."

"Janet, we've talked with all the people on our block, and they remember your brother and his wife with fondness. We're calling because my wife made a shocking discovery yesterday in the garden. It's important to us to know how a gun came to be hidden beneath the Laceleaf Japanese Maple at the center of the garden."

Janet gasped.

His blood raced with excitement. "That's not all, I'm afraid. Our neighbor Mrs. Winkel was badly hurt when the gun discharged."

"Oh, dear God, no."

Lyssa reached for his hand, and he gave hers a reassuring squeeze.

"Have you any knowledge of the gun that was hidden in the garden?" he asked.

"No, of course not!" she said, but the sharp intake of breath that preceded her snappy delivery suggested she knew something.

"You've no idea who might have stuck a gun under the tree?" He'd keep the pressure on until he had answers.

No reply.

Lyssa spoke into the silence. "Perhaps Rikki objected to a gun in the house and put it where no one would look?"

"There was never a gun in Tommy Tuttle's home." Janet's voice quavered with indignation.

"Or perhaps the son—"

"We never speak of Vince!" Janet shouted.

Lyssa mouthed to Kyle, "You try."

"This is upsetting, Janet, I agree." He made his voice compassionate but firm. "My wife is very uneasy living here since she discovered the gun, and our neighbor Mrs. Winkel is still in the hospital recovering from a gunshot wound that might have killed her, if not for my wife's quick action. If you know anything that could help us understand how a gun came to be planted in our rose garden, we implore you to tell us."

"I suppose . . ." Janet's voice was a whisper now.

He increased the volume on the phone.

"Maybe Vince did something and tried to hide it?" Janet's speculation was difficult to hear, even at the highest setting. "We never understood why he left suddenly and didn't return, even when Tommy was dying."

"When was this, Janet? When did Vince leave home?" he asked.

"No, enough!" Her shout rocked them back on their stools. "Leave it alone."

Janet Tuttle disconnected.

They sat, stunned, for a minute, Kyle leaning on his forearms, Lyssa gripping the edge of the counter.

"We're coming close to the answer, aren't we?" Lyssa said. "How did we manage that?"

"I'd say we blundered into it, my love." He looked sideways at her. "In hindsight, we should have met her face-to-face, I suppose. She's shut down now."

"But we touched on the truth. And it shocked her. Something horrible happened, and she knows some part of it."

He slid off his stool and pulled her into his arms. "If we're going to get any further, we need to know more about the son, Vince Tuttle."

She closed her eyes. "God help us, Kyle. Do we really want to know?"

"We've done enough for now. We need the police to look into this, not two amateurs." He wanted her away from all this stress. Could he insist she take a vacation? And while she was away, he'd poke around on the Internet and at the college.

Her arms tightened around his waist. "Yes, we're definitely amateurs."

"And you're shaking. Let's get you upstairs, into a hot bath. I'll finish up a spot of work and be up soon."

"Sounds perfect."

An hour later, Kyle closed his laptop and stretched his arms overhead. He'd like nothing more than an hour at the piano, but he didn't want to disturb Lyssa's sleep. Not tonight when she was so keyed up.

Perhaps just one Bach Invention. She'd told him once that Bach relaxed her when nothing else would.

He plugged both their phones into the charger and wandered into what was meant to be a formal dining room. His baby grand filled the space. After a warm-up piece, he played straight through two of the quieter Inventions. The final chords hung in the air for a moment. In the silence, he felt a peace that had eluded him for days.

Take that peace to your bed with Lyssa.

His foot was on the first stair step when his phone trilled from the kitchen.

"I apologize for ending the call so abruptly," Janet Tuttle told him. He imagined her sitting stiffly upright, her mouth pursed.

"We realize our message was disturbing, Janet. Anything you remember, or anything you can tell us, will help."

"I want you to leave it alone. I don't know what Vince has done, but I won't allow Tommy and Rikki's reputation to be tainted by it."

"We've no intention of sullying everyone's fond memories of your brother and his wife. Please, what can you tell me about Vince? We know nothing about him."

"It's so puzzling. He had always been a good boy, a star student, and everyone knew he had a promising career ahead as a teacher. And then that girl came home with him one weekend, and it all turned."

"Tell me about that, Janet. Anything you can."

Janet exhaled heavily, and Kyle heard the tinkle of glass on glass, followed by a few glugs. *Pouring wine, is she?*

"Rikki was furious when he and the girl left so rudely. And she and Tommy never saw Vince again. No letters, no phone calls, no visits home, no invitations to Green Bay. I suppose Rikki deserved it after the way she spoke to the girl, but it broke Tommy's heart."

Kyle tested his understanding. "So Vince and his girl moved to Green Bay, where he was a teacher?"

"Exactly."

"Did you meet the girl when they were at the Tuttles before they left?"

"Just for a moment. Tommy and Rikki picked me up for the wedding. We'd be away two days, and Tommy was fussing with the luggage and garment bags when Rikki realized she'd forgotten the wedding gift. We swung back for it, and Tommy suggested I meet the girl. Patty was her name. Or was it Kitty? Well! Vince and the girl were entwined on the sofa with a baseball game on TV, though they weren't watching. She had the good grace to stand and shake my hand. Dyed blond with too much makeup. Sexy, you know.

"I asked her if she was good to my nephew and she said, right away, 'I adore Vince.' I believed her until Rikki told me on the way to the wedding how pouty she'd been, as if she was offended we were all going to the wedding instead of entertaining her. I guess that's when Rikki said something she shouldn't have."

"Vince's wedding, do you mean?"

"No, you're not listening. Tommy and Rikki and I planned to attend a wedding out of town that weekend. Vince showed up, completely unexpectedly, with this person they'd never heard about. 'This creature,' Rikki called her.

Tommy didn't care for her either, said she was crude and had her hooks in his boy.

"When we got back from the wedding in Utica on the Sunday, they'd already gone. There was some kind of note, I think. Rikki was furious."

"Very upsetting for your family."

"And do you know what Rikki did after Tommy drove me home?" Janet asked with a hollow chuckle.

"What did she do?"

"Tommy said she marched out to her garden and got back to work. Well, that opened a can of worms. You see, she'd just had the tree planted, and she wanted to get everything in order for the garden tour at the end of June."

"So all of this happened in late spring?"

"Just before some holiday. Couldn't have been Fourth of July, because the garden tour was always the end of June and it hadn't taken place yet. Must have been Memorial Day. It was still a little chilly. The weekend before Memorial Day, yes. That's when they had the wedding."

"In Utica," Kyle said just to prove he was listening. "And how did the gardening go for Rikki?" He held his breath.

"That's what I'm trying to tell you. She took one look at the tree and realized it was crooked. All the money Tommy had spent on that gorgeous little tree, and the nursery had planted it crooked. That's what Rikki said."

Or someone disturbed it and slipped a gun beneath its roots. "I see. Very upsetting."

"She had a fit, Tommy said. She made Tommy walk all around the little tree with a plumb line while she jiggled it and wiggled it and stomped on the soil all around, until it was dead straight. You'd have died laughing to see Tommy act it out. Then she stripped off her garden gloves and tossed her apron on the ground. 'I'm going to give them a piece of my mind!' she told Tommy.

"She made him drive her there, to the nursery, and he read the newspaper while she ripped them up one side and down the other." She gave a dramatic trill to the *r* in ripped. "Everyone at the nursery just stood with their mouths open, Tommy said. After that, Tommy took her out for breakfast and she told everyone at Lynnie's Chestnut Lake Café what a horrible job the nursery had done. Do you see what I'm saying?"

"Yes, she was terribly put out about the tree, I can see that."

"No, Kyle, it wasn't about the tree at all. It was all about the girl, you see. Rikki wanted to fix that Kitty person who had her hooks in Vince. But, of course, she couldn't. She took it all out on the tree and the poor fellow who planted it."

But it is about the tree.

"Janet, why do you think the tree was crooked all of a sudden?"

Janet's answer had nothing to do with his burning question. "Rikki hated seeing her son taken in by this girl, and he'd gone off with her while we were in Utica." Janet burst into tears. "And he never came home again. It broke Tommy's heart. Vince didn't even come when Tommy was so sick or when Tommy died. They'd raised him well, and this girl changed all that."

"It's a terribly sad story, Janet. Very upsetting for all of you." He closed his eyes and debated what to say next. The scent of roses and lily of the valley washed over him.

Lyssa came beside him at the island and placed a soft hand on his shoulder. He pressed her hand. She motioned for him to put the phone on the counter, and she touched the speaker icon.

He rallied. "Janet, we'd like to talk with Vince. Do you have an address for him?"

"No!" Her shout made Lyssa tense. "No, I've just told you, he never gave his parents the address, just sent a photo of the condo he'd bought on the bay. How he could afford it on a teacher's salary, I have no idea."

"Perhaps the girl had money?"

"That's what I thought, but Tommy said the girl was trash."

"Janet, before I forget, you mentioned the wedding was just before Memorial Day. Was that five or six years ago?"

"Oh, heavens, I have no idea."

"Whose wedding? Do you recall?"

"The son of a classmate of Tommy's. I also knew Rich from the neighborhood. We grew up a few streets from the college. Our father was a professor, you know."

Kyle sorted through it. "Rich was the classmate whose son was married?"

"Rich Wessels, yes. The Wessels lived across the lake in some big showy house. The son who got married was Vince's age, and the bride used to summer on the lake, which is how they all met. Vince wasn't invited. Rikki didn't say so, but I suspect Vince made a fool of himself over the girl when she and the groom were first dating, and that's why he didn't get an invitation.

"The bride was from Utica, you see, so the wedding was there. Huge Italian wedding, four hundred people, magnificent food, quite the occasion. The parents took over the hotel and provided rooms for all the out-of-town guests. That's why we were away the two nights. And Vince was already gone to Green Bay, with that creature, when we returned home."

Kyle pinched the bridge of his nose.

Lyssa scribbled on the notepad, "Drunk?"

He nodded. "Janet, I can't thank you enough for telling me all this. I hear how upset you are, and I'm very sorry our phone call has brought up so much unpleasant history. Will you be all right?"

Janet's reply made it clear she intended to finish the beautiful bottle of wine she'd opened and then go to bed.

"Quite right." Kyle saw another note Lyssa had scribbled. "Janet, if you think of any more detail–the last name of the girl Vince went off with, which year all this happened, the name of the nursery that planted the tree, anything at all like that–please ring us back. You can leave a message if we're not answering right off." Which they wouldn't be. He planned to switch off his phone for the night.

Janet promised she would.

He ended the call and massaged his temples in small circles.

Lyssa kneaded his shoulders. "What did she have to say about the gun?"

"Not a bloody thing. We need to find Vince."

"You think he's responsible?"

Chapter 6

"What's this?" Kyle asked, his voice delighted as a child's on Christmas morning. He watched over Lyssa's shoulder as she centered a poached egg on slices of avocado atop half an English muffin. "Eggs Florentine?" He cupped her hips with loving hands.

"We ate all the spinach last night, so it's Eggs California. I thought we needed sustenance after our night of pleasure."

"Yes, wasn't it? It certainly chased away all thought of this week's unpleasantness, for one night anyway."

Lyssa smiled and added a dollop of hollandaise sauce, then licked her thumb when she handed him his plate.

He ferried the plate and a mug of coffee to the breakfast bar and dug in. "Delicious, sweetheart."

She added the lemony sauce to her dish and joined him. "Busy day ahead?"

"Quite. The spring cleanup work is tougher than we anticipated, and we have another big interview today. The last one's tomorrow, thank the Lord."

"This is for your position?"

"For the permanent CIO, yes. One of my techs has decided it's not for him, but the other, Paul, is still in the running."

"Think he's ready to be CIO?"

"He needs a bit of work on his people skills and politicking, but he has all the technical skills and intuition for the job. If I'm nearby to advise him for a time, I think he'd succeed admirably."

"Any good candidates from outside?"

"One has been eliminated, but the one we're talking with today looks promising. Unfortunately, he's asking more money than we're prepared to offer. And, by the way, I won't be home for lunch."

Lyssa's fork paused in midair.

"Problem?"

"Just wondering if you can squeeze in a phone call or two today. We should check with the police to see what, if anything, they're doing with the gun and let them know what Janet told us last night. I'd call myself, but they'll be much more likely to talk to you than to me."

"Except Harriet said they have no interest in the gun's past, criminal or otherwise. Correction, they emphatically have no interest." He sectioned off another bite-sized piece. "I've never had this. It's smashing." He popped the forkful in his mouth.

"Glad you like it. Remember that Hank Moran is interested in the gun. He let that slip when he and Bree's brother were here yesterday morning. I'm not sure how to track him down, except that he's Peter's old buddy."

"Peter's just gone off shift and is probably heading for bed," he said with a glance at the clock. "I'll try him this afternoon."

"Thank you. You aren't really thinking about driving to Myrtle Beach to talk with Janet Tuttle, are you?"

"I did say something about that last night, didn't I? Do you think we should?" He rested his forearms on the table. "Make a long weekend of it?

Lyssa smiled but shook her head. "While I'd love to walk on a sunny beach with you, there's a world of information online that might tell us what we want to know about Vince Tuttle. And I really want to get the garden planted this week, though the planting has to wait until the fountain is installed. Which reminds me."

He held his tongue, rather than say, for the seventeenth time, there was no hurry with the garden and she could just as well hire someone to do the entire project. They'd done that argument to death, and he still didn't understand her thinking. He ate the last bite of the delicious Eggs California.

She'd scooted her stool closer and placed her iPad between them. "We need to order our Zen water feature. The celestial design is my favorite." She waved her fingers over the crescent moon and carved stars.

Kyle curled his lips down at the corners and bared one tooth.

"You're snarling!" She laughed and braced his shoulders. "You hate it, don't you?"

"I can't look at that thing every morning. It would curdle my coffee."

"So that one's out." Lyssa covered the offending design with her thumb. "How about the others, the cube or the globe?"

"The granite block with the carved channels. Is that too large?"

"The cube? It's not quite two feet on all sides. Perfect."

"And you like it? It's not too dull for you?"

"It was my second favorite. It lets the roses steal the show. Shall I order it?"

"Wait. It weighs hundreds of pounds. How will you put it in place without destroying your back or crushing your roses?"

"You're completely right. I have to hold off planting until the fountain is in place, so I really need to order it today and line up someone to install it. The website recommends hiring a landscaper—actually a hardscaper, someone who specializes in retaining walls and pathways and irrigation systems and all that. He'd create the foundation—lots of small stones and layers of drainage—and get the plumbing working. And he'd have a winch or something to lift the thing into place, then hook it up, and make sure it's working correctly."

"I'm impressed by all you've learned, but the fact is, hiring someone to install the beast will double the cost of the fountain."

"Yes, probably." Lyssa sucked in a breath. "Still want it?"

"You won't ask Dick Davis to do all this, correct?" he asked in a tone that left no doubt about the correct answer.

"Of course not. Joel will know someone else."

"Good then." Her brother-in-law owned property all over town and was on a first-name basis with builders and landscapers. "I need to call Joel anyway, my love. Why don't I ask him about someone to do the installation."

She rewarded him with a cheery smile and a kiss on the cheek.

"What else do you have planned today?" He took another swallow of coffee.

"This morning Bree and I were planning to talk through the steps for planting the roses, but since it's pouring out and we can't really do anything until the fountain is in, I should call and cancel. I can scour the Internet for all traces of Vince Tuttle and Nathan Westover. And I can get a lead on the garden club and on the nursery Mrs. Tuttle used. I thought I'd call Joel about those last two."

"Since I'm making a call to Joel, I can add those questions to my list. No need for you to do all the legwork."

"Thank you, my darling husband."

"Who's lurking at the edge of our garden?" He narrowed his eyes and peered through the panes of the French windows.

"It's Bree. She's early." She opened the French door and called to Bree to join them.

"Morning, Penningtons," Bree said as she kicked off her sneakers on the patio.

"Bring them inside out of the rain," Lyssa told her.

"Have some coffee, Bree," Kyle offered.

"Thanks. How's the investigation going?" Bree filled a mug for herself and lifted the carafe toward them. "Anyone else?"

"I'm done," Kyle told her.

Lyssa shook her head and gave Bree the bad news about the delay caused by the need to install the fountain before planting.

"Just as well," Bree said. "I got soaked walking across your backyard."

"Thanks for being flexible." Lyssa carried their eggy dishes to the sink.

Kyle waited for Bree to settle with her coffee before asking her, "How would I reach Hank Moran? Is he with the sheriff's department?"

"State police, but he works with the counties, too. I have his cell." She scrolled through her contacts and held out her phone for Kyle to copy the number. "Man, I need this coffee. Ask Hank what they're doing with Lyssa's gun," she requested.

"It is not my gun." Lyssa shivered as she rinsed their plates.

Kyle chose not to correct her. She knew full well it was legally hers. "So the state police have the gun? Not our city police?"

Bree nodded. "Lyssa, you remember how clean that gun was, right? Hank said they found blood on it."

The plate slipped from Lyssa's hand, struck the granite countertop, and crashed in pieces on the tile floor.

Kyle bolted to her side and shut off the faucet. "Are you hurt?" She shook her head, and he steered her to a stool and made her sit.

"Human blood?" she asked Bree.

"Yes, Hank says whoever cleaned it left some important evidence behind."

Once the fountain had been ordered and Bree had gone off, Kyle enticed his wife to visit their neighbor in the hospital.

Toffee Winkel's eyes lit up at the sight of her neighbors. "Lucky me, visited by the dapper Brit and the pretty redhead who saved my life." Her voice was thin and shaky.

Lyssa touched her fingers to Mrs. Winkel's pale hand on the blanket. "We want to know why you're called Toffee."

The white-haired woman responded with a feeble chuckle. "Oh my, it feels good to laugh. It's been so serious around here. My sister Mary, God bless her, is a nervous wreck. Kyle, can you crank up the head of my bed just a little?"

While Kyle got the slope just right for Toffee, Lyssa wheeled over a stool that put her at a comfortable height for Toffee to carry on a conversation.

"My late husband, Larry, gave me that nickname when we were dating all those years ago at Tompkins College. My hair was never quite as red as yours, Lyssa. Larry said it was the color of toffee, and I wore it long and loose. From that point on, everyone called me Toffee. What fun we had in those days."

"I won our bet," Kyle said with a teasing smile for both women. He'd been studying her bandages and tubing and the machines all around her. One of the plastic pouches on the IV rack was Demerol. The nurse had just started the drip as they arrived. Toffee's tongue would be loose as long as she was awake, but who knew how long that would be?

"Kyle likes to think he's smarter than me," Lyssa told Toffee. "I let him be right sometimes."

Toffee chuckled. "You're both brilliant, according to the grapevine. The college is lucky to have you. Our alma mater went downhill over the years, and I hear that's turning around with the new president, Cushman, who's said to be courageous and smart."

"He is that. I'm proud to be counted among his oldest friends," Kyle said. "He actually introduced Lyssa and me when Lyssa was working in London, where my company is headquartered."

Toffee Winkel's answering "for heaven's sake" may have been weak, but it was a sweet melody to his ears. "We need to mind our time, though, and I have some questions for you."

He asked them in priority order while he paced back and forth near the foot of the bed. "Toffee, what can you tell me about your young neighbor Nate Westover in the months following his parents' death in the rockslide?"

Toffee gasped.

Lyssa patted her hand. "It must have been hard for all of you in the neighborhood when that happened."

"Hardest on young Nate," Toffee replied. "That poor, orphaned boy was in a hospital out West for weeks and then home with an aide for a time and getting physical therapy for his injured leg.

"I walked our dog, Trixie, every morning. We'd check on Nate, take him his favorite cookies. Cowboy Cookies, he called them. He had the recipe in his backpack, and the pack survived the rockslide. Oatmeal chocolate chip with pecans and cherries."

"I might want that recipe from you," Lyssa said.

"Remind me when I'm home again. I'd tell you wrong today. I'm a little fuzzy with that happy juice they're dripping into me."

"You're doing fine, Toffee," Kyle said.

"Where was I? Oh, yes. One morning that autumn, after his parents' death, I found Nate on the front porch, passed out. He'd apparently been drinking heavily, and I suspect he had been for some time. People do that to block out a horrible experience, I understand."

Lyssa asked, "What did you do when you found him passed out like that?"

"Fortunately, our neighbor Nick the teacher was just leaving for school and he came to our aid, and I think he got the boy into a rehab. I remember Nate protesting. Maybe he couldn't afford it, but Nick talked him into it. He had a way with young people, Nick did." Her voice trailed off, and her forehead puckered.

"So Nate went into rehab, you think?" Lyssa asked. "And Nick footed the bill?"

"We didn't see Nate for a while. Larry told me not to worry about the boy's finances. He had his college degree already, and he planned to teach. Later, Nick confided to Larry that the boy had plenty of money. Maybe his parents had life insurance."

"Where is Nate Westover now, Toffee?" Kyle asked.

"I don't know what happened to him after that. I'd see him around the neighborhood at night sometimes when Trixie and I were out later than usual for our evening walk. But the Westover house sat deserted. Then that lovely woman, Natalie, bought it."

"Kyle and I met her earlier this week."

"Toffee, do you recall the time Rikki Tuttle planted an ornamental tree in her rose garden?" Kyle asked.

"Oh my, what fuss and bother came from that. But, really, what else could she do? More than half her prize roses had been killed by the ice storm. When was that ice storm?"

"Five years ago, we heard."

"That's right. Our downtown had that big We Survived weekend a few months ago. Carlene Bischoff and I gave out cookies at her daughter Anita's dress shop. Bitter cold weekend. We froze our tushes off, but it was so much fun to be out."

Lyssa smiled. "You and Carlene made the scene."

"We did. Thank you, dear, that reminds me, I must ask Carlene to get together once I'm back in action. But Kyle was asking about the tree. Rikki decided, rather than invest in two dozen new rose bushes to replace the casualties, she'd redesign the garden with a Laceleaf Japanese Maple at the center. They'd seen one in Charleston that spring on a garden trip with Road Scholar, I think it was. Tommy just loved its shape, and when they heard the leaves turned a rose color in the fall, he was smitten.

"Tommy bought one of the trees for Rikki from some nursery down south and had it shipped to a nursery up here for planting. He wouldn't even tell her how much it cost. And oh my . . ." She rolled her eyes. "When Rikki Tuttle planted the tree right in the center of her prize-winning garden, instead of replacing her dead roses, the Tompkins Falls Garden Club had a fit. I wouldn't be surprised if they're still talking about it."

Kyle smiled politely. "She planted it shortly before Memorial Day weekend, did she?"

"Yes, and I know that because all hell broke loose next door at the Tuttles a day or two later."

He stopped pacing at the foot of the bed and gripped the bed frame. "What happened, Toffee?"

"Vince brought a girl home, that's what. Unannounced. He'd just finished his master's degree and had been offered a teaching job in Green Bay. I think that's it, with the football team Vince Lombardi coached. He told his parents he and the girl planned to marry. From what I saw, she was a blond bombshell. 'Good for Vince,' my Larry said."

"Did you meet her, Toffee?" Lyssa asked.

"No, but we saw her in the driveway when they arrived. It's common knowledge that, in Rikki's opinion, the girl was trash—that was her word—not at all what she wanted for her serious responsible son."

"Her name was Kitty?" Kyle asked.

"Oh, no, she may have been a sex kitten, but her name was plain old Patty. I'm sure of that."

Kyle asked. "Do you know the last name?"

"I'll think of it in a minute. It was an easy one. Anyway, Tommy and Rikki had plans to go to a wedding in Syracuse or Utica or someplace, and they went anyway. Vince was put out about that, but Tommy told him to put a sock in it and they'd talk when they were back from the wedding.

"The next night, while the parents were away, we woke up to such commotion and slamming of doors, as if a party was breaking up and everyone was leaving at once. No, wait."

"What is it, Toffee?" Lyssa asked. "Can I get you something?"

"No, dear, I just remembered, there was some loud noise that woke us up before all that ruckus. I remember thinking kids had set off fireworks nearby, although it was too early. Memorial Day was still a week away. Anyway, the last big noise we heard was a vehicle that was due for a new muffler. That was the last straw for Larry. He looked out—our bedroom was that front corner nearest your house—and told me the Westover boy's truck was pulling out of the Tuttle's driveway."

"I suppose Larry went over the next morning to complain to Vince?" Kyle asked.

"Next morning it was dead quiet over there, and there were no cars at all in the driveway, not even Vince's old Honda. Vince and his girl were gone. Rikki had a fit when she and Tommy and Janet returned from their weekend.

Tommy dropped off Rikki and took Janet home. Then Rikki started shrieking in the garden."

"Why?" Kyle asked.

"I peeked over the hedge and saw that her gorgeous little tree was leaning toward the house, and it looked like a couple of the roses were disturbed, too. I told her I thought Vince had a party and some of the guests had probably trampled the garden, but Rikki wouldn't hear it. She insisted it was the nursery's fault. She fixated on the horrible job they'd done when they planted the tree, and that's all she'd talk about for weeks."

"She was terribly upset about her garden, was she?" Kyle asked.

"You know, Kyle, I think it was really all about Vince and the girl. Beck. Patty Beck. That was her full name. Do you know, Vince never once came home for a visit? Never. He and Tommy had those harsh words that weekend, and they never spoke again. Rikki was very hurt."

"Was Tommy hurt, too, or was he angry?" Lyssa asked.

"It broke Tommy's heart, my dear. Literally. He had a heart attack not long after. He survived, but he never really recovered. And when he did die, Vince didn't come for the funeral, even though Rikki sent a copy of the obituary to Vince at his school. She didn't have a home address for him. Can you imagine that?"

"Why was that?"

"I never knew for sure. I know Rikki said some things she regretted when he told them he planned to marry the girl. That was when the four of them were still out on the driveway that Friday morning. Larry and I couldn't hear Rikki's words, but her voice was like an animal growling, low and menacing. And Vince had to hold the girl back, she was so mad at Rikki." Toffee sniffed. "That girl was a feisty fighter, you could tell, and Rikki was lucky Vince held her tight until Tommy made Rikki go inside. Then Vince and Tommy had words." She shook her head. "And it wasn't just 'Put a sock in it'. I can't repeat what they said even to you, Kyle. But Vince never came home again."

"Terrible thing, eh?" Kyle asked.

"When I heard that nasty fight, I held my tongue. I held out hope Rikki would confide in someone."

"And did she?"

"I think she talked it over with her minister, but I never heard her say another word about it. Until Tommy's funeral. Rikki stood up in front of everyone and said that girl had changed Vince. I know it was an unchristian thing to say, but how else can you explain it?"

"Did they marry, Patty and Vince?" Lyssa asked.

"Oh, yes. Didn't invite Rikki and Tommy, though. Larry and I only knew because something came in the mail, and Rikki brought it over, crying. She didn't want Tommy to see it. There was no return address and no letter or note. Just two photos. Patty in a princess wedding gown—you know, with the puffy sleeves and big full skirt and long train. And a picture of a luxury condo on the waterfront in Green Bay with "Home Sweet Home" on the back, written in purple ink in big loopy letters. I think the girl sent them, rubbing Rikki's nose in it."

That was odd. "Just Patty in the wedding picture, not Vince?" he asked.

"Just Patty in the dress and some people out of focus in the background, all in formal attire. Lots of flowers all around her."

"And you're sure it was a luxury condo on the bay, although Vince just had his teacher's salary?" Lyssa asked.

"That's exactly what Rikki said. She was sure Patty was trash, but evidently she came from money. Vince certainly didn't have anything more than his teacher's salary. Tommy and Rikki expected him to be responsible with his money, and Vince understood they wouldn't support him after college because they needed to save for retirement. Vince worked hard every summer and after school to save, and he paid his own way when he went to Geneseo for that teaching degree."

"Did Vince send a condolence card or flowers for Tommy's funeral?"

"Nothing. Nick across the street came to the funeral and told Rikki he was sure Vince was an excellent teacher. And I think he must be, because he was always so good with the little ones, first and second grade, when he worked summers at the Tompkins Falls Library."

"Wasn't it kind of Nick to say that?" Toffee asked them. "Rikki held onto those kind words about her son after Tommy was gone. She'd tell people her son had a gift for teaching young children." Toffee Winkel gave them a sad smile. "God bless Rikki Tuttle, she tried to be proud of her son."

Lyssa rode with Kyle from the hospital to campus. Both of them were too stunned by Toffee's revelations to talk about it.

They shared Lyssa's umbrella on the walk to the administration building. At the entrance hall, he gave her a peck on the cheek. "We'll touch base later."

She dove down a flight of stairs to the Alumni Office to gather more information about Vince and Nate. After some small talk with the clerk about how busy the campus would become next week and for the remainder of the semester, Lyssa stated her business.

"I'm looking for information about two young men who grew up in Kyle's and my new neighborhood. Nothing confidential, I don't think. Let's start with Vince Tuttle, who lived in our current house, 57 Seneca Street. I'm guessing his middle name was Thomas. What can you tell me about him?"

The clerk's fingers flew on the keys. "Got him. What do you need?"

"Things like when he graduated, what he did after graduation, you know."

"First, you're correct about his full name being Vincent Thomas Tuttle. He graduated six years ago this May. Dual major Art and English. Immediately started a master's degree at Geneseo State College."

"Where's that?"

"Very close. It's south of Routes 5 and 20, maybe twenty miles west of here, then fifteen miles south. I'm guessing on the distances. It's in the Genesee River valley, which is where the name comes from. Excellent school."

"I heard he got his degree in May just one year after he finished at Tompkins College."

"Yes, that's right. Childhood Education." She hummed with raised eyebrows. "Good for him."

"What?"

"He accepted a teaching job in Green Bay, Wisconsin, to start that September. Very impressive. He must have been a top student with really strong recommendations.

Elementary teaching jobs are almost impossible to get for someone who's just graduated. I know that because three of my kids wanted to be elementary teachers and ended up with very different jobs."

"Interesting."

When Lyssa asked about Vince's residence, though, the answer was, "We have no record of his current address."

"Is that just a polite way of saying that data is private?"

"No. I mean it *is* private, and I wouldn't have been able to tell you where he lives. But I really don't have that information. No contact information at all. To be honest, I was so surprised by the blank field that I just blurted it out."

"Why do you think that is? My Alumni Office is always tracking me down, no matter where I've moved."

The woman frowned at the screen. "I don't know what to say. We're pretty relentless, too."

"Doesn't matter. What can you tell me about our other neighbor, Nathan Westover, 53 Seneca? I'm pretty sure he finished here the same time as Vince."

Nathan William Westover had majored in History and Business and had graduated the same year as Vince. He'd had been accepted at Geneseo into the same program as Vince, but there was no information about his having completed the program, and there was no work history for him.

"Any chance you have a current address?"

"Same thing. No current address or contact information of any kind."

"Strange. Neither is deceased, as far as you know?

"Not according to our records, no. And they were local to Tompkins Falls. We would know, I'm sure."

"Where would I find photos of Vince and Nate?"

Chapter 7

The IT department's interview with the external candidate had revved them up, and Kyle knew beyond a doubt he'd be taking the young man to dinner at the president's house. Not what he wanted to do when an investigation into possible murder had fallen into his and Lyssa's laps. Although . . . He palmed his phone, hoping to persuade Lyssa to join him for the dinner at Justin and Gianessa Cushman's. Gianessa was sure to have a healthy feast, and Lyssa would enjoy time with the twins.

Before he could press her number, a tap sounded at his office door.

"Yes?"

His senior analyst, Paul, poked his head in. "Got ten minutes, boss?"

"Only if it's something intriguing," Kyle said with a wink as he pocketed the phone.

"I'd say it's baffling," Paul said with a grin.

"Even better." Kyle waved Paul to the chair across from him and spent the next few minutes listening to his exceptionally clever second-in-command describe a security breach that stumped him.

When Paul had wound down, Kyle summarized, "So it's a nasty little gremlin that serves no purpose other than to lead you on a merry chase and disappear just as you prepare to nab it, and then, sometime later, it recreates itself?"

"Perfect description. How do we get rid of it?"

"You're certain it's not a known virus?"

"I checked every description that was even remotely close."

"Including 'gremlin,' I've no doubt. All right, then." He tapped his pencil and marshaled his thoughts.

But Paul hadn't finished. "I asked everyone on staff about video games they might be working on, just in case it was a prank they were playing."

"Good hunch." Kyle sat back and gave him an admiring tip of the head.

"Everyone swears they have nothing to do with it. Like I said, I'm baffled."

Kyle agreed to take over the hunt, not for the gremlin but for the network user audacious enough to waste their time. Perhaps they had a genius student exercising his or her brain. Or it might be a Trojan horse embedded by the outgoing CIO last fall and set to activate months after his ignominious departure.

He cleared two-thirds of his desktop by transferring stacks of reports and books to a nearby chair. "Ready."

Paul filled the empty space with printouts to jumpstart his investigation. "Boss, I can't wait to hear how you figure this out."

Kyle had pored over the evidence of their elusive gremlin for twenty minutes when a fragment of memory shocked him into a cold sweat. *What on earth?*

He set down his pencil. *Fascinating how the mind protects us by burying trauma.* What had made him remember his genius classmate, Wollings, today of all days?

Whatever the trigger, Kyle knew his power of concentration had shifted irrevocably away from tracing a security breach at Tompkins College. Instead, he was fully absorbed in an incident at the school he'd been sent to as a boy, a private school that admitted only boys who had exceptional mental prowess. Like Wollings and himself.

He was ten at the time, younger and smaller than his thirteen- and fourteen-year-old classmates. The incident, involving the new lad, Wollings, must be popping up now because it held some key to the mystery of the gun in their backyard. *But what?*

He glanced out at the quad, deserted on this rainy afternoon, and emptied his thoughts. In a matter of seconds, the wretched details of the accident came into focus in his mind's eye, as fresh as if it had happened last night. The whole truth, including his part in it.

He could even smell the rushing muddy creek that flowed between the private school and the cricket field, tempting young lads to cross it, rather than walk around via the bridge half a mile upstream. His team had won the match and were in high spirits and didn't care a fig that it was pitch dark each time the full moon hid behind a cloud. The lads who lived in town had gone their separate way, leaving the six boarders to return to the cluster of buildings that constituted Mullett Academy.

Because he was the youngest and smallest, Kyle was subjected to bullying from day one. He was no match for anyone's brawn but he very quickly found a solution. That night, after cricket, he walked close behind beefy Hodgkiss, whom he'd chosen as his protector. Though Hodgkiss had some hold over most of the other bullies, he was no match for Kyle's superior wit. He'd played flunky to Hodgkiss's bluster for two full months now, and it had saved him from several poundings.

While they tromped across the field, the jolly cricket players trumpeted their victory and rehashed their rivals' defeat with insults and cuss words. Kyle stayed quiet. He was wet and tired. It had rained the entire match, until the final twenty minutes, when the sky brightened just before sunset. Kyle'd had the foresight, when the rain started, to pile their jackets under a tarp. He hoped the dry jackets on the return trek might prevent pneumonia, since everyone's shirts and pants were soaked through.

Owing to the hours of rain the stream, when they reached it, was much higher and raced powerfully. No one would be fool enough to wade across tonight, which left the jumble of fallen logs as their only way across. Kyle saw disaster ahead. They would dare one another or shove someone off—him, probably, or the new lad, Wollings—unless he took some preemptive measure.

With mock timidity, he said to Hodgkiss, "Logs will be slick. Who do you suppose should cross first?" Though he knew Hodgkiss would send him across as the test case, he gave his protector time to play it his way and used the time to select which log he'd traverse. The topmost one, though it afforded no handholds, was a straight wide way, marred only by one menacing bump nearer the far bank of the stream.

Hodgkiss puffed himself up and ordered his liege into danger. "Pennington goes first. See if he survives." That brought hoots of laughter from the other two thugs among them and sympathetic looks from the rest.

Kyle had no doubt he'd succeed, nimble and sure-footed as he was. Nevertheless, he played his role to the max, teetering a couple of times and once touching his hand down to the wet log, which earned him gasps and jeers. Hodgkiss would be reveling in that.

When he reached the shore thirty feet across, he silently congratulated himself for showing the lot of them the best route and throwing in the dramatics so they'd use caution.

One more lad, Hurst, followed without incident. It was when the new boy, Wollings, came across that things went horribly wrong. Just before he reached the tricky part, where a knob the size and shape of a fat pattypan squash impeded travel, Wollings looked back at the remaining hecklers on the far shore with a fierce scowl, probably sick of their hoots, which were meant to distract and unnerve. The three lads elbowed each other and quieted.

Without watching his footing, Wollings took one more step forward, which brought him to the edge of the knob. Kyle dared not call out a warning, for that would earn him a roughing up once they'd all crossed over, and he was too exhausted to spend the night in a wet field, unconscious. He suppressed a shiver in the chilly wind and prayed that the boy would watch his step.

As Wollings returned his attention to the journey, though, the moon hid itself, and Wollings' next step was straight into disaster. His foot twisted on the knob and he lurched sideways, arms flailing, and plunged with a howl and a sickening thud onto his back on the intersecting logs below.

With his heart thundering in his chest, Kyle slid down the bank and edged onto the log that had broken Wollings' fall. He reached the boy just as the moon revealed the scene.

Wollings' face was dead white, his back bent unnaturally, legs splayed. Kyle reached for the wrist closest him and felt for a pulse.

Hurst, a few feet behind him, asked, "Is he dead?"

"No, his pulse is strong, but I think his back's broken."

"Agreed." Hurst's face was nearly as white as Wollings'. Hurst, fourteen, planned to be a doctor. "We daren't move him. Bloody hell."

"Trade places?" Kyle asked.

"No, I'll go for help. I'm faster. Stay with him, Pennington." Hurst peeled off his jacket. "Try to keep him warm." He shouted to the others to drop their jackets as they came across. Without waiting for a response, he cat-walked back to land, and raced away into the night.

In the minutes that followed, the remaining three lads navigated the top log in complete silence. Though Kyle called a reminder as they passed above him, none left their jackets for Wollings. Once they assembled on the bank, they departed the scene wordlessly, leaving Kyle alone with Wollings and two jackets, his own and Hurst's.

He covered Wollings' torso and legs the best he could and settled down to his watch, huddling close to Wollings' broken body, his hand resolutely on his teammate's wrist. The only sound was the surge and whirl and hiss of the stream.

When help arrived, it was Hurst with the school doctor and two burly men, one carrying a backboard. Petrol fumes told of a vehicle idling nearby. The three adults carefully stepped onto the fallen logs.

"Out of the way, boy," the doctor ordered.

Kyle hauled himself to the top log and scrambled to shore, where Hurst waited.

"We're to walk back," Hurst told him. "He's still alive, eh?"

Kyle answered with a nod.

"Did he regain consciousness?"

"No, not once."

"Thank the Lord. The men will take care of him. He'll be all right, you know."

Kyle didn't think so, but he knew for sure he'd have preferred a pounding by the bigger lads to the guilt that churned in his gut. *I should have warned him.*

Kyle lifted his eyes and surveyed his office, disoriented for a moment. Why had he remembered Wollings just now? What did it have to do with their gun?

Lyssa fished out her phone as she ascended the steps from the basement of the administration building, reached Bree's voicemail, and left a message, "I need to drive to the college in Geneseo tomorrow or Friday, and I'm hoping you can come with me."

At the top of the stairs, she turned left to the Information Technology department, which consisted of a cavernous space on the right with maybe a dozen cubicles, followed by a conference room large enough to hold the full IT staff. On the left was a glass-enclosed climate-controlled room jammed with racks of servers, routers, and other mysterious equipment. At the far end of the hall was Kyle's office with the door wide open.

The conference room door was closed as she passed, but she heard excited discussion within, punctuated by laughter. If that was the interview in progress, it was going well.

Kyle was not at his desk. His computer monitor showed only his screen saver, a coastal scene he'd photographed in

Cornwall on a hike with her last summer. He wouldn't have gone off and left his office unlocked, even if he was just next door for the meeting.

She sat in his desk chair, and her gaze wandered to the rain-ravaged quad. There was Kyle with his hair plastered to his head, hands stuffed in his jacket pockets, studying the sidewalk as he crossed toward the administration building.

Something was very wrong. Should she rush to the side entrance with a dry sweatshirt? Should she leave as if she'd never been there? Or just wait? A rising panic attack helped her decide. She focused on her breathing, in for six counts, out for eight, over and over, and consciously relaxed each muscle starting with her toes.

She'd made it to her shoulders when he entered the office, blotting his hair with a wad of paper towels. His face scared her. It was as if he'd aged twenty years since morning. Worry lines creased his forehead and mouth, and his eyes were pinched nearly shut.

"Kyle, what's wrong?" The question startled him.

"Hello, my love." His eyes brightened at the sight of her, and he seemed more himself.

"Is everything all right? You left your door unlocked, your jacket is soaked through, and you never have a hair out of place except when we're caught on the coast path in a storm."

He stripped off his jacket and parked it, dripping, on a hook behind the door, then reached for a Tompkins College sweatshirt on top of the bookcase and drew it over his head. When he arranged for half an inch of shirt cuff to show below the sleeve of the sweatshirt, she knew he'd not completely lost his mind.

"That's better. You're right, I did all those things, but I can't tell you what's wrong, not just yet." He stepped around the desk and drew her into a fierce hug. "We'll talk tonight, all right?"

She pressed back to see his face, which he averted. "You promise?"

"Yes. Have any luck with the Alumni Office?"

"No new data, but I have photos of Vince and Nate that will blow you away. How's the interview going?"

"It's going so well that I'll have to take the candidate to dinner at Justin and Gianessa's. Come with me?"

She rested her head on his shoulder for a moment. His body was rigid with tension. *What is wrong?* She wanted to take him home, feed him, give him a massage, and draw him out. She swallowed before she spoke and made her voice light. "I will pass, but it's sweet of you to ask. Will you be late?"

"I'll make every effort not to wake you."

Before she could remind him he'd promised her tonight they'd talk over whatever was bothering him, the neighboring conference room disgorged a super-charged IT staff.

Kyle stepped back from the embrace, reached for a pencil, and had it jiggling in his fingers seconds before one of his staff peered into the office. "Be with you in a moment," he said. "Close the door, please." He returned his attention to her.

"Be *sure* to wake me." She sputtered with anger. "Whenever you get home. As you promised, we *will* talk tonight about whatever's going on." She brushed past him, threw open the door, and stalked down the hall.

"Lord, save me from myself," Kyle said under his breath. He'd just treated his wife as his lowest priority and he deserved her rebuke. Perhaps his ten-year-old self could be forgiven for a set of priorities that allowed innocent people to be hurt, but not his adult self.

He muttered, "asshole," at himself and waded into the pool of computer geeks swimming outside his office door. Without acknowledging the marital spat they'd all just witnessed, he told them, "I can tell from your level of excitement the discussion went well." To their candidate he said, "Congratulations for surviving the shark tank."

The young man's answering chuckle made all of them relax. "What's next?" the young man asked him.

"I'll escort you to the provost. On the way I'll address any questions you have for me. Ladies and gentlemen," he said to Paul and the rest of the crew, "take a moment while it's fresh in your mind to complete the feedback form for Human Resources. Then back to work. We've no time to spare today. Thank you."

His head pounded all the way to the provost's office and, in spite of his stated intention, he gave the candidate's questions short shrift. He announced to the provost's assistant, "I'll take a moment to speak with her first, if you don't mind." With no concern for the assistant's yelp of protest, he barged into the provost's inner sanctum. She was, mercifully, alone.

"Sorry to burst in on your yoga. Don't stop. I need an enormous favor. Lyssa's under the weather, and I can't make the candidate dinner tonight with Justin and his beautiful wife at their home. The candidate's very strong, asking too much money, but superbly qualified. His dinner merits your presence in my place, rather than someone from HR. I'll leave it to you to decide."

"Kyle—"

"Sorry, must dash."

And he did, head down, hands fisted at his sides, straight to his office. He closed and locked the door, turned off the overhead light, and hunkered at his computer. The system would tell him which professors had taught Vince Tuttle and Nate Westover and who among them still worked at the college. *We have to find those boys.*

Chapter 8

"Furious!" Lyssa told her sister. She wiped a bubble of spit from the screen of her iPhone and directed her attention out the French windows to the soggy back yard. She'd be out there planting if they didn't have to wait for the fountain to go in first. "I need a meeting. Any chance you can meet me at Happy Hour?"

"Sure," Manda said. "Want to tell me about it? I've got five minutes."

"Kyle's lost his mind." She ranted about finding his office door unlocked and seeing him sopping wet out on the quad.

"Sounds like he's in a bad way. Is it work, do you think?"

"Fool that I am, I actually worried about him. And then he said he'd tell me about it, whatever it was, tonight. I thought he meant over supper at home but, no, he has to take someone to dinner and did I want to join them? Puh-leeze."

"So you turned down dinner, and then what?"

"Then, when I asked if he'd be late, he said he wouldn't wake me."

"Wait, what happened to 'I'll tell you tonight'?"

"Exactly!" Lyssa stomped her foot. "So I said to him loud enough for his whole staff to hear, that he'd better wake me up because we're going to talk about it. Whatever it is."

"Bad move, Lyssa."

"I don't bloody care!" Lyssa snuffled as tears spilled over. "I want my sweet normal husband back. I want my safe pretty house back."

"Planning to drink?"

"No. Nor smoke pot."

"Good. I'll see you at Happy Hour. Call your sponsor."

"Ah, Professor Chivarri, I'm glad I caught you in your office." Kyle paused, expecting the silver-haired English scholar to offer a seat or at least a handshake.

Chivarri didn't get up, merely cocked his head. *Lord, spare me from egos larger than my own.*

"I'm Kyle Pennington, interim head of IT," he introduced himself from the doorway. "Do you have a minute to spare?"

"What have I done?" Chivarri asked with a wide playful smile.

"Not a thing, as you know. I'm looking for information about a former student whom you may remember. Vince Tuttle?"

Chivarri's gaze tracked to the left corner of the room. "Graduated six years ago. Girlfriend threw him over the same weekend."

"What was that about?"

"She was off to Yale for an MBA, didn't think Vince was good enough for her high-powered career. What do you want with him?"

"My wife and I bought the house in College Heights where the Tuttle family lived, and we've found some things Vince might want. Have you any contact with him?"

"Other than the odd email message, none. Disappointing. He was one of my best students and I'd hoped to stay in touch, hear about his career."

"Someone said he's teaching in Green Bay."

"Wisconsin, yes, home of the Packers. Are you a football fan, Dr. Pennington?"

"Not at all," Kyle said with a laugh.

"What's the accent?"

"Cornwall."

"Penzance?"

"Not far."

"The students are putting on Gilbert and Sullivan's Pirates of Penzance this year. I have a bit part. Rollicking good time." He attempted a British accent and failed utterly. "Come, bring your lovely wife, first week of November."

"We'll be there. How did you come by Vince's email address?"

"High-tech wizardry," Chivarri answered with a supercilious smile. "I went to the website for the school district, noted the way email addresses were constructed, plugged in Vince's name, and got through to him." He opened his hands.

"Well done. What sorts of messages got responses from him?"

"The one that caught his interest was about a classmate who'd died. Senseless accident. Anthony Rosario, Andy, another of my outstanding students. He was a local boy, like Vince, and I think they were friends even before college.

Anyway, I let Vince know about Andy's death, and he asked what happened. I sent him a link to the obituary."

"Did he respond?"

"I don't think he did, no."

"Do you recall any other friends of Vince's? Perhaps local boys?"

Chivarri rose from his chair with a laugh. "You'll want to look up Mark and Mike." He moved toward Kyle. "Twins. Very popular with the ladies. Hung with Vince and Andy and another young man who looked like Vince."

Kyle stood his ground in the doorway. "Their last name?"

Chivarri's forearm rested along the edge of the door, and his body barred reentry. "Weaver. Big name in restaurants around the area."

Joel must know them.

"Thanks for your time," Kyle said with good cheer as the door shut in his face. He drew out his phone to call Joel.

Lyssa glanced up as Manda slid onto the folding chair next to hers. "Sorry I'm late," Manda whispered. "I was talking with a friend of yours in the hall."

Lyssa smiled and returned her attention to the speaker, a woman friend who'd just put together a year of continuous sobriety. When the woman said, "I feel like a miracle," Lyssa nodded.

She'd celebrated two years clean and sober herself a few weeks ago. She rarely had the desire to drink or use anymore, but today had tested her. After ending her call to Manda, she'd called Gianessa. Her sponsor reminded her not to get too hungry, angry, lonely, or tired. The acronym HALT was a tool she often forgot to use in dealing with life sober. She'd fixed a sandwich then and gone grocery shopping.

When the AA speaker's talk ended, Lyssa clapped along with the other meeting-goers. The discussion for the remainder of the hour-long meeting focused on the importance of sponsorship. *Perfect.* She raised her hand and shared her sponsor's wisdom about today's crisis.

When she finished, Manda poked her arm and whispered, "Are you sponsoring anyone yet?"

Lyssa stifled a laugh. "Be serious. Who'd want me? I'm too new."

"You're not. You did everything right today. We all have days like that. You used the tools of the program and called people and showed up at a meeting."

"I was also a raving lunatic," Lyssa whispered.

"Stark raving sober," her sister whispered back.

Someone behind them shushed them. "Sorry," Lyssa said and tuned back into the discussion.

After the closing Serenity Prayer, someone helped Lyssa lift her tote onto her shoulder. "Thank you." She turned with a smile to the helper and was met with a fragrant bouquet of pink and red roses. "What—?"

"I owe you a very great apology, my love." Kyle said.

A few people clapped as she went into his arms. "I owe you one, too," she told him.

"Let's sort it out at home. Can we heat up that risotto you made that was so good?"

"You're not going out with the candidate?"

"The provost is handling that responsibility. Or delegating it, I don't care which." He gave her a crooked smile. "I hope they fire me."

~ ~ ~

"Kyle, you only slouch like that when you're thinking of that awful school your parents sent you to as a boy." Lyssa said it lightly, but she really was worried about him. Gone was the good cheer when he'd come for her at Happy Hour.

In spite of her conversational gambits, he'd been silent through dinner, elbows on the table, face hovering inches above his plate of mushroom risotto. He was as distracted now as he'd been on the quad in the pouring rain.

"What's happened that's got you in a funk?"

"I'm broody, am I?" His head came up, and he cleared his throat. "It's scary how well you know me, my love."

"What's happened to bring up all that history? Something about our missing victim?" She reached for his hand, but he withdrew his and rose from the little table by the French windows where they'd just finished their meal.

"Sorry, I was just fishing. Did someone go missing at your school?"

He leaned back against the island, between two stools, and regarded her from a distance of ten feet. "No, and it wasn't a horrible school, so much as a horrible bunch of classmates."

She recognized that strategy—shifting the discussion away from her question to give him time to decide how he wanted to answer. She'd cut him some slack for a minute, so long as he let her circle back. "You really haven't told me much about them. I know you were much younger, and they bullied you. But I seem to remember you got the best of the deal by signing them up as your clients at Pennington Secure Networks once they'd made their fortunes."

"Only some of them." He bit off the words.

"I never knew that." She lightened her voice, making it sound like a game. "Who made the cut and who didn't?"

"Those who made the cut had to sign in blood"—he used a Dracula voice—"they wouldn't use the network for any illicit activity."

She forced a laugh. "And why was that necessary?"

"You're aware I ingratiated myself with the bullies by offering to encrypt all their communication and files to keep them safe from prying eyes?"

"Prying eyes like the headmaster and parents and who else?"

He huffed out his breath and stared at a point on the ceiling. "The local constabulary and various intelligence agencies."

"Now you're teasing."

"No, actually, I'm not." He faced her with a solemn expression. "Some of the lads frequented the brothels and indulged in porn, traded materials and tips and secrets among themselves."

"They were young teens, weren't they?"

He nodded and crossed his arms.

"And you protected that?"

"I did, yes, and I'm not proud of it. Once I'd left school for university, I vowed not to protect any such activity, particularly with my own business. That's when I developed the monitoring software that enforces my credo."

"The one they agreed to by signing in blood?"

"Precisely. My clients understand that, in addition to blocking any and all intrusions from the outside, I monitor our network for all manner of theft, fraud, blackmail, money laundering, embezzlement, and exchange of national secrets." He took up position at the French door, hands in his pockets, his gaze scanning the unlit patio and beyond to the darkened yard. "I especially watch for any talk of violent or abusive behavior and any sign of human trafficking, arms trafficking, drug trafficking, and porn."

She knew all this. Why was it important for him to say it all now? "I see." She slid off her chair and stood beside him, a foot away.

"To your question about why I thought of the old school today, it's something I remembered after our session with Toffee. An unforgiveable incident that was hushed up."

A pit opened in her stomach. *What did my perfect husband do?*

"What did you remember?" She hated that her voice quavered.

"An accident that permanently disabled one of the lads." His gaze shifted in her direction but quickly returned to the backyard.

"Please share."

He cleared his throat and recounted for her the Wollings affair. She couldn't help interjecting words like "Horrible!" and "My God!" through the telling. Finally, he leaned into the window, touching only his forehead to the glass. She held her tongue to the count of ten and chose just one of the questions that crowded her head.

"What became of him?"

"Wollings? He was paraplegic. His parents had plenty of clout and went after the three who heckled him and who left the scene so callously. They insisted the three boys' families pay for all his surgeries and rehabilitation and equipment. Wollings didn't return to our school, but he had a brilliant mind. I heard at some point he'd gone into intelligence work or some think tank."

"Did he blame you for his fall?"

"No."

"Do you blame yourself?"

"For not speaking up, yes. I should have warned him. I was saving my own hide."

"Think of all you did to get everyone across safely."

"That doesn't justify it!" he yelled.

Lyssa cowered at his roar. He never raised his voice. Never. No one had done that to her since her father when he was still alive, when he was drunk.

"It was wrong of me!" Kyle pounded his palm with his fist.

She covered her mouth to keep from crying out, took a step back, and watched him carefully. Her body went on red alert as a flashback sucked her from the present to the past. Her mother screaming at her and Manda to flee. The two girls desperately wanting to gang up on their father to save their mother. "He'll rape you! Get out! I can take it," their mother shouted as she shielded her head from the swing of a chair.

The police had never come when they called, never helped, so twelve-year-old Lyssa didn't bother to call. Instead, she gripped Manda's arm and propelled them through the kitchen door into the rainy night.

"What is it, Lyssa?"

Disoriented by the flashback, she beseeched him, "Don't hit me." Hearing her voice—the young panicky voice she'd used toward her father in middle school—shocked her back to the present. She blinked and drew in a ragged breath. *I'm an adult, and I'm standing in my kitchen with my loving husband.*

Kyle was watching her, his mouth open, eyes questioning.

"When you yelled and smacked your fist, I thought you were my father for a second." She struggled with the words, wanted to add she was okay, but all she could do was breathe in and breathe out. *God, restore me to sanity right now.*

"My love, how could I have forgotten your past, your father's rages?" He took a step toward her and back again. "I would never raise a hand to you. I'm sorry for yelling like that."

She nodded and choked in another breath. "I'm okay," she managed to say, but the shakes followed her spurt of adrenaline. She wrapped her arms around herself.

His features crumbled. "Good Lord, what have I done?"

"Really, I'm okay. Panic attack or something. Can I have some water?"

He rushed to the sink, pulled a glass out of the cupboard and lost his grip. It shattered on the tile floor. "Blast!" he said. "Sorry, sweetheart."

Lyssa let go a laugh. "Don't worry. Please don't get cut." He took down another glass with trembling hands, filled it, and brought it to her.

She drank half of it down with noisy gulps. The next breath was easier. "That was intense."

"Have you always had panic attacks?" His arms were folded tight, fists under his armpits.

"Since adolescence. I drank and smoked pot to take the edge off them."

"And now you don't have either of those escapes. Should you be taking medication for them?"

She shook her head. "My doctor in Austin left it up to me, and I declined. Yoga had been helping."

"You didn't do yoga just now, or did I miss it?" He loosed his arms and gave her one of his lopsided Cornish smiles.

It made her laugh, just enough to feel in control again. "I used a yoga breathing technique."

"I see." He leaned back against the island and watched her sip the rest of her water.

"More?" he asked when she held out the empty glass to him.

"No, thank you."

He set the glass on the island. "You're really all right?"

"Yes, and I apologize for suddenly making this discussion all about me. You were very upset about what happened with Wally."

"Wollings."

"Wollings, thank you."

"Yes, upset for him, and deeply remorseful for my part in it." He shook his head. "I've never confessed that to a soul. In fact, I'd quite forgotten the whole despicable incident. Perhaps finding our two missing men, Vince and Nate, as well as the truth of the gun in our backyard, will somehow redeem me for my part in Wollings' having to spend his life in a wheelchair." He shook his head. "Wollings got lots of help after the accident, but Toffee told us Nate was on his own."

"Orphaned, she said."

"I need to know he's all right." He boosted himself onto the island and swung his legs. "Or not."

Lyssa laughed. "You never sit up there."

"For a moment I felt like a boy again and wanted to do something normal ten-year-olds do. Join me?"

It was on her tongue to say, "You were *ten*?" But she'd been twelve and Manda eleven in her flashback, so ten was not so hard to believe.

She moved aside one of the stools, hoisted herself onto the island beside him, and swung her legs. "I'd forgotten how much fun this can be." She planted a kiss on his stubbly cheek. "You're all right?"

"I'm splendid," he said with a chuckle.

"Are *we* all right?"

His arm came around her, and she rested her head on his shoulder. "We are, though we'll need to do more of this laughing and leg-swinging if we want our sanity to survive this business of the gun."

Chapter 9

After a quick breakfast of toast and coffee, Kyle proposed they divvy up the next steps in the investigation and share their findings over an early dinner at home. He vowed to query Joel for someone to install their fountain, coerce the police to investigate the gun's criminal history, and follow up with Vince's friends.

Lyssa would scour the Internet for information about Vince and Nate during the past five years and anything she could find about Nate's parents' accident and their estate. As he took one last swallow of coffee, she requested, "Can you also ask Joel if he knows someone in the garden club?"

"Right. That ought to keep us out of trouble for a few hours, eh?"

Kyle reached Joel Cushman five minutes before the final CIO candidate, Paul, was due at his office door. "I'm looking for a couple of people you might know, and I'm desperately hoping Lyssa and I can get away to Myrtle Beach for the weekend. Can you help?"

He'd called the right person. Joel agreed to find Lyssa a contact for the garden club. He also assured Kyle it was feasible to fly to and from Myrtle Beach if he was willing to hire a pilot and a plane, and Joel happened to know a pilot who wanted very much to golf for the weekend.

"Let's get that started, shall we?" Kyle decided. "I'll work on convincing Lyssa."

When Joel offered his groundskeeper as a resource for the fountain and irrigation system, he added, "Why don't I ask Harold about planting the rose bushes for Lyssa, too?"

"Ah . . . no. She's invested a lot of time already buying supplies and studying the best way to go about it. I'm sure she's not ready to let that go."

Lyssa tried every trick she knew to find Vincent Thomas Tuttle and Nathan William Westover on the Internet. "No one's that invisible," she said to Kyle when, after two frustrating hours, she called to ask him for ideas. "I've used Google and two other search engines, plugged in every possible variation on their names, done the same with Facebook, Twitter, Pinterest, Instagram, and every other form of social media I can think of. Plus, I went back to my ancient MySpace account and poked around."

"Perhaps they're invisible on purpose."

"I don't know what that means."

"Nor do I. And it may not be true, but it's a possibility we shouldn't ignore."

"You don't have any more tip or tricks I can use, Dr. Pennington?"

"You've already tried more that I'd have thought of. But we do know Nate's parents died in a rockslide. You should be able to find something about that."

"Good thought, thanks. How's your morning?"

"Busy, and I won't be home for lunch. I'm meeting two friends of Vince and Nate. One of the professors here put me on to them, and Joel set up a lunch for us at the Manse. Care to join us?"

"Tempting," she told him. "However, I'll keep plugging here and, if I come up empty on the Westover parents, I'll take my search to the library."

"Just be aware you may hear from Joel about a person to install our fountain."

"Perfect, they're delivering it tomorrow late morning. Love you, darling, bye."

It took half an hour to find a reference to William and Marjorie Westover in the *Tompkins Falls Press* archive. There, Lyssa found the notice for a memorial service for the Westovers and obituaries for each parent.

She searched backward in time and found a *Press* article that told her the Westovers' only child was one of three survivors of a rockslide in the Vermillion Cliffs. At the time of the article, the son, a recent graduate of Tompkins College, remained in the hospital in Flagstaff and was expected to undergo more surgery to his damaged left leg. The Westovers' church had opted to hold a memorial service within days of the accident. That seemed callous. *Why not wait for Nate to return to Tompkins Falls?*

The same *Press* article linked her to a story in a national wire service reporting the accident. A guided group hike in the Vermillion Cliffs area of Arizona had suffered heavy casualties, twenty-seven deaths, including the guide, in a massive rockslide. William and Marjorie Westover were listed among those killed. Their bodies were not recovered. Lyssa shuddered. That might explain the immediacy of the memorial service, but she still wondered why they would hold it without Nate. How long had he been hospitalized? Did the church feel no obligation to support him in his loss? Had a next of kin made the decision after talking with Nate?

She phoned the church office. Though the minister had moved on a few years ago, the office administrator remembered the Westovers. Without having to consult the files, she explained that Nate was his parents' next of kin and there were no other relatives on either side. He really had been orphaned, as Toffee said. The church community was horrified by the deaths of Bill and Margie, and church council felt strongly a memorial service would help them heal from the tragedy. As for how the church assisted Nate during his recovery, she couldn't recall. Lyssa thanked her and asked if she knew Nate's current status. She had no idea.

Fifteen minutes searching for related or follow-up articles turned up nothing. Why was there so little said about the event and its aftermath? She snapped her fingers. Maybe there was a lawsuit and nobody was allowed to talk about it. *Bet you a quarter.*

Regardless, what had it been like for the three survivors, all of them badly injured? Would an experience like that scar a person for life psychologically, if not physically?

But Nate had gone on for a master's degree from Geneseo. The Alumni Office at Tompkins College had not been able to tell her if he had finished that degree. In her heart, she imagined him teaching, still friends with Vince, sharing their lives and careers and families. What was the reality?

She needed to make that trip to Geneseo soon to see what else she could learn. The only other information they had about Nate was what Natalie Horowitz had said, that Nate had sold her the house after a tense negotiation. He'd come to the closing, was cold toward her during the proceedings, and rushed out right after, back to his teaching job. Was it Nate's hand that reached up to her from the pit of her garden?

Finally, in a fifteen-minute window between meetings, Kyle had an opportunity to call Hank Moran's cell phone. He launched into his rehearsed speech.

"Hank, Kyle Pennington, 57 Seneca Street. Thanks for reassuring my wife and our friend Bree there's no body in the backyard. We're grateful for your expertise, and we need every bit we can get with this gun thing." *Please, Lord, don't let him hang up.* "I wouldn't be calling you on your cell, but Lyssa and I are in over our heads with this.

"We're bumbling our way through the neighborhood, apologizing and asking questions, and that has led us to two previous owners of our property. Along the way we've caused everyone pain and worry. Lyssa is torn up by the thought of whoever was harmed by the gun before it was buried, and I'm worried sick about our legal culpability and, frankly, our safety, supposing a murderer is aware we've discovered the hidden gun." He swallowed hard at the thought. "If that weren't enough, we've both got jobs we should be attending to with all our energy, just as you have. We need your expert help."

The man on the other end cleared his throat. "Why don't you take a breath, Dr. Pennington, and we can talk about how you think I can help?"

Kyle exhaled a laugh and filled his lungs. "Thank you." *How does he know about my PhD?*

"I would have hung up, Kyle, but you're someone I've been wanting to meet. Everyone praises the work you're doing at the college with network security. I understand it was a disaster before you stepped in."

"It's shaping up," Kyle said.

"Tell me what you know already about the gun."

"We've worked out for ourselves that it was most likely planted under the tree shortly before Memorial Day five years ago, in May the same year as the infamous ice storm."

"I remember that storm. February that year. How did you arrive at May as the time frame?"

Kyle told him about the wedding the Tuttles had attended immediately after the tree was planted. "Rich Wessels' son was the groom, and the wedding was in Utica."

"I'll use that information to pinpoint the date, thank you."

"You're investigating officially, are you, Hank?"

"I wouldn't say that."

"But you do have Lyssa's gun and there is blood on it, according to Bree. Whose blood?"

"Human blood that was missed when someone cleaned the visible surfaces of the weapon sometime before burial."

"So there are no fingerprints other than the Davis lad and Bree Shaughnessy?"

"Correct. The blood doesn't match anyone in our databases, and it isn't from one of the Westover family."

"Including the son Nathan?" Kyle pressed.

"I can't say."

Bloody hell. Why not?

"Hank, does one of your databases concern unsolved homicides?"

"It does."

"New York State only?"

"Correct. What else can *you* tell *me*, Kyle?"

Kyle supposed he was lucky to have gotten that much information. "The weapon was buried in what was then the

Tuttle's backyard, probably while the parents were away for the Wessels wedding. Of the Tuttle family, the parents Tommy and Rikki are both dead. The son Vince, we believe, lives and teaches in Green Bay, Wisconsin, but we have no address or phone number, nor does his Aunt Janet Tuttle."

"Got it." Key clicks suggested Hank was entering Kyle's new input into his notes.

"We also know there was a girl visiting the Tuttles with Vince that weekend—Patty Beck. The neighbor who's still in the hospital heard arguments to the effect Vince planned to marry the girl, and the parents objected, very strongly. Vince and the girl had departed by the time the parents and Janet returned from the wedding. Janet says the young couple settled in Green Bay and purchased an expensive lakefront condo, although Vince was said to be a schoolteacher."

"Got it."

"So you'll be following up with those people? That would save us having to do it ourselves."

"I can't say. Truthfully, Kyle, I don't see that happening."

Kyle blew out his frustration. "I guess Lyssa and I will be traveling to Green Bay soon. Or perhaps Bree and Lyssa will go on their own for a wild-goose chase and, possibly, stumble into a killer who's determined not to be found." *Let him chew on that.*

"I don't recommend anyone make that trip."

Kyle silently agreed. He changed tactics. "Hank, my geography of the states is sketchy, but I believe there are half a dozen states between Tompkins Falls, New York, and Green Bay, Wisconsin. If a body were transported in a vehicle traveling from Point A to Point B and dumped along the way, data about that victim's blood and the gunshot wound might have found its way into one of those states' homicide databases, mightn't it?"

"Where are you going with this?"

"Lyssa and I are keen to know if the blood on our gun is a match for any of those unidentified bodies. In a technical sense, I am well qualified to hack those databases, although I have no intention of doing so. Any chance you'll be checking that?"

"Might be a good idea." Hank said.

Kyle's relief came out in a whoosh. "Thank you."

"Kyle, I need to know how you got this phone number."

"From Bree."

"Let me rephrase that. *Exactly* how did you get this number?"

"Ah. I didn't hack it from anywhere. Bree had coffee with us one morning this week. When she said you had the gun and the gun had blood on it, I asked how I could reach you. She then searched the contacts on her phone and held the phone out for me to copy your cell number."

"I'll have a word with her, thank you. Now let me explain something about my unofficial interest in this seemingly innocuous case of a weapon discharged within the city limits of Tompkins Falls."

Which would not be something of interest to the State Police. "Right."

"I assume you're aware that Bree is my buddy Peter's kid sister. She was pretty close to the gun when it discharged, close enough to get detailed photographs of the weapon before the shooting. She could have been killed when the gun discharged. Probably the same is true for your wife?"

"Lyssa was actually in the line of fire and managed to move aside before it discharged." Kyle swallowed hard and sucked in a breath.

"That's motivation enough to do a few things not in the procedure manual, even without hard evidence your gun is associated with another crime."

"I see. I'm grateful. Officer, I'm aware that the law considers the gun to be the homeowner's property, and that would be my wife, Lyssa." Kyle enunciated each word of his final point. "In my wife's best interest, I need to know whose gun was buried and unearthed on our property and whose blood is on the gun."

A raspy exhale on the other end of the connection told Kyle he'd pushed as far as he dared. "Registered to William Westover of 53 Seneca Street, Tompkins Falls, deceased. According to the TSA, the gun did not accompany him out West when he and his wife were killed. That's all I can tell you."

Hank ended the connection.

Kyle sat back in his chair. *So who took possession of the gun?* Probably Nate Westover.

His finger stopped short of pressing Lyssa's number. But not necessarily Nate. The house had been unoccupied for months before Nate sold it to Natalie Horowitz.

Lyssa arrived at the Tompkins Falls Public Library at eleven, just as two dozen small children and their moms poured out through the double doors. She held the door open for them and enjoyed the commotion. "Storytime?" she asked one mother, who nodded and said how terrific the children's librarian was, especially during school breaks.

Stories, crafts, and lessons were scheduled every day of the week. *Will we have storytime in Cornwall for our children?*

Once inside, Lyssa pulled together her notes before approaching the desk. The librarian, Kathy Regis, reviewed what Lyssa had done to date. As the next step, she recommended a few of the library's proprietary online directories and databases.

After looking into Wisconsin teachers, public schools, and Green Bay real estate, they scoured the archives of local and regional newspapers for the Green Bay area. Their search netted them only a few bits of information about Vince, nothing about Nate, and one crumb about Patty.

Vince had won Green Bay Area Teacher of the Year twice. He had, for the past three years, coordinated the volunteers for a citywide primary-grades reading enrichment program. Before that he had served for two consecutive years on the board for his condominium complex on the waterfront. They found no photos of Vince, no speeding tickets or other mention in the newspaper, and only one mention of his wife.

Lyssa asked Kathy, "This last article about Vince's award says his wife, Patty, works in the hospitality industry. What does that mean?"

"She could be anything from a receptionist to an event planner to a manager at a hotel or a casino, anything like that."

"Let's try to find out more about her."

They shifted their focus to business organizations, casinos, resorts, hotel chains, and commercial sites. There was nothing for Patty Beck or Patty Tuttle.

"And you've you tried Facebook and other social media sites. If you need a photo, yearbooks may be your only option at this point. College or high school libraries will have copies."

"I did find photos of Vince and Nate at Tompkins College in their senior yearbook. Now I know his school and the condo complex where he lives. That's more than his own aunt knows."

"Oh." The librarian's tone of surprise made Lyssa pause.

"What are you thinking?"

"If that's true, they may be protecting their privacy. For any number of reasons. And they're smart to do it."

"You mean, they might be deliberately limiting their online exposure to protect their identities or ensure no one bothers them in their private lives?" That was a twist on Kyle's theory about Nate and Vince wanting to be invisible, one without negative connotations.

Lyssa thanked Kathy for all her help. Tomorrow she'd go to Geneseo, whether Bree could go with her or not. For now, she was hungry. No wonder. It was after two already.

Back at the house, she wrapped herself in one of Kyle's warmest sweaters and settled at the patio table with a mug of green tea and a salad topped with goat cheese. Out of the corner of her eye, she noticed a car roll silently up her driveway.

Promptly at one o'clock, Kyle had arrived at the Manse Grille for lunch with the Weaver twins, generously arranged by Manse owner Joel Cushman. Joel had told the brothers only that lunch was on him, and that his close friend, Kyle Pennington, wanted information about an old classmate of theirs at Tompkins College. After seating the twins and Kyle at a choice table by the window, Joel said, "These guys are my toughest competitors."

"At least you admit it," the twin with the shaved head said with an easy laugh. "I'm Mike." He pointed to his brother, who was identical except for a full head of curly brown hair. "My kid brother, Mark, six minutes younger, and the financial brains of our family's restaurant business."

Mark told Kyle, "Joel's mostly kidding about being in competition. Here in the Finger Lakes, where the economy is up one year and down the next, we have a common goal to attract tourists to the area and keep the locals coming out for good food and conversation."

"Well said. I'll leave you to enjoy the Manse's good food and your own good conversation." Joel departed with a wave.

Once their orders were in, Kyle eased into his questions. "Professor Chivarri told me your family has a home somewhere on the lake."

"That's our family's property," Mike said, pointing across the lake and to the right. "The big red barn is an organic farm, and that's our parents' house, the gray one to the south. Mark and I have smaller homes for our families, past the tree break. You can't really see them from here."

"Sounds like you're making the Finger Lakes your home, both of you?" Kyle asked.

"Wouldn't live anywhere else," Mike answered.

"Kyle, Joel said you have questions for us," Mark said. "Maybe we should get right to them."

"Good." He straightened the fork and knife at his place. "By any chance did you have a classmate named Wessels?"

"Charlie Wessels, yeah," Mike answered. "Up until high school. Then he went to a prep school somewhere in New England. We didn't see him much after that."

Mike's on board, Mark's not. "Perhaps I should back up a little and tell you why I sought out Professor Chivarri." Kyle looked directly at Mark.

"That'll work." Mark thanked the waiter for his iced tea.

"Quick background: my wife and I bought the house at 57 Seneca Street in College Heights, and we understand the Tuttle family lived there before us. Chivarri thought you were in college with Vince Tuttle and might be able to tell us about him, possibly get us in touch with him."

"One of the old gang." Mike clapped his brother on the shoulder. "Where is Vince these days?"

"Green Bay, last I heard," Mark answered.

"No way. He was a Seahawks fan."

"I guess the Seahawks didn't offer him a job, bro," Mark said with a chuckle that was music to Kyle's ears. "He went into teaching, remember?"

"I forgot about that. I always had him pegged for corporate advertising," Mike said. "He had a lot of talent as an artist and also had a way with words. I remember, now, when we tried to get him to wait tables, he turned us down to work at the library in their reading program."

"He loved teaching kids. Thanks." Mark took a roll from the basket Kyle passed. "Why do you want to find him?"

"We found some things when we moved in that belong to his family, and we thought he might want them."

"I knew his dad had passed. His mother, too?" Mike asked.

"She died within the year, in Myrtle Beach, where she'd been living with Vince's aunt. The aunt doesn't have contact information for Vince."

Mike cocked his head. "We don't either, do we?"

But Mark's attention was on Kyle. "Does this have anything to do with the gun that turned up?" His voice had changed from good-guy friendly to no-nonsense manager.

"Er, yes," Kyle answered.

"What gun?" Mike wanted to know.

Mark held up one finger and carried on a side conversation with his brother that explained the discovery of the gun and the accidental shooting of the neighbor.

"As for the gun, none of us hunted, as far as I know," Mark told Kyle.

"It was a small revolver."

"I can't imagine the Tuttles having a gun in the house."

As he spoke, their food arrived, and Mike proposed a toast, "To good food."

All three raised their glasses, and Kyle took the first bite of his trout. "Delicious. I'll have to ask how they season this."

"Good steak here," Mark said. "And crisp salad."

For several minutes, the only sound at the table was clinking silverware and chewing.

"So, the lady who got shot, is she going to be all right?" Mike asked midway through his burger.

"She's recovering nicely and should be home in a week or so," Kyle said. "Her sister's staying at her home, and the neighbors are pitching in with lawn care and shopping and the like."

"The gun was actually buried in the garden?"

"Yes." Kyle set down his fork. "Lyssa said it was wrapped in several layers—a leather pouch, covered by a bandanna, wrapped in oilcloth that looked like part of an old picnic tablecloth. All that was stuffed in an adult-size lunchbox. Does that make any sense to either of you?"

The twins traded a squinty-eyed look. "Bizarr-o," they chorused.

"We thought so, too," Kyle said. "From what we've been able to piece together, the gun was buried the weekend before Memorial Day five years ago, the year of the ice storm. We've no idea why it was buried that way or how it had been used before it was buried."

"What do the police think?" Mark asked and ate the last bite of his salad.

"The police are not interested in anything about the gun, prior to the shooting this week."

Mike shrugged, but Mark said, "If I found something like that, I'd wonder what the deal was. I mean, nobody in their right mind would do something like that."

"Come on, bro, it was probably a joke." Mike got his mouth around the last of his burger.

"A gun? I don't think so. Did the police know if it had been fired? Other than the shot that almost killed your neighbor?"

"There was human blood on it," Kyle said quietly.

"Jeez, I wish I could help you." Mark set down his fork. "Five years ago was one year after we all graduated from Tompkins College. Mike got married that summer."

"In June, right. Vince accepted the invitation but didn't show," Mike said. "Nice that he had a job somewhere, but that pissed me off. How hard is it to travel in June?"

"Did Nate Westover come to your wedding?" Kyle asked.

Both twins looked wordlessly at their empty plates. The busboy arrived to clear the dishes.

Kyle started fresh. "When would you have seen Vince last? Do you recall?"

"Before my wedding, for sure," Mike said. "He was working on a master's degree, so probably spring break, a few months before the wedding."

"That sounds right. Andy had a party when the snow finally melted that year, and Vince came." Mark thanked the waitress for the dessert menu.

"Yeah." Mike snapped his fingers. "He had that hot chick with him, remember? Blond, real sexy. Somebody he met in grad school. I can't think of her name." Mike finished his beer and set the glass down with a thud. "Man, she was all over him."

"You're shaking your head, Mark," Kyle prompted.

"She was *so* not his type." He blew air through his lips. "I couldn't see that working."

"You've got a point, bro." Mike lifted a finger and ordered another beer.

"You never knew him, but Vince was a real serious guy," Mark said. "Don't get me wrong, he had a great sense of humor, but he had his head on straight about what he wanted to do with his life and how to make a good living and support a family. He had it all mapped out. Except this chick didn't fit. She was so not going to be a soccer mom and president of the PTA."

Mike snorted. "Totally. You're driving, right, bro?"

"I'm driving. Anyway that's the last time I remember seeing Vince. I wonder if they got married?" he asked his twin.

"Nah, he would have invited us, for sure." Mike ran his hand over his shaved head. "But what was he doing with a gun that Memorial Day?"

"The neighbors thought there was a party at the Tuttles, and the parents were away for the weekend," Kyle said.

"Wait, you're saying Vince had a party at his house and didn't invite us?" Mike squawked. "No way."

"Why's that?" Kyle asked.

"We were best buds—Vince and Nate, Mark and me, and Andy."

Mark nodded, his face creased with pain. "Yeah. I don't know if you heard, our buddy Andy Rosario passed away a couple of years ago?"

"Professor Chivarri told me, yes. I'm sorry for your loss, both of you," Kyle said.

"Thanks, man."

"What can you tell me about Nate Westover? He lived a couple houses away from the Tuttles."

"It's hard to talk about Nate," Mark said. "Something happened to change him."

People said that about Vince, too. Kyle kept the thought to himself.

"I understand his parents were killed in a rockslide," Kyle said. "It must have been a horrible trauma for Nate."

Mark drew in a deep breath and let it out. "He was never the same. Drank a lot, argued about everything. Wait, you asked about Charlie Wessels when we first sat down. Why was that?"

"Just curious about something Vince's aunt said. The tree where the gun was buried was planted the weekend of Charlie's wedding in Utica, and the Tuttles were in Utica all weekend for the festivities. Except Vince hadn't been invited to Charlie's wedding. Were you at that wedding?"

"Us? No. We never really hung with Charlie. We all knew each other from the lake, and we were in the same class in elementary school, like I said, but that's all."

"Did you know the bride?"

"No," Mark said.

"Yes," Mike corrected him. "Remember he introduced her when she came to meet the parents? Pretty girl."

"I would remember a pretty girl, but I'm drawing a blank, bro."

"Black hair, lots of eye makeup. Not your type. He brought her to the summer festival and introduced her around. Probably the year after college."

Mark just shook his head.

"So she didn't spend summers on Chestnut Lake?" Kyle asked.

"No, they met in college. They both went to Cornell and stayed for law school."

"I see, thanks." *Janet led us on a wild-goose chase.* "One more thought. Was Nate at Andy's party that spring break when you last saw Vince?"

"No," Mark answered.

"Sure he was," Mike said.

"No, he wasn't," Mark gripped his water glass with white knuckles. "Andy didn't invite him." He told Kyle, "Not for public discussion, but Vince's parents barred Nate from their home. I don't know the details. But I guess

Andy's mom found out. I think they were both in some club together."

"Garden club?" Kyle suggested.

"Could be. Anyway, Mrs. Tuttle refused to let Nate come into her house, so Mrs. Rosario banned him from Andy's party," Mark said.

"I can see her point," Mike said. "But nothing was the same without Nate. He had a way of making us feel like family. He didn't have brothers or sisters or aunts or uncles. Other than his parents, we were his family."

"True." Mark asked his brother, "Has anyone seen him?"

Mike turned his beer glass around with his fingers. "You and I haven't. Does he still live in your neighborhood?" he asked Kyle.

"No, that house was sold four years ago. No one seems to know where he lives," Kyle said. "I asked several of his professors from Tompkins College, and he hasn't stayed in touch with any of them. We're waiting for Nick Nunzio to come back from Florida to ask him."

"Nunzio!" Mike slapped his brother on the back. "Remember him from high school? What a douche bag."

"He wasn't your favorite teacher?" Kyle declined dessert and asked for coffee.

"Try least favorite." Mike shook his head and swigged the last of his beer. "Wait, he's your neighbor?"

Chapter 10

Lyssa's heart thudded as a car nosed past the corner of the house into full view and glided noiselessly to a stop. Relief flooded her when she recognized the VW Passat hybrid with her brother-in-law at the wheel. She smiled broadly at Joel and tapped her hand over her heart.

"Did we scare you?" Joel asked as he crossed the patio.

"Kyle said you might be in touch, but I never imagined you'd drop in unannounced. Welcome, both of you."

"Lyssa, this is Harold, my director of buildings and grounds at the Manse."

She left her salad untouched and held out her hand to the stern-faced man. "Pleasure to meet you, Harold."

"Same. Is that big ugly hole the garden you're working on?" A twitch at the corner of his mouth might have been a smile.

Joel confirmed it with a wink.

"That's my garden," she said with a laugh. "Did Joel tell you we plan to drop a granite block into the very center and have it issue forth a soothing, silent flow of water for eternity? Know anyone who can do that for us, Harold?"

"All you need is the right professional, I always say. Tell me how you plan to do the rest—I mean, prepare the soil so your roses will thrive?"

Challenge on. She motioned him forward, and the three of them strolled to the edge of the garden. "My husband's gardener in Cornwall gave me instructions, and we'll follow them to the letter." She gestured to her stack of fertilizer, cow manure, and bone meal, then to the separate mound of peat moss, as she explained the work she and Bree planned to do after the fountain's installation—spreading materials and mixing them together to prepare a bed for the rose bushes. "Including bone meal, which I understand is poo-pooed in some circles."

"I use bone meal, too," he said. "Were you planning to tamp the soil down every time you mix?"

"Yes, we figure we'll look like we were stomping grapes. Thank heaven our neighbor is still in the hospital and won't see us."

"How large is the block of granite, and how deep is your center hole?"

She told him the dimensions and was glad to see Harold nod.

"By the way, I checked out the company in my business databases and called a few customer references," she told them. "They're reputable and so are their products."

"You've done a good job so far. Here's what I recommend. We'll create a foundation for the fountain with layers of stone and sand and gravel, position the fountain, and surround it with decorative stones. Before that, though, we'll need to run power for the pump, and a water line."

She clunked her forehead with the heel of her hand. "I forgot about power."

"And, as long as we're bringing water to the fountain, we could set up irrigation to the whole garden and extend the lines to your back yard, if you want."

"Definitely. That's fantastic, Harold."

"When's the fountain being delivered?"

"Sometime this Friday. Oh my gosh, that would be tomorrow."

"I'll get someone over here this afternoon to lay the water lines and run some power out to the garden."

"So quickly? That's amazing, thank you."

Harold shrugged. "We've had extra hands this week. A few of our summer helpers asked for work over their spring break, so work at the Manse is ahead of the game. We'll lay the foundation tomorrow, bring in a winch Saturday morning and get the fountain positioned, hooked up, and running. Are all four sides of the granite block the same?"

"Yes, and we'd like it square to the yard, no quirky angles."

"That makes it easy. You and Kyle don't even have to be here. If need be, we still have Sunday to work out any glitches. How does that sound?"

"Fantastic. Wonderful. Thanks a million. And thank you, Joel."

Joel nodded without comment. He stayed where he was, as Harold returned to the VW. "Nice job with the research. You've done a lot of hard work. You might want to consider having Harold do the actual planting, too."

A red flag went up. "Whose idea was that?" She hated her harsh tone.

"My idea, no one else's. Just a thought."

"Thanks, but I'm looking forward to the planting, and Bree Shaughnessy is, too. In fact, she's counting on it. Thanks a million for making this fountain project happen so quickly."

"Glad to help. I'm hoping you and I can have a conversation, if you're not too busy."

"Kyle's due home for dinner at five or before. What's on your mind, brother-in-law?"

"I have to return Harold to the Manse. Any chance you can ride along and have coffee with me there? Manda or I can drive you back here."

"Sure, I guess." Her heart pounded just the way it had when he'd stolen silently into the driveway a few minutes ago. "Can you give me a hint?"

Joel squinted into the distance. "What you and Kyle are doing has me worried. I may be able to help."

Lyssa's mouth opened, but no words came out.

Her brother-in-law had reserved an intimate room off the main dining room at his Manse Inn and Spa. White linen tablecloth, gleaming silver spoons, delicate china mugs, steaming carafe of coffee, and a sweeping view of Chestnut Lake. *Why is he doing this?*

When Joel finished telling her what her husband had done, the illusion created by the luxurious setting shattered. Phrases like "threatened the state police in six states" and "hacking high-security databases" flew at her.

Lyssa sat rigidly, her coffee untouched as she squinted out the window. She identified with the churning dark blue water and the white caps that looked like horses' manes thrown back in frenzy. *Kyle, what were you thinking?*

Abruptly, she raised her hand and cut Joel off with a snappy, "Give me a minute."

She palmed her phone, pressed a number that she'd added to her contacts yesterday morning, and smiled benignly at Joel as the connection went through.

"Who is this?" Hank Moran's gruff voice greeted her on his personal cell.

"Professor Lyssa Pennington calling. What exactly did my husband, Kyle, say to you that has my family telling me he's put us in jeopardy and can't be trusted?" Lyssa huffed out her breath at Joel.

Joel reached for her hand on the table. "Don't, Lyssa."

She snatched her hand away, stood up, and strode to the window.

"Mrs. Pennington," Hank told her, "you'll want to talk to your husband about that."

"I intend to, Hank. And don't patronize me. My brother-in-law, Joel Cushman, is telling me my husband threatened to hack your databases and those of every state police agency between here and Green Bay. Is that the truth?"

"That's inaccurate. He made me aware that he's technically capable of such a crime and that he has no intention of committing that crime. My take is he was trying to convey the desperation you both feel at the nonresponse of law enforcement to your discovery of the weapon in your garden."

"Thank you for being so precise with your words." She pressed her hand to her chest, tried to slow her galloping heart. "Is there anything else I should know about your conversation with my husband?"

"He's aware that you and he are over your heads with investigating any crime that might have been committed with the gun. I agree with him. Is there anything else *you* should tell *me*? New information you've turned up, for example?"

"Since Kyle and I last talked, I've located Vince Tuttle." She drew in a steadying breath before giving him the few facts she and the librarian had found earlier.

138

"Good work. Now, stay out of harm's way and watch your backs. If there's a body somewhere, and I'm inclined to think there is, we'll find it. And if there's killer out there, he's clever enough to have gotten away with murder for years. Don't mess with him, Lyssa. You or Kyle."

"Understood. Thank you." *God, help us. This is serious.* Panic rose in her chest, and she fought it with breathwork.

Hank's voice startled her when he growled, "And don't give this number to anyone." He broke the connection.

Lyssa pressed the heels of her hands to her forehead. With a squeak of relief, her tears spilled over. Kyle hadn't been stupid, but what was he thinking? And what game was Joel playing? And whose body was it? Not Vince Tuttle's. *I have to be able to trust the men in my life, in my family.*

Joel's hands were warm on her shaking shoulders, and he pulled her into a hug.

She pounded her fist harmlessly against his arm. "You were wrong, you know." She twisted away. "How dare you make false claims about my husband! What exactly was your point, Joel?"

"That wasn't my intent. Sit down, let's have some coffee, and you tell me what Hank said."

"Caffeine is the last thing I need."

"It's decaf. And your sister just strolled in. Okay if she joins us?"

Lyssa whirled in Manda's direction. "Your husband just lied to me about Kyle's phone call to Hank Moran, and suggested we're moments away from having Homeland Security on the our doorstep. I don't need this." She flashed angry eyes on Joel. "Kyle and I have dropped everything to investigate a possible murder in our backyard, and he was just trying to get police support. Why would you suspect him of committing a crime against the government?"

Joel stood with his mouth open.

Manda stopped just inside the doorway. "Lyssa, you're overreacting. Are you having a panic attack?" she asked, her voice grave with concern.

"Yes," Lyssa snapped. "Triggered by your rich and powerful husband, who is of the opinion my husband is a menace to police in six states."

"Stop, Lyssa, you know that's not true," Joel said. "Manda, please close the door."

Lyssa countered, "Do not close the door. I will tell you what Hank Moran just reported to me, and then we will not speak of Kyle's phone call again. Agreed?"

Husband and wife exchanged a look. From the shifting of eyes and twitching of cheeks, Lyssa gathered they were not in agreement. Manda dropped her eyes with a little puff of frustration.

Joel nodded curtly. "Agreed."

Lyssa recited her entire conversation with Hank, without interruption. After a moment's silence, she said, "Manda, if you still want to grill me about it in the morning, let's you and I go to the Early Risers meeting and then walk along the shore after."

Manda pursed her lips and glanced at the main dining room beyond their private space. "Sounds good. I'll pick you up at six-fifteen."

Following the direction of Manda's gaze, Lyssa noted that the dining room was filling up with people dressed in business attire. Was it five already? Kyle would be home and worried about her.

With a pointed look at the fourth chair, Lyssa asked Joel, "Is someone else invited?"

Joel's face froze. He worked his jaw back and forth and put on a smile. "Sounds foolish, I know, but I thought it would be nice for you and Kyle to have an early dinner with Manda and me."

Lyssa gave a hollow laugh. "He and I committed to having dinner together tonight so we could catch each other up on our investigation. Which is when I'd have learned from him about his conversation with Hank. The real one. You've preempted that by inviting him here, and I suppose he agreed, as I did, to the command performance."

Joel nodded and attempted a smile. "You hate me right now, don't you?"

"Could you just explain how it is you know about Kyle's conversation with Hank before me?"

"Even though I got it wrong?" Joel sat in one of the chairs and motioned Manda and Lyssa to join him at the table. "According to Bree's sister-in-law, Gwen, Hank called Bree to chew her out for giving out his personal cell number. Gwen told me Bree's version of what Kyle said to Hank."

"Gwen being Officer Peter Shaughnessy's wife?" Lyssa asked Manda, who nodded. "Did it occur to you Bree might have embellished the story?"

Joel tapped his fingers on the immaculate white tablecloth. "I'm sorry. My intent was to get all of us on the same page and see where and how Manda and I can be of help. I *do* know people and I *can* help, Lyssa, if you'll let me."

She chose her words deliberately. "I am ravenous because I came with you instead of eating the lunch I'd just fixed, which the birds are probably enjoying right now on my patio. Kyle is probably hungry, too. I'd like to have dinner with you, but if you bring up Kyle's phone call again, or lecture us, I'm walking out. I'll walk home if I have to."

Manda's eyes blazed at her sister. "We're trying to help, Lyssa," she said, her voice shrill.

Joel cleared his throat to get his wife's attention, but she ignored the warning. "He and I are afraid for you and Kyle. You shouldn't be doing any of this investigating. It's making you crazy. Hello? And it's probably dangerous."

Joel pressed Manda's forearm. He told the two sisters, quietly, with a smile, "You ladies chat for a bit while I apologize to my clientele and intercept Kyle on his way in."

Lyssa noticed several concerned diners craning their necks for a better view of the private room. She smiled brightly and gave them a finger wave.

Joel closed the door behind him as he exited to the main dining room.

She fiddled with a coffee mug. Manda leaned toward her, hands reaching halfway across the table. "I mean it, Lyssa. We want to help, and we're scared."

"I'm pretty scared, too, Manda. About Mrs. Winkel, who's still in the hospital. About foolish Richie Davis, who's still in jail, poor kid. And I'm even more worried about the violence that goes with that gun. Kyle and I are doing our best to understand what crime was committed, when, and by whom. So far, we have the 'when'."

She reached for a clean mug, poured a fresh cup for herself, loaded it with cream and sugar, and drank half. "And I've located the young man who disappeared with his girlfriend the night of the crime, Vince Tuttle. Hank Moran was glad to get that information, and I'm hopeful someone in authority will follow up with Vince. He can tell us what really happened that night."

She eyed her sister, and her tears spilled over. "Manda, I'm serious when I say they wouldn't have been interested in those facts, unless Kyle had said what he did to Hank." She took a big swallow of her coffee. "Much as I hate what he did." The mug banged as she set it down, and coffee sloshed onto the white linen cloth.

Kyle suspected Lyssa's light laughter and cheery conversation during their impromptu family dinner were just a cover. On the drive home, he glanced at her from time to time, and each time she sat rigid in the dove-soft leather seat, her head averted. Only when the two of them were in the kitchen, sorting mail and charging cell phones, did he test the waters. "Fancy some tea, my love?"

She nodded without comment, her face set in a frown.

Worse than I thought.

The pot of tea sat brewing under its cozy before he ventured again into troubled waters. "Out with it. I can see you're fuming."

There was to be no warm-up. Eyes burning, voice hard, she told him, "Don't ever put me in this situation again, for any reason. I may have saved your butt with Joel and Manda tonight, but I need you to hear me when I tell you that I honor my citizenship in New York State and the United States, and I don't want either of those bureaucracies believing I'm in cahoots with, or even married to, someone who threatens law enforcement."

"I did not threaten—"

"Kyle, anyone with a brain—even your intellectually inferior wife who happens to have a PhD from a major research university—can see the implied threat in what you said to Hank."

"Hold on. Did we not agree that we needed the police to take responsibility for protecting us?" Prickles at the base of his brain warned him to get his temper in hand.

"Absolutely we did."

"And did you not ask me to make the phone call to Hank because he was more likely to take me, a man, seriously than you, a woman?"

"I did. But surely there was a less inflammatory way to go about it?"

"Why do you say 'inflammatory'?"

"When I finally turned my phone back on after the library, I saw a million texts from Bree, and Joel and Manda were ready to eat you alive tonight."

"If you'd had your phone turned on you'd have gotten my call about my conversation with Hank. I didn't feel it was appropriate to leave a message."

"Yes. Agreed. But let's hope Bree and Gwen and Joel and Manda haven't blurted their interpretation to anyone else. We'd have Homeland Security at our front door. Isn't it bad enough we've got a gun in our backyard with someone's blood on it?"

"Why do you think Homeland Security—?"

"Because we're living in an age of terrorism and cybercrime. Kyle, I implore you, don't identify yourself with one of those crimes. Because as soon as you do, I'm implicated as well, and I won't have it."

"Sweetheart, I have an impeccable, international reputation as one of the good guys relative to cybercrime." That made her swallow hard. It was, after all, an irrefutable fact. He'd built his career on his distinctive expertise with encryption, and his integrity was above reproach.

"And was that the only tactic you had that would get Hank Moran to listen?"

"As it turned out, yes. And the state police are now cooperating with states between here and Green Bay to see if there's a match between the ballistics and the blood on our gun, and their unsolved homicides. Correct me if I'm wrong, but none of that was happening yesterday."

She took a step back and studied the tea cozy. "Are they doing that?" Her voice reflected surprise and, perhaps, relief.

While he'd made his point, her ragged breathing signaled another panic attack in progress. *Best tread carefully.*

"Yes, they are," he said gently.

"Good." Her lower lip trembled.

He took a step toward her, but she shied away and crossed her arms in front of her chest.

"Kyle, I can't believe you would use threatening tactics like that. What were you thinking?"

His teeth set in a snarl. She meant it rhetorically, but he answered her snarky comment anyway. His finger jabbed the counter with his every phrase. "Classic argumentation. When he praised my work at the college, he showed me my expertise with network security was my ace in the hole. He forced me to use it. I did. It got results."

"I'm not sure I believe he 'forced you to use it.' Is it possible you were just showing off or maybe—"

"Let's hear how you would have made them pay attention." *Oh Lord, that was a mistake.*

"I don't know at the moment, and I won't without a good night's sleep, which I'm not likely to get, thanks to you."

"Thanks to your family's interference, you mean." Now he'd done it.

She burst into tears, stomped up the stairs, and turned left at the top.

"Lyssa," he implored.

She shut the door to the guest room.

"Bloody hell," he muttered as he headed into his music room. He poured himself a brandy and sipped it as he shuffled through sheet music. No peaceful Bach Inventions tonight. He'd tackle the Chopin Scherzo. Controlled fury with clever intervals.

Fat lot of good that'll do your marriage.

Lyssa sobbed and punched her pillow through the Chopin, wept through the Brahms, and fell into a peaceful sleep the moment the Bach began.

Sometime after midnight, a hand rose from the hole in the center of the garden, found her in the guest room, and grabbed her by the throat.

She bolted upright and sucked air with noisy gasps. Stroking her throat, she scanned every corner of the room. She was alone.

White window curtains fluttered as the heat came on. She studied the lacy pattern traced on the linen panels by the streetlamp as it shone through the branches of a tree.

Her breathing eased, and her hand slid instinctively lower, to her breastbone, where she massaged with soothing pressure. Her newfound calm brought awareness. She wasn't alone.

Death was in the room with her.

Her mother's screams echoed in her head. Unbidden, images of the accident that had claimed her parents' lives played across her memory. They'd been drunk when they'd driven off the road into a ravine. Their car plunged through bushes and saplings, its headlong descent arrested when it wedged between two trees.

But that wasn't it. Those were not her mother's screams she'd heard in the dream. "Who is the woman screaming in my dream?" she asked the lacy image on the curtain.

"What is it, my love?" Kyle's voice was gentle as he settled on the mattress beside her.

"Our parents died instantly. The state police told us that."

"Look at me, Lyssa." He touched her shoulder. She faced him, eyes wide with terror.

"I didn't hear you come in." Her body was trembling.

"You were gasping and shouting. Bad dream?"

She nodded.

"Your parents?"

"Yes—no. I thought so, but first it was . . . Kyle, the hand reached up from the hole." She rested her head on his shoulder. "And choked me."

"It's all right, sweetheart. The police are handling it now. We'll be all right."

"Will we?" She clutched at his pajama top.

"Of course, my love. Why do you say that?"

"I'm so frightened by what you said to Hank, threatening to hack the law enforcement databases. That was insanely risky."

"I felt I had to say what I did. We needed the police to help, and now they are helping."

"Please, don't ever do anything like that again without considering the consequences to me."

"You know I chose my words carefully."

"Don't start that argument again. You can't win it with me."

"My statement stands, but all right. How's this then? I'll make every effort to talk with you before I take another risk. Honestly, I don't know how I could have warned you ahead in this case."

"At the very least, let me know right away afterward. I don't want to hear it from a third party. Any third party." She stuffed down the vision of Homeland Security escorting her husband away in handcuffs. "I can't have you dragged off to prison. I won't live that way."

"Agreed. And you'll do the same?"

"When would I ever...?" Her voice rose an octave.

"You've been known to put yourself in danger, sweetheart. I couldn't take it if anything happened to you."

Chapter 11

Just when she'd steeled herself for battle with her sister, she answered the front door to, not Manda's scowl, but Gianessa's dazzling smile.

"Good morning, Lyssa. It's just me."

"Where's Manda? What's going on? Why are you here?"

"Manda and I hashed over what happened yesterday, and I was voted to take you to our early AA meeting in her place. Ready?"

"Come in for a second," Lyssa said. "Kyle's having coffee. I'll get a sweater, since it's so chilly out."

As she ran up the stairs, she heard Gianessa tell herself in a singsong voice, "Good morning to you, too."

"Sorry, good morning," Lyssa called back.

She stopped at the mouth of the closet and drew her phone from her back jeans pocket. Her sister answered on the first ring.

Without waiting for a greeting, Lyssa said, "I'm sorry, Manda. For all of it. I'm a mess, I admit it. I'm glad you sent Gianessa. She'll help clear my head."

Silence. She filled her lungs, waiting, hoping Manda would forgive her.

"We're so worried about you, Lyssa. What happened with Mrs. Winkel was traumatic. It rocked your world."

"You're right, and it's not just Mrs. Winkel. Someone was murdered in this house and it's gone unnoticed and unpunished for five years."

"Oh. I didn't know that."

In the gathering dawn, Lyssa could just make out the pit of the garden through the bedroom window. "I have to know the truth."

"You have to get to a meeting and stay sober today, big sister."

"Right. First things first. Thank you. I love you."

"Dress warm."

"I almost forgot I came up here for a sweater."

"Make it a heavy hoodie." Her sister's voice dropped an octave on "heavy hoodie," and they both laughed.

They said their goodbyes, and Lyssa ran down the stairs. As she shrugged into her warm layer and stuffed her phone in the pouch, she overheard them in the kitchen.

Kyle was saying, "We've worked things out, but she had a terrible nightmare. At times I wonder if she's a bit psychic."

"When we talked after the shooting, I could tell she was very sensitive to the energy on the gun," Gianessa said.

"And to the house, too, it seems. I'll let her tell you the dream."

"You're talking about me, aren't you?" Lyssa made her voice light.

They started and turned wary eyes to her.

"I couldn't get through this horrible mess without you both," Lyssa said.

Kyle reached a hand toward her, and she gave him a hug and told him, "Love you, have a good day."

His arms tightened around her. "Roses and lily of the valley. My favorite way to start the day."

She kissed him. "I called Manda to apologize."

His face relaxed, and a smile lit his gray eyes.

Lyssa carried the picture of his smiling eyes with her out the front door, down the front steps, and out to the car. *God, don't let me damage my marriage and my friendships any further.*

Gianessa started up the SUV, and they rolled down Seneca Street.

Lyssa flipped down the mirror on her sun visor. "I look horrible, don't I?"

"Kyle said there were nightmares."

"Just the one. I'll tell you on our walk."

After the meeting, they headed to the willow path along the lakeshore. The deep blue water shimmered this morning. Gianessa stretched her arms overhead.

Lyssa followed her example, her face welcoming the brisk breeze on her face, letting it sweep away her tension. With the next inhale, her belly relaxed.

"I can't believe how much this helps," she told Gianessa.

"Good." She gestured for Lyssa to walk beside her. "I know they're predicting rain, but I'm loving the brilliant sunshine the universe has given us right now. Let's embrace it."

Lyssa relished the sun's warmth on her face, arms, and torso. She stood taller and matched her steps to Gianessa's as they quickened their pace. They had plenty of company this morning–runners, walkers, and bikers–on the two-mile path at the north end of Chestnut Lake.

After a quiet quarter mile, Lyssa slowed her steps and faced her sponsor. "When Kyle said I'm a bit psychic, you used the word sensitive. Whatever it is, it scares me."

Gianessa's violet eyes held a connection with Lyssa's for a moment. "My healing energy used to scare me, too. Once I accepted it as a force for good, I cultivated it and began using it to help people. You get to choose what you do with your psychic ability."

"Mine doesn't feel like a force for good." She trembled inside as she said it.

"Tell me."

Lyssa related the nightmare of the hand rising from the garden and choking her, the screams she'd heard that she'd mistaken for her mother's, and her reimagining of her parents' car descending into a ravine.

"I think you've left out some important details."

"Have I?"

"Close your eyes. Very quickly, tell me what you see."

"There's a white curtain at the window, and it has on it a shadow from the tree outside that looks like lace." She shuddered. "Or maybe a spider web." Chills ran down her back. "Yes, a web."

"What else?"

"I remember thinking I was alone and then realizing Death was there, too."

"What do you think that's about?"

An icy chill rushed through Lyssa. *God, help me, what's happening?*

"You're shaking. Tell me," Gianessa said insistently.

"I'm so afraid."

"What's the sensation? Tell me."

"Freezing cold, all through my body. Help me."

Gianessa wrapped her in a hug and rubbed her back vigorously. "Icy cold is how people sometimes describe evil."

"Someone died in our pretty little guest room, didn't they?" Lyssa choked on the words.

"If that's the truth, it will be revealed. Let's keep moving, get you warm again." They started forward at a brisk pace.

Lyssa focused on the movement of her pink sneakers, left foot, right foot, on the gravel path. After a few hundred steps, she looked out to the sparkling lake. "It's glorious this morning, isn't it? That color is like Manda's and my eyes. Kyle calls it sapphire."

"Nice recovery." Gianessa smiled. "Let's turn back. Does anything still bother you about yesterday, about the way you handled things?"

"Yes. Kyle and I had set aside the dinner hour yesterday to catch up on what we'd found in our investigation. We try to talk every evening so things don't get out of hand. The last two days defeated us. Fortunately, Wednesday Kyle set aside his job responsibilities, and we talked as we should have. Then we both caved to Joel's master plan yesterday. Honestly, Kyle did try to call me after his talk with Hank, but my phone was switched off. And . . ."

"And what? Tell me."

"I should have called Kyle, rather than Hank, when Joel lit into me."

"Why didn't you?"

Lyssa opened her mouth, then paused to think it through.

"I wasn't sure I trusted Kyle to tell it to me straight. Or maybe I didn't trust myself to know the truth when I heard it.

I do trust Kyle. But obviously Joel didn't trust him or he wouldn't have been all over me about Kyle's call to Hank. Then, once Hank told me what Kyle had really said, I didn't trust Joel either. I shut everyone down." She smiled ruefully and looked over at her friend. "I should have called you."

"You think?" Gianessa winked.

"Instead, I blasted Joel and Manda and froze Kyle out over our delicious dinner at the Manse." Lyssa closed her eyes and felt the quickening breeze swirl around her, lifting away her regrets. Refreshed, she told Gianessa, "I want to trust my husband. Implicitly."

"You should tell him that." Gianessa nodded toward the parking area, where Kyle stood beside his Lexus.

When they reached the edge of the lot, he came forward but stopped a few feet from Lyssa. "I've taken off the next few hours for us to talk."

"Thank you," Lyssa said, her voice barely a whisper. She swallowed the lump in her throat.

He reached out and she went into his arms. She heard the Cushman's SUV start up and crunch across the gravel. Kyle stroked her back, and she inhaled the scent of him, ginger and cypress with a hint of musk.

"Since it's going to rain any minute, what say we hop over to Lynnie's Chestnut Lake Café and catch up over breakfast?"

Kyle was mesmerized by the team logo, a sparkly orange bovine, on Lyssa's University of Texas Austin ball cap. When Lyssa doffed the hat and set it to her right, his gaze followed.

"What is there about my hat that fascinates you?" she said with a touch of annoyance.

"Sweetheart, your cow may be the solution to our security dilemma."

"That is not a cow," she said through her teeth. "That is a Texas Longhorn." She touched her index finger to the tip of each long horn. "Not. A cow."

"No, of course. Silly of me. But what is the name of the Texas team with the famous cheerleaders?"

"Dallas."

"Dallas what?"

"Dallas Cowboys."

"Exactly." He reached for his phone. "I promise, this will take only twenty seconds."

"Darling." She covered his hand. "Why not tell whatever it is to your new CIO Paul and have him handle it?" He'd told her in the car on the way over that the college had brought their search to a close at seven this morning by naming Paul, the department's senior analyst, as Tompkins College's new CIO.

"Brilliant." *Never mind it's exactly what I was about to do.*

"Thank you." With a shake of her head, she left the table. When she returned a few minutes later, he was still on the phone, laughing with Paul. As she slipped onto her chair, he signed off and pocketed his phone.

"I will not take it out again, I swear."

She put her hat on backward. "How are Paul and the longhorn solving your security dilemma?"

"Had we remembered our arithmetic, we'd have solved it a month ago, when the trouble started. We've six of us in the department with administrative privileges, but there are seven privileged accounts. I never asked why. I never checked who was using what account."

"And the odd account is named Cowboy?"

"You're hired." He lifted his coffee mug to her. "I suspect the account and its little gremlin were left behind by the disgraced former CIO for us to remember him by. At any rate, for the next twenty-four hours, Paul will record and scrutinize every move Cowboy makes, and he's double-checking with the group to see what they know about Cowboy. We've been bloody stupid about it. Nice job, my love. Where were we?"

She looked at the notes she'd made on the back of a paper place mat.

"We had finished laying out everything we know about the gun, ending with it was small enough to fit in a pocket. See, I drew a line under the whole lot and started the next section, which is labeled—"

"No, don't tell me! Next on our list was the house. Or the tree?"

"The tree." She smoothed out her peanut-butter-smeared napkin where she'd written, on a relatively clean patch, the list of topics for discussion. She tore off the patch and anchored it with a saltshaker. "The unlikely burial place for the gun was a Laceleaf Japanese Maple tree."

"Which Tommy Tuttle ordered and had planted by a nursery on Friday of the weekend before Memorial Day weekend, five years ago. That was May 19th, by the way. I finally looked it up," he said. "So the gun was buried the 20th, and Patty Beck and Vince Tuttle left town that night."

She looked up from her scribbling. "Noted, thank you, good work. The nursery probably did a good job, yet when the Tuttles returned from their wedding in Utica, the tree was crooked."

"And a few nearby roses had been disturbed, according to Toffee."

"Which leads us to believe someone dug up the tree just enough to bury the gun." She took another messy bite of her bagel and wiped her fingers on yet another flimsy napkin.

"Have enough napkins, do you?" His eyes twinkled with mischief. He'd brought a stack of them from the dispenser by the register, and she'd commandeered the lot of them.

She toed him under the table, but her mouth quirked up in a smile. "What else is important from our session with Toffee in her hospital room?"

"Lots of commotion heard by Larry and Toffee Winkel on the night of May 20th. Something like a firecracker woke them. Maybe that was the gunshot. One or more shots, we don't know. Lots of noise, Toffee said. She thought a party was spilling into the backyard as it broke up and people left, but I learned yesterday from the Weaver twins, Vince and Nate's good buddies, there was no party or they'd have been invited. Doors slamming, noisy truck backing out. Larry Winkel identified the truck as Nate Westover's. If Toffee thought it was a party, there must have been multiple voices, excitement, maybe shouts."

She spread peanut butter on the remaining half of her bagel. "Did the Winkels call the police?"

"I don't believe so. But that's a good thought. Perhaps someone did."

"I can have Kathy Regis search the newspaper archives for anything on the police blotter that weekend, for our block of Seneca Street."

"Worth doing, yes." He stroked the handle of his mug, secretly pleased she'd delegated a task for once. "When the

Tuttles returned, Rikki straightened the tree with Tommy's help."

She chuckled. "That's right, Janet said Rikki made him walk around it with a plumb line."

He smiled. "He must have been a card." At her puzzled frown, he explained, "A funny guy, quick to turn a tense situation into a joke or a story."

"Everyone loved him, that's for sure."

"Which brings us to the house," he said with a glance at the list on the napkin.

"Ours?"

"Ours. What do we know about our house that's relevant to this investigation?"

She didn't answer, simply stared at a clean, folded white lunch napkin on the next table. Her expression was so solemn, he didn't think she was looking for a better option in paper napkins.

"What is it, my love?" He brushed a stray lock of hair from her cheek.

She blinked rapidly. "When I had the nightmare, I woke up and saw the white curtain stir. Death was with me in our little guest room."

He rested his forearms on the table. "I suppose our guest room would have been Vince's room."

"I think someone died there," Lyssa told him. "But it was all mixed up with a woman's screams and a car plunging into a ravine. No, not a car." She slapped her hand on the table and swiveled to face him. "It was a body thrown into a ravine, Kyle." Her voice was hushed, her eyes were wide. "Those images feel like facts to me. I know that doesn't make sense."

"I think we need to trust them." When her questioning gaze didn't stray from his face, he nodded and squeezed her hand. "So the shooting took place in Vince's room, and the body was dumped in a ravine somewhere on their route."

"On Vince and Patty's route to Green Bay, yes." She drew in a ragged breath and rubbed her arms briskly.

"Cold?"

"A passing chill, nothing more."

"Here's one possible scenario that fits our facts," he said. "Vince and Patty had the house to themselves for the weekend. They were making love in Vince's bed when Nate barged in on them. He was furious at Vince for his success. Nate had his father's gun in hand. Patty screamed." Kyle cocked his head for her reaction. "Nate shot one of them."

"Okay, or when Patty screamed, he went to shut her up, but had to put down the gun. Vince picked it up and shot Nate."

"Right, otherwise Nate would have strangled Patty. Then she and Vince cleaned up the evidence, carried the body to Nate's truck, buried the gun, and later dumped Nate's body."

"But Nate is alive, we think. Oh my gosh, I totally forgot to tell you." She drew out the copies of Vince and Nate's yearbook pictures and laid them side-by-side. "Nate and Vince as seniors at Tompkins College."

"Which is which? Except for the nose, they could be brothers," he said. "I wonder if they were similar in height, too?"

"Janet would know."

"Nate has no current address, no employment history, nothing like that in the college records at Tompkins College. Nor on the Internet."

"You're right. But wasn't Nate seen more recently than May 20ᵗʰ five years ago?" She snapped her fingers. "The house closing with Natalie. Didn't she say she'd lived there four years?"

"Yes, but Natalie wouldn't have known what Nate looked like. It could have been Vince at the closing of the Westover house."

She picked up her bagel and put it down again. "True, but the attorney for the closing would have known if it was Nate, wouldn't he?"

"Possibly, assuming the attorney was the Westover family attorney."

She shook her head. "So confusing. Feels like we're going in circles."

"There's still hard data we can gather," he said. "The closing date, for example. The attorney's name. Your librarian can find those."

"Yes, good. And Bree and I want to talk to Nick Nunzio when he's back."

"Good idea." Kyle sat back. "Or maybe not. The Weavers called him a douche bag. Sorry, their word. Makes me wonder how reliable his word is." He studied Lyssa's pinched face and tense body. "Besides, sweetheart, both of us are stressed beyond what's healthy. Your beautiful face is pale and troubled. Your shoulders are rigid and nearly at your ears."

He demonstrated, screwing up his face and hunching his shoulders, and she giggled at his mock-monster.

"That's better. And I'm as bad as you. I've been running like a maniac since the day we returned from our honeymoon. I deeply regret taking on the CIO position."

"Gianessa says you're a caretaker, and that's how you got yourself into it."

"She's usually right," he said. "I suppose I was taking care of Justin, eh? Trying to support his dream of a revitalized college that operates with integrity. Worthy goal, but stupid move on my part."

"Worth thinking about." She tapped the pencil eraser on the tabletop.

He lifted the pencil from her fingers and cradled both her hands in his. "Let me propose something fun for us. Since the fountain project is in Harold's expert hands for the entire weekend. And since the newly appointed CIO, Paul, is chasing down the elusive Cowboy security breach, thanks to you, what say you and I steal off to a beach for the weekend? Fly somewhere tonight. Walk on the sand, make love, eat seafood, rest."

"Yes." Her eyes danced.

"Yes?" He sat open-mouthed for a moment, but she didn't retract her agreement or her hands. "Splendid. Joel's eager to make it up to us for his blunder, and he's poised to make all the arrangements. I've entrusted him with my credit card number. I'll give him the go-ahead, will I?"

"Yes." She slid her phone across the table, and he stared dumbly at it. "You vowed not to use your phone again."

Kyle laughed deep in his throat as he pressed in Joel's number. He watched Lyssa while he counted the rings. "Will you pack for us both?"

She nodded, smiling, happiness written in her sparkling eyes.

"Is Myrtle Beach okay, my love?"

"I knew you were going to say that. Yes."

"We'll apologize to Janet Tuttle for dredging up all this unpleasantness, feed her, and see what else she can tell us." He shook his head. "Voicemail. Yes, Joel, it's Kyle. Lyssa's delighted. We can be packed by five o'clock. We're very grateful." Before he handed back her phone, he thumbed an app. "Temperature for Myrtle Beach is in the sixties. Sunshine all weekend."

"I feel better already."

"And Joel told me last evening he has in mind an all-purpose resort right on the beach, with a pool and a spa for you and a fitness room for me. He has a friend, a pilot, who's been dying for a few rounds of golf, who'll fly us in a private plane direct to Myrtle Beach and stay at a golf resort nearby."

She leaned close for a kiss. "How can I ever thank you?"

"I suspect we'll find several ways."

"More coffee?" Lynnie stood beside the table, straight-faced, with a carafe in her hand.

"Yes, please," Lyssa answered. "It's quieted down. We're not in anyone's way, are we?"

"Not at all, honey. You still working on those bagels? Want something fresh?"

Lyssa and Kyle locked gazes. "Do you, by chance, have cinnamon-raisin sticky buns?" Kyle asked.

"There are two left. I'll bring them right over."

Kyle stood and stretched. "We have three more items on the list. We need the energy boost these will give us."

"You can always rationalize a sticky bun." Lyssa glanced at the list. "Two families, the Tuttles and the Westovers, and the girl Patty Beck who, according to Toffee, married Vince Tuttle."

"We've an odd assortment of facts for all that." Kyle sat down again as Lynnie set their pastries on the table.

Lynnie cocked one hip and pointed at Lyssa's place mat full of notes and then at the neighboring tables, all set for the lunch crowd. "No more place mats may go missing."

"You have our word," Kyle said and held up his hand in solemn agreement.

"She is a treasure," Lyssa said with her gaze on Lynnie's retreating back.

Once Kyle had chomped the first bite of his sticky bun, he said, "We know William Westover owned the gun, and no one registered it in another name after he died. The Westovers celebrated their only child's college graduation with a trip to the National Parks in the West. A rockslide wiped out most of a group hiking in the Vermillion Cliffs, including the guide and Nate's parents. Nate was injured. Toffee said it was a leg injury."

Lyssa took up the narrative. "While he was still in a hospital in Flagstaff, a memorial service was held here in Tompkins Falls for the parents. The church council felt it was important for the congregation's healing. Nate was next of kin, by the way. No siblings, aunts, uncles, etcetera. What else do we know?"

"We know Toffee Winkel looked in on Nate once he returned. He was at home, visited by aides and physical therapists. Sometime in the fall, she and her little dog, Trixie, found him passed out on his front porch and asked Nick Nunzio for help. She thinks Nunzio got him into a rehab, because Nate was gone for a time. She didn't say how long." He scarfed one more bite of the pastry.

"After that, the Westover house stood empty, though she'd sometimes see Nate around the neighborhood after dark when she was out with Trixie," Lyssa said. "I didn't think about that before. That's really odd, isn't it? As if he wasn't supposed to be in the neighborhood and wasn't living in the house. Why? I think the city police know more than they're saying about Nate."

"We need to find out what else they know. And that's where Joel can help us. He has connections that go back before Peter Shaughnessy joined the police force. Their lack of interest in the gun's past still does not make sense to me. In truth, it makes me suspicious."

Kyle reached across the table for her phone and left a quick voicemail for Joel, summarizing what they wanted to know.

Around a mouthful of sticky bun, Lyssa said, "Next item. The Tuttles. Well-liked by everyone."

"Except Mr. Jonas during the garden tour." Kyle noticed Lynnie eyeing them. He gave her a thumbs-up. "Outstanding. Just the right amount of cinnamon and raisins." She beamed.

"Tommy Tuttle liked a good laugh," Lyssa said. "Rikki Tuttle had a green thumb. Vince Tuttle was a good student, majored in Art and English at Tompkins College, master's degree from Geneseo, immediate job offer from Green Bay. By the way, Kyle, I learned from our librarian that Wisconsin is said to have the highest quality teachers of any state, so for him to get that job says that he was standout. I wonder if he picked Green Bay because he was a Packers fan?"

"No, he was a Seahawks fan." At her raised eyebrows, he added, "His buddy Mike Weaver supplied that tidbit. They, by the way, never saw a fit between Vince and Patty. Oh, and by the way, Vince's girlfriend broke up with him immediately after graduation, thought he wasn't good enough for her. I suppose that made him vulnerable to someone like Patty."

He sat back. "Vince has since won teaching awards and was superlative in every way—every way, my love—until he came home with Patty Beck. From his behavior after that, Janet Tuttle says the family wrote him off. They wouldn't have done that without cause."

"You're right. The change in Vince dated from the weekend the gun was buried under our tree, didn't it?" she asked. "He took Patty's side in that horrible fight with Rikki that nearly ended in a chick fight. Can you imagine easygoing Tommy Tuttle ordering his wife to go inside? And then having words with his son in front of the whole neighborhood?"

Kyle nodded. "Still, I don't think the change in Vince's behavior was just because of the parents' slight to Patty Beck. Something changed him dramatically, and I think whatever it was happened the night the gun was buried."

"Remember, as soon as we told Janet about the gun under the tree, she said Vince might have done something and needed to hide the evidence."

"And, like Nate, Vince has no record with the Tompkins College Alumni Office, beyond his master's degree and job offer from Green Bay, correct?"

"Correct. No address, no contact information."

"And no presence on the Internet?" Kyle asked.

"Only the teaching awards. Come to think of it, not even a photograph to go with those."

"He's hiding something, my love, don't you think?"

"He could just be protecting his privacy. Kathy Regis pointed that out."

"I suppose, but still, hiding is completely out of character for Vince Tuttle, isn't it?"

"Yes. So is turning his back on his parents." Lyssa splashed water from her glass into her cupped hand and used it to wash the sugary coating from her fingers.

"You clever girl." Kyle copied her. "I'm sure it's gauche, but it works quite well, doesn't it?"

"We shouldn't do it in Myrtle Beach, Kyle."

"No," he agreed with a laugh. "Sweetheart, we don't know much at all about Patty Beck, who is the final item on our list. I wonder if she's the one who was killed with the Westover gun?"

"We know Vince brought her home to meet his parents, which suggests he was very serious about her."

"The Weaver brothers said they were mismatched. She wouldn't ever be a soccer mom or PTA president. Tommy thought she was trash, and Rikki called her a creature." Kyle's shoulders shook with a stifled laugh. "Creature," he repeated under his breath.

"Stop." Lyssa rested her forehead against the heel of her hand and chuckled.

"Wait a minute. Wouldn't Vince have returned to settle the estate after Rikki died?"

"According to Janet and Toffee, he didn't come when Tommy died. I don't recall Janet saying anything about either will," Lyssa said.

"Another question for Janet. Do we know anything more about Patty?" Kyle asked.

"Sort of. We know that the evidence of Patty and Vince's marriage was simply the photo of Patty in a princess wedding dress. The photo could have been a fake. Something she had done at the mall."

"So it's possible they never married," Kyle mused.

"Except the write-up of Vince's most recent award refers to his wife, Patty, who works in the hospitality industry. That's another thing, Kyle. The other photo in the letter, the luxury condo. We know from my library search that Vince served on the board of that condo association, but I still don't see how they could afford a luxury condo on the waterfront.

"I want to follow Vince's money story beyond what we already know about him being a hard worker and paying his own way through Geneseo."

"Brilliant. That's your expertise, my love, and it will serve us well with this investigation."

"As for Patty's money story, we know nothing. Either she had money, or there's a whole bunch of money associated with the crime committed with our gun, but I can't imagine what."

"That's a leap, connecting the gun and a large sum of money." His fingers played a tricky practice scale on the tabletop. "All that can wait until we're back from the beach, eh?"

"Agreed."

Kyle spotted Lynnie approaching, carafe in her hand. He placed his hand over his mug. "I'm done, Lynnie. Lyssa?"

"I've had enough. Thanks so much, Lynnie. This was just what we needed." Lyssa scraped back her chair, stuck her head through the neck opening of her hoodie, and shimmied into it.

"Don't forget your hat." Kyle left two twenties on the table, drew on his cashmere coat, and clicked the remote starter for the Lexus. "It's stopped raining for the moment. Besides packing for our trip, what are you doing today?"

"I'm going solo to the college in Geneseo to see what more we can learn about Vince and Nate and maybe even Patty. Bree can't join me, but she strongly advised taking a box of doughnuts from the Bagel Depot."

Chapter 12

Triple the size of Tompkins College, the campus of the state college at Geneseo spilled down a steep slope from Main Street to the highway along the Genesee River. Lyssa huddled in front of a kiosk on the edge of campus with an upright campus map. Her box of doughnuts was safe in a plastic bag while the morning rain misted her hair and tickled the back of her neck.

Her fingers roamed the map and her lips moved silently as she worked out her route. It was simple. Continue down Main Street to Park Street, take that past the circle, and the Education building was the second building on her right, across from the alumni building.

The Alumni Office, predictably, refuse to give her any information, even for Vince Tuttle, who she knew had completed a master's degree program. *Waste of a coconut doughnut.*

Anticipating the Education department office would also refuse to give any information about students, past or present, Lyssa decided to ask the administrative assistant if any of the professors happened to be on campus. If she could appeal to them as a colleague she might tease out some bit of information.

She entered the cavernous silent building and remembered it was Friday of spring break. *I may strike out.*

She squared her shoulders and trudged to the third floor.

The administrative assistant smiled warmly as she entered with her box of goodies in hand. "How may I help you?"

"Lyssa Pennington, Tompkins College. I'm hoping some of your childhood education faculty are around."

"Down the hall, all the way to the end. You'll see a couple of doors open across the hall from each other. They got roped into presenting at a conference at the last minute, and they're pulling something together."

"Have one." Lyssa held out the box. "Will these convince them to take a five-minute break?"

"I never could say no to a Boston cream," the assistant said and plucked her favorite from the pack. "They'll love you for this."

Laughter erupted from the end of the hall.

"Sounds like they're in a good mood." On her way down the hall, she silently blessed Bree.

"Hi." Lyssa knocked perfunctorily and breezed into the faculty office on the left, holding out her box.

"Yum." Dressed in torn blue jeans and a Geneseo hoodie, hair in a ponytail, a woman professor sat cross-legged on the floor surrounded by children's books.

"I can tell you love your job," Lyssa said.

"Who doesn't love children's books, right?" The woman selected a chocolate-covered. "I'm Rosie," she said, after swallowing her first bite. "What can I do for you?"

"I'm Lyssa Pennington, economics professor at Tompkins College." At Rosie's grimace, she added,

"Boring, I know, right? Anyway, two young men from my neighborhood graduated from your program, and one of them is teaching now in Green Bay, Wisconsin. In fact—"

"Vince Tuttle, yes. Everyone knows Vince. Phenomenal student. Really great with kids. He's on one of our recruiting posters, I don't know if you noticed."

"It's so good to hear that. I'll watch for it on the way out." They chatted a few minutes about Vince's success, but Lyssa realized she knew more than Rosie. "Have you kept in touch with him?"

"No, I intended to, but he never got in touch with me. I'm sure he's doing really well, and I'm glad to know about the awards. That's a feather in *our* cap, too."

"It certainly is. Did you also know my other neighbor, Nate Westover?"

Rosie blinked and hinged backward a few inches. "I was Nate's advisor. Very troubled young man. I'm convinced he had all the potential Vince had, maybe more, but he couldn't get out of his own way."

"How do you mean?" Lyssa asked.

Rosie set aside the picture book in her lap, drew up her knees, and hugged them. "As you probably know, Nate lost his parents in a horrible accident that he survived. Avalanche or something like that."

"Rockslide, yes. I'm sure it was traumatic for him. Everyone in the neighborhood was concerned for him." She realized as she said it, it wasn't true. Toffee and Nick had supported Nate, but no one else had mentioned his ordeal. She wondered if the Tuttles had helped him. And what had been Vince's response to the tragedy?

"He probably should have taken a year off to get his head together," Rosie was saying. "What do I know?" She waved a hand. "I'm not a psychiatrist. He acted like he had PTSD. He'd suddenly get angry and aggressive for no reason. And he was constantly putting Vince down for getting ahead of him in the program." Her voice trailed off.

"They probably had an understanding they'd finish together. From what people have said, they'd been best friends for a long time and had similar goals."

"Identical goals," Rosie said with a loud laugh. "Oh my gosh, when we interviewed them, Phil said they were like twin sons from different mothers."

"Heard my name." A man dressed in chinos and a purple polo shirt appeared at Rosie's door. "Phil." He held out his hand to Lyssa, but his gaze zeroed in on the box. "I love you." He fingered through the remaining selections and lifted out a jelly-filled. Confectioners sugar dropped on the floor as he brought it to his mouth for the first bite.

"Anyway, Nate kept sabotaging his own efforts," Rosie said. "Personally, I think he drank to deal with the horror of the accident. That's just my theory. The thing is we couldn't give him a placement."

"I don't know what that means." Lyssa looked from Rosie to Phil.

Phil told her, "To get certified, students have to do more than a hundred hours in classrooms—first as observers, then assisting young learners, then teaching a lesson. They do that at various grade levels in their certification area. In our case, grades one through six, and children with special needs."

"Sounds like really good preparation. I'm impressed," she said.

"Thank you," Rosie said. "We're very proud of our program. And all that work Phil talked about comes before they do student teaching."

"How is student teaching different?" Lyssa asked.

"As student teachers, they're supervised by a host teacher and by us, but they're completely in charge of a classroom for a period of time. They do all the lesson planning, classroom management, instruction, grading, meet with parents and with the committee at the school that oversees students with special needs. It's a tremendous responsibility, and they have to be thoroughly prepared, screened, interviewed, and fingerprinted before they're even given a placement."

"That's what you meant by placement. I see," Lyssa said. "So Nate was denied a placement for some reason?" When the reason was not forthcoming, she said, "A good reason, I have no doubt."

Rosie loosened her hold on her knees and stood. "I really wish Nate had taken time and gotten the help he needed to recover from the trauma."

It was clear from her rigid stance that she'd said all she was going to.

"I've taken up enough of your time, Rosie. Thanks a millions for talking with me."

Rosie cocked one hip. "Why are you asking about Nate, if I may know?" Her gaze bore into Lyssa's.

"Honestly?" Lyssa said, trying to buy a few seconds to concoct a based-in-truth answer to a question she should have seen coming.

"Preferably." Rosie's smile was a straight line.

"When I looked him up at Tompkins College, I was upset to see that, unlike Vince, Nate hadn't finished the program at Geneseo, even though people knew he was eager to teach. I identified with that passion to teach. He'd obviously gone through hell, and it bothered me that he might not have fulfilled his dream." She thought of Natalie saying Nate had rushed away from the closing to return to his teaching job. "But someone else told me he *is* teaching. I was curious how that was possible and if it was really true."

"Where exactly is Nate teaching?" Rosie's tone was hostile, and she'd bunched her fists.

Good time for an exit. Lyssa replied as she backed toward the doorway, "The woman didn't know."

She bumped into Phil, who steered her into the hall and pointed to his open doorway. "Wait there," he whispered.

From the neutrality of the hallway, Phil called to Rosie, "Why didn't you tell her about Patty?"

Lyssa gasped.

Rosie stormed out of her office, passed Phil with a glare, and disappeared down a side corridor, her throat emitting a fierce *grrr*.

Rikki had growled like an animal at Patty, too, according to Toffee Winkel.

Phil held up a finger, listening. A door slammed shut. "Ladies' room. We have two minutes. Patty is infamous in this department. You've heard of her?"

"Not relative to Nate, I haven't."

"Rumor was Nate lived with Patty because she, quote, knew how to massage his injured leg." He cleared his throat. "Patty worked part time at a coffee place on Main Street in the village. She bartended, too, I think. Try asking at the coffee shop with the giant blue cups painted across the front windows."

"Thanks. Why did Rosie have that reaction when you mentioned Patty's name?"

"Patty came in here a few times and got in Rosie's face about denying Nate a placement. You can't even imagine the fight that followed. Very bad. I heard she made a scene at the placement office, too, more than once. It never worked."

"Nate never got a placement?"

"Right, but I give him credit. He kept on with his courses and did well in them. Except for student teaching, he finished the program. Rosie's right. He might have been a great teacher in this state if he'd been given the chance. But something he'd done on his own time was communicated to the college and subsequently verified with the authorities." A door closed, and Phil cast a worried look down the hall.

"That's all I can say, and you didn't hear it from me." He pointed to a stairway sign past Rosie's office. "You need to leave."

Lyssa shoved the box of doughnuts at him and made a run for the stairs.

As she emerged from the building, she yanked her hood over her hair and directed her steps up Park Street to the village. On the trek, she rehashed what she'd heard. Before Patty hooked up with Vince she was Nate's personal masseuse? This was starting to sound like a love triangle.

Or had Phil juiced up the facts to make good gossip?

Either way, Patty had advocated for Nate with the placement office and with his advisor, and before that she'd given him a place to live and helped him recover from his injury. She cared about him and his dream. *Or his employment potential.*

Vince probably cared about Nate, too. They'd been friends forever. Vince and Patty had a mutual interest, Nate's health and happiness, and they eventually hooked up.

And how did Nate view that? Probably jealous, possibly angry. Lyssa doubted he was cool with it. Rosie had said Nate put Vince down for running ahead of him in their master's program. Stealing Nate's girl was a much worse offense, wasn't it?

What about Patty? She sounded like an opportunist. First, she and Nate were hot, but she dumped him because he wasn't going anywhere career-wise, even with her obnoxious attempts to help him. And Vince was succeeding, so she glommed onto Vince? *No, that's not right.* Lyssa doubted Vince would marry a woman like that, and he'd definitely planned to marry her. Patty must have good qualities.

Lyssa hunched deep in her hoodie as the rain picked up. She spotted the storefront decorated with blue cups a block away and picked up her pace.

Either way, Nate was probably angry at both Patty and Vince. Patty had let him down by not getting him a placement, the only thing standing between him and his dream job. And Vince was succeeding where he'd failed. Or, viewed another way, Vince stole his girl, and Patty deserted him. Regardless, Lyssa didn't see Vince and Nate's friendship surviving those conflicts.

Her hand went to her heart and she massaged it, aware of the depth of her feeling for the young men, both of whom could have been her students. She remembered her intuition after talking with Natalie—that somehow the Westovers' death in the rockslide was at the root of whatever had happened with the gun planted in the garden a year later.

His parents' shocking death and his own injury had changed Nate's life. And the gun was his, after his father's death.

Eager to learn all she could about Patty from her old boss, she pushed open a door with foot-high blue cups painted suggestively side-by-side on the glass. A jingle bell announced her, and a man who looked to be in his late thirties emerged from the back and took up position behind the counter. He straightened his spine when she shrugged out of her wet hoodie, and she gave him a wave.

"Help you?" he asked.

"I feel like a drowned cat," she told him. As she looped her hoodie over a coat rack by the door, she sensed his gaze sweeping from her ankles to her red hair.

"Hot coffee, please," Lyssa said with her sunniest smile as she slid onto a stool.

"Anything with it?"

"Yes, how about a sesame bagel with veggie cream cheese?"

"No veggie. Plain okay?"

At her nod, he asked, "Toasted?"

"Absolutely. Nice place."

When he'd set her up with her order, he stood with his hands on the counter and asked, "What brings you to town?" His eyes strayed to her left hand, and he frowned at the wedding ring.

"I'm looking for information about Patty Beck who might have worked here five or six years ago."

Eyes wary now, the café owner drifted back against the sandwich station behind him and folded his arms across his chest. "What do you want to know?"

"I'm actually on a mission to get in touch with her husband, Vince Tuttle," Lyssa said. "Vince grew up in the house where I live, on Seneca Street in Tompkins Falls. His professors here at the college don't have contact information for him, nor do his old professors at Tompkins College, except that he teaches somewhere in Green Bay. Someone I talked with on campus just now remembered that Vince's wife, Patty, worked here when they were dating. I'm desperately hoping you can help me find Vince and Patty."

"Why do you want to find them?"

She embellished the reason Kyle said he'd used with the Weaver twins. "My husband and I have been sorting through the attic and cleaning up the yard. We've found some things we think Vince and Patty might like to have. I understand from our neighbor, Mrs. Winkel, that Vince didn't spend any time cleaning out the place after his mom passed. Maybe it didn't matter to him, but I know I'd love to have photos and jewelry that belonged to my parents. He might be regretting that." Her voice caught, genuinely.

She shook her head and reminded herself this was all acting, and, besides, she'd soon be in Myrtle Beach with Kyle. And she was hungry. She took a big bite of her bagel and schmear.

"I know what you mean," the man told her. "When my dad died and left this place to me a few years ago, I thought everything in the basement was junk. Until I went through it last winter and found a whole family history packed away down there, even things from the old country. My name's Ralph, by the way."

While Lyssa dabbed cream cheese off her cheek, she said, "I can't believe your name is Ralph. Our favorite burger place in Tompkins Falls is Ralphs."

"No way."

"Really. So you remember Patty?"

"Yeah, I knew her real well. She worked here afternoons for a few years, right when my father was teaching me the business. There was another kid from your town hung out here, too."

"Do you mean Nate Westover?" Her excitement grew.

"Yeah, that was his name. I kind of think Nate and Vince were buddies, until Patty."

"What do you mean, 'until Patty'? The neighbors say they were inseparable growing up."

"Patty was real pretty, flirtatious. Kind of manipulative, if you want the honest truth. First, she and Nate were an item for maybe six months. None of my business, but they lived together."

"Sounds like it was serious," Lyssa said.

Ralph shrugged. "Patty used to say she was taking care of him because he'd been hurt really bad in some accident. Me, I think he didn't want to spring for a place of his own and he played the pity card." He flapped one hand. "Whatever. During that time, when things got quiet in here, I'd see Patty with Nate over there in the corner booth. It wasn't like they were making out or nothing."

"So what do you think they were talking about?" Lyssa asked.

"I figured Patty was hitting him up for money because tips were slow. Patty was always looking for money but, from the look of it, Nate didn't have a dime to spare. And then, after the holidays, Vince starts coming around with Nate, and the two guys would sit together. Sometimes Patty would join them, and the three of them would joke around."

"In the corner booth?" Lyssa swiveled to see it. The backs of the benches were high enough for a private conversation and the booth was far enough from the door so the occupants could go unnoticed. She started to say, "Looks cozy," but a sudden headache made her stop. Gianessa would tell her to pay attention to a physical sensation like that. *What does it mean?*

Ralph's voice cut into her musing. "They all had a great time together at first. Next thing you know, it's spring, and Nate's not coming around as much. And Patty, she's all over Vince. They're definitely making out in the corner booth. I've never seen anyone fall so hard." Ralph chuckled. "He was a goner."

Tommy Tuttle said she had her hooks in his son.

"I'll bet Nate and Vince had a big blowout about Patty, right?" Lyssa said.

"Nah. My old man wouldn't have put up with that in his restaurant. You ask me, though, Nate was jealous, no question. Once Vince started dating Patty, Nate wouldn't give him the time of day. Vince'd walk in, Nate'd walk out. Then Nate stopped coming around."

"It's too bad it broke up their friendship."

"Yeah, but you know there was something about Nate I didn't like." He jerked his thumb to the right. "Patty said he got into a few fights at the bar next door."

"How would she know that?"

"She bartended there nights. Always trying to make enough money for the next course at the college. She wanted to be a teller at a casino, she said. Hah! She loved money. But Vince, he was a real stand-up guy. I was glad when she picked him."

"So she didn't have rich parents putting her through college?"

"Are you kidding? Raised by a single mom who lived in a trailer someplace in Pennsylvania."

"That had to be rough. It sounds like you watched out for her. That was kind of you."

He shrugged, but a smile played around his mouth. "She had a hard life. Her mom drank, and there was no alimony or nothing like that. Patty worked here three or four years, plugging away at her college degree, working her way through. She didn't date much until Nate, but whenever she did, it was always a tall dark handsome guy. Nate was really hot for her, but, like I said, I didn't want her dating a guy that couldn't hold his booze."

"I'm thinking Vince and Nate were both tall and dark, weren't they?" She reached in her purse for the photocopies she'd made of Vince and Nate from their yearbook.

"Yep, same type."

She placed the two headshots next to each other, facing Ralph. Two clean-shaven good-looking young men, with white smiles, dark eyes, and straight dark hair.

Ralph laughed. "He had a honker all right," Ralph said as he jabbed the photo on the left with his beefy finger. "Maybe not as tall or handsome as Nate, but he was a good guy. I was glad for Patty when she hooked him."

Joel had left her a voicemail saying the Tompkins Falls Garden Club was meeting at the library at two-thirty this afternoon. Knowing she could make it with time to spare, she tucked her phone back in her purse and started the car. The rain intensified as she steered north out of town.

Her intention to think through all she'd learned at the college and from Ralph was thwarted by a blast of westerly wind that shoved the car over the rumble strip.

A gust of wind slamming rain against his office windows interrupted Kyle's train of thought. Was Lyssa still on the road? *Lord, protect my love.* He paced to the window and gazed at the puddle-dotted quad. Wind-driven rain like this was common in Cornwall, less so in the Finger Lakes. The first time he'd held Lyssa in his arms they were caught in a fierce squall on the cliff path more than a mile from Pennington House.

She'd slid on some mossy stones and sprained an ankle. He'd had a time of it coaxing her up a set of slippery steps so they could cross the cliff top to a sheltered track that led down to the road. She'd never once asked him to carry her, which he'd been all too willing to do. Until that day, he hadn't given her credit for her pluck. She'd shown it many times since. *She'll need it driving in this howl.*

Another gust sent him back to his computer, where he'd nearly finished his escape plan. Lyssa's faculty contract did not require her to stay in Tompkins Falls through the end of June, which was unusual. Probably Justin had made that concession, knowing how strongly the Penningtons felt about spending the summer at Pennington House.

He and Justin went back nearly two decades to their respective PhD programs at University of Chicago's London campus. Justin knew well Kyle's passion for his native Cornwall. The two of them had spent many weekends rambling over the countryside with their cameras.

Unfortunately, his own contract required him to stay through June. He had no intention of deserting Paul or his staff, but he also had no reason to be physically present at the college now that Paul had accepted the job as CIO. He could support the IT department adequately from the UK. Or possibly he could convince Justin to save money by releasing him early from his contract.

Bottom line, he and Lyssa could be in Cornwall by June 12th.

To that end, he'd spent the morning producing a timeline for his exit and noting how he would provide support for various contingencies. Already his headache had eased. If only the storm would blow over before their flight to Myrtle Beach. He doubted even a golf fanatic would be foolish enough to fly a small plane in this weather.

Lyssa battled the wind north on Route 39 until she reached US Route 20, a major east-west route that went right through Tompkins Falls. After a few miles of easier travel, she pulled the car into a parking lot for a break and massaged her aching hands, which had gripped the steering too hard for too long. Thinking Kyle was probably wondering about her, she texted him she was okay and on her way to a garden club meeting at the library.

Getting no response, she set aside her phone and continued the journey. She reflected that, if Vince and Nate's program of study was stringent with its requirements for privacy and credentialing, the school where Vince was teaching must be stringent as well. They'd had to interview him face-to-face. They'd probably even fingerprinted him when he was there, regardless of whether New York State had done it prior to his student teaching.

He would have interviewed sometime before the weekend of May 19th five years ago, started the job in Green Bay that fall and, according to the database Kathy Regis had consulted, was still at the same school. "So Vince is alive," she told the dashboard. There was no way someone else could have shown up in his place in September five years ago claiming to be him.

And Patty had sent a photo of herself in a wedding gown to Rikki Tuttle after she and Vince had been living in Green Bay for a while. That argued for Patty being alive and still doing mean things to Vince's mother.

I really should have compassion for Patty. She'd come from a poor home with a drunk for a mother and had worked her way through college. Had she graduated? Lyssa knew not to bother asking the Alumni Office.

She felt depressed suddenly, probably a by-product of battling the wind. No, it was more than that. If Patty and Vince were alive, it must be Nate who'd been killed by the gun under the Laceleaf Japanese Maple. She'd rather it be Patty who died that night. *So much for compassion.*

The article she'd read at the library about Vince's latest teaching award had said his wife Patty worked in the hospitality industry. Ralph had said she'd joked about wanting to be a teller in a casino. Maybe now she was. Lyssa couldn't remember if she'd checked Facebook and Instagram for Patty Beck. Anyway, she wouldn't have time this afternoon. Besides the garden club meeting, she had to pack for herself and Kyle.

She made a mental note to stop by Kathy Regis's desk before the garden club meeting and ask her to check the police blotter for the weekend the gun was planted. And to find the date, real estate agent, and attorney for the closing on the Westover home. And to see if she could find any mention of Nate Westover in any of the teacher databases.

Bree had promised to find out where Nick hung out. When she and Kyle got back, she and Bree would buy Nick a beer at his favorite watering hole and see what they could get out of him relative to Vince and Nate.

And I'll follow Vince and Nate's money stories. She had the weekend to come up with a strategy for that.

Kyle returned from a meeting to find Lyssa's text. He smiled, wishing he could meet her at the garden club meeting. He'd give anything to be a fly on the wall and figure out who was the brazen hussy, the one who'd barged into Estella Capellita's backyard while she and Toffee Winkel had tea on the patio. The nerve of the woman, chastising Estella for not keeping up the rose garden.

"You ladies know how make a stormy day look like a walk in the garden," Lyssa said to the lady with the pink dress who greeted her at the door.

"Grab a scone for yourself. We'll start the meeting in one minute," was the response.

The dozen women nibbling scones around the tea urn were dressed for spring. Hats in shades of lime green, bright pink, or sunshine yellow. Flower-print blouses over silk skirts or linen pants. Silk scarves printed with tulips or lilies or the muted colors of a Monet garden. Flower lapel pins, flowered rings, and bright-colored bracelets that flashed as the women gestured in conversation.

She made a mental note to bring back from Myrtle Beach spring-colored scarves for her friends. As she poured tea for herself, a woman in a lavender silk dress draped with a dark purple scarf introduced herself as Melissa, the garden club president.

When the meeting began, Lyssa settled in a chair at the back of the room. She'd just taken two sips of tea when the presider asked her to introduce herself. She stood and told them, "Ladies, my husband and I are the new owners of 57

Seneca Street. Some of you recognize the address of Rikki Tuttle's beautiful rose garden."

A murmur of excitement rippled through the group. Lyssa said, "I don't mean to impose on your meeting time, but I wonder if anyone remembers which nursery supplied the Laceleaf Japanese Maple that Rikki planted in the center of her rose garden following the ice storm. I believe that was five years ago."

Comments along the lines of "Ruined the garden," and "What was she thinking?" floated over the group. One woman rose to her feet and confronted Lyssa. "If your intention is to sue the nursery for what we all know was Rikki's own arrogance, you'll not get that information from us."

"No, of course that's not my intention," Lyssa said. "I just want to talk with . . ." Her words were lost in a swell of protest and argument.

The presider banged a gavel. "Let's exercise decorum, ladies. I'm sure Louisa simply wants to talk with Hans at Woodard Nursery about replacing the tree. Isn't that right?"

Lyssa opened her mouth to set the record straight about her name and her purpose, but realized she'd just gotten what she'd come for. *Good time for an exit.*

"Exactly. Thank you, ladies." She hustled out of the library and back to her car.

Her iPhone app told her Woodard Nursery was halfway to Geneva, on the left. She thumbed a quick text to Kyle about her next stop.

"I told that woman's husband the tree wouldn't survive in this climate," Hans Woodard barked at Lyssa. He smacked his hands on his shop counter, leaned his considerable weight on them, and glared at her. "But would he listen? 'My wife has a green thumb. In her garden, everything thrives,' he says to me."

Lyssa licked her lips and said, in her calm teacher voice, "Yes, I understand Tommy Tuttle saw the tree on a trip to South Carolina and wanted it for the garden. I believe you planted the tree for Mrs. Tuttle in late May five years ago. Is that right?"

Hans *harrumph*ed as he searched the tablet next to the register. "Friday before Memorial Day weekend, right."

"May 19th?"

"That's a fact, Liza."

"Lyssa."

"And on Monday she's in here shrieking like a Banshee about what a lousy job we did. Woodard Nursery knows how to plant trees. If it was crooked at the end of the weekend, somebody else made it crooked. That's what I told her then, and that's what I'm telling you now."

"I see. I understand there was a party held at the Tuttle house that Saturday night. What would it have taken for the tree to go crooked in two days time? Could people bumping into it as they stumbled around drunk have loosened it, for example?"

"That wouldn't do it. Maybe if a few big guys like me got in a fight and somebody fell into the tree, that could maybe do it. You ask me, though, somebody tried to steal it, started digging it up, and got interrupted."

"That's really interesting," she said. "Why do you think that, Mr. Woodard?"

"Common sense, the way that woman described the disturbance. A couple of the rose bushes right next to the tree were crooked, she said, but nothing else was out of

About the Author

C. T. Collier grew up in Seneca Falls, NY, left the area for college and jobs, and always wanted to return to the Finger Lakes. Today she lives in a beautiful small city on one of the prettiest of the Finger Lakes, not unlike fictional Tompkins Falls on lovely Chestnut Lake. Most days you'll find her writing in her tiny office looking out on a woods populated with fox, deer, wild turkeys, and songbirds. In her career as a tech-savvy college professor she has been endlessly fascinated with campus intrigue. Entirely fictional, Tompkins College is no college and every college.

Learn more at https://drkatecollier.wordpress.com

Made in the USA
Middletown, DE
06 August 2016